To some real "Texas characters":

My son, Caleb
My husband, Craig
My father, Gene
My big brother, Toby

Texas Spitfire

Catherine Creel

ZEBRA BOOKS
KENSINGTON PUBLISHING CORP.

ZEBRA BOOKS

are published by

Kensington Publishing Corp.
475 Park Avenue South
New York, NY 10016

First printing: December 1987

Printed in the United States of America

TOO WILD TO TAME

Without a word, Ross gathered Dallas in his arms and brought his lips crashing down upon hers. She moaned low in her throat and felt her head spinning. The next thing she knew, her arms had come up to entwine themselves about the corded muscles of his neck.

She grew more and more light-headed as a result of the demanding pressure of his mouth upon hers, and no matter how vigorously her more rational instincts commanded her to resist, she could not prevent herself from kissing him—wholeheartedly and with very little regard to the fact that she was clad only in her nightclothes.

Suddenly, as though someone had emptied a bucket of cold water over her head, she pulled away from him and cried, "No!"

"What the—" Ross ground out, his eyes blazing down at her. His hands shot up to seize her wrists in a none too gentle grip, but she would not be subdued. Fighting like a tigress, she twisted and kicked and squirmed furiously against him. He held fast, his sun-kissed features growing savage as he sought to bend her to his will.

"Get out of my way, damn you!" she hissed. "I'll scream and bring the whole household running!" she threatened in a low voice quavering with fury and shame—and outright fear.

"If I wanted to take you, you flame-haired little spitfire, it wouldn't matter how much you screamed," Ross told her. His smoldering gaze raked possessively over her, and a faint, mocking smile touched his lips when he vowed softly, "And take you, I *will* . . ."

Prologue

Corsicana, Texas . . . 1894

Dallas Harmony Brown shifted the small wicker basket to her left hand. Frowning as her deep blue gaze dropped to observe the thick layer of dust which had settled upon the pointed toes of her "wondrously practical and splendidly stylish"—at least that was what the advertisement in the Sears, Roebuck & Company mail order catalog had promised—laced leather boots, she released an audible sigh of exasperation and reached up to tug the broad brim of her straw hat lower upon her upswept auburn locks in order to shield more of her face from the relentless, burning rays of the Texas sun.

Reflecting that it was only the ninth of June and already "hot enough to wither a fence post," as her father loved to say, Dallas told herself that the summer promised to be a real scorcher indeed. As always, there would be little relief from the heat. She would have to make a point of granting Cordi and Etta permission to go swimming with their friends down at the creek as soon as their daily chores were finished.

Smiling warmly in acknowledgment of the nods and greetings of several acquaintances, she quickened her steps and headed southward along Twelfth Street. She was oblivious to the admiring glances directed her way by a good many of the town's masculine residents, both young and old, as she gracefully swept the full skirts of her striped green calico shirtwaist upward in order to cross the tracks of the Cotton Belt Railroad. Her actions unintentionally provided the men working in the railyard with a brief glimpse of trim, shapely ankles and a lace-edged white petticoat.

Dallas Brown was without a doubt a very striking young woman—a real beauty, if one did not mind the light brown freckles which danced across her pert, upturned nose in stubborn defiance of repeated efforts to bleach them with a supposedly tried-and-true lotion made of buttermilk and salt. A faint smattering of freckles, decidedly not in vogue during this age of creamy white complexions, was also in evidence upon the otherwise flawless skin of her arms below the long sleeves she had negligently rolled up to her elbows while preparing her father's dinner.

Although the accursed freckles, inherited from her red-haired mother, might be considered by some to detract from her appearance, there was certainly no denying the perfection of her figure. Her waist was slender enough to meet the current standards of fashion without the torturous constraint of a corset, and her bosom was already full and firm, in spite of the fact that she had only recently turned seventeen. Hips that were trim yet well rounded tapered down into long, shapely limbs. A little more than five feet five inches in height, Dallas was taller than either of her younger sisters, and taller than the greater majority of the girls who had participated in commencement exercises with her two weeks earlier.

She transferred the basket of food to her other hand again as she neared the spot, a block south of the tracks that bisected the town from east to west, where she knew her father to be working that day. Abner Brown, a Corsicanan by birth and a blacksmith by trade, had been retained by the men drilling the first of three new artesian water wells to repair and sharpen their tools. Though it was certainly not his usual custom, he had offered his services at a fee far below the going rate, for he was as anxious as everyone else in town to secure the additional water supply required by his hometown.

Along with several other local businessmen and concerned citizens, Abner had decided that something had to be done. Corsicana, founded in 1848 and located in the heart of a fertile prairie region, was similar to dozens of other communities in the rich black-belt agricultural territory of North Central Texas in that it relied almost exclusively on cotton for its economic livelihood. Unfortunately, the fluctuating cotton prices had faltered during the first years of the 1890's, creating the need to diversify and attract new industry to the seat of Navarro County. But such hopes could not even begin to be realized until the water problem was solved.

The main source of water, a lake appropriately known as the "Waterworks" some two miles southeast of Corsicana, had proven hopelessly inadequate when it came to keeping up with the city's growing demands.

Hence, a special company of well drillers had been brought in, and they had wasted little time in erecting a wooden derrick and setting up their old cable tool rig to find water there beneath the parched Texas soil.

Dallas's eyes widened in surprise as she took note of the crowd of onlookers gathered about the drilling site. It wasn't that unusual to find a handful of townspeople clustered about the derrick to observe and comment as the drillers did their work, but it *was* unusual to see such a large number of men and women standing out in the heat of the day to observe efforts that could hardly be described as fascinating.

"What on earth?" Dallas murmured to herself in puzzlement. Hurrying forward to satisfy her rapidly increasing curiosity, she spied her father near the derrick. Big and burly, with a disposition to match his gruff demeanor, Abner Brown towered above most of the other men. His craggy, weathered features were drawn into a ferocious scowl, and his dark green eyes glittered angrily beneath the brim of his hat. A very worried Dallas made her way to his side.

"Papa? Papa, what is it?" she asked breathlessly, her bright, perplexed gaze making a hasty sweep of the crowd. The reactions displayed on the faces of the spectators ranged from incredulity to disgust, and it seemed that everyone was talking at once while the drillers stood staring at one another in momentary confusion.

"Oil, damn it!" Abner ground out, nodding curtly toward the derrick.

"Oil?" She turned her head, her eyes widening again as they fell upon the dark brown crude spurting over the floor of the drilling rig and soaking into the ground around the well.

Good heavens, *oil!* Why, nothing more unexpected had ever happened in Corsicana than . . . than *this!* Oil was something found "up North"—not here in Texas!

While an amazed Dallas and the other onlookers stared at the growing pool of petroleum, the hapless drillers, whose job was to find water, not crude, cursed their luck and pondered their next course of action. The oil would somehow have to be sealed off—that much they knew—and soon, if they hoped to avoid contaminating the warm artesian water they still intended to tap. To the drillers, the oil was a hazardous nuisance and nothing else. To many of the onlookers, it was little more than a source of conversation.

To Abner Brown, however, it was something entirely different. He alone, it appeared, realized the significance of the troublesome discovery. After letting out a string of highly expressive curses, he muttered, "Damned ugly black stuff will ruin the town if we let it!"

"Ruin the town, Papa? What do you mean?" asked Dallas, raising her face to the bearded, glowering darkness of his.

"Cattle and cotton, not *oil,* made Texas what it is! I'll be damned if I'll stand by and watch this state become another Pennsylvania! No, by damn, we'll not let them come down here and turn Corsicana into—"

"Papa, what *are* you talking about?" Her fingers curled anxiously about the hard thickness of his upper arm as her wide, luminous sapphire gaze caught his fierce green one. "What's all this about Pennsylvania?"

"I've seen it, Dallas, I've been up there and seen it! The land here won't be fit to grow rocks if we don't

11

keep quiet about this!"

She was about to question him further . . . but never got the chance.

A short, dark-haired man standing near the derrick chose that moment to light his pipe. This was accomplished with a swiftness and ease borne of much practice, and nothing of any consequence would have come of his actions, were it not for the fact that the ground near the well shaft was by now thoroughly saturated with oil. Taking a long draw on the tobacco, the fellow carelessly tossed the still flaring match downward—and all hell broke loose.

Flames immediately sprang to life and engulfed the derrick. Curses and shouts burst from the drillers' lips as they flung themselves away from the well in an instinctive quest for survival. Screams and gasps punctuated the flight of the onlookers as they scattered like so many chickens. Dallas's father yanked her backward to safety, then stood watching with her in helpless and stunned disbelief while the oil-fed blaze quickly consumed the wooden derrick.

The fire was extinguished shortly thereafter. Miraculously, no one had been injured. The spectators returned, their numbers steadily increasing as news of the exciting goings-on down near the Cotton Belt tracks spread all over town.

Dallas remained at the site with her father, who was soon called upon to labor at the forge that had been set up near the well. Several pieces of equipment required the blacksmith's immediate attention. The drillers, impatient to get on with their task, were aided by some of the railroad workers in erecting another, rather makeshift derrick. In almost no time at all, the old cable tool rig was boring down through the damnably oil-bearing stratum once more.

But disaster soon struck again.

A spark from Abner Brown's forge was the culprit this time. The hot, tiny flicker of light, shooting outward as if ordained by providence, was all it took to ignite the ground about the well. Drillers and onlookers took off like a shot yet again, and the second derrick perished in the same manner as its predecessor. Dallas was always to wonder if perhaps her oil-hating father had not "willed" the spark to cause the destruction.

Before someone finally hit upon the idea of constructing a ditch by which the oil seepage would be routed to an earthen tank a few yards to the side of the well, a total of three derricks had gone up in flames. This particular tally became something of a joke among the townfolk, who continued to flock to the drilling site to offer the workmen comment or advice or a less than appreciated bit of levity about the situation.

The near bankrupt drillers finally finished their water well. The local businessmen promoting the wells had been annoyed with the delay caused by the oil. They repeatedly asserted that, since no real market existed for the "smelly black stuff" in Texas—what with no way to refine it, store it, ship it, or even be certain it was of commercial value—there was absolutely no plan of utilizing the discovery.

But, as if deliberately taunting Abner Brown for the fears he had voiced to his beautiful eldest daughter, fate decreed otherwise . . .

I

Corsicana, Texas . . . 1898

"No, Cordi. Meeting Mr. Kincaid at the station is a necessary evil I'd rather perform alone!" Dallas asserted in a voice edged with simmering indignation. Her anger was not directed toward her sister, but rather toward a man she didn't even know.

Rossiter Maverick Kincaid. Why in the world would someone choose to give their child such an incredible-sounding name? More importantly, Dallas asked herself with yet another frown of intense annoyance, would the bearer of this thoroughly ridiculous moniker turn out to be as arrogant and ill-mannered as she envisioned?

"Why must you be so obstinate about everything all the time?" Cordelia Brown's wide-set, blue-green eyes flashed with sisterly irritation as she placed her hands on her hips and challenged, "Simply because Mr. Kincaid is a few days late, is that any reason to—"

"Not a few days—a *week!*" Dallas amended sharply,

her own sapphire gaze shooting sparks. "I suppose we should count ourselves fortunate that he *deigned* to send us word of his belated arrival at all!" Two bright spots of color stained the lightly freckled smoothness of her cheeks, and the fire in her eyes deepened as she recalled the disagreeable fact that, until the arrival of his telegram yesterday, she and her sisters had been left to worry and wonder if the rogue was ever going to show up at all.

"There may be a perfectly logical explanation for his delay, you know!" the pretty, sandy-haired young woman of eighteen pointed out. She was close on her older sister's heels as Dallas marched into the front entrance foyer and impatiently settled a small, perky hat of pale-blue straw atop lustrous auburn curls arranged in the "pompadour" style that had become the rage throughout the past year. Cordi heaved a sigh and tried one last time to reason with the hot-tempered redhead who had been both mother and sister to her for the past ten years. "I should think you'd be glad of my support when you finally come face-to-face with him! From what Sam's told Etta about these drillers, they're not exactly what one would call easy to deal with. Why, according to Sam, they can be positively belligerent! Come now, surely you must see that it would be best if I came along to—"

"No, Cordi," Dallas firmly reiterated while her right hand moved to close about the brass doorknob. Looking very much like someone preparing to do battle, she lifted her head proudly, squared her shoulders, and flung the door open. "When I *do* come face-to-face with Mr. Kincaid," she paused to declare while her breasts rose and fell rapidly beneath her

16

starched white blouse, "I fully intend to let him know how utterly disgraceful I find his behavior to be! And having either you or Etta present would only serve to make the confrontation even more unpleasant than I expect it to be!"

Dallas swept briskly down the steps of the front porch and made straightaway for the sorrel mare and "slightly used" spring wagon she had only recently procured from the Mitten Livery Stable. The wagon's presence before the large white, gable-roofed house on the outskirts of the city was something of an extravagance, particularly when given its new owner's usually prudent management of the family finances, but Dallas had convinced herself it was a wise purchase nonetheless. After all, with their father gone, a reliable means of transportation was a necessity for the three Brown sisters.

She climbed up to the worn leather seat, arranged her dark navy broadcloth skirts about her, then took up the reins and quickly drove away. Well aware of the fact that the train had been due to arrive a full quarter of an hour earlier, she smiled to herself in smug satisfaction and mused that it would do Mr. Rossiter Maverick Kincaid a world of good to realize that he was not the only one who could keep people waiting!

Her smile faded in the next instant when George Proctor's kindly face swam before her eyes. It was George who had arranged for the man to come to Corsicana, and it was George who, all too familiar with his beloved goddaughter's headstrong and independent nature, had made her promise to "bend over backwards" to get along with the driller.

Dallas released a long sigh and gave a sharp flick of

the reins. Promise or no promise, she wasn't about to "bend" at all—either backwards or forwards or in any other direction! Mr. Kincaid would have to realize that *he* was working for *her* and not the other way around! Although there was every likelihood that to exert her authority in so blunt a manner as she intended would earn her a stern reprimand from George, she wasn't about to play the part of a meek, helpless female. No, she had come too far for that . . .

Thoughts of George inevitably brought back memories of her father. He had been gone nearly six months now, and yet his presence could still be felt in the house. Overbearing and gruff and often downright cantankerous as Abner Brown had been, his daughters had loved him dearly and had never doubted they were loved by him in return. Dallas's mouth curved into a sad little smile of remembrance as she told herself that their life together may not always have been happy, but neither had it been dull.

Plagued by a fresh wave of guilt, she frowned and shifted uneasily upon the leather seat. She could not shake the feeling that she was betraying her father. To the very end, he had refused to follow the example of his friends and neighbors. He had stubbornly clung to his belief that oil would ruin the land, and no amount of argument or method of persuasion had been able to make him agree to joining in on the boom.

Forgive me, Papa, she silently beseeched. There was little doubt in her mind as to what Abner Brown's reaction would have been if he'd known of his daughter's plans to have an oil well drilled right smack-dab in the middle of their backyard. Recalling George's teasing remark about his old friend turning

18

over in his grave, she sighed again and cast her troubled blue gaze upon the familiar sights she was passing on her way across town to the Southern Pacific Depot.

She found herself reflecting once more upon how very much everything had changed since the fateful time, almost exactly four years ago, when oil had first bubbled up out of the ground to transform the city's quiet, orderly existence into that of a crowded, hustling, and boisterous boomtown's. Willingly or not, Corsicana had entered the rough and tumble world of oil that day, and there was no going back.

Scores of oil scouts, drillers, and potential investors still flocked to participate in Texas's first oil boom. The hotels and boardinghouses were full to bursting, houses that had been vacant for years were now rented at exorbitant prices, and nearly everyone who wanted employment encountered no difficulty whatsoever in finding it. Other outsiders of lesser virtue also sought opportunity—indeed, it wasn't long before residents began complaining about the great number of tramps and "roving characters" who infested the town and whose invasion begat a rash of crimes ranging from burglary and pilferage to the unusual but highly irritating theft of garments drying on clotheslines.

While the feverish oil excitement brought with it a welcome boost to the local economy, it also spawned a rapid proliferation of saloons, gaming halls, and bawdyhouses. Most of the activity of *this* caliber took place down near the railroad tracks, but everyone for miles around was aware of what was going on. Business, particularly brisk on paydays, was carried on at all hours with little restraint on the noise or nonsense, though the city officials had recently given in to repeated pestering by the conservative element of the town and decreed that these notorious establishments would at least close their doors on Sunday. Periodic reports of violence and mayhem emanating from this more "lively" section of town were frequent. Only last week, Dallas recalled with an expressive wrinkling of her slightly upturned nose, there was an incident wherein a Pennsylvania pipe-gauger was severely battered with a brick by an inebriated townsman who apparently took exception to the Yankee's boast about *his* native state's contribution to Corsicana's good fortune.

Times had certainly changed for the former cotton town, she mentally concluded, her grimace turning into a smile of appreciative irony when another memory suddenly drifted to the forefront of her mind. Four years ago, as the drillers struggled to bypass the crude and complete the artesian well that would inadvertently launch the boom, the *Dallas Morning News* found the most noteworthy happening in the area to be that of a valuable mule being struck and killed by a freight train near Corsicana . . .

Having reached the depot by this time, Dallas maneuvered the wagon alongside the raised wooden platform and tugged on the reins. Her dark auburn brows knitted together into a frown when she saw that the train had not yet arrived.

Late as usual, she mused in annoyance. Setting the brake, she gathered up her skirts and climbed down, then took her place among the other people gathered in front of the small brick building to wait. Although not precisely in the mood to make idle conversation, she politely returned the greetings of several acquaintances and murmured an evasive response to questions regarding her presence at the station. She finally wandered over to the ticket window, where the depot agent saluted her approach with a nod and a broad grin.

"Mornin', Miss Dallas. Gonna be another hot one, ain't it?"

"I'm afraid so, Mason." Knowing that it was expected of her, she dutifully shaded her eyes against the sun's bright rays and peered up toward the cloudless blue sky. If there was one thing Mason Parnell loved to talk about, she told herself with an inaudible sigh, it was the weather. Today, however, he surprised her by changing the subject.

"I heard tell you got yourself a driller comin' in today. Your pa wouldn't be too happy 'bout that, now, would he? 'Course, me and the missus—"

"How did you know about Mr. Kincaid?" Dallas abruptly cut him off. Why, no one save herself and her sisters . . . *Etta,* she thought in growing suspicion. It would be just like Etta to have told Sam. And Sam could nearly always be counted on to relate anything of interest to his father, who in turn would of a certainty tell his wife. After that, Dallas reflected with an inward groan of exasperation, the whole town would be privy to the information!

"It's my business to know such things, ain't it?" the short, balding man before her quipped with a self-satisfied smile. Mason Parnell prided himself on the fact that he ruled the depot in every way possible—he brought the news first, sold tickets, mastered the intricacies of baggage checks and waybills, man-handled freight on and off the cars whenever his

21

assistance was needed, fielded complaints, and passed along the "colorful" stories he heard from the drummers on their way to and from town.

Dallas was tempted to ask him, sarcastically, if he also knew what she'd eaten for breakfast that day, but she wisely held her tongue. She managed a cool smile, then turned away from the ticket window and wandered restlessly over to the side of the building. Raising a hand to one of the reddish-brown bricks, she absently fingered the letters, *C-O-R-S-I-C-A-N-A,* stamped within the center. The Whiteselle Brick and Lumber Company, a local firm, was quite proud of the fact that each and every brick used to build the depot bore the city's name. A soft, crooked smile touched her lips when she thought back to how her father had made no secret of the fact that he considered the building's "uniqueness" to be nothing more than—

The shrill whistle sounding in the near distance signaled the train's arrival. Every muscle in Dallas's body tensed, and she was dismayed to feel her stomach doing a sudden flip-flop.

Dallas Brown, you're as nervous as a long-tailed cat under a rocking chair! she chided herself in disgust. For goodness' sakes, what was there to be so jittery about? She was merely going to say what had to be said. After all, she thought as she lifted her chin in a gesture that was unconsciously self-defiant, her anger with the man was righteous anger, was it not? Mr. Kincaid had responded to her generous offer of employment by keeping her on tenterhooks this past week while he did God-only-knows-what up in Pennsylvania. If not for the severe shortage of competent drillers, she would have demanded a return of the money she had advanced him and arranged for someone else to drill her well!

Realizing that it wasn't like her to form such an intense dislike for someone she had never even set eyes on before, she nonetheless could not help feeling that she and Rossiter Maverick Kincaid were destined to clash . . .

Several minutes later, after the majority of the other passengers had disembarked and she had begun to fear the driller would not appear, she spied a tall, raven-haired man stepping leisurely down from the train. Her eyes grew enormous within the delicate oval of her face as they fastened upon him, and she was totally unprepared for the way her heart suddenly took to pounding.

Good heavens, it's him!

There was no way of being certain, of course, she breathlessly reasoned with herself, but she somehow *sensed* he was the one. Rossiter Maverick Kincaid—in the flesh. Only, she had never dreamt he would turn out to be so . . . so . . .

Devilishly handsome, an inner voice obligingly finished for her. She couldn't help but agree. He towered above the others milling about on the platform, so that, for the space of several long moments, she was afforded with the opportunity to critically appraise him—or rather his face—without detection.

Though she couldn't see as well as she would have liked, due to the fact that a distance of quite a number of yards separated her from the spot where he stood negligently perusing the crowd, she was able to discern that he was a good deal younger than she had expected—no more than thirty. His features were strong, chiseled . . . undeniably masculine . . . and the rugged perfection of his face and neck had been tanned to a deep golden hue, giving evidence of the fact that he apparently spent most of his time out-of-doors. Her fascinated gaze traveled up to his hair, which was black as midnight and currently set afire by the sun's radiance. It was thick, slightly waved, and cut short above his collar—

Dallas inhaled upon a gasp when her eyes suddenly met his. Hastily averting her gaze, she could feel the hot color flooding her face. She was furious with herself for having been caught staring—and furious with *him* for catching her!

Stealing a quick glance in his direction again, she was nonplussed to observe that he was now making his way through the crowd toward her. It was impossible not to watch him as he drew closer, for his superior height demanded—and ultimately received—notice.

Maybe he isn't Mr. Kincaid after all! she hopefully told herself, fighting down an inexplicable surge of sheer panic. Perhaps she had merely allowed her imagination to run wild, perhaps he wasn't coming over to speak to *her,* but to someone else.

Anxious to gain support for this latter theory, she hurriedly looked around, only to note with a sinking feeling of dread that she was the only person occupying space on that particular side of the depot. The last of her hopes were dashed when she turned back to find him looming ominously above her.

Stifling another gasp, she instinctively dropped her eyes to the worn, dusty wooden planks of the platform. She stared at a pair of dark brown leather cowboy boots for a painfully long moment before her luminous, deep blue gaze was drawn irrevocably upward. Her widening eyes beheld long, hard-muscled legs molded by a pair of fitted denim trousers . . . narrow hips beckoned attention to a trim waist and a tooled leather belt with a large silver buckle that glinted in the sunlight . . . a pale-blue cotton shirt was stretched tight across a broad chest and a set of wide, brawny shoulders . . . and a slow, insolent smile spread across a countenance that was a perfect match for the lean, unabashedly virile body below it.

Dallas swallowed a sudden lump in her throat and forced herself to meet the man's gaze. She was shocked by the powerful tremor which coursed through her when her eyes encountered the amused intensity of his. Of a brilliant apple-green hue, his eyes glowed with a strange, unfathomable light that was positively unnerving.

Dismayed to feel another blush staining her cheeks, she retreated behind a wall of prim-and-proper aloofness. She drew herself rigidly erect and fixed the man with a look that would have withered lesser men. Her fingers clenched about her reticule as she narrowed her eyes up at him. Since he stood nearly a foot taller than she, she was forced to tilt her head back in order to face him squarely.

"You *are* Mr. Rossiter Maverick Kincaid, are you not?" she asked, her words more of a challenge than a question. She despised herself for the telltale quaver in her usually well-controlled voice.

"George didn't tell me you were so young," the man drawled lazily, his own voice deep and resonant and full of a noticeable appreciation of the humor in the situation. Dallas almost blurted out that there was a good many things George hadn't told *her,* but she instead chose to demand in a brisk tone edged with impatience, "I suppose I may take that to mean you are indeed Mr. Kincaid?"

He didn't answer right away. She was infuriated when his penetrating gaze made a bold, leisurely appraisal of her face and figure. Plagued by the strange, thoroughly disquieting sensation that he was somehow able to see a great deal more than she would have liked, she found herself fervently wishing she had accepted Cordi's offer of support. There was something about the man before her, something she could not yet put a name to, that made her feel as though he were dangerous . . .

"You can take it to mean anything you like." The merest hint of a mocking smile touched his lips before he finally confirmed, "But yes, I am *Ross* Kincaid."

"And *I* am, as you correctly surmised, Miss Brown. Now that we've got the matter of our identities settled, perhaps you'd care to tell me exactly *why* you are a week late?" Her beautiful face was flushed with a dull, angry color, and her eyes darkened as they flashed accusingly up into his. Though she had been initially quite taken aback to discover he was not at all what she had expected, she found her indignation over his delayed arrival returning to hit her full-force. "I must tell you, Mr. Kincaid, that I most assuredly do *not* appreciate the manner in which you have conducted our business together thus far! My sisters and I were quite naturally worried when you did not show up on the appointed date. For some unknown reason, George Proctor's inquiries regarding your whereabouts proved

26

entirely fruitless, and—"

"George knows me well enough to vouch for my good character," he declared in a low voice brimming with laughter.

"What do you mean, 'George knows you well enough'?" she asked in sudden bewilderment. "Why, he . . . he never said anything about having made your acquaintance—"

"I suppose he had his reasons." Apparently dismissing the subject, and Dallas's questions, altogether, Ross lifted a hand to replace his snakeskin-banded Stetson atop his head. Dallas was startled when he moved to her side and took her upper arm in a firm grip. Resisting his attempt to pull her along with him, she demanded breathlessly, "Wha—what on earth do you think you're doing? Let go of me!"

"Look, *Miss Brown,*" he countered, his tone one of exaggerated patience as though he were speaking to a child, "don't you think we've wasted enough time? I came to do a job, and I'd like to get to it."

"You came to—" she echoed in disbelief, then sputtered indignantly, "Why, you . . . how dare you!" She jerked her arm from his grasp and took a furious step backward. Her eyes blazed up at him as she balled her hands into fists and planted them on her hips. "I'm fully aware of the fact that you have work to do! In the event you have forgotten, I happen to be the one employing you! And as for wasting time—may I remind you that *you,* Mr. Kincaid, bear sole responsibility for an entire *week's* delay!"

She paused to try and regain her composure, only to lose it again when she observed the impertinent humor dancing in Ross Kincaid's eyes. *Why, the arrogant*

Yankee was actually laughing at her! If there was one thing she hated, it was being treated with this . . . this masculine irreverence she encountered all too often. She was a grown woman, not some silly, simpering little schoolgirl, and she'd be damned if she'd allow this man to treat her as such!

"We might as well get things settled here and now, Mr. Kincaid," Dallas feelingly asserted. The rapid rise and fall of her breasts and becoming rosiness of her cheeks left little doubt as to the present state of her emotions. Oblivious to the fact that she and the handsome but overbearing driller were standing alone on the platform now—and also to the fact that Mason Parnell was leaning far out of the ticket window at the opposite end of the depot and straining to catch every word she uttered—she folded her arms tightly across her firm young bosom and declared with as much dignity as she could muster, "Although George Proctor was the one who first approached you about the matter, *I* am the one who hired you to come to Corsicana. I am the one who advanced you more than five hundred dollars to purchase the necessary equipment. And I, Mr. Kincaid, am the one who was forced to sit around and wait for seven days while you did not even see fit to advise me of the circumstances surrounding your delay!"

She dropped her arms to her sides and took a deep breath. When she spoke again, it was with only slightly less vehemence.

"Whatever your reasons for not arriving on the appointed day—well, I don't suppose they really matter now. What does matter, however, is our relationship as employer and employee. I don't think you quite understand the way things are, Mr. Kincaid. You see, *you* work for *me,* and I demand that you accord me the—"

"No, Miss Brown," Ross disagreed in a low, deceptively level tone. All traces of amusement had vanished now, to be replaced by a faintly menacing air of forcefulness. He took a step toward her, and his unwavering, light green eyes seemed to bore down into the glistening blue depths of hers as he quietly proclaimed, "I'm afraid you're the one who doesn't understand. I work for myself."

"But that . . . that simply is not so! George said you agreed to the terms of our arrangement. While it's true that your compensation will be in the form of a small percentage of the profits, it is also nonetheless true that I will be paying for all the equipment and labor required to drill the well—not to mention providing food and board for you throughout the duration of your stay here—which therefore means that you will indeed be working for *me!*" Her whole demeanor issued a silent challenge to him as she stood there with her beautiful chin set at a defiant angle and her hands clenched within the folds of her skirt.

Unbeknownst to Dallas, something deep within Rossiter Maverick Kincaid stirred in that moment, something he could not quite put a name to. He told himself it was nothing more than a begrudging appreciation of her loveliness and spirit, but his heart was unconvinced. What the devil was there about this uppity, fiery-eyed little redhead that made him experience such a strange combination of irritation and admiration and—damn it!—the desire to reach out, yank the pins from that mass of flaming hair, and watch it tumble wildly down about her face and shoulders?

She's different from the other women you've known. You could tell that almost from the first moment you set eyes on her, a small, inner voice in his mind expounded. Cursing himself for a fool, Ross impatiently lifted a hand to tug the front brim of his hat lower. His eyes glittered coldly and a tiny muscle twitched in the bronzed ruggedness of his left cheek as he reiterated, "It makes no difference who's paying the bills—I'm still my own boss. George should have made that clear to you. I never take orders from anyone but myself, *Miss Brown.*" The sound of her name on his lips gave the distinct impression of mockery. "I work at my own pace, hire my own crew, and make all my own decisions regarding the well. To put it bluntly, I'll be damned if I'll put up with any interference from you or your sisters! Now either you accept things the way they are, or you can find yourself another driller."

Dallas visibly seethed. The arrogant scoundrel had her over a barrel, and he knew it! Glaring murderously up at him, she was torn between the urge to drive off and leave him standing there beneath the hot Texas sun, and the desire to slap his insolent, handsome face for him. Thankfully, however, the voice of reason prevailed and she did neither. Never, in the entirety of her twenty-one years, had any man infuriated her in quite the same manner as *this* one had, and most particularly not after only two minutes' acquaintance! How in heaven's name was she ever going to be able to do business with him? Worse yet, how was she ever going to be able to tolerate his presence in her backyard for the next several weeks?

Making a silent vow to show Ross Kincaid that she possessed enough brains and backbone to keep him from running roughshod over her—as he was apparently used to doing with everyone else—she took a brisk step forward, looked him straight in the eye, and said, "You leave me little choice. But let us have an understanding, Mr. Kincaid. I will not tolerate discourtesy from you while you are on my property, *nor* will I tolerate it from any members of the crew you assemble. My sisters are both young and impressionable, and I will not have them exposed to the sort of . . . of 'vulgarity' which I've noticed is quite common among men of your profession! In short, Mr. Kincaid, if you or your—"

"In short, Miss Brown, you want me and my men to be on our best behavior," he supplied, his deep voice laced with what she could have sworn was contemptuous humor. Without responding one way or the other to her demands, he seized her arm again and did not allow her time to protest before leading her over to where another man stood solemnly watching them in front of the depot.

"This is Erik Larsen, my partner," Ross casually informed her, his long, work-hardened fingers maintaining their dominant grasp upon her arm. "Swede, this is Miss Brown."

Erik Larsen's somber, unmistakably Nordic features were transformed by the dazzling smile he turned upon Dallas. He was nearly as tall as Ross, and only a year or two younger. With the flaxen hair and cobalt blue eyes that were the familiar signature of his heritage, he was the striking antithesis of his darkly handsome partner.

"I am honored to meet you, Miss Brown," the

31

attractive young Swede gallantly proclaimed, sweeping his brown felt hat from his head. Though his speech was tinged by a noticeable accent, his English was flawless and his manners impeccable. *In that, he is also the opposite of his associate!* Dallas resentfully mused.

"Thank you, Mr. Larsen." She was unable to refrain from answering his smile with a brief one of her own. "Mr. Kincaid neglected to mention the existence of a partner," she then remarked with a narrow, pointed look up at Ross. Pulling her arm free at last, she happened to catch sight of the smirk on Mason Parnell's face. The depot agent sat perched atop his stool on the other side of the ticket window, and he made little effort to conceal his eavesdropping. His all-too-knowing expression made it seem as though he were saying, *I told you so, Dallas Brown. I told you you shouldn't have gone against your pa's wishes.* She did her best to ignore him, but she was all too aware of the fact that every detail of what had happened between her and "one of them Yankee drillers" would soon be related to anyone and everyone even remotely interested. There were times when she almost wished she had followed through on her plans to move to the city for which she had been named!

"Are you coming or not?" The clear, resonant tones of Ross Kincaid's voice broke in on her troubled thoughts. Blinking up at him, she realized that he was waiting for her to lead the way to the wagon—and not too patiently, either, judging from the way he stood virtually glowering down at her.

"What about the equipment?" she defiantly shot back, her eyes flashing once more. What was there about the man that put her on the defensive every time he so much as looked at her? "Your telegram said it would arrive yesterday, but we've seen nothing of it yet!" Ross's own gaze kindled with a responsive spark as his mouth tightened into a thin line of anger.

"To tell the truth, *Miss Brown,* I don't know what the hell happened to it," he said, obviously hating to admit the problem.

"What?" Dallas breathed in outraged disbelief. "You . . . you mean to tell me that five hundred dollars' worth of equipment has simply disappeared?"

Ross's scowl deepened, and his temper flared to a dangerous level. He was furious with himself for having trusted the equipment out of his sight—and furious with his beautiful young "employer" for interrogating him about it.

"The railroad prefers to term it a 'temporary misplacement'," he muttered tightly. "Someone between here and Pennsylvania's got it, and you can damn sure bet Swede and I will find out who! Until then, we'll have to make do with whatever we can scrape together in Corsicana." Settling his hat lower upon his thick raven locks again, he snatched up the two battered valises at his partner's feet and began striding back toward the other end of the platform. Erik smiled at Dallas, his hat in his hand as he politely waited for her to make the first move.

Still fuming, she gathered up her skirts and swept regally across the wooden planks. She refused to spare so much as a glance at Ross when she approached the wagon. He stood ready to help her up, but she willfully ignored his outstretched hand and raised her foot to the stepping board.

A loud gasp broke from her lips as she suddenly felt

two strong hands closing about her waist. With startling swiftness, she was hoisted up into the wagon, then tossed unceremoniously—almost roughly—upon the front seat. She opened her mouth to offer a scathing assessment of such manhandling, but Ross effectively cut her off by climbing up beside her in one lithe motion and forcing her to either move over or risk being flattened by his tall, hard-muscled frame. It wasn't until he had taken up the reins and released the brake that a thoroughly provoked Dallas recovered voice enough to demand, "What in heaven's name do you think you're doing? This is *my* wagon, Rossiter Maverick Kincaid, and I'll not have you—"

"It's *Ross* Kincaid," he corrected with a noticeable edge to his voice. Then, giving a cursory but expert snap of the reins, he guided the wagon about and headed it toward the center of town. "We'll take a look at your property first," he decreed in the self-confident, authoritative manner of a man used to giving orders—and having them obeyed.

"By all means," Dallas parried with biting sarcasm. "But unless you are possessed of a remarkable clairvoyance, you will require directions!" She thought she heard a low chuckle behind her, where Erik had bent his own tall frame upon the rear seat. A faint smile touched Ross's lips.

"Only after we get through town. I know the general location of your place—I always make it a point to learn all I can about a field's production beforehand. Besides," he added, his gaze idly surveying their sun-drenched surroundings, "I doubt if Corsicana's changed so much that I won't be able to find my way around."

34

"You mean you . . . you've been here before?" Her eyes widened in surprise.

"More than once. The last time was nearly five years ago."

"But what could have brought you to Corsicana back then? Oil wasn't even discovered until—"

"It had nothing to do with oil."

Dallas waited for him to elaborate. When he did not, she heaved a sigh and questioned with more than a hint of renewed exasperation, "Well, what *did* it have to do with, Mr. Kincaid?" She was unprepared when he suddenly turned to her and smiled. His eyes twinkled across at her in disconcerting amusement, and she was almost certain she glimpsed a not-entirely-proper warmth within those gleaming viridescent depths.

"George Proctor. I stopped by and paid a visit to him on my way back from the ranch."

"Ranch?"

"My family's place in Fort Worth."

"Fort Worth? But I thought you were from Pennsylvania!" She gazed at him in dawning realization while her eyes grew very round. "Why, you . . . you're not a Yankee at all, are you?" she demanded accusingly, as if he had set out to deceive her.

"I never said I was."

She stared openmouthed at him for a moment, then pivoted angrily back around. *Hell's bells, nothing was going as she had planned!* Here she was, with a Yankee driller who wasn't a Yankee at all, with two men to provide room and board for instead of one, and with five hundred dollars' worth of equipment that had mysteriously disappeared. And to make matters worse, she seethed inwardly, the man beside her was a supercilious, dictatorial, devil-may-care rogue who had probably left a trail of broken hearts from Texas all the way up to Pennsylvania!

Dallas shot him a quick, wrathful glance. Her mouth curved into a smile of purely feminine mischief as she mused that it would give her the greatest of pleasure to knock Rossiter Maverick Kincaid off his self-erected pedestal . . .

Ross, meanwhile, had turned his attention to the boomtown. He was not surprised to see the vast number of derricks scattered through Corsicana and dotting the green, gently rolling countryside—he had expected as much. Still, it was something of a shock to view the familiar panorama right there in his home state. The quiet little community he remembered had become a veritable forest of oil towers, all of them stretching eighty-five feet into the sky. The wooden giants loomed over the housetops, in backyards and front yards and gardens and horse lots. And in some areas the derricks stood within only a few feet of each other, signifying a drilling practice he knew to be profitable but reckless.

Recalling something he had read in a newspaper recently—"Corsicana is one city in Texas that is full up"—he observed the truth of that statement as he drove the wagon down Beaton Street. The busy scene was one of noise and movement and a heady excitement that could actually be felt. Men, women, and children hurried along the crowded boardwalks flanking the main road, which had been "paved" some ten years earlier by way of a unique method using eight-inch Bois d'Arc blocks; it was rough all right, but not so muddy when the rains came.

People of all shapes and sizes, ages and backgrounds were in the process of frequenting a wide assortment of establishments—banks, hotels, drugstores, barber shops, a telephone and telegraph company, grocery and hardware stores, livery stables, doctors' offices, bicycle shops, dry goods stores, two newspaper bureaus, attorneys' and land agents' offices on the top floor of buildings housing undertakers and tailors, a photography studio, a bakery, and even a confectionary where candies were manufactured fresh on the premises. In the midst of all this commotion, pedestrians and horsemen continually blocked the path of the city's mule-drawn streetcar, only to find themselves cursed out of the way by the crusty, sharp-tongued driver.

Ross smiled to himself when he glanced up to note the ninety-foot gaslight tower still proudly standing guard at the corner of Collin and Beaton streets. The old, derrick-type structure looked especially incongruous with all the poles and lines running down each side of the street, but he recalled how it had created quite a stir when erected some thirteen years ago. The first of its kind, the light had burned brightly above the rolling plains before progress finally brought electricity to the town.

The memory of George Proctor's enthusiastic boasts about the "giant, innovative tower of illumination" brought another brief smile to Ross's lips. Heaven knew George loved progress as much as any good banker should, but there were apparently some things even George didn't want to see changed. Ross fully believed that was why his lifelong friend had chosen to accept the presidency of a bank in Fort Worth soon after the oil fever took hold of Corsicana—because he couldn't bear to stand by and watch the boom transform the peaceful, orderly existence of his beloved hometown into a chaotic whirlwind of activity.

Whirlwind. Why the devil did that particular term seem to so accurately describe the present state of his emotions? It sure as hell wasn't because of what was going on around him. No, he was a man well-accustomed to the fever and flurry which went hand-in-hand with the discovery of oil.

Dallas Brown. That damned little voice in his mind said it for him. What was there about her that fired both his interest and his blood? There was no denying her obvious charms, but he somehow knew it was more than that. Much more . . .

"Mr. Kincaid! Mr. Kincaid, are you listening to me?"

Mentally shaking himself, Ross frowned and looked at the young woman beside him. Her voice had sounded sharp and impatient, and her eyes were flashing the deep blue sparks he had already come to know so well. He felt an odd racing of his pulses. Breathing a silent oath, he gave an abrupt flick of the reins and responded with an unaccountably terse "What is it?"

"I thought it might interest you to know that we're supposed to bear left upon reaching the fork in the road ahead!" *Is the impossible man deaf as well as overbearing?* Dallas thought sourly.

"Tex has told me the main field encompasses the entire eastern half of your city, Miss Brown," Erik unexpectedly spoke up.

Dallas turned to face him, her gaze shifting to Ross and back. "Tex?"

38

"A fair exchange, do you not agree?" the young Swede quipped with an appealingly crooked grin. "In the oil fields of Pennsylvania, it is the custom to identify each man by nature of his homeland. Is it not so here in Texas as well?"

"To some extent, I suppose." She allowed a brief smile of irony to touch her lips as she added, "Of course, nearly every man in the state would classify as a 'Tex,' while I'm sure a large number of the others would share the distinction of *your* background, Mr. Larsen." Facing forward again, she was all too conscious of Ross's eyes on her. She forced herself to refrain from looking his way, instead fastening her gaze on a lone hawk circling in the hot air currents above.

The next several minutes passed in silence, broken only by the creaking of the wagon springs and the increasingly distant sounds of the city. By the time Ross pulled the wagon to a halt in front of her home, Dallas was once again doubting the wisdom of her scheme. After all, what did she really know of these men? Aside from George Proctor's recommendation—and even *that* seemed to raise certain nagging questions in her mind—how could she be certain the impudent driller and his partner wouldn't turn out to be thieves or rascals or . . . or worse?

Groaning inwardly at the way she was allowing her imagination to run rampant, Dallas alighted from the wagon before Ross could make a move to offer—or rather *decree*—assistance. She swept briskly forward until she stood within the shade of two massive oak trees lining the walk. Her eyes widened once more when she turned back to see that the men had retrieved their valises from the back of the wagon and were obviously intent upon following her into the house with them.

"Wha—what are you doing?" she queried with a frown of bafflement.

"Exactly what it looks like," parried Ross. He tipped his hat further back upon his head as he paused to give the house a swift but critical appraisal. His slightly narrowed gaze took in the typical Texas "shotgun" structure that had been remodeled and enlarged by Dallas's father a few years earlier. Painted white with green trim, it sported a three-gabled roof with a fish-scale shingled gable on the front, a wide gallery across the front and on the east side where it ended in a graceful gazebo, and a screened back porch which stretched across the south side of the house. In addition to the forty-year-old oak trees which stood guard before the house, the immediate grounds were well-landscaped with smaller trees and shrubbery, while rose bushes climbed high upon the white latticework at both ends of the front gallery. It was obvious to Ross that the place was well cared for, and he couldn't help but be reminded of the pride his own family had always taken in their home. The roses were a particular reminder—he smiled to himself at the memory of how his mother had once walloped the daylights out of him for having the misfortune to land in the midst of her rosebushes while roughhousing with one of his younger brothers.

"Your home is a very nice one, Miss Brown," Erik pronounced, his light blue eyes full of sincerity.

"Thank you, Mr. Larsen." The warm smile she bestowed upon him quickly faded when she met the other man's amused and faintly challenging gaze.

"It'll do," drawled Ross. Without another word, he brushed past Dallas and began sauntering toward the front steps. She stared openmouthed after him for a brief moment, then gathered up her skirts and hastened after him.

"I beg your pardon, Mr. Kincaid, but just *where* do you think you're going?" she demanded. She was forced to draw up short when he came to an unexpected halt and spun about.

"Once again, I should think the answer is obvious. My partner and I are anxious to get started, so if you'll just show us which rooms are ours, we'll—"

"Rooms?"

"Yes, Miss Brown—rooms," he confirmed in that tone of exaggerated patience she had already come to know and despise.

"Surely you don't think you're going to stay *here?* Why, I . . . I could never allow such a thing!" she indignantly proclaimed, her cheeks burning. "It is entirely out of the question for you and Mr. Larsen to live under the same roof with my sisters and myself!" Again, she glimpsed a light of roguish devilment in his eyes, and she was greatly alarmed to feel the manner in which her heart took to fluttering. "Besides which, I . . . I have already arranged accommodations for you in town, at the Molloy Hotel. I was extremely fortunate to find them, since all the hotels and boardinghouses in town are nearly always filled to capacity. Indeed, there are many weary oil men who must content themselves with a cot in a hotel corridor, or even a chair in the lob—"

"Then let one of those other 'weary oil men' have the room—*I* will be staying here. In order to do my job, I'll

41

have to be close by at all hours of the day and night. So, my dear Miss Brown, if you ever want to see that well of yours drilled, you'll just have to get used to the idea of seeing me around." That said, he tugged on the front brim of his hat in a gesture that was more mocking than polite and pointedly waited for her to respond.

Dallas cast another murderous look up at him and battled the wicked temptation to tell him precisely what he could do with his job. *Things are getting worse by the minute!* What in tarnation was she going to tell Cordi and Etta? More importantly, how was she going to explain to her friends and neighbors the presence of two young—and handsome, drat it!—men in her all female household? There would be talk, plenty of it, and it would be the kind of talk that could easily ruin any chance of her sisters making the advantageous marriages she coveted for them . . .

She heaved a sigh and gazed heavenward, only to be gifted with sudden inspiration. Perhaps she could find someone to act as a chaperone of sorts for the duration of Ross Kincaid's stay . . . yes, that would help a great deal. But who? she asked herself, then was almost immediately provided with the answer—*Ruby Mae Hatfield.* Thinking of the older woman who had been her friend for as long as she could remember, Dallas mused in smug satisfaction that if anyone could be counted on to protect the as-yet-untarnished reputation of the Brown sisters, that person was Ruby Mae!

"Very well, Mr. Kincaid," she finally acquiesced. Her sapphire gaze was shining with indomitable spirit as she lifted her chin and declared to the man who stood literally towering above her, "You and Mr. Larsen may stay in my house, but only if you

42

understand that there is to be absolutely no socializing with my sisters! You will be regarded as temporary guests and nothing more, so under no circumstances will you attempt to insinuate yourselves into our lives. If that is agreeable to you, then may I suggest we get on with things? You *did* come here to drill a well, did you not?"

Ross Kincaid studied the upturned countenance of the auburn-haired beauty standing so haughtily before him . . . and knew he was in trouble. Like it or not, there was no denying the way she set his blood afire. *Damn you, George,* he swore silently, though he did so without malice. And without much conviction, either.

"Whatever you say, Miss Brown," he responded with a mocking condescension that belied his words. Dallas bristled anew, but she clamped her mouth shut and marched rapidly up the walk. Ross and Erik exchanged looks of masculine indulgence before following at a more leisurely pace.

II

"See you tomorrow, Sam!" Etta Brown gaily called out, lifting a hand in farewell. She watched the slender young horseman who had brought her home rein about and ride away. Her mouth curved into a secretive, wholly feminine smile, and her golden eyes glowed with the confidence of triumph.

Tomorrow and every day for the rest of your life, Sam Houston Rawlins! she added silently. Twirling her beribboned straw sailor hat upon her fingertips, she gathered up the full skirts of her maize calico shirtwaist and traipsed lightly up the walk toward the welcoming coolness of the house.

Even on the hottest days, the twelve-foot ceilings, to-the-floor windows, and transoms over all the interior doors of the old house ensured a natural cooling process. The process was furthered by two sets of double sliding doors at strategic points, as well as two sets of French doors that also served to give certain closed-in areas a more open look. Etta, however, took all this architectural excellence for granted—much as

45

she took just about everything in life for granted. She had never actually stopped to notice or appreciate the beautiful oval of stained glass in the front door, the unique, decorative iron mantels which hung above the four separate fireplaces throughout the house, nor the tasteful and comfortable furnishings which had always helped to make the place a real home. This particular day was no exception, for her mind was completely preoccupied with thoughts of a romantic nature as she swept across the recently polished pine floor.

She released a soft sigh of contentment and felt as though she was floating on air while moving up the carpeted stairs to her room. But her dreamy state of euphoria was abruptly shattered when she swung open the door and spied the unfamiliar, battered valise resting squarely in the middle of her quilt-covered bed.

"What the—" she breathed in stunned disbelief, then suddenly remembered Dallas telling her the driller from Pennsylvania was due to arrive that day. Her eyes narrowed in growing suspicion. Giving an angry toss of her reddish-blond curls, she flounced about and went rushing back down the stairs in search of her sister.

Dallas was seated in the kitchen at that moment, trying—none too successfully—to get on with her work. Though staunchly determined not to allow the two men who were outside knowledgeably examining the lay of the land in her backyard to disrupt her life in any way whatsoever, she could not prevent her gaze from continually straying to the window. She managed to catch a glimpse of Ross Kincaid's tall form every now and then, and each time she did her eyes fell hastily back to the bowl of apples on the table before her.

Why should it bother her so much that he was

attractive? she wondered crossly after several long minutes of doing battle with herself. For heaven's sake, one would think she'd never seen a good-looking man before! Well, she had, she thought as she raised her chin defensively. She had seen plenty of them, and she'd be willing to bet her eye teeth that Ross Kincaid's dark and dashing good looks would pale considerably if viewed alongside even the second best Corsicana had to offer!

She released a long, disgruntled sigh, then became aware of the sound of footsteps on the staircase overhead. Musing with a frown that it probably owed its origin to Cordi, who had mysteriously disappeared by the time she had returned from the train station with the drillers, she steeled herself for the inevitable barrage of questions she knew to be forthcoming.

"That's *his* valise on my bed, isn't it?"

Dallas groaned inwardly at the sound of Etta's voice behind her. Her youngest sister had always been the most difficult to handle. Rising almost wearily to her feet, she turned to watch as the petite, strawberry blonde stormed into the sunlit kitchen.

"Just what in the blue blazes are that . . . that stranger's belongings doing in *my* room?" Etta demanded indignantly.

"I'm afraid things haven't quite worked out the way we expected," Dallas admitted with a heavy sigh. Her lips curled into a faint, bitter smile. "It seems Mr. Rossiter Maverick Kincaid is full of surprises."

"I don't care what he's full of! How dare you allow that Yankee to—"

"He isn't a Yankee, Etta. And he didn't come alone—he brought a partner with him. I had to put one

47

of them in your room and the other one in Papa's. I'm very sorry, but you'll simply have to double up with Cordi for a while. You see, they're . . . well, they're going to be staying here until the well is completed."

"They're going to *what?*" Her voice rose on a shrill note.

"They're going to stay here until the well is completed," Dallas calmly reiterated. "But there's no need to worry—I've already spoken to Ruby Mae and she's agreed to move in with us until they've gone." She crossed to Etta's side and placed a comforting arm about the seventeen-year-old's shoulders. "It won't be for long. And with Ruby Mae here, I don't think there will be any questions raised about—"

"What about Sam?" an unconsoled Etta demanded, her eyes sparkling with sudden, angry tears. "Goodness gracious, Dallas, what do you think he's going to say about this little 'arrangement' of yours?"

"It may surprise you to hear this, my dearest sister," Dallas replied in a tight, low voice as she returned to the kitchen table and took up the paring knife once more, "but I don't feel the least little need to defend my actions to Sam Houston Rawlins or anyone else in this town!"

"Is that so?" retorted Etta. She folded her arms across her rounded yet still-blossoming bosom and challenged, "Then why did you ask Ruby Mae to come and stay with us?"

"For the simple reason that I don't want you or Cordi to suffer any embarrassment!" She sank back down into the chair and ruthlessly stabbed the point of the knife into a plump, unresisting apple. "I don't want them here any more than you do, but I had very little choice in the matter!" Her sapphire eyes flashed in renewned pique.

"Just when I have Sam all primed and ready to begin thinking seriously about settling down, you have to go and—"

"Don't you dare start that again!" Dallas sharply cut her off. She fixed the girl with a stern, maternal frown. "Not only are you still too young to marry, but you know good and well I'm not going to allow you to throw your life away on someone who hasn't any future ahead of him!"

"You can't stop me from marrying whenever and whoever I please, Dallas Brown!" her sister cried in youthful defiance. "And Sam does too have a future— a very good one!"

"Oh, Etta, we've had this same argument a dozen times before! What good do you think it's going to do us to have it again now? As a matter of fact," she insisted with a quick scowl toward the window, "this is the worst possible time for you to go into hysterics over matters of the heart, so why don't you simply accept things the way they are and—"

"Why don't *you* accept things the way they are?" parried Etta, looking for all the world like a stubborn little bantam hen as she placed her hands on her hips and angled militantly toward Dallas. "You know very well that Sam and I have been devoted to each other since . . . well practically since we were children! And no matter what you say or do, our love will not be denied!" she finished with a melodramatic flair.

Dallas was preparing to make an appropriately sarcastic retort about the type of "devotion" that had always made her sister and Sam Rawlins quarrel almost incessantly, when Ross Kincaid suddenly threw open the back door and ducked inside without warning. Dallas abruptly rose to her feet, her color high and her eyes ablaze at his presumption. Etta stood glaring across at the intruder as though he were among the lowest forms of life on earth. Amusement flickered briefly across Ross's handsome face before Dallas swept forward to confront him.

"Mr. Kincaid," she said, her voice slightly tremulous with anger, "I thought I made it perfectly clear that you are not entitled to the same rights and privileges as the other members of this household. In future, I would appreciate it if you would have the decency to knock before entering!"

"Tell me, Miss Brown, is *that* how you enforce the rules around here?" he challenged dryly, the downward shift of his gaze indicating the knife Dallas still clutched in her hand. She flushed in embarrassment and hastily whipped her arm behind her back.

"Of course not!" Raising her chin in yet another gesture of defensiveness, she declared a bit primly, "I have never found it necessary to employ threats of physical violence."

"Never?" There was a hint of underlying laughter in his deep, resonant voice, and his eyes gleamed down at her in that same disturbing manner that had unnerved her at the train station. Dallas swallowed hard and was glad for her sister's intervention.

"I take it that *you,* sir, are the man who has come to drill our well?" Etta demanded, her tone of voice leaving little doubt as to her true feelings in the matter. Marching forward to stand beside Dallas, she tilted her head back and eyed Ross dubiously.

He responded with a brief smile and a nod. "At your service, ma'am," he drawled, then looked back to Dallas.

"Mr. Kincaid, I should like to present my sister, Henrietta," she hastily declared, finally remembering her manners. If there was one thing she had always prided herself on, it was that every visitor in her house was treated with courtesy and respect. She mentally consigned Ross Kincaid to the devil for having gone and made her betray the sacred code of Texas hospitality!

Etta, meanwhile, was apparently not at all impressed with the driller's rugged good looks. Drawing herself haughtily erect—which still left her a foot and a half shorter than Ross—she glared up at him and feelingly proclaimed, "You may have been able to bamboozle your way into this house, Mr. Kincaid, but don't think for one moment that *I* fail to see you for what you are! The sooner you do your job and get out of here, the better!"

"Etta!" her older sister dutifully scolded. The unrepentant seventeen-year-old merely cast Ross another speaking, unamiable look, then flounced from the room. Left at an uncomfortable loss for words, Dallas avoided meeting Ross's gaze. She was both surprised and relieved when, instead of offering comment on Etta's rudeness, he quietly announced, "I came to tell you I'll be taking the wagon into town." Giving a curt nod back over his shoulder toward the spot where Erik was staking out a wide patch of tree-shaded ground, he added, "The drilling site's a bit close to the house, but that can't be helped. I've got to see about getting together a rig and crew."

"Which brings us back to the matter of that five hundred dollars I sent you!" Her eyes kindled anew as they flew up to meet his. "Until George arrives, I've no more money to—"

"Money's not a problem."

"Wha—what do you mean it's not a problem?" she sputtered. "Of course it's a problem! Surely, Mr. Kincaid, you're aware of how much will be required to purchase the necessary equipment and hire the men to oper—"

"Perfectly aware, Miss Brown." He donned his hat and tugged the front brim low upon his sun-bronzed forehead. A mocking smile played about his lips as his green eyes twinkled irreverently down at her. "And like I said—it's not a problem." Turning about on his booted heel, he sauntered back outside with an easy, masculine grace and pulled the door to behind him.

Dallas stared blankly after him, not knowing what to make of his enigmatic words, not knowing what to make of *him*. He had entered her life less than an hour ago, and yet he had already managed to thoroughly upset her peaceful and orderly existence! Etta was positively up in arms over his presence, Ruby Mae Hatfield was sacrificing her much-valued privacy in order to provide a necessary stamp of respectability, and Cordi . . . well, Cordi was no doubt going to prove entirely useless for the next several days, since she was the sort who was always so "affected" whenever an attractive young man was near.

"Maybe you were right after all, Papa," she murmured aloud, her gaze drifting upward and thus in the vicinity of where she believed Abner Brown to be an avid observer of her progress in his absence.

Dallas breathed a sigh and smiled ruefully to herself. Wandering back to the table, she resumed her seat and took up the same apple she had pierced in anger a few moments earlier. The sudden glint of light on metal caught her attention, and she stared fixedly at the knife she held in her right hand. Of its own accord, her mind conjured up the startling image of a pair of vivid green eyes that seemed to convey a warning she could not, or would not, even make an attempt to identify . . .

A short time later, Cordi Brown returned home after making a hurried trip to the post office. Her haste had been prompted by the discovery of a letter she had promised to send off the day before—it was an important communication from Dallas to George Proctor, its hastily written contents informing him of Rossiter Maverick Kincaid's imminent arrival and imploring him to come to Corsicana as soon as possible.

Not only was he Dallas's godfather and the adored "uncle" to all three Brown sisters, but George was also, in accordance with Abner Brown's will, the trustee for the deceased man's estate. Dallas could not draw so much as a nickel from her father's account without George's consent and signature, a fact which galled her mightily. To add insult to injury, Abner had decreed that there would be no end to this arrangement until his eldest daughter either reached the age of twenty-five or married, whichever occurred first. It had pained Dallas greatly to learn that, although her father had relied upon her for the past ten years to manage his household and fill the role of mother for Cordi and Etta, he still did not consider her mature enough to be trusted not to squander away the small fortune his late wife had inherited long ago—a small fortune that he would never allow to be touched, even when the family finances were at their absolute worst.

Shuddering to think of Dallas's reaction should it ever come to light that the letter to George had been posted a day late, Cordi heaved a sigh and reached up to carefully disengage her new pink velvet hat with Mercury wings from atop her meticulously pompadoured curls. Her sandy-colored hair was, unfortunately, not nearly as thick as her older sister's auburn tresses, making it necessary for her to use a "rat" to help pad the full, brushed-up style that was so admired. Each night found her repeating the time-honored ritual of retrieving loose hair and combed-out tangles from her brush and placing them in the little covered dish which rested alongside the three precious vials of toilet water on her dressing table.

She frowned to herself just as a sudden, smoke-scented breeze gently billowed the skirts of her printed lawn gown. In the process of scurrying past the barn on her way to the back door, she was almost certain she heard a noise coming from within the large, musty building which housed nothing but her father's blacksmith paraphernalia and a few old relics from the often turbulent marriage of Abner and Lillian Brown.

Her ears detecting the clanging sound again, Cordi decided that it was definitely coming from inside the barn. A quick glance toward the front of the house told her that the wagon was missing, and another hasty look in the direction of the fenced-in pasture off the backyard yielded no sign of the horse. Had Dallas not returned from the station yet? she then wondered. Good heavens, the train must have been even later than usual, for she'd already had time to walk all the way to the center of town and back!

Who could be in the barn? Gathering up her skirts, she marched forward to investigate. It wasn't until she had nearly reached the open doorway that a note of warning sounded in her brain. Suppose whoever was inside was trying to steal some of her father's tools? she paused to consider. After all, there had certainly been a great deal of such purloinment taking place around town of late. Perhaps she'd better exercise caution and run on over to Ruby Mae's for help. Ruby Mae could always be counted on to handle even the most difficult and dangerous situations! she mused in appreciation of the older woman's stalwart nature.

No sooner had she decided to retreat, however, when she found herself face-to-face with the man who suddenly came striding out of the barn with an ax in his right hand and a coiled length of rope slung over his left shoulder. Cordi gasped in alarm and took an instinctive step backward, only to lose her footing when the high heel of her black kid-and-cloth shoe trounced upon an ill-placed specimen of good and porous Corsicana rock. A tiny, breathless shriek broke from her lips as she felt herself falling.

Recovering from his own initial surprise, the man sprang into action. He flung the ax aside and lunged forward just in time to prevent Cordi from landing inelegantly on her backside in the dirt. His strong arms slipped around her trembling softness and effortlessly hauled her upright, while she could only blink dazedly up at the tall, handsome stranger in a mixture of gratitude and fear . . . and a strange exhilaration.

"Who—who are you?" she demanded shakily, her

turquoise eyes widening as they encountered the arresting Nordic blue of his. "And what were you doing in our barn?" In spite of a disturbing reluctance to do so, she pushed against him and, with as much grace and composure as possible, extricated herself from his supportive embrace. Her stomach did a sudden little flip-flop when he swept the hat from his blond head and smiled disarmingly down at her.

"I am sorry if I frightened you," he apologized in his proper yet noticeably accented English. "My name is Erik Larsen, but I am called 'Swede.' And you—you are one of Miss Dallas Brown's sisters?" Cordi suffered a sharp intake of breath as a result of the way his gaze flickered briefly but thoroughly over her, and she was forced to gently clear her throat before replying, "Why, yes, yes I am. But how did you—"

"Forgive me once more," he interrupted with another smile, one which Cordi couldn't help thinking made him appear even more appealing in a wonderfully masculine way. "I should have told you in the beginning. You see, I have come with my partner to drill the well. I searched in the barn to see if I could find anything to be of use in our work." He bent and retrieved the ax before declaring with irresistible sincerity, "I did not mean to cause you alarm."

"Oh, I . . . that is," she stammered, then finished in a rush, "please, Mr. Larsen, think nothing of it!" Her eyes sparkled engagingly up at him, and her mouth curved into a smile of pure delight. "Indeed, I owe you a debt of gratitude for your timely assistance, sir."

"Consider the debt paid, Miss Brown, in return for the pleasure of helping such a pretty young lady," Erik gallantly proclaimed. Nodding down at her, he donned his hat and took himself off to finish the task of preparing the drilling site for the derrick which would be constructed the next day.

Cordi stared after him, transfixed. She had never dreamt that her sister's plan would yield such an attractive and utterly charming benefit. Yes indeed, it seemed that fortune had smiled upon them already!

Erik Larsen, she silently repeated as a faraway look came into her eyes and a number of questions ran together in her mind. Was he married? Did he perhaps have a girl waiting for him back in Pennsylvania? Would he turn out to be like the other drillers in town, the hard-living, hard-drinking, and hard-fighting men Dallas had warned her to avoid at all costs? Might it be possible that his tastes ran toward slightly impoverished but highly respectable young women of eighteen with light brown hair that wouldn't hold a curl and eyes that were an odd mixture of blue and green?

Her cheeks flushed and her fascinated gaze constantly drifting to where Erik stood critically perusing the surrounding countryside, Cordi gathered up her skirts again and made her way unhurriedly across the yard to the back steps. She seemed to take little notice of the kitchen's heretofore lone, apron-garbed occupant as she opened and closed the door, then leaned back against it with a sigh.

Dallas took one look at the other woman's face and knew that something was amiss.

"Cordi, where have you been?"

"Been? Oh, nowhere in particular," murmured Cordi. As if in a daze, she glided farther inside the pleasantly cinnamon- and apple-scented room and lightly gripped the back of a chair. She smiled dreamily and released another sigh before declaring, "My dearest sister, I'm so glad you made the decision to have the well drilled!"

"Are you indeed?" Dallas parried with a noticeable touch of sarcasm. Briskly dusting the flour from her hands, she opened the door of the black, cast-iron stove oven and slid the last of the pies inside. An expression of sisterly suspicion crossed her features when she straightened and turned back to Cordi. "And what, may I ask, has brought about this miraculous change in attitude? As I recall, it was only yesterday that you were proclaiming my decision to be of disastrous proportions!"

"Yes, but that was before I . . . well, before I truly understood how advantageous it could prove to be!" A telltale blush rose to Cordi's face while her eyes were aglow at the memory of a tall, fair-haired gentleman's arms about her.

"I see," Dallas replied with a skeptical frown. She was all too familiar with her sister's impressionable nature—particularly where men were concerned—and she now sensed that the reversal of Cordi's opinion somehow owed its origin to a member of the opposite sex. "Tell me, Cordi, did you by any chance happen to encounter anyone while on your way inside?" Although her first thought was of the young Swede working in the backyard, she then wondered if Ross Kincaid had perchance returned from town already. She hastily uttered a silent prayer that he had not. If Cordi was to become infatuated with one of the drillers, she'd rather it be with Erik Larsen, for he was most assuredly the lesser of two evils!

"Why, yes, I did!" admitted a wide-eyed Cordi,

obviously a bit amazed by the accuracy of her older sister's conjecture. "And oh, Dallas, he is not at all what I expected! He was very proper and didn't even try to take liberties, even though he certainly could have under the circumstances! Don't you think he is terribly attractive? You know, his eyes are so kind, and—"

"Who?" Dallas impatiently demanded, telling herself that the man in question couldn't possibly be Ross Kincaid, for *his* eyes were full of devilment, not kindness. As a matter of fact, she mused to the accompaniment of a sudden, inexplicable tremor dancing down her spine, everything about him spoke of a sort of mischief she dared not name!

"Mr. Larsen, of course! Why didn't you tell me Mr. Kincaid would be bringing along a partner?" It appeared that she was much too engrossed with thoughts of Erik Larsen to bother being curious about the other man.

"Because I didn't know!" snapped Dallas, her nerves understandably beginning to wear thin. She heard the grandfather clock in the hallway chiming the hour of twelve, prompting her to release a heavy sigh and tell Cordi, "I'll have to explain everything later. Right now, we've got to see to dinner. From what I know of him thus far, it would be thoroughly in keeping with that insufferable man's character for him to demand a five-course meal three times a day!"

"Surely you're not referring to Mr. Larsen!" Cordi vigorously protested in defense of the young man who had already managed to capture her profound interest.

Rolling her eyes heavenward in yet another burst of exasperation, Dallas bit back the retort that rose to her lips and spun about to snatch the covered plate of day-old bread from its place near the stove. She didn't care *what* Mr. Rossiter Maverick Kincaid demanded—sandwiches were all he was going to get! And if he dared to say one word, *one word,* she'd inform him in no uncertain terms as to what he could do with his complaints . . .

Fortunately for Ross, he said nothing. In fact, both he and Swede seemed quite appreciative of the cold chicken sandwiches, judging from the fact that they consumed half a dozen between them while standing beneath the trees in the backyard and discussing their next course of action.

Dallas had been astonished to learn upon his return from town a short time earlier that he had arranged for a wagonload of lumber, drilling equipment, and other supplies to be delivered first thing the next morning. Eyeing him warily, she had questioned him as to precisely how he had managed to achieve such results without benefit of ready cash. He had remained evasive and told her they would square accounts later. She had decided not to press the issue, consoling herself with the thought that there would be plenty of time for explanations and settlements once George Proctor arrived—particularly for explanations!

Cordi stole frequent glances out the gingham-curtained kitchen window at Erik every now and then while helping a still fuming Etta condition her hair with whipped egg whites and then rinse it with a mixture of bay rum and rose water.

"For heaven's sake, Cordi Brown, stop ogling the man! Don't you have any pride at all?" Etta scolded, her voice sounding rather muffled as a result of her being bent head-first over the sink.

"I am not 'ogling' him!" a miffed Cordi denied. She began scrubbing at her sister's long, reddish-blond curls with a great deal more vigor than was necessary. "And as for pride—just who is it that's been going around making an absolute fool of herself over Sam Houston Rawlins?"

"Why, you—I have not!" sputtered Etta.

"Everyone's talking about how you've been chasing after him all these years and how he—"

"That's a blasted lie!"

"Stop it, both of you!" Dallas finally intervened, her voice ringing out sharply. Distressed to see how much her sisters had already been affected by the men's presence—though, to be honest, Cordi and Etta had always been inclined to quarrel—she practically flung the last of the pies onto the cooling board and swept angrily from the room. *Damn Ross Kincaid!* she swore inwardly. She wished she'd never heard of the man!

Hurrying upstairs, she immediately set about busying herself with the household chores. By this method she was usually able to restore her emotions, at least for a while, to their normal level of intensity. She could forget her troubles and concentrate solely on the satisfaction to be gained from simple, physical labor.

That day, however, soon proved an exception. She was placing freshly laundered towels in the bathroom when a new and unpleasant thought suddenly rose in her troubled mind. Her face colored hotly as her sapphire gaze, wide and full of embarrassment, was drawn in turn to the unique, Grecian vase water closet and claw-footed bathtub facing each other across the gleaming pine floor. *How on earth were four women*

*and two men going to manage with only one bathroom
between them?*

"I must have been insane to agree to this!" she
muttered, then shook her head while belatedly lament-
ing her own folly. She turned to leave the room, only to
catch sight of her reflection in the large oval mirror
hanging on the rose-papered wall above the washstand.
It was as though another woman stared back at her, a
woman whose deep blue eyes glistened with mockery
and a knowing amusement . . .

Later that same day, an increasingly restless Dallas
ventured outside to speak with Ross again. She was
grateful for the fact that both Cordi and Etta had taken
themselves off to help Ruby Mae gather up her things
for the short-term displacement. Recalling how Etta
had strongly suggested they all move to Ruby Mae's
instead of the other way around and how Cordi had
offered a retort about the way some people were too
stubborn to even try to make the best of things, Dallas
breathed a very unladylike oath and stepped out into
the sweltering heat of the late Texas afternoon.

She shaded her eyes against the sun, then frowned
slightly when she heard the unmistakable sound of an
ax connecting with wood. Turning her head, she was
aghast to discover the same handsome, raven-haired
driller who had played havoc with her thoughts all day
in the process of chopping down the large chinaberry
tree which had faithfully shaded the rear portion of the
house for as long as she could remember.

"No!" gasped Dallas in horrified dismay. Why, that
tree had been planted by her grandfather! It was the
first tree she had ever climbed—it was also the first one
she had ever fallen out of. The beloved old chinaberry

was an important part of her family's history, and now she found Ross Kincaid bent on its destruction!

Her skirts flew up about her ankles as she instinctively went racing down the steps and across the yard to put a stop to the annihilation. Without pausing to consider her own safety, she seized the handle of the ax just as Ross swung it upward to deliver the next killing blow.

"Stop! Stop it at once!" she cried with heartfelt vehemence.

"What the—" he ground out, easily wresting the ax from her hands and rounding on her with a thunderous expression that immediately brought to mind the old saying about looks being able to kill. "Damn it, woman, didn't anyone ever teach you not to come barreling up behind someone like that? Just what the devil did you think you were doing? You might have been split in half!" His green eyes had darkened to jade and were ablaze with castigating fury. Momentarily taken aback by the violence of his reaction, Dallas breathlessly countered in a voice that was not altogether steady, "Well, I . . . I wouldn't have found it necessary to come barreling at all if not for the fact that you were chopping down my tree!" Her own anger gave her renewed courage, and when she spoke again, it was with a good deal more conviction. She doubled her hands into fists and planted them on her hips while her eyes flashed reproachfully up at Ross. "How dare you take it upon yourself to destroy my property! I will not tolerate this, Mr. Kincaid! You were hired to drill a well, not mutilate the premises! You have no right to . . . to *murder* anything that gets in your way around here!"

"It's only a tree," he replied in a low tone brimming with amusement. His rage had evaporated as suddenly as it flared, so that now a wry grin tugged at his lips and a roguish light sprang to life in his eyes. Musing that the flame-haired beauty before him appeared even more magnificent when angered, he felt another powerful stirring of his blood. His fingers curled more tautly about the wooden ax handle.

"A tree may not be able to speak or draw breath, but it is a living thing nonetheless!" Dallas obstinately contended. Folding her arms tightly across her bosom, she raised her chin in a proudly defiant gesture that dared him to laugh at her. "And besides that, this particular tree is of sentimental importance to my sisters and myself!" Bristling when she glimpsed what she believed to be a look of derisive humor crossing the rugged perfection of his features, she fixed him with a chilling glare and remarked scornfully, "But I wouldn't expect you to understand such things, Mr. Kincaid, since I am quite sure you do not have the capacity to care deeply about anything other than . . . than your own selfish desires!"

Shocked to realize that such words of condemnation had actually come from *her* lips, Dallas inhaled sharply and gazed up at Ross with wide, luminous eyes. Whatever had possessed her to say such a thing? She scarcely knew the man—how could she pass judgment on him like that? *Dear Lord, what is happening to me?*

"Maybe you're right about that. And maybe you're not," drawled Ross, his handsome countenance inscrutable now. "But you can take me at my word when I tell you there are a lot of other things I'd rather be doing than standing out here in the heat taking an ax to

64

your chinaberry tree."

Dallas's eyes flew back up to his. A dull flush rose to her face when she took note of the way his gaze traveled downward to rest—with what appeared to be bold significance—upon the swelling curve of her breasts. Dropping her arms abruptly back to her sides, she fought down the cowardly tendency to whirl about and run inside the house. *Don't you dare, Dallas Brown! Don't you dare give him the satisfaction!*

"Just what, may I ask, made you decide to take an ax to my tree in the first place?" she finally questioned with icy composure.

"Everything within fifty feet of the derrick will have to be cleared."

"Why?"

"Because I say so."

"Oh? And I suppose that means you intend to dismantle part of my house as well?" she demanded sarcastically.

"If I find it necessary," he parried with maddening nonchalance.

Dallas wanted to hit him. His green eyes seemed to taunt her, and the look of masculine superiority on his damnably handsome face provoked a wealth of feelings—none of them at all charitable—deep within her. Never in her life had she met such an arrogant, insolent, overbearing, downright infuriating man!

"Perhaps, Mr. Kincaid, I *should* find someone else to drill the well!" she declared, giving an angry toss of her head. A wayward tendril of shimmering, reddish-brown hair curled down upon her silken brow, and she swept it impatiently aside while struggling to maintain at least some semblance of control over her rising temper. "It is becoming increasingly obvious that you and I cannot get along!"

"I never give up on anything before it's finished," he told her quietly. He knew his statement was not entirely true—there had been an occasion not all that long ago when, following a heated disagreement with an employer who'd made the mistake of offering too much "advice," he'd moved on to another job without seeing the project through. He was no different from other members of his profession when it came to such things, for all drillers were notoriously independent and demanded total control over a well and crew. Much like the pilots who had once captained the great riverboats, they were in short supply and could well afford to tell a boss to go to hell if they disliked anything about the setup or working conditions.

But Ross had no intention of doing that now. Not when the "boss" was a spirited young redhead by the name of Dallas Harmony Brown. Try as he might to convince himself that he was staying on because of his friendship with George, he could not honestly deny that there were other reasons as well.

"Are you . . . are you actually saying that you *refuse* to leave?" Dallas stammered in disbelief, her blue eyes growing very round. Gifted with the joint, uncomfortable sensations of smallness and apprehension when Ross suddenly took a step closer, she found herself blushing anew as her gaze was drawn to the exposed, glistening smoothness of his broad chest where the top three buttons of his shirt had been unfastened in hopeful expectations of a cooling breeze. She could literally feel the heat emanating from his hard-muscled body, and when she inhaled upon a soft gasp, she caught the uniquely masculine scent that was a combination of soap and tobacco and leather.

"What I'm saying, *Miss Brown,* is that you ought to go back inside the house where you belong and let me get on with the work I came to do." His deep, resonant voice was full of exaggerated patience, and Dallas felt indignation washing over her once more as she glanced up to find a spark of patronizing humor lurking in his gaze. Furiously reflecting that if there was one thing she hated, it was being treated like a child, she was driven to say the first thing that came into her head.

"Why, you egotistical bastard!" Her eyes were ablaze with a brilliant, deep blue fire. "What makes you think you have the right to tell me where I do or do not belong? This is *my* property, and—"

"And I'm here to drill *your* well, which I'll never have the opportunity to do if you're going to waste my time arguing about whether or not women are better suited to cooking and cleaning rather than plowing fields and playing poker. Now off with you!" With that, he took her arm in a firm grip, spun her about, and bestowed a brisk pat of dismissal upon her shapely backside.

Dallas's eyes flew wide in shocked outrage. *No man had ever dared to touch her with such bold familiarity!* Explosive fury shot through her from head to toe, and she hesitated only an instant before rounding on the tall, unrepentant transgressor with a vengeance. She brought her right hand up as she whirled and would have achieved the desired result of delivering a brain-rattling slap to Ross's handsome face, if not for the fact that he moved with surprising agility to dodge the blow.

A loud gasp broke from Dallas's lips when she struck

nothing but air. Further dismayed to find herself spinning all the way around with an embarrassing lack of grace, her full skirts and petticoats tangling about her legs, she gave a soft, breathless cry and instinctively clutched at the only available means of support—her intended victim. Almost before she knew what had happened, she was swept forward against the granite-hard breadth of Ross Kincaid's chest.

She stared, wide-eyed and speechless, up into the rugged, disturbingly solemn features of the man who held her. His strong arm was clamped like a band of steel about her slender waist, and her body was pressed so tightly against his that it seemed she shared every breath he took. His eyes appeared to darken and smolder as they raked across her flushed, lightly freckled countenance.

Dallas knew that she should struggle, that the last thing in the world she should be doing was *this,* but she could not make her unaccountably traitorous flesh obey the more sensible dictates of her mind. She could only rest complacently within the driller's hard embrace and, as if mesmerized, wait for something to happen.

When it did, it shook her to the very core . . .

Losing the battle with his own nobler instincts, Ross muttered a curse and brought his warm, demanding lips crashing down upon hers. He knew the moment his mouth made contact with the softness of hers that his desire burned even hotter than he'd suspected. But he tried, nonetheless, to fight it. *Hell, he didn't even know her!* His other hand still gripped the ax, and his fingers now tightened upon the smooth wooden handle until his knuckles turned white.

Dallas caught her breath and felt wildfire coursing through her. While it was true that she had been kissed before, it was most definitely *not* true that she had ever received the sort of kiss Ross Kincaid was presently forcing upon her! She trembled violently and could find neither the strength nor the inclination to protest when the kiss deepened and she was gathered even closer to Ross's hardness. Acutely conscious of the way her full breasts were molded intimately against his chest, she moaned inwardly as his warm, velvety tongue suddenly thrust provocatively between her lips and began exploring the virgin sweetness of her mouth.

His steely arm tensed about her waist and threatened to cut off her breath, but she was aware only of the liquid fire racing through her veins, and of the strange, hotly yearning sensation which made her strain upward against the man who was awakening her to the first stirrings of passion she had ever truly known . . .

Without warning, the kiss ended. Her eyes clouded with startled bewilderment, Dallas was left to blink dazedly up into space as Ross abruptly released her and turned away. She swayed dizzily for a moment, then gaped at the driller in a mixture of amazement and disbelief when he lifted the ax and blithely resumed his demolition of her beloved chinaberry tree.

Her face crimsoned as dawning indignation crept over her. Why, the arrogant scoundrel was behaving as though nothing had happened, as though she were nothing more than some . . . some painted-up *floozy* and that the kiss they'd shared was of such little consequence that it could be dismissed without either justification or explanation or—heaven help her— *continuation!*

Her blazing sapphire gaze directed invisible daggers at the broad, lean-muscled back of the man who wielded the ax with a practiced skill she was in no frame of mind to appreciate. Musing with wrathful facetiousness that she could avenge her outraged honor by fetching the shotgun hanging above the parlor fireplace and shooting Ross Kincaid stone-cold dead—for that was undoubtedly what her father would have done if he'd caught a man grabbing one of his daughters—she smiled a bitter, inward smile and told herself that George would be highly displeased if, upon his arrival, he found that she'd killed the only available driller for miles around.

Satisfying her vengeful instincts by leveling one last murderous glare at Ross's dark head, Dallas pivoted angrily about and beat a hasty retreat inside the house. She was quite flushed and out of breath by the time she reached the sanctuary of her room, but she adamantly refused to admit that her inflamed condition had anything at all to do with the feelings—other than righteous indignation—provoked by Ross Kincaid's bold, wildly stimulating embrace.

III

"Dallas, honey, this coffee's strong enough to haul a wagon." Ruby Mae Hatfield took another long drink of the hot, fragrant brew and grinned broadly. "Makes me think you don't want me dozin' off at all tonight. Are you really *that* worried about those two out there?" she asked, giving a quick, sideways nod of her head toward the back door to indicate the men she had encountered on her way inside minutes earlier. Her brown eyes glistened with unflappable confidence. "If you are, don't be. I've handled a lot worse than their sort. They could turn out to be wild as an acre of snakes, and I swear I'd not let them get close enough to you or the girls to do anythin' more than—"

"Oh, Ruby, it isn't that I'm afraid they'll actually *do* anything!" Dallas insisted with a heavy sigh, then blushed and grew noticeably flustered when she recalled the humiliating incident that was still so fresh in her mind. She cursed the fact that her lips tingled anew at the memory of a certain tall, black-haired rogue's kiss. "It's just that I . . . well, I was . . . I'm

71

concerned about appearances. You know how vicious gossip can be in this town, especially when aimed at the daughters of the same man who stood up in front of all those people at the Opera House that night and delivered a rousing lecture on the evils of oil!" She leapt out of her chair and snatched up the coffeepot. "Great balls of fire, why did Papa have to make his opposition to the boom so public? It's made things very difficult for us!" Indeed it had, she added silently. On one hand, she felt like a traitor; on the other, like a woman finally coming out of the Dark Ages.

"I guess Abner did what he thought he had to do," the older woman theorized with a philosophical shrug of her mulberry-crepe-covered shoulders. Lowering the empty china cup to the table, she slowly eased her unusually tall and stout-framed form upright until she stood a full six inches higher than Dallas. Sunlight was gradually fleeing the room, and its subsiding rays cast long shadows across both women.

Ruby Mae's dark brown hair was coarse-textured and streaked with gray, and her features were rather severe, the lines etched into the weathered smoothness of her face providing outward evidence of all that she had endured throughout fifty years of living, but Dallas knew there was not a more honest or good-hearted woman in all of Texas.

"Your pa never was one to hide how he felt about anythin', was he?" murmured Ruby Mae, her mouth twisting into a brief, wry smile. "But I'll say this for him—he did right by you girls. Any other man might have farmed the three of you out when your ma died, but not Abner. He tried his best to make sure none of you ever lacked for nothin'. Knowin' Abner, I'm sure he never put it into words too much, but he loved you dearly. And I don't think he'd want you frettin' yourself over what's in the past."

"I suppose you're right," Dallas concurred with another sigh. She had just turned around to place the coffeepot on top of the stove when both of her sisters came bustling into the warm, cheerful room which had always served as the focal point of the Browns' familial life.

"What did you think of him?" Cordi excitedly questioned Ruby Mae. "Isn't he terribly attractive?"

"Would you please try to talk some sense into *her* now that you're here?" Etta simultaneously requested of the woman with a meaningful frown in Dallas's direction.

"Yes. No. And don't you think it's high time the two of you set about helpin' your sister get supper ready?" Ruby Mae suggested in a stern voice, then softened the effect with an indulgent smile down at them. "We can all stay up late and talk enough to keep a windmill goin' just as soon as we get through eatin' and doin' the dishes. Now come on," she said, stepping behind Cordi and Etta and placing an arm about each of them, "let's get to it. I don't mind sayin' that I'm a mite curious to find out more about these two young bucks that've got you gals all riled up!"

"I am not the least bit 'riled up'!" Dallas protested too vigorously, earning her looks of mild astonishment from three pairs of eyes. She set the coffeepot down with a clatter and turned a stormy face toward the window. Her own eyes kindled with several conflicting emotions as they immediately lit upon Ross Kincaid.

You're cocksure of yourself, aren't you, Mr. Kin-

73

caid? she silently challenged, her heart pounding erratically. *Well, this is one small-town Texas girl who won't allow herself to be taken in by your display of swaggering bravado!*

As if aware of her scrutiny, Ross suddenly turned his head and met her gaze. His mouth curved into what appeared to be a knowing smile. Dallas caught her breath upon a soft gasp and felt hot, guilty color flooding her face. Hastily moving away from the window, she ignored Ruby Mae's inquisitive stare and left the room with a murmured excuse about freshening up for supper . . .

Supper proved to be even more of an ordeal than she had expected.

Without waiting to be directed to a seat, Ross installed himself at the head of the table. Cordi was all too happy to guide Erik to the chair next to hers, while Etta chose to sit between Dallas and Ruby Mae at the opposite end. A veritable feast awaited them upon the spotless white linen tablecloth—fried chicken, mashed potatoes, fresh snap beans, buttermilk biscuits and cream gravy, corn-on-the-cob, and the apple pies Dallas had baked earlier that day. While none of the sisters appeared to be very hungry, there was obviously nothing wrong with Ruby Mae's appetite, nor that of either Ross or Erik, who consumed amazingly vast quantities of everything but the snap beans—both men confessed to a particular dislike for "greens."

Every time Dallas looked up from her plate, it was to find Ross's unfathomable green gaze upon her. Although she could not force the vivid memory of his kiss from her mind, she did her best to ignore him and was grateful for the fact that Ruby Mae kept things lively with a barrage of questions directed in turn at the amiable young Swede and his less talkative partner.

"How is it you came to know George Proctor?" the older woman asked Ross at one point.

"George and my father are old friends," he answered with a faint smile.

"That so?" Ruby Mae's eyes narrowed a bit, as though she were mentally sizing him up. "Dallas tells me you're from Fort Worth. Why've you been spendin' all your time up in Pennsylvania instead of down here where you belong?"

"Because until now, Miss Hatfield, there hasn't been any oil down here where I belong." His eyes were brimming with amusement when they met hers.

Ruby Mae smiled inwardly in growing relief and satisfaction. There was something about him she liked, something she couldn't explain but something there all the same. She cast a quick glance toward a secretly attentive Dallas before continuing. "Why should oil have a hold on you? Seems to me there's plenty to interest a young feller right here in Texas, what with all the cattle and cotton to be seen to."

"Maybe so," he allowed with another brief smile, "but I just happened to stumble into the oil industry while attending college up North."

"You went to college?" interjected Cordi. She tore her fascinated gaze away from Erik long enough to bestow a look of wide-eyed surprise upon Ross. "Well, then why on earth are you working as a driller?"

"Drilling is a most lucrative and honorable profession, Miss Brown," Erik gently defended before Ross could reply. He smiled down into the youthful loveliness of her upturned countenance, and Cordi felt her heart melting. Etta took note of the all-too-familiar, adoring expression on her sister's face and grimaced to herself in disgust before echoing in tones of obvious contempt,

"Honorable?" Wadding her napkin into a tight ball, she threw it down beside her scarcely touched plate of food. "What's so all-fired honorable about men who fill the saloons to overflowing each and every night and spend the rest of the time chasing after practically anything wearing skirts?" she accusingly demanded, her gaze shifting furiously back and forth between the two men. "My father tried to warn everyone, you know. He didn't want any part of the greed and craziness that's taken over this town. As far as I'm concerned, you and your kind are no more welcome here than polecats at a picnic, and I wish to goodness things could be the way they used to be!"

"Shame on you, Etta Brown!" Cordi indignantly scolded. "Mr. Larsen and Mr. Kincaid are our guests, and you've no call to—"

"They're not our guests!"

"They most certainly are, you little shrew!"

"Etta! Cordi! That's quite enough!" Dallas intervened in a low, tight voice. Her cheeks were aflame, and her eyes were filled with sisterly reproach as she told the two young combatants. "If you are unable to behave civilly to each other, then at least do us the courtesy of leaving the table!"

"Gladly!" retorted Etta. The spindled legs of her cane-bottomed chair scraped noisily across the polished pine floor as she abruptly rose to her feet. Lifting her chin haughtily, she proclaimed, "In future, I shall be only too happy to take my meals in my room!"

With that, she wheeled away from the table and stalked from the room in a huff. It was a common manner of exit for the hot-tempered young blonde and had been almost since the first day she learned to walk.

Common or not, Dallas was perturbed at her sister's childishness. She stared after Etta for a moment, then gazed uneasily back down toward her plate. She could feel Ross's eyes upon her, and when she finally forced herself to look up, it was once again to find no mockery or condemnation in his steady, strangely intense gaze. In fact, she could have sworn that an invisible current of understanding passed between them. She was so nonplussed by the sensation that when she made an attempt to quench a sudden thirst, her fingers trembled and refused to take an adequate hold upon the glass. Her eyes widened in dismay as the heavy amber goblet tipped over and a river of cold milk went streaming across the tablecloth to land in Erik's denim-clad lap.

"Oh, Mr. Larsen, I . . . I'm so sorry!" she gasped out, hurriedly righting the glass while the gallant young Swede remained perfectly calm.

"It is nothing, Miss Brown," he hastened to assure her with a warm, genuine smile of acquittal. After casually soaking up the bulk of the liquid with his napkin, he accepted the offer of Cordi's napkin for the completion of the task. He was, in all good conscience, however, obliged to prevent her from adding her efforts to his, which she appeared set upon doing until she suddenly realized the strategic importance of *where* the milk had fallen. Blushing fiercely, she desisted.

"Good thing it wasn't hot coffee," Ruby Mae commented dryly between generous bites of apple pie.

Dallas's eyes flew back to the raven-haired man

seated at the opposite end of the table. Appreciative humor at the situation was clearly written on his handsome, sun-bronzed features, and he cast her a lazily mocking smile before remarking in a low, mellow tone, "An 'interesting' meal indeed, Miss Brown. It's almost like being at home again."

"Oh? And why do you say *that,* Mr. Kincaid?" she demanded tartly, her deep blue gaze visibly bridling. Hellfire and damnation, she swore inwardly, the man was laughing at her! He'd already had the audacity to manhandle her, and now, *now* he was obviously enjoying himself at her expense!

"I happen to come from a large family—a family of ten, to be exact. Mealtime was never exactly dull at our table, either."

"Ten?" Ruby Mae echoed, then slowly shook her head while marveling aloud, "Land's sakes, your ma must've had the patience of a saint! Why, if I'd ever seen fit to get myself married, my man would've had to chase me all over hell and half of Georgia to get me to bear more than three or four young'uns!"

Dallas groaned inwardly and could feel her cheeks growing warm once more. She loved Ruby Mae Hatfield dearly, but there were times when she wished her friend weren't so quick to voice her opinions— especially the more "colorful" ones! Refusing to meet Ross's gaze, for she knew all too well what she would find therein, she looked instead to Cordi.

"Would you please go see to Etta?"

"Now?" asked Cordi in disbelief, her eyes growing very round as they shifted hastily toward Erik and then back. "But, Dallas, don't you think I should—"

"Do as your sister says, honey." Ruby Mae was

quick to lend her support. "The two of us can manage the dishes all right by ourselves."

For a moment, it appeared that Cordi would resist, but another glance in Erik's direction evidently changed her mind. Both men politely stood as she left the room in a soft rustle of skirts. She turned and flashed Erik one last innocently beguiling smile before disappearing into the hallway. Dallas and Ruby Mae rose to their feet as soon as she had gone, thereby signaling an official end to the meal.

"Thank you for the supper, Miss Brown," said Erik. "It has been a long time since I tasted food such as this." His blue eyes twinkled down at her when he added, "My mouth and my stomach tell me it is special, and not at all like the fare Tex complains about in Pennsylvania."

"Miss that good ole Texas home cookin', do you?" Ruby Mae quipped with a triumphant smirk at Ross. "That right there ought to tell you somethin' about stayin' put where you belong!" Without waiting for a response, she began gathering up the dishes and transporting them to the sink. She airily waved away Erik's offer of assistance, murmuring something about his evening being better spent with Cordi in the parlor.

"I'm afraid there won't be any time for that tonight," decreed Ross. Retrieving his hat from one of the pegs near the doorway, he turned back to Dallas and quietly informed her, "Swede and I are going out to round up a crew."

"At this time of night?" she demanded, her eyes widening in bemused surprise. She lowered the plates she had been stacking back to the table. "How on earth do you expect to be able to find—"

"The saloons will be crowded with roughnecks by now." He handed the other hat to his partner and was already reaching out to grip the brass doorknob when Dallas's voice rang out in direst tones of disapproval.

"The saloons?" She folded her arms tightly across her bosom and feelingly declared, "I will not tolerate rowdy drunks around my place, Mr. Kincaid!"

"You won't have to. It's always been my custom to hire only those men capable of holding their liquor. In other words, Miss Brown," Ross clarified with another faint, mocking smile across at her, "any man who's so drunk he can't hit the ground with his hat in three tries will never work for me." His piercing green eyes silently dared her to challenge his authority, to engage in a battle of wills with him right there and then in front of Ruby Mae and Erik, but Dallas bit back the scathing retort which rose to her lips and settled for flinging him a look that effectively conveyed the current, highly precarious condition of her temper. His smile merely broadened. Negligently donning his hat, he opened the door and sauntered outside into the warm, moonlit darkness. Erik paused to bid both ladies good night before following after Ross.

"They're an unlikely pair, ain't they?" murmured Ruby Mae. Scraping the leftover food from the plates with swift, vigorous motions, she started the water running into the galvanized steel sink and added a handful of soap slivers. "Kincaid strikes me as bein' a bit much to handle, while that young Swede's nothin' short of a real gentleman." She turned to peer closely down at Dallas, who crossed the room in an obviously preoccupied manner and placed the last of the dishes on the marble-topped cabinet table beside the sink. "I don't need anyone to tell me that you'd just as soon put a rattlesnake in his pocket and ask him for a match!"

"Who?" asked Dallas, pretending innocence while the telltale color stained her cheeks. She silently cursed the fact that she blushed so easily—she'd never been able to lie convincingly because of the damned rosiness which always gave her away!

"You know who. And don't go tryin' to tell me that what I just saw happenin' between the two of you doesn't mean anythin'! It's plain to see you and Ross Kincaid haven't hit it off too well. What I want to know is why. If he's givin' you trouble, maybe I can help."

"He's not giving me trouble," she denied, then hastily averted her face. "It's simply that Mr. Kincaid and I have different ideas regarding . . . well, regarding a good many things." Her sparkling sapphire gaze was clouded with a mixture of confusion and anger—anger directed at Ross Kincaid *and* herself—as she took up the kitchen towel and prepared to dry the dishes Ruby Mae washed. With a will of their own, her eyes strayed out toward the backyard, which was aglow with the silver luminescence cast by the full moon above.

"A full moon means trouble all right," the woman beside her suddenly remarked.

Dallas flushed guiltily once more and attempted to hide her disquiet with a forced smile while she accepted the first slightly soapy plate. "Perhaps for some, but not for me!"

"Oh? And just why is it *you* should be spared?" Ruby Mae asked with a quiet laugh. "Every creature on the face of the earth seems to go at least a little bit crazy whenever the moon's full. Man, woman, or beast—it's a known fact that we all feel a mite itchy at such a time."

Her brown eyes were full of loving amusement as she smiled at Dallas and added, "Yes, sir, I'd venture to say even Ross Kincaid's feelin' itchy right about now."

"Would you mind very much if we talked about something else?"

"All right," Ruby Mae consented readily enough, though her eyes continued to dance with good-natured raillery. Her lips twitched as she handed the younger woman another plate to dry. "You know, I heard somethin' mighty interestin' when I was over at McKinney's yesterday."

"Oh? And what was that?" Dallas murmured a bit absently. Try as she would, she could not banish the driller's devilishly handsome image from her mind. And to make matters worse, Ruby Mae's playful remarks concerning the effects wrought by a full moon had conjured up all sorts of thoroughly wicked visions. Foremost (and most disturbing) among them was the one wherein she and Ross Kincaid stood entwined in the silvery radiance outside, kissing and caressing each other in a mad, abandoned rush of passion as they sought to ease the desperate "itch" created by the moon's hypnotic spell . . .

"Justin Bishop's back in town."

Dallas inhaled sharply and very nearly dropped the plate in her hands. The warm, telltale color crept up to her face again, but she wasn't certain whether it owed its origin to what Ruby Mae had just told her, or to the recent, extremely alarming turn of her thoughts.

"Justin's back?" she echoed in a small, breathless voice. Her head spun dizzily as the image of Ross Kincaid's face was momentarily supplanted by another's. It was the face of a man who, upon leaving

82

Corsicana to escape the inevitable tragedy facing him if he remained, had vowed to return someday and take Dallas away as well. That had been more than five years ago. *Dear Lord, why now?* she asked silently, then was surprised to realize that where there should have been at least a twinge of sadness or pain, there was only a vague numbness.

"Jewel Coppinger said Mason Parnell told her he saw him gettin' off the train yesterday mornin'. Accordin' to Mason, Bishop looked like a dime novel on a spree, wearin' a lot of fancy riggin' and smokin' one of them skinny little cigars that—"

"Justin's been here since yesterday morning?" Her mind was still reeling with the news. It seemed impossible that she was the same girl who had once fancied herself in love with that defiant, rambunctious young man from the wrong side of the tracks. So much time has passed, so much had happened. Even if Justin had not changed, *she* certainly had.

"You mean you haven't heard from him yet?" the older woman questioned in disbelief.

"No. But I don't suppose I should expect to. After all, I've received no word from him since he went away." She finished drying the last plate and stacked it atop the others. Smiling at her friend's thoughtful frown, she untied the strings of her white cotton apron and placed it on the table beside the sink. Her blue eyes sparkled with humor as she paused to give a temporarily speechless Ruby Mae a quick hug. "Save all your matchmaking plans for Cordi and Etta, for I fear I'm a hopeless case!" She was already out in the hallway when she heard Ruby Mae chuckle and exclaim, "No one as young and pretty as you, honey, could ever be called hopeless!"

With an indulgent shake of her head at her friend's irrepressible nature, Dallas gathered up her skirts and went in search of her sisters. Ruffled feathers need to be soothed, she mused with a sigh, then blushed anew at the sudden thought of how Ross Kincaid would probably choose to soothe *her* ruffled feathers . . .

Dallas awoke with a start.

Her eyes flew open to find that the room was bathed in darkness. Turning her head upon the pillow, she gazed at the tiny slivers of moonlight escaping from either side of the fringed window shade. She became aware of the comforting bulk and warmth of Ruby Mae's flannel-encased body beside her in the bed, and it was then that it finally dawned on her she was safe in her own room instead of lost in a dream world.

A soft sigh escaped her lips as she relaxed her tensed muscles and pulled the covers up to her chin. Telling herself with an inward smile that it was no doubt Ruby Mae's snoring that had jolted her awake, she closed her eyes again and sought a return to blissful unconsciousness.

Suddenly, her eyes flew wide as she heard the noise again—a muffled thump that seemed to reverberate throughout the entire house. *That* was certainly not Ruby Mae's snoring! she concluded with a troubled frown.

Her heart pounding, she tossed back the covers and slid from the canopied four-poster. She snatched up the Watteau-pleated silk wrapper lying at the foot of the bed and tossed it about her shoulders, hastily plunging her arms into the full sleeves and tying the belt while making her way to the door.

Stealing one last glance back at the other woman's peacefully slumbering form, she hesitated. Perhaps she should ask for help in investigating the strange noise. But she hated to disturb Ruby Mae, and after all, she calmly reasoned with herself, it was probably nothing more than mice in the attic again. If only Cordi would stop "rescuing" the cats from their duties, there wouldn't be any of those horrible little creatures rattling around up there at all hours of the night!

Dallas slowly eased open the door and peered outward. Her eyes, adjusted to the darkness by now, swept up and down the length of the narrow hallway. Seeing nothing, she slipped quietly from the room and padded barefoot across the cool wooden floor toward the staircase. Her lustrous auburn tresses had been secured into a single thick braid, which hung down her back almost to her hips and swayed gently to and fro as she moved forward in a soft rustle of silk.

"You'll not escape *this* time, you lazy ingrates!" she muttered just under her breath, but without any real malice. Planning to march downstairs, retrieve a snoozing feline or two from their favorite nighttime perch on the back doorstep and press them into duty up above, she was too preoccupied with thoughts of her mission to notice the tall, dark form looming before the bathroom doorway immediately to her left.

A breathless cry of startlement broke from her lips as a large hand suddenly closed upon her arm and pulled her quite forcefully off her course. She had no time to struggle before being propelled about, and she gasped loudly as she was brought up hard against the warm,

85

broad expanse of a man's bare chest. Her eyes grew round as saucers when they traveled hurriedly upward to her half-naked captor's face. He was clad only in a pair of denim trousers. Somewhere in the benumbed recesses of her mind, it occurred to her that the noises she'd heard must have been generated by the removal of his boots . . . she should have recognized the sound, for her father had always taken off his boots and let them fall the same way . . .

"You!" Even in the darkness, she could make out the rugged, strangely inscrutable features belonging to the one man she would never willingly choose to be alone with in a dark hallway! Her pulses leapt wildly, and she was afraid for a moment that her weakening knees would disgrace her by buckling, though precisely *why* they should do such a ridiculous thing was totally beyond her comprehension. Striving to regain her composure, she attempted to tug her arm free, all the while demanding in a furious if slightly tremulous whisper, "What in heaven's name do you think you're doing? Take your hands off me at—"

Suffering a sharp intake of breath, she suddenly found herself enfolded by the smooth, steely hardness of Ross Kincaid's arms. His fathomless green eyes, suffused with an intense glow that sent an involuntary shiver running down her spine, seemed to be trying to bore into her very soul as he stared down at her. She tried to move, tried to speak—but could not.

Dallas Brown, you can't be doing this! her mind pleaded with her in growing desperation. *You've got to leave, you've got to get away before . . . before . . .*

But it was already too late. And what was worse, she had known it would be.

Without a word, Ross gathered her even closer to him and brought his lips crashing down upon hers. She moaned low in her throat and felt her head spinning. The next thing she knew, her arms had come up to entwine themselves about the corded muscles of Ross's neck, while her lips parted of their own accord and allowed him full access to the sweet nectar of her mouth.

The faint yet unmistakable aroma of liquor hung about him, but Dallas found herself dazedly reflecting that he did not taste of strong spirits. His warm, velvety tongue probed and caressed with provocative expertise. She grew more and more light-headed as a result of the demanding pressure of his mouth upon hers, and no matter how vigorously her more rational instincts commanded her to resist, she could not prevent herself from kissing him—wholeheartedly and with very little regard to the fact that she was clad only in her nightclothes and he in nothing but a pair of trousers—right back.

She blinked up at him in stunned bewilderment a few moments later when he released her. Just when she was certain he meant to turn his back on her and offer her the same humiliation she had suffered earlier that same day, he surprised her by swinging open the bathroom door, yanking her inside with him, then forcing her almost roughly back up against the door as he closed it again.

Dallas opened her mouth to hotly protest such treatment, but Ross gave her no opportunity to voice her outrage. He crushed her relentlessly against him once more, his mouth branding hers in a swift, possessive manner that left her dizzy and gasping for breath. Clinging weakly to his powerful, granite-hard shoulders, she was startled to feel his hands sweeping down her back to close boldy upon her thinly covered hips. She gasped inwardly and tried to draw away, but Ross held fast, his strong fingers spreading across the shapely roundness of her buttocks and molding her intimately, shockingly close to his undeniably masculine hardness.

Dallas's eyes flew open, their brilliant sapphire depths clouded with the overwhelming effects of a passion she had never realized lay smoldering deep within her. She pushed feebly against her handsome "assailant," but she was quite effectively imprisoned within his scorching, irresistibly masterful embrace. Indeed, did she truly *want* to escape this rapturous awakening of her womanhood? Wrong or right, she could not put a stop to things just yet . . .

Suddenly, Ross's mouth freed hers. She had done no more than draw a deep breath, however, when her lungs expelled the mind-clearing air in yet another gasp as he began nibbling at the delicate flesh of her earlobe. His warm lips lingered there for several long moments, eliciting more than one soft moan from his beautiful "victim," before trailing a fiery path downward to the sensitive hollow of her throat.

His fingers abruptly relinquished their hold on her buttocks, only to move purposefully upward to the belt of her wrapper. With amazing swiftness, the belt was untied and the edges of the blue silk garment swept aside. Dallas trembled as his arm clamped about her slender waist to hold her captive for his pleasure . . . and pleasure there was, with a more than equal amount falling to her.

She gasped anew when his hand unexpectedly claimed one of her breasts, its rose-tipped fullness protected only by the sheer fabric of her high-necked, embroidered cambric nightgown. Her fingers curled almost convulsively upon the bare warmth of his shoulders, and she was certain she would faint dead away with the sensations he was creating by the skillfully evocative movement of his fingers upon her sensitive, nearly naked flesh.

Dallas swayed dizzily back against the door, her breath nothing more now than a series of short gasps. Never before in the entirety of her twenty-one years had she felt so . . . so marvelously *alive!* It was wicked, she knew. Wicked and wanton and—heaven forgive her—so utterly wrong. But oh, it was also sheer ecstasy! If she were ever going to have anything to repent of, then let it be *this* with *him!*

"Oh!" she cried out softly, her passions careening even more wildly upward as Ross suddenly bent his head and captured her breast with his mouth. His lips suckled possessively at the silken flesh beneath the thin cotton, while the moist hotness of his tongue swirled round the sensitive rosy peak. The wonderfully erotic sensation of his actions prompted Dallas to arch instinctively against him while bringing her hands up and threading her fingers within the raven thickness of his hair . . .

The shade at the single window had not been drawn, so that the room was filled with moonlight. This would not have mattered in the least to Dallas, who was being carried away on the wings of desire for the first time in her life, if not for the fact that she just happened to open her passion-glazed eyes and catch sight of her reflection in the gilded oval mirror hanging above the washstand. Before now, Ross's tall, lithely muscled form had been blocking her vision of the mirror—but no longer. She gazed in stupefaction at the image of herself standing half-naked and pliant within the arrogant driller's embrace while he kissed and stroked the womanly charms she had always guarded so zealously.

It was as though someone had suddenly emptied a bucket of cold water over her head.

"No!" came her strangled cry. Grabbing handfuls of his hair, she gave an expectedly forceful yank and jerked Ross's handsome head away from her breast.

"What the—" he ground out, his eyes blazing down at her in the room's soft, silvery luminescence. His hands shot up to seize her wrists in a none-too-gentle grip, but she would not be subdued. Fighting like a tigress, she twisted and kicked and squirmed furiously against him. He held fast, his sun-kissed features growing savage as he sought to bend her to his will.

Finally, in a burst of frenzied desperation, Dallas opened her mouth and sank her teeth into the bare, bronzed flesh of his right forearm. Ross let out a blistering curse and relaxed his hold just long enough for her to wrench away and spin about to grasp the doorknob with violently shaking fingers. She somehow managed to get the door open, but was dismayed to suddenly find the immovable force of Ross's hard, virile body planted directly in her path to freedom.

"Get out of my way, damn you!" she hissed, her eyes shooting brilliant, midnight-blue sparks up at him. "I'll scream! I swear, I'll scream and bring the whole household running!" she threatened in a low voice quavering with fury and shame . . . and outright fear.

Raising her hands and doubling them into tight fists, she began pounding at the broad target of his chest, then gasped sharply when her wrists were seized once more and forced roughly behind her back. Her breasts were nearly flattened against his warm hardness. She stared, wide-eyed and breathless, up into his dangerously impassive features as her traitorous body tingled from head to toe.

"If I wanted to take you, you flame-haired little spitfire, it wouldn't matter how much you screamed," Ross told her, the deep resonance of his voice making her flush hotly. His smoldering gaze raked possessively over her, and a faint, mocking smile touched his lips when he vowed softly, "And take you, I *will*, Dallas Harmony Brown. You know it as well as I do. But it sure as hell won't be in a bathroom, and it won't be before you ask for it."

"That's something I'll *never* do!" Dallas vehemently denied. "Now let go of me, you . . . you conceited jackass! She renewed her struggles with a vengeance, only to find herself abruptly released. Eyeing Ross mistrustfully, she watched as he stepped away from the door and leaned nonchalantly back against the washstand. She hesitated a brief moment longer, wondering if perhaps he were secretly planning to pounce on her again, before drawing her wrapper tightly about her body like a shield and sweeping from the room with as much dignity as she could muster under the mortifyingly *un*dignified circumstances.

"Next time, wildcat," she heard him promise before she rounded the corner and fled back down the hallway, "you won't get away so easily."

Her breath caught in her throat, while another tremor of mingled fear and excitement shook her. Reaching the safety of her bedroom at last, she wasted no time before peeling off her wrapper and scrambling back into bed. She was greatly relieved to see that Ruby Mae was still fast asleep, for the last thing she wanted to do was try and explain away her current state of agitation.

I behaved like a common trollop! she thought with an inner groan of pure anguish, her face aflame. Was it truly *she,* the prim and proper Miss Brown, who had allowed a man—a virtual *stranger*—to touch her that way? How could she ever face him again? How could she face herself?

I might as well go join all those other fallen angels down by the railroad tracks, she mused bitterly as hot tears started to her eyes, *or maybe I should choose the other extreme and become a nun . . . only whoever heard of a Presbyterian nun?*

It didn't help matters any when she became aware of the lingering dampness of her nightgown where Ross Kincaid's mouth had wrought such sensuous enchantment. The vivid memory of the bold, intimate caresses his lips and hands had bestowed upon her breasts prompted a tingling warmth to spread upward from somewhere in her lower abdomen. Further dismayed to feel the way her toes literally curled when her mind flashed back to when he had imprisoned her within his hard embrace and kissed her with such intoxicating fierceness, she released a heavy, ragged sigh and shifted restlessly beneath the covers.

"Dallas? You all right, honey?" Ruby Mae's voice startled her in the darkness.

Dallas froze, her eyes widening in consternation. Mentally upbraiding herself for waking her friend, she toyed briefly with the idea of pretending to be asleep, then took a deep breath and answered in a deceptively steady tone, "I'm fine. Just a bit fidgety, I suppose. I'm sorry I disturbed you."

"Don't worry about that none," Ruby Mae chuckled softly, turning over on her side and settling back down within the deep, welcoming cushion of the feather mattress. "I'm a light sleeper. And my hearin's so good, I can hear a lot of things I probably shouldn't."

Dallas turned beet-red at the unmistakable implication of the older woman's words. She was tempted to ask Ruby Mae exactly *what* she'd heard, but immediately decided against it. Telling herself that having her curiosity satisfied might very well serve to make her feel even more miserable than she already was, she tightened her grip upon the pillow and murmured a rather tremulous good night to Ruby Mae.

It was all Ross Kincaid's fault. She'd be damned if she'd ever give him another chance to humiliate her!

And take you, I will, Dallas Harmony Brown. His vow suddenly echoed anew throughout the turbulence of her mind.

"When hell freezes over, Mr. Kincaid!" she muttered wrathfully, forgetting that Ruby Mae's hearing was so good. Releasing another long sigh, she closed her eyes and drifted off into a troubled sleep.

IV

Relief was too mild a word for what Dallas felt when she came downstairs the following morning and found that Ross had already gone outside to supervise the delivery and setup of the equipment. Swede had been dispatched into town at first light with the wagon to fetch the men hired by his partner the night before, and the six of them assembled in the backyard as the rising sun set the sky ablaze. Crowding around a table laden with steaming mugs of hot coffee and fresh biscuits stuffed with sausage—provided through the efforts of the perennially early rising Ruby Mae—they were all young and full of life and eager to get started.

"Looks like them girls are plannin' to sleep the whole mornin' away," observed Ruby Mae as she and Dallas sat down at the kitchen table with their own coffee. "I've never understood how a body can lollygag in bed so long after the sun's come up." She took a drink, after which her mouth curved into a grin and she remarked amiably, "Speakin' of which, it seems to me you're up and about a mite late yourself."

"It must be something in the air." Dallas offered the lame excuse with an equally unconvincing little smile. Her eyes were underscored by faint circles that gave testimony to the fact she'd slept little, while there was a noticeable pallor to her usually glowing features. Carefully sipping the hot brew whose wonderfully rich aroma seemed to fill every corner of the house, she cast an uneasy glance toward the window. "I suppose they'll start drilling today."

"Probably so. 'Course I can't claim to be any kind of expert on the subject, seein' as how that well of mine turned out to be nothin' but a dry hole. You'd think the good Lord would've seen fit to put just a little bit of that black gold under *my* place," the large, brown-haired woman mused with a quiet laugh.

"What's under your place?" Cordi interjected, making an appearance downstairs at last. She bypassed the table and headed straightaway for the window with a hasty "good morning" to the other two women.

"Nothin' but dirt. Land's sakes, you look dressed to kill," Ruby Mae noted wryly as she raised the cup to her lips once more. Her brown eyes glimmered with knowing amusement as they met Dallas's.

"Nonsense! I always dress neatly whenever I'm going to work," Cordi replied with a defensive toss of her meticulously arranged curls. Attired in a brand-new, stylish dress of natural-colored pongee with a bertha collar trimmed by black silk bands, she would have looked much more at home at a formal garden party than in the small, dimly lit office where she would be operating a switchboard for the better part of the day. Without a doubt, she would be the most elegantly dressed employee of the Southwestern Telephone and Telegraph Company.

"Oh, Cordi," sighed Dallas, "don't you think you're carrying this a bit too far?"

"I haven't the faintest idea what you're talking about," the sandy-haired young woman loftily declared. She was about to turn away from the window when a particular member of the new derrick crew caught and held her attention. Her blue-green eyes widened in surprise as she exclaimed, "Why, it's Sam! What on earth is he doing here?"

"Sam Rawlins is one of them?" Dallas asked in disbelief. She stood and hurried to join her sister at the window. Her own eyes quickly verified what Cordi had just said. "It *is* Sam!"

"I knew there was somethin' I forgot to tell you," Ruby Mae confessed with a low chuckle. "I figure Etta'll be purrin' like a kitten in a creamery once she finds out he's one of the roughnecks Kincaid signed on. And it sure ain't gonna hurt Sam Rawlins none to get his hands dirty for a change. If those folks of his would start treatin' him like a man instead of a kid, he might just make somethin' of himself after all."

"What can he possibly make of himself?" murmured Dallas, her thoughts drifting elsewhere. Her silken brow creased into a frown as her eyes searched in vain for any sign of Ross Kincaid. *He's out there somewhere,* she told herself with an imperceptible clenching of her jaw, *and I'll bet he's still smugly congratulating himself over what happened last night!* Her dreams had been haunted by inescapable memories of his wildly passionate embrace, and she cursed herself for being unable to forget how much her body had thrilled to his

97

masterful touch. *Never again. Never, ever again!* she silently vowed.

"Oh, Dallas, you're such a snob!" This came from Cordi, who suffered her own brand of disappointment when she saw that Erik Larsen was already starting work on the construction of the derrick. Transferring her bright gaze to her sister, she accusingly proclaimed, "You think just because Sam didn't finish college that he'll never amount to anything. Well, it so happens there are a lot of people in this world who—"

"It isn't just that Sam didn't finish, Cordi," insisted Dallas, her frown deepening as she returned to her seat at the table. "In case you've forgotten, he was booted out after only one semester! The whole town knows how wild and unpredictable he can be. He's never held steady employment. Hell's bells, he's never really had to do an honest day's work in his entire life!"

"Yes, but is that *his* fault?" the younger woman retorted. She whirled about and leaned back against the sink while folding her arms tightly across her breasts. "Sam certainly can't be blamed for the fact that his father's one of the richest men in town! I think you're being terribly unfair to Etta. After all, a person can't choose who to fall in love with! It isn't so easy for the rest of us to bury our emotions like you've done!"

"I have not buried my emotions!"

"Yes you have! And you want Etta and me to be just like you, able to turn your feelings on and off at will. Why, I daresay that if you had your way, we'd either marry wealthy, *suitable* men or remain old maids for the rest of our lives!"

"Your sister only wants what's best for you, honey," Ruby Mae intervened at this point. She smiled across

98

at Cordi, and her expressive brown eyes were aglow with kindness and the wisdom gained by living as long as she had. "No one else loves you the way she does."

"I . . . I know that," Cordi murmured guiltily, her anger visibly evaporating. Her outbursts of temper were far less frequent than Etta's and quickly over with. "I'm sorry, Dallas," she apologized with a genuine expression of remorse.

"So am I." Crossing back to give the eighteen-year-old a quick, conciliatory hug, Dallas smiled and suggested, "Why don't we sample some of Ruby Mae's sausage and biscuits? After that, I'll be happy to give you a ride to work on my way to the hotel." Since it was a Saturday, she would be delivering a dozen apple pies to the Molloy Hotel, just as she had done for the past several months. It gave her a great sense of satisfaction to be putting her culinary talents to such good use, and besides that, the extra money had certainly come in handy.

"All right," Cordi agreed, her own features relaxing into a smile. She and Dallas proceeded to share a companionable breakfast, during which Ruby Mae regaled them with a humorous account of what it had been like growing up with eight siblings instead of a mere two.

Refusing to heed her sister's pleas that they leave the house by way of the back door a short time later, Dallas carried the boxes of pies down the tree-shaded walk to the wagon and settled them carefully upon the rear floorboards. Cordi, none too happy about the fact that a certain young Swede had not been granted the opportunity to feast his eyes upon her elegant attire, tried to console herself with the thought that there was still the evening meal . . .

Etta, meanwhile, came downstairs not long after her sisters had gone. Upon discovering, much to her amazement, that *her* Sam was a member of the crew sawing and hammering in the backyard, she immediately flew outside in a whirl of blue calico, her long, strawberry blond hair streaming like a banner behind her. She was oblivious to the stares and smiles of the other men as she insistently drew a slender, boyishly attractive young man of twenty aside and demanded to know what in tarnation he was doing there.

"What the hell does it *look* like I'm doing?" Sam Houston Rawlins snapped in response. He whipped the hat from his head, took Etta's arm in a rough grip, and led her across the yard to the other side of the barn. His hazel eyes glittered angrily down at her when he came to a halt and spun her about to face him. "Why didn't you tell me they'd be living here?"

"Who?" parried Etta, her own eyes flashing fire.

"Kincaid and Larsen, that's who! Damn it, Etta, you knew I'd find out eventually!" Releasing her arm as though the contact suddenly burned him, he ground out a curse and raked a hand through his thick dark brown hair. "There I was, minding my own business in the Two Sixes Saloon last night, when in walk these two characters who let it be known they're on the lookout for a crew. Thinking it might prove interesting, I signed on." He'd done it on impulse, telling a bold-faced lie regarding the extent of his oil field experience. "*Then* what do I find out when Larsen picks us up this morning—" he ground out, glowering down at her from a height that topped hers by nearly six inches— "but that it's *your* well we'll be drilling, and that those

100

two sonsabitches are actually living under the same roof with *my* girl!"

"I didn't know about that until after you brought me home yesterday!" Folding her arms across her heaving bosom, Etta glared defiantly up into her beloved's stormy countenance and proceeded to give him back every bit as good as he gave. "Hellfire and damnation, Sam Rawlins, do you think I *want* them here? I told Dallas you wouldn't understand! I tried to tell her it was wrong to let them stay, but she refused to listen! Just what in blue blazes was I supposed to do—throw them out of the house with my own two hands?"

"You could have told me, and *I'd* have thrown them out!"

"Oh really? Well then, if you think it will do any good, you're perfectly welcome to give it a try! Only don't expect me to shed any tears over what's left of you when you're through trying!" She started to march furiously past him, but his hand shot out and closed upon her arm again.

"Oh no you don't! You're not going anywhere until we get this straightened out between us!"

"There's nothing to straighten out! You've made your feelings quite clear! And you've got work to do, remember?" she reminded him with biting sarcasm. Hot, angry tears sparkled in her golden eyes as she uttered reproachfully, "How dare you, Sam Rawlins! How dare you so much as insinuate that I would have anything to do with any other man! It wouldn't matter whether he was living in my house or in . . . in Timbuktu!"

Sam, his heart melting as it was always wont to do at the first sign of Etta's tears, released a long sigh and made a valiant attempt to smooth things over. His fingers grew gentle upon her arm, while the blaze of fury in his gaze became nothing more than a soft glow of loving contrition.

"Hell, sweetheart, I didn't mean to make you cry. It's just that . . . well . . ." He stuffed both hands into the front pockets of his denim trousers and finished in a low, husky tone as though he hated to admit it, "Damn it, Etta, it's just that I can't stand the thought of any other man getting close to you!"

"Oh, Sam," murmured Etta, her glistening eyes full of affection and immediate forgiveness as she cast a watery smile up at him, "don't you know by now that I could never care for anyone else but you?" She was rewarded for this heartfelt declaration of eternal devotion when Sam wrapped his arms about her and drew her close. Several long moments passed before either of them spoke again.

"At least I'll be here where I can keep an eye on things," Sam finally murmured against the top of her head, then added with a quiet chuckle, "Who knows? Maybe I'll turn out to be such a success at this drilling business that I'll stick with it a while."

"What? And have folks thinking the son of Franklin Oliver Rawlins is nothing but common, oil field trash?" Etta teased with an answering giggle. Her eyes were alight with feminine mischief when she raised her face to his. A meaningful, innocently seductive smile played about her lips. "You know, Sam, if you *did* by any chance decide to stick with this, you might just end up making enough money to—"

"Sorry, Etta, but I've got to get back to work now!" he cut her off. Dropping a light kiss on the tip of her nose, he donned his hat and beat a hasty retreat back around the corner of the barn. The petite, headstrong young woman he left behind heaved a sigh and frowned thoughtfully to herself.

"Someday, Sam Houston Rawlins," she vowed, her words spoken in little more than a whisper, "I'm going to pin you down and *make* you propose marriage to me!"

With that, Etta marched away from the barn and back across the yard toward the house. She smiled when Sam glanced up from his work to meet her gaze, but her smile rapidly disappeared when she turned to start up the steps and encountered Ross Kincaid, who stood towering above her with a strange half-smile on his face and a disquieting gleam in his green eyes. Refusing to be intimidated by his presence, she tilted her head way back so that she could look him square in the eye and declared in an emotion-charged undertone, "You'd better know what you're doing, Mr. Kincaid. Because if anything happens to Sam—"

"The only danger facing your friend, Miss Brown, is the loss of a job," he calmly informed her, the quiet, authoritative nature of his voice only serving to irritate her further.

"And just what do you mean by that?" she demanded a trifle acidly.

"Simply that if you persist in coming out here and luring a certain member of my crew away from his duties, you'll soon find—"

"Luring?" she indignantly gasped. Her eyes narrowed until they were mere slits of golden-tinged fury. "I don't have to go around *luring* Sam away from anything!"

103

"Nevertheless, you'd do well to take my advice and keep your distance from the men. They've been hired to do a job, not cater to the whims of a spoiled little vixen who's sorely in need of a lesson in manners."

"Why, you . . . you . . ." Etta sputtered in outraged disbelief. Ross merely tipped his hat in a mockingly polite gesture, then strode away and left her standing there with her color very high and her body quaking with anger from head to toe. Her eyes flew back to Sam, but he was too busy helping the other men lift a newly completed section of derrick into place to be aware of the brief yet significant confrontation between his ladylove and his employer.

"Now that you've had a chance to talk to Sam, maybe I can talk you into eatin' some breakfast," said Ruby Mae when Etta came bursting through the back door.

"I'm not hungry!" the petite young blonde fairly shouted as she stalked from the kitchen and up the stairs. Ruby Mae mentally counted the seconds until she heard the anticipated *slam!* of a door resounding throughout the old house.

"No wonder that girl ain't any bigger than she is," the buxom woman mused, shaking her head at the peculiarities of youth. Then, heaving a sigh, she poured a fresh cup of coffee and helped herself to another biscuit.

Across town, meanwhile, Dallas carried the last of her pies into the spacious, clean-as-a-whistle kitchen of the Molloy Hotel. With a barber shop, cabinet shop, tailor shop, telegraph office, grocery store, restaurant, and twenty rooms upstairs, the comfortable and well-run establishment had for several years been a particular favorite of the many drummers who passed through town. There was even a special Drummer Room in the rear area of the dining room, where the eager young salesmen were permitted to display their wares. Before the boom hit, older boys who were anxious to attend school but who lived too far out in the country had been permitted to obtain lodgings at the hotel in exchange for chores and firewood. But now, Dallas reflected with more than a touch of sadness as she placed the box on the worktable beside the huge cookstove, the worthwhile pursuit of education had given way to the more feverish pursuit of quick riches.

"You know, Dallas, I could buy twice this many from you and still run out before suppertime!" Fanny Woodward marveled with an accompanying laugh. Dallas smiled and gratefully accepted the money the Molloy's head cook counted out into her hand.

"If I thought you meant that, Fanny, I'd bring *two* dozen next Saturday!"

"Well then . . . it's a deal!" the plump, attractive brunette, some ten years older than Dallas, startled her by agreeing.

"Are you serious?" asked Dallas, her eyes widening in disbelief.

"Perfectly! And why don't we make it a dozen apple and a dozen cherry next time? That way, the Saturday regulars will have a chance to try both. You know, it's still just about the only day of the week we get the local folks in. But I can't say I blame them for not wanting to come in the evenings," she added with a sigh. "Things do tend to get pretty wild after sundown. It's a wonder my Jim lets me stay on here at all!"

Marveling over her good fortune—and wondering at the same time how in the world she was ever going to produce two dozen pies in a single day—Dallas bid good day to the cook and strolled back through the hotel's cheerfully decorated lobby. She instinctively raised a hand to shade her eyes from the sun's brightness as she emerged outside, then frowned a bit at what her eyes beheld.

The boardwalks were starting to get crowded, while the streets had already long since come alive with the noise and almost frenzied motion with which she was all too familiar. The dust kicked up by the horses' hooves and wagons' wheels, not to mention the booted feet of a veritable swarm of human beings, was borne aloft by the hot Texas wind to settle lightly upon her securely pinned auburn hair and her usual, eminently practical attire of white cotton shirtwaist and dark blue skirt.

"Dallas?"

She started at the sound of her name. It flashed through her mind that the masculine voice was familiar . . . and yet not. Still, there was something about it that made her pulses take to racing and her cheeks pinken. Swallowing a sudden lump in her throat, she whirled about and found that her suspicions were correct.

"*Justin!*" she gasped in stunned astonishment. Her deep blue eyes grew very round as she stared across at him.

He had certainly changed—she could see that right away. He was taller, the gauntness of his frame a thing of the past, and his impeccable attire bespoke a certain polish and worldliness she would never have believed it

106

possible for him to attain. His coat and trousers were of the finest gray serge, his double-breasted vest of a shimmering, red brocade satin, while his custom-made shoes had been fashioned of the best English enamel calfskin. He held a black felt bowler in one hand and a cigar in the other. His dark blond hair, parted in the middle, was slicked down and shone dully above the collar of his white linen shirt. Yes indeed, Dallas mused dazedly, the smoothly attractive, sophisticated man before her was a far cry from the troubled youth she'd once known . . .

"You're even more beautiful than I remembered," he murmured quietly.

Her eyes flew back up to his face. There was a certain, undeniable hardness to his features, but his gold-flecked brown eyes glistened warmly across at her and his mouth had curved into a smile of such genuine pleasure that she could not help responding in kind.

"Hello, Justin," she said finally, her own smile rather tentative. For a brief, fleeting moment, she felt as though the past five years had melted away, as though she and Justin Bishop were the same people they had once been. *But we're not,* she then thought, *we're not lovestruck kids anymore. And my heart isn't shattering into a million pieces like I was once so sure it would do if ever I saw him again.*

"We have to talk, Dallas." He tossed his cigar to the ground and slowly crossed the distance between them, his expensive leather shoes treading softly upon the dusty boardwalk. "It's been a long time. There are a lot of things I want to explain—"

"You don't have to explain anything to me, Justin. You see, you're right—it *has* been a long time." Unable

107

to keep a telltale note of reproach from her voice, she tempered it with another smile, this one a bit more relaxed than the first. "What's past is past, Justin. But I'm glad to see you again. I've often wondered where you were and what you were doing." She had thought about him a great deal at first. Somewhere along the way, though, he had taken his place among the other rarely summoned memories tucked away in a corner of her mind.

"I haven't forgotten, Dallas. And I don't think you have, either." He stepped even closer and stared deep into her widening gaze. "I have to talk to you!" he reiterated, his low tone charged with emotion.

"But we—"

Suddenly, they were jostled by a particularly rowdy group of young men passing them on the boardwalk. A tiny, breathless cry escaped Dallas's lips as she was propelled forward against Justin. He swiftly brought his hands up to steady her, his fingers closing upon her slender waist.

Justin Bishop experienced a powerful surge of red-hot desire at the contact. His dark, almost hawkish gaze raked hungrily over the beautiful young woman who had haunted his dreams for five years. *Damn, but he wanted her more than ever! In all this time, he had never stopped wanting her.*

Dallas, blissfully ignorant of the effect she was having upon him, blushed and made all haste to extricate herself from his tight, unnecessarily continuing embrace. Drawing firmly away, she stepped back and raised a hand to sweep a wayward curl from her forehead. She was surprised to realize how self-conscious she felt, then was thoroughly nonplussed when the unbidden image of Ross Kincaid's face suddenly swam before her eyes.

Though she tried not to, she found herself comparing the man standing before her—a man she had once known very well—with the man who had entered her life for the first time a mere twenty-four hours ago. That Ross Kincaid was the more handsome of the two, she could not deny. Neither could she deny that he possessed a more commanding presence, a quality of . . . well, of *manliness* that was both compelling and infuriating at the same time! He would tower above Justin by at least four or five inches, and his manner of dress was the antithesis of the suave, dandified look Justin affected. And though she hated to admit it, she had felt awkward and uncomfortable when she had been thrown against Justin a moment ago, but when Ross Kincaid had touched her it was as though— merciful heavens, it was as though she had been struck by lightning . . .

This is ridiculous! she told herself angrily. Why should what had happened between her and that insolent rogue have anything at all to do with how she did or did not feel about Justin Bishop?

"I . . . I have to be going!" she murmured in a sudden rush. She raised her face to Justin's and forced another smile to her lips. "Perhaps we'll see each other again sometime while you're in town." Startled when he suddenly captured one of her hands with both of his, she gazed expectantly up at him, her eyes wide and full of bemusement.

"I'll be coming by this evening, Dallas," he solemnly proclaimed. The tiny golden flecks in his eyes seemed to darken and glow as he added, "At least give me the chance to explain. For old time's sake, if nothing else."

Dallas didn't know what to say in response. On the one hand, she was curious to learn why he had stayed away for so long; on the other, she was hesitant to recall the painful memories of the past. The heart of a sixteen-year-old girl is a fragile thing indeed, she reflected with an inward sigh, and although hers had not exactly broken in two, the betrayal of first love *had* left it scarred.

She finally nodded her assent and did not protest when Justin took her arm to lead her over to the wagon. Climbing up and quickly settling her skirts about her, she turned her head to stare down into the confidently smiling features of the man who had obviously done what he'd set out to do. Hank Bishop's son had triumphed over his unfortunate past and had returned to his hometown to show those who had once scorned and ridiculed him that he was now a force to be reckoned with. He had forgotten nothing.

"Good-bye, Justin," said Dallas. She sensed an intense, disquieting air of purposefulness about him, but she told herself it did not matter.

"Until tonight," promised Justin. Stepping away, he watched as she gave a flick of the reins and maneuvered the wagon back into the seemingly endless flow of traffic on Commerce Street.

We both know why I came back, Dallas, he silently told her, his dark gaze remaining fastened on her until the wagon rounded a corner and she disappeared from view. Then, negligently drawing another cigar from his vest pocket, he continued on his way down the boardwalk toward the "red-light district" at the opposite end of town.

Dallas Brown was his. She had always been his. And come hell or high water, he meant to claim her . . .

Insisting that they needed to make the most use of the remaining light, Ross declined to take Ruby Mae's suggestion that he and his men call it a day and come inside for supper. Dallas, who had been dreading the prospect of facing him, tried to conceal her profound happiness upon hearing that he would not be present at the evening meal. Though despising herself for her cowardice, she had not ventured outside even once since returning from town. She could not help but be relieved when Ruby Mae took it upon herself to speak to Ross about the progress of the work going on in the backyard. The derrick, Ross had informed the older woman, would be completed by nightfall if all went as planned, and by that same time tomorrow, they hoped to have the rig, boiler, and engine set up and fully operational.

Dallas was grateful for the fact that there had been so much to keep her mind occupied. Enlisting the aid of a reluctant Etta—who had unwisely complained of having nothing to do, what with Sam working and unable to entertain her as he had so obligingly done ever since her graduation two weeks earlier—she had subjected both the kitchen and the parlor to a thorough cleaning. That done, she had collected a sinkful of delicate white undergarments, washed them by hand and dipped them in milk, then pressed them while they were still damp for the purpose of giving them a crisp, fresh look.

A fiery blush had stained her cheeks when, upon

111

wondering why she always went to the trouble of making certain her underthings were so soft, white, and utterly perfect when no one besides herself would ever see them, yet another vision of Ross Kincaid's rugged, devilishly appealing countenance had insinuated itself into the forefront of her mind. Recalling what her father had always told her about "an idle mind being the devil's playground," she had hastily put the offending garments away and taken herself off to find Etta again.

Later, after taking a bath and washing her hair, she agonized over what to wear that evening when Justin Bishop came to call. She wanted to look her best; whether it was because she harbored some secret desire to impress the man who had apparently found it so easy to leave her behind, or simply because she was a woman and therefore naturally inclined to care about her appearance no matter what circumstances existed, she did not know. Finally, exasperated with herself, she impatiently tugged a gown of pale-blue organdy from the tall, carved oak wardrobe and sent it floating downward to land across the foot of the bed.

Upon facing herself in the mirror a short time later, Dallas wasn't sure whether she liked what she saw or not. The dress, with a tucked lace inset on the front of the unusually low, square-necked bodice, long gathered sleeves trimmed with matching lace, and skirts that fitted snugly over her hips and then flared outward at the hemline, had always seemed a bit too frilly, too unabashedly feminine for her tastes. She had worn it only once, and even then she'd had second thoughts about doing so. Still, she staunchly decided, it *was* the prettiest gown she owned, and she'd be

112

hanged if she'd face Justin Bishop looking like some dried-up old maid!

Brushing her hair until it shimmered and appeared to take on a life of its own, she twisted it upward into a tight knot, then suddenly changed her mind and arranged it into a softer style that rested low upon the nape of her long, slender neck. She reached over to her dressing table and took up the most treasured piece of jewelry her mother had left her—a small gold watch hooked on a delicate fleur-de-lys ornament. After fingering it lovingly for a moment, she pinned it near her left shoulder.

"Well, I suppose you're as ready as you'll ever be," she murmured to her reflection. *Ready for what?* the young woman staring back at her seemed to retort.

Dallas did not even try to answer. Heaving a sigh, and feeling unaccountably discontented, she turned away from the mirror and swept from the room.

Supper was uneventful, and a trifle dull, though none of the women at the table, not even Ruby Mae, ever actually said as much. Both Cordi and Etta kept stealing glances toward the back door while picking disinterestedly at their food. Dallas, equally preoccupied as alternating thoughts of Justin Bishop and Ross Kincaid whirled round in her head, managed to carry on the barest conversation with Ruby Mae, who subjected all three of the sisters to her closely scrutinizing gaze at regular intervals throughout the meal. As usual, Ruby Mae Hatfield missed little.

Following supper, the four of them retired to the parlor. Cordi sank down upon the piano stool and began to play a rather sad, plaintive tune. Etta wandered over to stand beside the old upright piano, which was missing three keys entirely and tended to make odd little thumping sounds every now and then. In spite of his daughters' persistent complaints, Abner Brown had never allowed it to be repaired. Ruby Mae settled herself on the flowered-chintz-covered sofa and smiled softly in remembrance of how she had once told Abner, only half in jest, that he was so tight with his money it was a wonder he'd ever brought himself to part with any of it at all. Dallas took a stance at the front window, where she fingered the lace curtains with a rather distracted air while gazing outward at the gathering twilight.

"He'll be along soon, honey," Ruby Mae assured her.

"I almost hope he doesn't come at all!" She let the curtains fall back into place and spun about, folding her arms tightly across her breasts. "It's not going to change anything. As a matter of fact, I'm not at all sure I *want* to know what he's been up to these past five years!"

"He's probably got a wife somewhere," Etta theorized idly as she crossed the room to plop down onto the sofa beside Ruby Mae. "Or at the very least, a mistress."

"Henrietta Brown!" gasped a shocked Cordi. She stopped playing and twirled about on the piano stool. "You ought to be ashamed of yourself, saying an awful thing like that! Why, the very last thing Dallas needs to hear is that the man she's loved for so long hasn't remained true to her or to their—"

"I don't love Justin Bishop!" Dallas hastened to set the record straight. She moved forward until she stood directly behind the sofa, and her eyebrows knitted

114

together in a somber frown as she declared, "Perhaps I once fancied myself in love with him, but no longer!"

"But you've waited for him all these years, haven't you?" demanded Etta.

"No, I most definitely have not!"

"Then why didn't you marry any of those other men who asked you?" Cordi took up the interrogation. "Some of them were really quite nice, and yet you turned them away without giving any serious consideration at all to their proposals!"

"How in heaven's name would you know what sort of consideration I gave them?" challenged Dallas, her eyes flashing as her temper began to rise. She abruptly unfolded her arms and brought her hands down to grip the back of the sofa. "This is absurd . . . the subject of my love life is not open for discussion!"

"You don't *have* any love life," Etta noted with a superior lifting of her nose.

Dallas flushed hotly and subjected the petite blonde to a narrow look of acute, sisterly reproach. Growing concerned over the intensifying emotions in the room, Ruby Mae quickly sought to ease the tension.

"Land's sakes, I don't know what's gotten into you girls! But I think we've enjoyed just about all of this we can stand, don't you?" She turned to Cordi and directed, "Why don't you play somethin' to liven it up around here?" Then, to Etta, she said, "I expect Sam'll be done soon. You might better go on out back and make sure he doesn't leave without a good-bye kiss." Etta was only too happy to take her suggestion. Cordi was obliging with the strains of "The Yellow Rose of Texas." Dallas looked down at the older woman with the twinkling brown eyes and smiled ruefully.

"Oh, Ruby, I don't know what's gotten into us, either," she remarked with a sigh. "Everything was just fine until . . ." She was going to say *until Ross Kincaid came into our lives,* but fortunately caught herself in time and amended it to, "until I decided to have that blasted well drilled!"

"It might well be because of that," Ruby Mae thoughtfully allowed, "but it might also be nothin' more than the fact that your sisters are growin' up and changin'. You've had to be a mother to them for so long now, I guess it's kind of hard for you to realize they're not girls anymore."

"I suppose you're right," Dallas conceded with another sigh. She stepped from behind the sofa, her skirts and petticoats rustling softly as she sat down on the same cushion Etta had just vacated. Listening to the music, she and Ruby Mae drifted into a companionable silence that ended all too soon when a knock sounded at the front door.

Dallas virtually leapt to her feet. Her widened eyes cut to Ruby Mae's, and she was immediately bolstered by the warm encouragement she read therein. She took a deep, steadying breath, hastily smoothed her skirts, then forced herself to cross slowly into the entrance foyer. There was only the merest hint of a quaver in her voice as she swung open the door and said with a politely welcoming smile, "Good evening, Justin. Won't you come inside?" He looked quite dashing indeed, she mused, standing there as he was in his elegant black evening suit and not a single dark blond hair out of place. He looked almost *too* perfect . . . was there nothing remaining of the ragtag, unruly boy he had once been?

"I'd rather we talked out here, if you don't mind." His reply was unexpected, and Dallas, glancing uncertainly toward the parlor, hesitated to consent. Justin's features relaxed into a brief yet highly persuasive smile. "It won't take long."

"All right," she acquiesced, though she still felt a nagging uneasiness about the whole thing.

She stepped out onto the front porch and gently pulled the door to behind her. Acutely conscious of Justin's dark eyes upon her, she followed a long-held custom by strolling over to the whitewashed porch swing and sitting down. Justin waited until she had arranged her full skirts about her before taking a seat as well. The wood creaked beneath his weight as the swing took to rocking gently back and forth.

The light from the parlor shone outward, bathing the porch and its two occupants in a soft golden glow. There was nothing but silence between them for several long moments, during which time they were only dimly aware of the pleasant, familiar sounds of the approaching night. Leaves rustled softly, crickets serenaded, and the windmill near the barn quietly pumped as the gray, weathered blades were set in a continual motion by the warm summer breeze. The air was scented with a mixture of woodsmoke and roses and the heat rising from the fertile, sun-baked land.

"I meant to come back before now, Dallas," Justin finally began. His voice was low and tinged with what seemed to be genuine sorrow. Dallas turned her head and met his gaze.

"Then why didn't you?" The words—angry and accusing in spite of her resolve to maintain a cool detachment—were out of her mouth before she could stop them. She cursed herself for sounding like a bitter, scorned female. Scorned she may have been, but she had not grown bitter as a result . . . *or had she?*

"Because my life didn't turn out the way I thought it would," he replied with a heavy sigh. "To tell the truth, I got sidetracked more than once along the way." Drawing a cigar from the pocket of his dove-gray vest, he made no attempt to light it, but instead merely held it in his right hand and studied it while his attractive brow creased into a frown. "At first, my only thought was to get as far away from Corsicana as I could. I made my way to New Orleans, where I spent the better part of a year working at whatever jobs I could find. Then one day, a friend of mine talked me into heading out West. We ended up in San Francisco for a couple of years. After that, well . . . I traveled around a lot. New York was my last stop." He paused here, his lips curving into a faint, humorless smile as he glanced at Dallas and saw that her beautiful countenance had taken on an aloof look.

"I know what you're thinking," said Justin. He unbent his wiry, impeccably attired frame from the swing and moved to take a stance beside one of the porch columns. When he turned back to Dallas, his brown eyes were gleaming with a strange, unfathomable light. "I never sent word to you for the simple reason that I didn't want you to know I had failed. I never forgot you, Dallas, never forgot my promise. But I couldn't come back until I'd made something of myself, don't you see?"

"No, I don't," she answered, slowly shaking her head. She was tempted to ask him so many things— how he had made a living all these years, what had finally occurred to bring him the success he coveted so much, if he truly expected her to believe that his feelings for her had not diminished after all this time— but she did not. It wouldn't make any difference, she realized. Nothing could change the past. Perhaps she should still feel something for Justin Bishop, since he had once meant a great deal to her, but her heart no longer came alive for him. Would it ever come alive for any man? she then wondered.

It came alive for Ross Kincaid only last night! that accursed inner voice in her mind gleefully reminded her. *As a matter of fact, every square inch of you came alive for Ross Kincaid—*

"I don't blame you for that," Justin murmured with another ghost of a smile, his voice drawing her out of her disturbing reverie. She colored hotly and hastily averted her gaze while he continued with, "I always knew it was too much to hope you'd understand. But I'll do everything I can to make it up to you. I've come back for you, Dallas, and I've not come back empty-handed."

"What?" She sat bolt upright and blinked dazedly up at the fair-haired man before her.

"I was lucky enough to participate in a real estate deal a short time ago that paid much, much more than anyone thought it would. And I've taken on a partner who specializes in oil investments. So you see, fate did finally lead me back to Corsicana. And back to you."

"But I don't love you anymore!" Dallas blurted out, then blushed and grew uncharacteristically flustered. Clasping her hands tightly together in her lap, she raised her sparkling sapphire eyes to Justin's dully gleaming brown ones and questioned in as calm and rational a manner as possible, "Surely you don't expect the two of us to . . . to continue our relationship as though five years had not passed?"

"You said you'd love me forever, remember? And I promised to return and take you away with me." There was an increasing tightness about his mouth, and his piercing gaze seemed to rake over her with a barely controlled hunger. "Well, I'm here, Dallas, just like I said I'd be. *I've come back!*" His voice had taken on an alarming intensity all of a sudden, prompting Dallas to rise abruptly to her feet.

"I can't believe this is happening!" she exclaimed in disbelief. "You disappear for five years, you never even take the trouble to let me know if you're alive, and then you actually expect me to fall into your arms as though you'd gone away only yesterday? I was a sixteen-year-old girl when you left, Justin, but I'm not a girl any longer. We were both different people back then. Time has proven that what we felt for each other was nothing more than youthful infatuation, the sort of thing—"

"How could you know what I felt?" Justin tersely cut her off. He took a step closer, his eyes glittering almost savagely down at her in the pale golden light. "How could any of you know?" He gave a short, bitter laugh. "Your mother wasn't a whore. Your father didn't spend his nights getting roaring drunk and his days beating the hell out of you!" His fierceness abated somewhat, and a faint smile of remembrance tugged at his lips when he told Dallas, "I hated this town, hated everything and everyone in it—except for you. You were different from the others. No, Dallas," he concluded with a slight shake of his head, "what I felt for you was something far beyond 'infatuation'."

"But it wasn't necessarily love, either," she argued gently, her eyes full of compassion as she, too, remembered the grievous circumstances of his life there. It suddenly occurred to her that perhaps she had cared for him *because* of that. She could not deny that she had pitied him, nor that she had initially felt drawn to him upon witnessing a fight in which he'd been forced to defend himself against a cruelly taunting group of young men. Though only eighteen when their paths had finally crossed, he had seemed hard and embittered beyond his years, and yet she had glimpsed within him a desperate yearning for love.

"Call it what you will," he decreed in a low, charged tone, "but the fact remains that you're mine!" Dallas inhaled sharply as his hands suddenly came up to close about her upper arms, and she flushed uncomfortably when he fixed her with a burning look and declared, "Your father can't keep us apart now. I know you've waited a long time, but the waiting's over. I'm going to make it all up to you, Dallas. I'm going to give you the sort of life you deserve."

"No!" she gasped out, her eyes widening in dismay. "Oh, Justin, it's too late! And I didn't wait for you, I didn't!" She tried to pull free, but his grip merely tightened. Something akin to panic rose within her, but she quelled it and endeavored to make him see reason. "I'm sorry, Justin, truly I am, but we can't go back, we can't—"

Her protests were cut short by the unexpected pressure of his lips. His arms wrapped about her startled softness and held her so closely against him that she could scarcely breathe. Shocked into temporary immobility by the embrace, she found her

121

thoughts flying back to the kiss Ross Kincaid had forced upon her the previous night—and realized that, in comparison with the present, practiced assault of Justin's mouth upon hers, it was the clear winner in terms of desired results! Whereas *his* kiss had set her on fire, Justin's achieved nothing more than a very faint stirring of her senses . . .

"I didn't know you had company."

Dallas's eyes flew open in startlement at the sound of the deep, undeniably masculine voice she had already come to know so well. Struggling to regain her breath as Justin released her with dizzying abruptness, she gazed past him to where Ross Kincaid stood poised on the bottom step of the porch. He was leaning negligently against the thick wooden post, his hat tipped back upon his head and his arms folded across his broad chest. His green eyes were alive with devilment . . . and something else she did not recognize.

"Who the hell are *you?*" Justin demanded, furious at the intrusion.

"The name's Kincaid." He unhurriedly tugged off his hat and straightened to his full height, which put him almost level with the other man in spite of the fact that Dallas's would-be suitor was glaring belligerently at him from atop the porch. A strange little smile, one that did not quite reach his eyes, played about his lips as he favored Justin with a pointed look of dismissal before turning his steady, penetrating gaze upon Dallas. "I came to tell you we finished the derrick."

She could feel the hot color washing over her. Though she didn't know why, it perturbed her immensely to realize that he had seen Justin kissing her.

"I . . . I'm glad to hear it," she stammered, her eyes falling self-consciously before his. *Dear Lord, why did she feel as though she were some naughty schoolgirl caught in the act of committing a misdeed?* At that moment more than any other, she wanted to do Ross Kincaid bodily harm.

"You've said what you came to say. Now get on about your business and leave us to ours!" Justin ground out. Having immediately sensed in Ross a potential rival for Dallas's affections, he was anxious to get rid of him. He had heard about the well being drilled; it was a matter of concern to him in more ways than one.

"I also wanted you to know that I think I've got a lead on that missing equipment," Ross told Dallas as though Justin had never spoken. "A man by the name of—"

"Damn you, you heard what I said!" growled Justin, his face suffused with a dull, angry flush. He was usually careful to guard his temper, but there was something about the driller that provoked him almost beyond reason—almost. Determined to impress Dallas with his handling of the situation, he took a firm grip on his emotions and asserted in a cold, clear voice, "Miss Brown and I were engaged in a private discussion before we were so rudely interrupted. We'd appreciate it if you'd take yourself off at once!"

Her eyes growing very round, Dallas watched in breathless anticipation as Ross moved up the porch steps with a slow, measured deliberation that boded ill for the other man. He tossed his hat to land square in the middle of the porch swing, then paused mere inches away from Justin and remarked in a deceptively lazy drawl, "I don't believe I caught your name."

"Maybe that's because I didn't give it!"

Dallas's wide, luminous gaze shifted anxiously from Ross to Justin and back again. She watched as the two men stared long and hard at each other, apparently, engaged in a sort of silent combat that she sensed would erupt into actual violence if something did not occur—and soon!—to prevent it.

"Justin Bishop is an old friend," she hurried to inform Ross. To Justin, she said, "And Mr. Kincaid is the man who is drilling the well for us."

"I've already heard about the well. You won't be needing it," Justin told Dallas, his dark eyes full of meaning as they fastened upon her. "I've got more than enough—"

"It's getting late, Mr. Bishop," Ross broke in to proclaim with that same, studied equanimity. "Hadn't you better think about heading on back to town?"

"I'm not leaving, Kincaid—you are!" Justin parried between tightly clenched teeth. His hands curled into fists as he took a menacing step forward.

"Am I?" A faint, dangerously mocking smile appeared on Ross's handsome face, and there was an unmistakable light of warning in his smoldering gaze.

This is unbelievable! thought Dallas. Indignantly musing that the last thing she needed was to have two grown men battling it out like tomcats on her front porch, she hastened to intervene once more. She placed a restraining hand on Justin's arm and forced a smile to her lips.

"Please, Justin, it really is getting a bit late. I think perhaps it would be best if you were to leave now. I'll . . . I'll see you at church tomorrow, that is, if you're planning to come?" She didn't really want him to come, but it was the first thing that had popped into her mind. Recalling how they had secretly arranged to meet and attend church together on several occasions in the past, she thought of her father. Although Abner had always been suspicious of those "chance encounters," he had been unable to prove anything, and there hadn't been much he could say against the matter—after all, his daughter *was* in the house of the Lord, even if it was with someone like Justin Bishop.

"Please, Justin," she repeated. Her eyes were softly shining and full of entreaty.

"All right," he finally agreed, though he did so with obvious reluctance. "But I want you to think about what I said." He stared down at her while settling his hat upon his head, and his eyes took on the same hard look of purposefulness that had disturbed her earlier. "I won't take no for an answer, Dallas." With that, he turned and shot one last speaking, malevolent glare at Ross, then moved across the porch and down the steps with long, angry strides. He had soon ridden away into the moonlit summer night.

Dallas waited until Justin had gone before venting her outrage on Ross. Two bright spots of color stained her cheeks, and her eyes were ablaze with deep blue fire as she rounded on him with a vengeance.

"Just who the devil do you think you are? Not only did you treat Mr. Bishop with profound discourtesy, but you had the unmitigated gall to stand there spying on us for God only knows how long before you deigned to inform us of your presence!" Her full young breasts, which rose and fell rapidly beneath the clinging organdy of her low, square-necked bodice, were accentuated even further when she crossed her arms tightly below them. She was too angry to notice the way Ross's darkening gaze was drawn downward before traveling back up to fasten upon her beautiful, stormy countenance. "Could it be that your intrusion was not an accident at all, Mr. Kincaid? Is it possible that you actually knew I had a caller?" she demanded accusingly. "Did you by any chance come around here with the express purpose of interrupting my conversation with—"

"Conversation?" Ross challenged, one eyebrow mockingly raised. A tight, sardonic smile played about his lips. "Is that what I interrupted?" He hated like hell to admit it, even to himself, but the sight of her being kissed by another man had provoked a jealous rage more intense than he'd ever known. It had taken every ounce of self-will to keep from bounding up those steps and literally tearing that oily little bastard away from her! His blood still boiled when he thought of her in Bishop's arms. *Damn, but you act like you're already a goner, Kincaid,* he told himself with an inward curse. *Anyone would think she's got you hog-tied and down for the count . . . and they might just be right.*

"What happens between myself and Mr. Bishop is none of your business!" she hotly declared.

"I'm making it my business," he avowed in a low, vibrant tone as he began slowly advancing upon her.

Dallas started in sudden alarm, her arms hastily uncrossing and her eyes growing round as saucers. She instinctively retreated a half-dozen steps.

"Don't you come near me, Ross Kincaid! If you dare to lay so much as a finger on me, I'll send you packing so fast it will make your head swim!" Hoping her words held a good deal more bravado than she actually felt, she nonetheless continued backing away until her hips came up against the gallery's spindled railing. *This is it—plain and simple,* her mind's inner voice told her. Unless she was prepared to either scream for help or shinny over the railing, there would be no escape . . .

Ross offered no response, other than maintaining his present, unwaveringly determined course in her direction. He did not come to a halt until he stood so close she could feel the heat emanating from his body. He towered above her in the shadows, his tall, powerfully built frame making her feel small and trapped.

She raised her eyes to his. Those smoldering green orbs seemed to burn into her very soul. She could not move, could not speak, and most disquieting of all, could not prevent herself from swaying toward him. Her eyes swept closed, while her lips parted ever so slightly, as though issuing an unspoken invitation.

Ross stared intently down at the beautiful, spirited young redhead who had sparked his interest—and his desire—like no other woman. Passion fired his blood, threatening to make him throw all caution to the wind and claim possession of that sweet mouth and those damnably enticing curves. It was all he could do to keep his hands off her, and yet he knew that if he touched her at all, he'd not be able to stop at one kiss . . .

Her eyelids fluttering open, Dallas watched in stunned disbelief when Ross spun about on his booted heel and strode away. She could do nothing more than stare speechlessly after him as he retraced his steps and disappeared around the corner of the house.

He'd done it again!

Fury and humiliation washed over her. How could she have allowed herself to stoop so low, to stand there meekly waiting for him to kiss her like that? And how could *he* have turned and walked away without so much as a by-your-leave?

"Dallas Brown, you are an idiot of the first magnitude!" she seethed disparagingly to herself. Casting one last, dagger-hurtling look in the direction Ross Kincaid had gone, she gathered up her frilly, flounced skirts and stormed inside the house.

Cordi and Ruby Mae, still sitting in the parlor, fell abruptly silent when they caught sight of Dallas flying up the stairs. Exchanging glances of profound bewilderment, they soon recovered their voices and spent the next quarter of an hour ruminating upon what might have happened to set her off. Neither of them could have guessed that it was Ross Kincaid and not Justin Bishop who should have figured so prominently in their speculations . . . nor could they have known that the night held even more surprises for them all.

V

The house shook as a violent blast rent the air.

"Dear God, what was that?" gasped Dallas. She and Ruby Mae, jolted from a sound sleep, tumbled hurriedly from the bed and tossed their wrappers about their shoulders.

"Lord have mercy, a noise like that'd make the hair of a buffalo robe stand up!" Ruby Mae offered. She flung open the door and nearly collided with Ross and Swede, who had hastily drawn on their trousers and were now speeding down the hallway to the stairs.

"Dallas! Ruby Mae! Did you hear it? What in tarnation could it have been?" Cordi and Etta took turns asking in breathless, wide-eyed alarm as they came rushing out of the room next door.

"I don't know, but I'm going to find out!" exclaimed Dallas. She quickly knotted the belt of her wrapper, then took off after the men, racing barefoot down the stairs with her nightclothes flying up about her ankles and her unbound hair streaming behind her like a brilliant red banner. The other three women soon followed, though a frightened Cordi and Etta remained close to the comforting, protective bulk of Ruby Mae while they moved through the darkened house.

The acrid smell of smoke came up to hit Dallas as soon as she reached the kitchen. She frowned in puzzlement at the strange, flickering golden light that filled the room, and her gaze flew to the back door to see that it was standing wide open. Her heart filling with dread at what she would find, she hurried outside.

She gasped and drew up short at the foot of the steps, thunderstruck at the sight that met her eyes. The newly erected derrick was no longer towering eighty-five feet into the starlit Texas sky—it was lying sprawled on the ground, its laboriously constructed timbers already well on their way to being consumed by the flames which threatened to spread across the sun-baked ground to the house and outbuildings.

"Get some water!" Ross shouted at her above the fire's roar. He and Erik were valiantly working to contain the blaze by shoveling dirt onto the edges of the fire. There was no way they could save the derrick; their efforts would now have to be spent on preventing any further destruction. "Water, damn it!"

Shaking her head as if to clear it, Dallas spun about and took flight. She scurried across the yard to the empty stock trough, snatched up one of the buckets hanging on the side of the barn, and began pumping water into it like mad. Ruby Mae materialized at her side before she had finished.

"Here, let me at that!" Taking charge as she was always wont to do, the resolute spinster grabbed the pump handle and curtly motioned to Cordi and Etta to lend a hand as well. Within seconds, Dallas and her sisters were racing back and forth between the pump and the leaping circle of fire, where they emptied bucket after bucket of water while the men continued waging their own battle against the encroaching flames.

The night air was thick and heavy with smoke. The heat from the raging conflagration was so intense that Dallas began to feel faint and short of breath. Increasingly fearful of the outcome, for it seemed impossible that they could succeed against the fire's relentless power, she paused for a brief instant and looked to where Ross and Erik were tirelessly working to contain the blaze. The smoke had blackened their faces, while the flames had singed the hair on their unprotected arms and chests. Still, they did not waver.

Dallas felt an odd twisting of her heart as she gazed at the tall, raven-haired man who was risking his life to save her beloved house. Dashing at the tears which gathered in her burning eyes—and sparing a hasty glance toward Etta, who had come to stand beside her with another bucketful of water—she was about to resume her own frantic efforts when a spark suddenly shot outward to ignite the skirt of Etta's gingham wrapper. Flames rapidly engulfed the lower portion of the garment.

A strangled cry broke from Etta's lips. Momentarily frozen in horror, Dallas could only watch as her sister dropped the bucket and staggered backward. The petite blonde's features were contorted in panic, and her mouth began to emit shrill, piercing screams as the flames started to eat their way through her wrapper to her nightgown . . .

Reacting with lightning-quick speed, Ross sped past

Dallas, seized Etta about the waist, and tackled her forcefully to the ground. He rolled over and over with her, effectively suffocating the flames before they'd had the chance to scorch her legs.

Her body finally obeying the frenzied dictates of her brain, Dallas rushed to her sister's side just as Ross was helping the much shaken young woman to her feet.

"Oh, Etta, are you all right?" She placed an arm about the seventeen-year-old's shoulders and peered anxiously down into her dirt-smeared features. Cordi and Ruby Mae came scrambling across the yard just as Etta breathed,

"Yes, I . . . I think so!" Still somewhat in shock from her ordeal, she was grateful for Dallas's arm about her. Her wide, benumbed gaze flickered hastily downward to fasten upon the ragged remains of her wrapper. "Dear God, I might have burned to death if not for—" She broke off at the sudden realization, and her eyes flew back up to her sister's face before traveling to where Ross had already resumed his place at the fire. Once he had satisfied himself that Etta was unharmed, he had wasted no time before taking himself off to fight the blaze again. "He saved my life, Dallas! He saved my life!" she uttered in profound amazement.

"We'd be mournin' you for sure if it wasn't for him!" Ruby Mae feelingly declared in complete accordance. She caught Etta up in a brief but affectionate hug, then smiled and directed, "You go on inside and lie down, honey. Lord willin', the rest of us will be in soon!" Turning away to hurry back to the pump, she called over her shoulder, "I do believe we'll have this dangblasted thing beat if we just keep after it a while longer!"

Both of Etta's sisters quickly embraced her one last time before following Ruby Mae's lead. Dallas stole frequent glances at Ross while she worked, her heart turning over in her breast as she recalled what he had done for Etta. He had displayed admirable wisdom and courage, had charged boldly ahead without sparing any thought for his own safety. *Who the devil is this man?* she asked herself in mingled awe and confusion. *And why has everything gone topsy-turvy ever since he came along?*

Strangely enough, she no longer feared that the fire would spread to the house. It was almost as if she were drawing on Ross Kincaid's strength, as if she sensed he would never allow himself to be vanquished by anyone or anything . . .

Her instincts were soon proven correct, for, mercifully, the tide turned in their favor shortly thereafter. Ross, hoisting his shovel upward to balance it in one hand, pronounced the fire contained at last. He added that he and Swede would maintain a vigilant watch over the blaze until it had burned itself out. The women all breathed a long sigh of weariness and relief as they tossed their buckets aside and sank down together upon the back steps.

"How on earth could this have happened?" murmured Cordi. Her wrapper was torn and dirty, and her face was smudged in a number of places. Dallas and Ruby Mae looked equally bedraggled, but they were too tired to care.

"Well, it wasn't no accident, that's for sure," the oldest of the three decisively opined. "That blast we heard must've been the explosives goin' off. It's a wonder the whole house didn't come tumblin' down

133

around our ears!"

"Why would anyone want to blow up the derrick?" Dallas wondered aloud. Her brow creased into a pensive frown as she reached up to loose the knot of hair she had hastily devised in order to keep her long auburn locks from getting in the way. She stared toward the dwindling fire in the middle of the scorched circle of earth that had once been her backyard, and her eyes shadowed with several conflicting emotions.

Perhaps this is an omen, she suddenly thought. She certainly could not deny that she'd had more than a few doubts about having the well drilled in the first place. Her father had always been dead set against it . . . neither one of her sisters had been in favor of it, at least not in the beginning . . . Justin Bishop, whose opinion really shouldn't enter into the matter at all, had also expressed disapproval of it . . . and, last but not least, there was Ross Kincaid. The fire's golden glow was reflected in the brilliant sapphire depths of her eyes as she gazed directly across at the man whose broad, naked back was turned toward her.

A highly perplexing shiver danced up and down her spine. Why did he have to be so . . . so downright *virile?* He was without a doubt the most all-fired masculine person she had ever encountered! And that was exactly what bothered her. He made her too disturbingly aware of her own femininity, made her do and think and say and—damn it!—*feel* things that kept her nerves on end every minute of the day.

She knew she couldn't take much more of this game of cat-and-mouse they had been playing. Tonight's disaster, coupled with her increasingly distressing relationship with Ross Kincaid, served to make her strongly suspect that her decision had been the wrong one after all.

"Looks like someone around here's trying to tell you somethin'," Ruby Mae observed with another heavy sigh. "I just wish we knew how and why and *what!*"

"That's obvious, isn't it? Whoever did this doesn't want us drilling the well," supplied Cordi. She rose to her feet and spared one last, wistfully longing glance toward Swede before turning to open the door. "I don't know about you, but I'm absolutely exhausted! Besides, we really ought to look in on Etta and let her know the danger has passed."

Murmuring her agreement, Ruby Mae climbed slowly to her feet and held the door while Cordi trudged into the kitchen. The older woman paused in the doorway, apparently waiting for Dallas.

"You comin' inside, honey?"

"Not yet. I . . . I've got to speak to Mr. Kincaid about something first."

"All right. But don't stay out here too long. Those church bells are gonna start ringin' earlier than you think tomorrow mornin'." Looking back at the dying flames outlined against the deep blue-black of the night sky, she shook her head and disappeared inside the house.

Dallas stood and drew the edges of her blue silk wrapper more closely about her slender curves, then quickly tightened the sash looped at her waist. She swept the tangled mass of auburn hair away from her face, squared her shoulders, and set off across the yard with the light of determination in her eyes.

"Mr. Kincaid, I should like to have a word with you," she announced, drawing to a halt at what she deemed to be a safe distance behind him. Ross stood talking quietly with Erik. He did not turn to face her right away, but instead spoke to his partner again.

"Go on," he told the young Swede. "There's no sense in the both of us staying out here."

Erik, his white teeth flashing in the midst of his smoke-blacked face, grinned at Dallas and bid her good night. She reciprocated with a rather weak smile and a brief word of thanks for his part in battling the fire, to which he gallantly replied that it had been an honor for him to be able to help her and the other Misses Brown. Then, he was gone, leaving her alone with the one man who frightened, infuriated, and inflamed her as no other man could.

"First of all, Mr. Kincaid, what is your opinion regarding this . . . this," she began, making an angry, sweeping gesture toward what was left of the derrick, "premeditated disaster!"

"My opinion, *Miss Brown,* is that this particular derrick is a total loss and we'll build another one tomorrow," he replied with a faint, mocking smile.

"That isn't what I mean and you know it!" Her voice rang out sharply in the still of the night. The only other sound to be heard was the soft crackling of the fire, which sent a shower of sparks reaching for the moon and cast long, intriguing shadows across Dallas's stormy countenance and Ross's unfathomable one. "Do you have any idea *why* my derrick was blown up?" she demanded with exaggerated patience.

"Competition." He took up both shovels and started off toward the barn. Dallas stared blankly after him for a moment before giving chase.

"Competition? What is that supposed to mean?"

"Simply that if someone's decided to drill on the property next to yours, they might be willing to do all they could to make sure your well's never completed."

"But I . . . I don't understand! How could that—"

"By virtue of a little something called the Rule of Capture," he anticipated her question. He stopped and turned to stare closely down at her while she gasped and came to an abrupt halt to keep from colliding with him. His eyes swiftly drank in the sight of her flushed and wide-eyed features, her wildly cascading hair, and her alluring, thinly robed curves. To him, she had never looked more beautiful . . . nor more dangerously irresistible.

"And what, pray tell, is *that?*" she queried with biting sarcasm. She cursed the fact that her eyes kept straying downward to the bronzed, hard-muscled expanse of his chest. Swallowing hard, she tried to ignore the wicked turn her thoughts took when her gaze followed the well-defined line of softly curling black hair that disappeared beneath the waistband of his trousers.

"Oil supposedly belongs to anyone under whose property it lies. But if someone wanted to get to the oil under your land, all they'd have to do is drill a well next to your place and drain it over to theirs."

"Even if that's what someone *is* trying to do, I still don't understand how they could stoop so low as to blow up my derrick! Why, we might have all been killed!"

"Men will do anything in the name of greed," he told her in a low, tight voice, his eyes darkening. "But they weren't out to kill anyone. Whoever did this used just enough dynamite to bring down the derrick."

Dallas fell silent. Her head spun as she pondered

what Ross had just told her, and she was only dimly aware of the fact that he had turned and was heading for the barn again. *Enough is enough. How can I possibly go on with this when everything seems to be pointing against it?* she mused with an inward sigh as she reluctantly admitted defeat.

Staunchly telling herself that she really had no other choice, she hurried after Ross and caught up with him just as he reached the front of the barn. A sudden warning bell sounded in her brain, but she ignored it, her only thought to get things settled before she weakened in her resolve.

"Mr. Kincaid, I've come to a decision!" She crossed her arms tightly against her breasts as Ross once again drew to a halt and turned to face her in the moonlit darkness.

"Have you?" he responded wryly, his words more of a challenge than a question. Dallas bristled beneath his steady, unnerving scrutiny.

"I most certainly have!" Her voice rose on a shrill note of annoyance, and she hastily sought to regain her composure. When she spoke again, it was with a determined, outward air of cool equanimity. "I have changed my mind about the well. I realize now that it was a mistake, a very big mistake, and one which must be rectified at once. What happened tonight only helped to show me the folly of my—"

"What you're saying is that you're giving up."

"If it pleases you to put it that way, then yes, Mr. Kincaid, I am!"

"You didn't strike me as the sort of woman who'd let anyone tell her how to run her life."

"I'm not letting anyone tell me anything!" Dallas

defensively retorted, her eyes sparking with anger.

"That's exactly what you're doing," insisted Ross, his voice taking on a hard edge. His mouth tightened into a thin line of displeasure as he paused to lean the shovels upright against the outer wall of the barn, and his gaze glittered coldly down at her when he straightened again. "Someone wants to keep me from drilling your well—who or why, I don't know. But the fact remains that he blew up the derrick in an attempt to dissuade us from continuing. Well, *sweetheart,* what he did may not concern you a whole blasted lot, but it galls the hell out of me! I'll be damned if I'll stand by and let some underhanded son of a bitch keep me from doing the job I came to do!"

"How . . . how dare you call me that!" she sputtered indignantly. "And how dare you—"

"I won't let you knuckle under on this," he declared in a low, slightly husky tone, his handsome face forebodingly grim. "We're damn well going to finish what we started, regardless of your dimwitted change of heart and regardless of whatever tactics anyone uses to try and make us turn tail!"

"Dimwitted?" Her temper flared to a perilous level, and it was all she could do to keep from striking him. She uncrossed her arms and held them stiffly at her sides, her hands balling into tight fists. Fairly quaking with the force of her outrage, she glared up at him with eyes brilliantly ablaze. "You have no right to dictate what I will or will not do, Ross Kincaid! This happens to be *my* property you're standing on! If I say there will be no well, then there will be no well! There isn't anything you can do about it! You're nothing more than an employee here, whether you choose to face the

truth of that particular fact or not, and I will not allow myself to be ordered about by a . . . by a *hired hand!*" she finished with a proudly defiant toss of her head, her lustrous auburn tresses swirling riotously about her face and shoulders. She cried out when Ross's hands shot out to take her arms in a none too gentle grip.

"I don't give a damn what you call me, you little wildcat, but I ought to teach you a lesson about—" Breaking off with an oath, he released her just as abruptly and fought for control over his own explosive temper. "Does this have anything to do with Bishop?" he suddenly ground out. "Is he one of the reasons you're so anxious to give up?"

"Justin? Why . . . why no, I . . ." she breathlessly started to deny, her voice trailing away and her face flaming as it occurred to her that Ross Kincaid had no right whatsoever to demand information regarding her personal life. Drawing herself rigidly erect, she fixed him with a narrow, chilling look and uttered scornfully, "As I said before, my relationship with Justin Bishop is none of your business!"

"And as *I* said before, I'm making it my business!" His lips curled into an insolent, taunting smile while a surge of unbridled jealousy shot through him. "He'd never be able to handle you, you know. What you need is a man who won't let you run roughshod over him, a man who will know how to tame that spirit of yours without breaking it."

"A man like you, I suppose?" she parried with a sarcastic expression of wide-eyed innocence.

"No" was his unexpected reply. Dallas blinked up at him in openmouthed surprise. His eyes were full of a strange, disturbingly intense light. She didn't seem to

140

notice when his hands slid back up the silk covering her arms to close upon the trembling curve of her shoulders. "Not a man *like* me," he clarified in a soft, resonant tone that sent chills running down her spine. "A man who *is* me."

She caught her breath upon a gasp. A sudden wave of light-headedness threatened to send her swaying forward against his bare chest, but she fought against it, just as she fought against the startling temptation to smooth her fingers across the hard, sinewy muscles rippling beneath all that gleaming bronzed skin—

"No!" she cried out, denying herself every bit as much as she was seeking to deny him. Her hands came up to push against his broad, oh-so-masculine chest while her eyes cleared and flashed. "Not again! Never again!" Struggling almost frantically within his relentless grasp, she lifted her bare foot and sent it flying forward into swift, painful contact with his shin.

His only response was to curse and tighten his hold upon her shoulders, his fingers digging into her soft flesh. It was then that she finally did what she had been tempted to do on at least two other occasions—she raised her right hand, doubled it into a fist, and brought it up hard against the rugged perfection of his left jaw, just as her father had once taught her to do. Her knuckles hurt terribly, but she consoled herself with the thought that the arrogant scoundrel's jaw hurt even more. At least the blow had achieved the desired effect of making him release her.

"Why, you little—" he bit out menacingly, his smoldering green eyes appearing downright savage while he rubbed at his throbbing jaw.

Dallas wheeled about in a desperate bid for freedom,

141

but it was too late. A soft cry broke from her lips when Ross's steely arm clamped about her waist and hauled her roughly back against him. She kicked and flailed and squirmed in a fierce yet entirely futile attempt to escape. Not only were his height and strength far superior to hers, but he was determined to subdue her . . . and Ross Kincaid was the sort of man who was seldom thwarted in anything.

She opened her mouth to scream in earnest, but his other hand immediately silenced her. He bore her purposefully inside the darkened, musty confines of the barn while she struggled against him in rapidly escalating alarm. Without warning, she was tossed unceremoniously backward to the ground. She gasped, her eyes flying wide when she landed backside-first upon a cushioning pile of hay. Wasting little time, she scrambled on to her hands and knees, then tried to climb to her feet, only to find herself hampered by the voluminous folds of her nightgown and wrapper.

Ross, taking advantage of her wholly feminine predicament, dropped to his knees and yanked her back down beside him. She struck out at him with all her might, her blows doing little damage as he rolled her over in the hay and imprisoned her furiously squirming body with his powerful, lithely muscled one. The folds of her wrapper and nightgown were now twisted immodestly up about her silken thighs.

"Let me go, damn you! Let me go!" Dallas raged hoarsely. Hot tears of helpless frustration stung her eyes. Her head tossed furiously to and fro, her shimmering auburn locks fanning out upon the fragrant, dried grass in glorious disarray. She threaded her fingers within the dark thickness of Ross's hair and gave a violent tug, just as she had done the night before, but without the same results. He merely seized her wrists and stretched them high above her head, holding them captive with one strong hand. She next tried to jerk her knees upward into a disabling collision with the most vulnerable part of his masculine anatomy, but he anticipated her actions and roughly jammed his own knee between both of hers. She gasped in shocked outrage to feel his hard, denim-clad lower body parting her bare legs.

"Get . . . off of me, you . . . you bastard!" she breathlessly demanded. She wriggled in vehement protest beneath him, which only made matters worse. Her eyes grew enormous within the delicate, fierily blushing oval of her face as she felt the undeniable evidence of his manhood against her sparsely covered softness. "No!" she exclaimed in very real panic. Her blazing sapphire gaze locked with the darkening green fire of his. "Damn you to hell, Ross Kincaid, if you think I'm going to let you—"

"Shut up, Dallas," he murmured gruffly, his voice edged with raw emotion. There was a dangerous intensity to his rugged features, and even in the darkness she could see the almost savage gleam in his eyes. "For once in your life, just shut up and don't try to fight what's happening to you!"

"Why, you arrogant, unscrupulous snake! You may have been able to get what you wanted from other women with that ridiculous, self-serving line of reasoning, but not from *me!*"

In the very next instant, however, Dallas proved herself a liar—or at least half a liar. Ross had no sooner brought his lips crashing down upon hers than she moaned low in her throat and felt unspeakable passion flaring to life within her. She trembled beneath him, shaken and confused by the wild flood of desire his touch never failed to create within her. He kissed her with a scarcely controlled violence, his lips hard and demanding, his body pressing hers deeper into the hay.

Her wrists were abruptly released as his arms gathered her close in a fierce, possessive embrace. Her own arms crept about his neck, and she strained boldly upward against him, returning his kisses with an answering fire that was far removed from the cool, prim-and-proper demeanor she usually affected.

She suffered a sharp intake of breath when he suddenly rolled so that she was atop him. Her long hair tumbled down about them both like a shimmering curtain, while her nightclothes became even more twisted up about her shapely limbs. Seized by a brief moment of returning sanity, she tried to draw away, but she succeeded only in prompting Ross to deepen the kiss and slide his hand downward over the slender, graceful curve of her back to the undeniably feminine contour of her buttocks. Before she knew what he intended, he had impatiently pulled the last protective folds of blue silk and white cotton upward.

Her eyes swept open as she felt a rush of cool air on her feverish skin. She was even more shocked to feel the strong warmth of Ross's fingers curling about her bare bottom. *Dallas, Dallas, what are you doing?* the voice of her conscience desperately implored. She might have come to her senses then and there, if not for the fact that Ross's hands had begun a gentle kneading and caressing of her soft, delectably rounded flesh. And as if that weren't enough to drive reason away and replace

144

it with intoxicating madness, he set his lips to roaming hungrily across her beautiful face and then downward along the column of her white throat to the sensitive hollow where her pulse beat with such alarming speed.

She moaned softly in protest as his hands suddenly left her bottom, but she was consoled when they moved to the high, lace-edged neckline of her gown. The row of tiny pearl buttons surrendered with startling ease. Ross tugged the gaping edges aside, his mouth branding her silken skin as it trailed a fiery path downward to her breasts. When the nightgown's gathered bodice still presented too much of a barrier to his wishes, he forced it to yield, tearing the delicate cotton and thereby exposing Dallas's breasts in all their full, rose-tipped glory.

A loud gasp broke from her lips, but she was given no time to resist—if resistance had indeed been her intent—before his mouth claimed one of the perfectly formed globes and his hands returned to fasten upon her captivating derriere. Lifted even further upward for his pleasure, she stifled a cry as his hot, velvety tongue flicked across the nipple with tantalizing lightness while his lips tenderly suckled.

She clutched almost frantically at the bronzed hardness of his shoulders. Gasping again and again while his strong fingers boldly explored the naked curves of her buttocks and thighs, she bit at her lower lip and blushed fierily when one of his hands glided forward across the smoothness of her hip . . . down toward the beckoning triangle of auburn curls nestled between her slightly parted thighs . . . then gently pried the soft petals of womanly flesh apart to pay loving tribute to the pink bud of femininity concealed therein.

Liquid fire raced through her veins when he touched her there. *Merciful heavens, what was happening to her?* It was as if he had touched off a veritable powder keg of emotion! She literally ached with a strange yet undeniable yearning, and she could not keep herself from emitting a series of soft, breathless moans. A deep tremor of passion shook her, and she strained upward, affording Ross's appreciative lips with even greater access to her beautiful breasts while her hands glided feverishly over the hard muscles of his arms and shoulders.

She was abruptly rolled onto her back in the hay again, with Ross's tall, virile frame pressing her down into its unresisting fragrance. His mouth returned to claim hers in a searing kiss as his fingers continued their hypnotic caresses.

Almost entirely incapable of rational thought, Dallas allowed herself to be swept away. She felt as though on fire . . . and knew that the only man capable of putting it out was the one holding her in his arms. There was little doubt she would have granted him the privilege of doing just that, if not for the fact that her arm suddenly brushed against a cold, metal object which had previously been buried in the hay.

She dazedly turned her head toward it as Ross's lips began to wander once more. It took only a moment for her passion-clouded eyes to make out its distinguishable outline in the darkness. There, right next to the spot where she was letting Ross Kincaid do the sort of things she had been warned never to let any man do, was a pair of her father's black forging tongs.

Papa! Dear God, what would he think if he knew she was on the verge of yielding her innocence to a man who wasn't her husband, a man she had known only two days? Dallas silently agonized.

He does know. As a matter of fact, he's probably watching you right now, you shameless hussy! the voice of her much-offended conscience took great pleasure in taunting her.

It was a sobering thought, to say the least. Reality came crashing down about her at last, and she wasted no time in breaking the spell Ross's sensuous magic had woven about them.

"No! Stop it, please, stop it!" she cried in heartfelt vehemence as she pushed against him.

Surprised by her sudden, quite fervent resistance, he raised his head and fixed her with a grim look that was half furious and half searching. His heart twisted painfully as he took note of the mingled fear and mortification in her wide, luminous eyes. Reason quickly returned to him as well. He cursed himself for having lost his head; he hadn't meant for things to go that far. *But, damn, she had driven him to near madness with her fiery beauty and indomitable spirit . . . he had never wanted a woman as much as he'd wanted her . . . as much as he still wanted her.*

"Dallas, I—"

"No! Don't . . . don't say anything! Just let me go!" she demanded brokenly, her gaze sparkling with tears and her face burning with shame.

Ross stared intently down at the tousled, auburn-haired beauty who could both enrage and arouse him as no other woman had ever done. His ruggedly handsome features tightened. Without a word, he slowly eased off her and drew himself upright. He reached a hand down to help her up, but she pointedly ignored it, instead climbing to her feet and drawing her wrapper about her in stiff, angry movements.

"If you ever dare to breathe so much as one word of this to—" she seethed.

"You have my word as a gentleman that what happened here tonight will remain *our* secret."

His mocking words did little to reassure her, or to soothe her wounded pride. The way he was looking at her didn't help much, either, for she glimpsed an unholy light of devilment in those magnificent green eyes of his. Lifting her head in a proudly defiant gesture that belied her present state of dishevelment, she swept regally past him and out of the barn.

A slow, meaningful smile spread across Ross's face as he stared after her. The smile faded into a scowl a few moments later when he recalled what Dallas had said about abandoning the well. Admitting to himself that his determination to finish the job stemmed more from a desire to remain near a certain, sharp-tongued redhead than out of any sense of duty, he swore roundly and took himself back outside to check on the fire which had now burned down into nothing more than a large, single mass of embers glowing softly against the nighttime horizon.

Dallas, meanwhile, had immediately flown upstairs and locked herself in the warm, lamplit bathroom, where she hurried across to kneel on the pine floor beside the bathtub. Wrenching the porcelain-handled faucets upward, she sat back on her heels and watched as the water streamed forth with a gentle roar.

She was aghast at what she had done—even more so at what she had *almost* done. There was no excuse for her wanton behavior, but neither was there an excuse for the way that infuriating, green-eyed rogue had taken advantage of her. She despised him every bit as much as she despised herself, in spite of the fact that he had made her feel more vibrantly alive than she'd ever felt before, and in spite of the fact that thoughts of him had filled her head nearly every waking hour of the past two days.

"I wish I had never heard of Rossiter Maverick Kincaid!" she muttered, snatching up the lavender-scented bar of soap on the side of the tub and flinging it into the water.

People in hell want ice water, too, that inner voice of hers retorted. It had been one of her father's favorite phrases when she was young. She had hated it then and she hated it now!

A short time later found her snuggled safely beneath the covers of her bed. Ruby Mae snored softly beside her. The window shade had been left up, and the moonlight streamed freely inside the room while the lace curtains stirred gently in what little breeze there was.

Dallas tensed at the sudden sound of footsteps. Though far from sleep, she had been lost in turbulent contemplation, and the realization that someone was coming up the stairs prompted her heart to pound erratically. Her eyes grew very round as the booted feet came to a halt right outside her door.

There was no doubt in her mind as to the identity of the person standing there. Envisioning him all too clearly, she listened, breathless and waiting, for what seemed like an eternity. Then, the footsteps resumed, growing steadily fainter and fainter until she could hear them no more.

Dallas felt herself flushing hotly from head to toe. She released a long, pent-up sigh, tugged the pillow from beneath her head, and cradled its fluffy softness against her. It provided little comfort, but it was at least something to hold on to while her body trembled and her head spun dizzily.

VI

Irritably musing that she was never so glad in her life to get out of a place, Dallas drove the wagon home at a near breakneck speed. Both Cordi and Etta set up a fuss over the fact that the wind was tearing at their hair, but Ruby Mae simply sat in knowing silence beside her highly perturbed young friend and held on tight.

Church had been a far from uplifting experience, at least in Dallas's opinion. Not only had Justin Bishop's presence there proven even more disquieting than she had anticipated, but the sermon itself had turned out to be an unforeseen ordeal. Asking herself why the preacher had chosen that particular day to present his infamous, monthly exhortation on the "evils and temptations of the flesh," she compressed her lips tightly together and felt her cheeks flame anew. It was as if he had been able to read the troubled thoughts whirling round in her mind, as if he had been speaking directly to *her* when he came to that part about guarding oneself against the "enticements of the devil!"

And then there was Lorena Appleton. As if things

hadn't been going badly enough already, the gossipy young widow, planting herself squarely in the midst of the crowd milling about on the steps outside after the service, had made a number of very pointed remarks about how "the Brown girls actually have two of those wicked Yankee oilmen living with them." Cordi had only made matters worse by defensively retorting that neither Ross Kincaid nor Erik Larsen were Yankees at all.

Hellfire and damnation! Dallas swore inwardly. Recalling the look of smug, malicious satisfaction on Lorena's face, she snapped the reins together and shifted angrily on the wagon seat. What really infuriated her was that Lorena Appleton herself had one of the very worst reputations in town. Why, it was a well-known fact that no man was safe once Lorena had set her sights on him!

She thought of Justin again, and her eyes sparked at the memory of his maddeningly possessive behavior. Not only had he remained at her side throughout every single minute, but he had maintained an almost constant grip upon her elbow. It was as though he had been trying to show everyone that she was his, as though . . . as though establishing *ownership,* for heaven's sake!

"I hate to tell you this, honey, but we just passed your house!" Ruby Mae's voice suddenly cut in on her unpleasant reverie.

"What?" Dallas murmured with a frown. Hastily turning her head, she saw that they had indeed gone right by her house and were heading out toward the Jockey Club's racetrack. Horse races were held there every Sunday, but attending them had definitely *not* been on her agenda for the day. Coloring in embarrassment, she slowed the horse to a halt, maneuvered the wagon about, and quickly covered the short distance back to the house. Cordi and Etta, for once calling upon the wisdom they had been given, offered no remarks concerning their sister's rare display of absentmindedness.

Once inside, Dallas directed her purposeful steps toward the aromatic brightness of the kitchen. Her sisters, anxious to look their best for Sunday dinner—or rather for the socializing they planned to indulge in afterward—rushed upstairs to straighten their windblown hair. Announcing that she had a few things to see to at home and would be back in "two shakes of a lamb's tail," Ruby Mae disappeared back outside.

Dallas paused to check on the progress of her pot roast before sliding it back into the oven and hurrying to take a stance at the window. Her beautiful sapphire eyes bridled with renewed anger and uncertainty at what they beheld.

The new derrick was already half-finished, the crew evidently having improved with practice, and Ross was at that moment swinging lithely up on to one of the timbers to nail another into place above it. He had taken off his hat and shirt, allowing the sun to bring a fiery radiance to the dark, slightly damp thickness of his hair and a lustrous sheen to the bronzed, hard-muscled smoothness of his upper torso.

Nonplussed by a sudden desire to be back in the circle of those strong arms, Dallas spun away from the window and crossed back to the stove. She forced her thoughts away from the inevitable wickedness of their present course, and turned them instead to the matter of the well.

Arriving downstairs shortly after dawn, it had become immediately apparent to her that Ross had meant what he'd said about not letting her give up. He had somehow managed to arrange for another load of supplies to be delivered on that early Sunday morning, then had wasted little time in beginning the construction of another derrick on the same, blackened site where the other one had stood. Dallas knew it would have been entirely useless to protest, for he had made his determination quite clear the night before.

Perhaps she should have marched out there with shotgun in hand and ordered him off the place! There it was again, she mused with a heavy sigh—that tendency toward violence. She had never really wanted to do anyone bodily harm until he came along. Why was it that she wanted to shoot him one moment and—*heaven forbid*—lose herself in his powerful embrace the next?

"George Proctor, where the devil are you?" she murmured aloud, fervently wishing her beloved godfather would materialize beside her. *And do what?* that dreaded inner voice of hers demanded. *Save you from yourself?*

There was no reason to hope the situation would improve, Dallas thought disconsolately as she closed the oven door again and set the coffee on to boil. She would most assuredly have to avoid Ross Kincaid from here on out. It wouldn't be easy, particularly since he was still living in her house and working in her backyard. Still, she could at least try and ensure that the two of them were never alone, for therein lay the danger—as long as they remained in the presence of others, there would be no reprisal of the sort of disastrous, humiliatingly intimate encounter that had taken place between them the night before. She would be safe just as long as she kept the insolent rogue at a distance. But, God help her, if he so much as touched her again . . .

"Dallas! Confound it all, Dallas, that hateful she-wolf is out there in *our* backyard!" Etta indignantly exclaimed as she and Cordi came tearing into the kitchen. "I could scarcely believe my eyes when I looked out of the window upstairs and—"

"Goodness gracious, Dallas, do you think Mr. Larsen is already acquainted with that awful woman?" Cordi breathed at a sudden, horrible thought.

"Who?"

"Lorena Appleton!"

"Lorena Appleton is in our backyard?" Dallas repeated in bemusement, her silken brow creasing into a frown of disbelief. Anxious to see for herself, she hastened back to the window. Her eyes grew very round as they ascertained the truth of her sisters' words. "Hell's bells, what is *she* doing here?" she muttered in obvious displeasure.

"You mean what is she doing out *there!*" amended Etta. She and Cordi quickly joined their older sister at the window. "Look at her! It's a wonder her eyelashes haven't fallen off before now, the way she bats them at every man she sees. And I'll bet those hips of hers could keep a windmill going!"

"Why, she's . . . she's making an absolute spectacle of herself!" added Cordi. Dallas remained silent, her gaze narrowing as she watched the shapely young widow's performance.

Lorena raised a hand to give a cursory pat to her meticulously arranged blond curls as she beamed a warm, beguiling smile up at Ross and Erik. Having interrupted them at their work on the pretense of looking for Dallas, she proclaimed that she just happened to have been passing by and thought she'd see for herself how the Browns' well was coming along.

"You know, Mr. Kincaid, I've already heard a great deal about you!" she simpered, fluttering her eyelashes in the manner Etta had always found so revolting.

"Have you, Mrs. Appleton?" Ross drawled lazily as he finished buttoning on his shirt. Lorena had lost no time in making her name known to them and demanding to know theirs in return. She had also lost no time in letting them know she was a widow.

"It was an honor to make your acquaintance, Mrs. Appleton, but I am afraid I must get back to work," Erik announced with a polite smile. "If you will excuse me please." He tipped his hat to her, then took himself back to where the other men were still laboring. Since his tastes did indeed run more toward sandy-haired young ladies with unusual eyes that were both blue and green, he found Lorena Appleton far less captivating than she would have liked to believe.

"Tell me, Mr. Kincaid, would you consider drilling a well for *me?*" Lorena queried once Erik had left them alone. Standing with Ross beside the cluttered worktable set up a short distance away from the derrick site, she thrilled to the nearness of his tall, undeniably powerful frame. Her pale-blue eyes glowed with a rapidly increasing resolve as she told herself that Ross Kincaid was without a doubt one of the most magnificent specimens of healthy, virile manhood she had ever seen! There was something about the driller that reminded her of her late husband, who had never failed to excite her in spite of the fact that he had been a faithless wastrel who had left her with a mountain of debts and a string of broken promises.

"That all depends, Mrs. Appleton," he replied with a faint smile. Though he couldn't keep his eyes from straying once or twice to the point where the heart-shaped bodice of her printed lawn gown stretched tightly across her ample bosom, he felt only a mild, passing twinge of masculine appreciation for her charms. She was pretty in a classically peaches-and-cream way, but not nearly as attractive to him as the spirited, lightly freckled redhead who fired his blood at every turn.

"On what?"

"On whether or not I decide to stay in Corsicana for a while."

"Well then, perhaps there is some way I can persuade you to do so," she virtually purred, moving a step closer and smiling up at him with an undisguised invitation in her eyes.

"You don't waste any time, do you?" he challenged in a low voice brimming with amusement. He had easily recognized her for what she was—the sort of woman who liked to think she held the upper hand when it came to men.

"Not when I've made up my mind about something." There was no use in playing coy, decided a thoroughly confident Lorena. Most men were delighted by her boldness, so much so that they were willing to do practically anything to capture her interest.

"It's always been a habit of mine to make up my *own*

157

mind." He was about to add that he had work to do and needed to be getting back to it, when his attention was caught by a movement at the kitchen window. Casting a quick, surreptitious glance in that direction, he smiled inwardly. He felt inordinately pleased to know that Dallas was watching him as he spoke with the young widow, and it occurred to him that he might as well make all the use he could of the situation.

"Maybe we should discuss this a bit more, Mrs. Appleton," he decreed with a sudden, devastating smile. Lorena appeared certain of victory when he took her arm and started leading her away.

Ross was not at all surprised when, upon escorting the comely blonde to the horse and buggy she had left waiting in front of the house, he looked up to see a beautiful, familiar face peering out at them from behind the parlor's lace curtains.

"So you really will consider drilling a well for me then?" Lorena asked for confirmation when they had reached the small, black and red buggy that had been a present from one of her many admirers. She gazed alluringly up into Ross's handsome, deceptively attentive features.

"I'll consider it." He spanned her corseted waist with his two large hands and lifted her effortlessly up into the buggy. She shivered in delight at his touch.

"But . . . but when will I know your answer?"

"When I'm ready to give it."

Unaccustomed to such evasiveness from a member of the opposite sex, Lorena frowned. Then, remembering that an adorable little pout was always more effective, she pouted. In the end, however, she was sent on her way with nothing more than a strange, noncommittal smile from Ross and the uncomfortable sensation that she had somehow been played for a fool.

In the wake of Lorena's departure, Ross hooked his thumbs in the front pockets of his trousers and cast a nonchalant glance overhead at the sunlit sky. His penetrating gaze traveled briefly to where Dallas still watched him from the parlor window. With slow, deliberate movements, he unbuttoned his shirt and eased it off again, slung it over his shoulder, and sauntered back to the opposite side of the house.

Dallas spun about and plopped down hard upon the sofa. Her eyes were ablaze with their distinctive deep blue fire, her breasts rose and fell rapidly beneath the embroidered white muslin bodice of her gown, and an angry blush stained her cheeks. She didn't know why, but what she had just witnessed galled the very devil out of her!

Lorena Appleton's performance had been laughably transparent, but Ross Kincaid, whom she had mistakenly believed to be a man in possession of at least a modicum of common sense, had apparently been thoroughly taken in by it. Not only that, but the whole, disgusting little scene had been played out on *her* property! It was bad enough that Lorena had flaunted herself before the men like that; it was even worse that Ross Kincaid, as their employer and therefore an example to them all, had been a willing participant!

Seized by the sudden, double temptation to snatch the manhunting young widow bald and deliver a resounding whack to Ross Kincaid's handsome head, Dallas breathed a most unladylike curse and leapt up from the sofa. She began pacing angrily back and forth, her arms folding tightly across her breasts and her best Sunday shoes making brisk contact with the lemon-scented pine floor.

"Dallas!" An obviously impatient Cordi had just arrived to stand framed in the parlor doorway. "Ruby Mae's back. Dinner's ready and getting cold. Now are you coming or not?"

Having quickly lost interest in Lorena Appleton once she had left the backyard with Ross—and thereby traveled safely out of sight of *their* men—Cordi and Etta had remained in the kitchen to watch the derrick crew work. They had been none too pleased when Dallas, before taking herself off to the parlor to maintain her impulsive surveillance, had charged them with the rest of the preparations for dinner.

"Dallas!" Cordi tried again.

"I'm coming, confound it!" snapped Dallas. Instantly contrite when she viewed the stricken look on the younger woman's face, she released a long sigh and crossed the room to link her arm through Cordi's. She smiled and said with a forced airiness, "Pay me no mind. I've become something of a bear of late!" Cordi's own features relaxed into a smile.

"That's perfectly understandable, considering all that's been happening around here." She appeared to take no notice of the sudden, telltale color which rose to her sister's face as they moved companionably back down the hallway to the kitchen.

Ruby Mae and Etta had already begun carrying the food outside, and Dallas and Cordi hastened to lend a hand. Ironically, it had been at Dallas's insistence that the special Sunday dinner had been arranged; since Ross had refused to allow the men time away from their duties to attend church services, she had countered with the proposal that they could at least observe the Lord's day with a traditional meal. Surprisingly enough, Ross had agreed. And Dallas, putting aside any lingering reservations about the sort of men he had hired, had actually managed to convince herself that she was doing her Christian duty by providing nourishing food and wholesome fellowship for the members of the crew.

Now, however, she found herself wishing she could call the whole thing off! She was feeling decidedly out-of-sorts, though she did her best to put on a cheerful front, and the prospect of sitting down to dinner with Ross Kincaid held even less attraction for her than she had expected!

Does he really find that . . . that frilled-up barracuda attractive? she suddenly wondered as she stood beside the stove dishing mashed potatoes into a bowl. Lorena Appleton's smirking face swam before her eyes. Dallas frowned darkly and brought a spoon smacking down in the midst of the potatoes.

Why should it matter to you one way or the other? Her mind's voice played devil's advocate. *After all, you don't want him, so why shouldn't Lorena—or any other woman, for that matter—have him?*

"Hurry up with those potatoes, honey!" Ruby Mae good-naturedly urged when she returned inside to fetch the last plate of cornbread.

Dallas started guiltily at the sound of her voice and whirled about so fast that the spoon went flying across the room. She watched in openmouthed dismay as it struck the opposite wall and dropped to the floor with a dull clutter, leaving a trail of mashed potatoes as it fell. All of a sudden, she felt like doing a perfectly absurd

161

thing and bursting into tears. The impulse to do so must have been written on her face, for Ruby Mae wasted no time in bustling forward to reassure her.

"There there now, it's only a little bit of potatoes!" the buxom older woman pronounced with a broad grin. Obtaining another spoon from the cabinet drawer beside the stove, she took up the plate of cornbread as well as the bowl of potatoes and started back to the door. "Just leave that mess till after dinner and come on out. We're gonna have ourselves one heck of a picnic today, you just wait and see!"

Wishing she shared her friend's enthusiasm, Dallas drew a deep, somewhat ragged breath and steeled herself for the ordeal ahead. Ordeal it would definitely be, what with Ross Kincaid waiting out there to taunt her with those dancing green eyes of his. His presence would serve as a constant reminder of her painful, all too human weaknesses, and she knew it would be that way until he was out of her life for good!

The dinner, as it turned out, was both a success *and* a disaster.

There was no need to ask the men if the food was to their liking—their enjoyment of it was quite obvious. For some of them, it was the first home-cooked meal they'd had in a long time; for others, it was a far sight better than the meals they'd had at home. Although it was a trifle warm sitting in the sunshine beside the partially erected derrick, no complaints were heard.

Dallas was able to avoid meeting Ross's gaze throughout most of the meal. On the very few occasions when she did happen to glance his way, she was rewarded with an intense, strangely somber look that sent a rosy color flying to her cheeks and an

162

involuntary shiver running down her spine. She did her best to hide her discomfiture, but it was impossible to conceal the shadow of perplexity in her eyes. Ruby Mae commented on her young friend's unusual reticence a couple of times, but Dallas simply waved her concern aside with something about feeling a bit under the weather. Reflecting that she couldn't very well tell Ruby Mae she was being unsociable because Ross Kincaid was undressing her with his eyes, she squared her shoulders and went about her duties as hostess with renewed determination.

A dessert of cherry cobbler and vanilla ice cream had just been served when Etta, making the rounds with the coffeepot, paused beside Ross. He gazed up at the petite young woman, musing to himself that she had an angelic face but the devil's own temper, and waited patiently for her to speak.

"Mr. Kincaid, I . . . well, I just wanted to thank you for what you did last night!" she finished in a rush. It was obvious that her gratitude, though sincere, was begrudgingly expressed. Etta was the type of person who found it difficult to admit she'd been wrong about anyone or anything, but she knew she had judged Ross Kincaid too harshly.

"No thanks needed," he replied quietly. Etta was about to turn away again when he suddenly flashed her a wry grin and added, "Next time you decide to try and put out a fire with your wrapper, take it off first."

Peering closely down at him, she glimpsed the unholy light of amusement in his eyes. Her brow cleared and she actually found herself smiling back at him.

"I'll remember that!" she promised with a soft laugh,

then continued on her way with the coffeepot. Her features were lit with an expression of loving mischief when she finally came to where Sam stood alone near the side of the house watching her every move. "I declare, Mr. Rawlins, you've scarcely spoken a word to me today! Why, anyone would think you and I—"

"Don't play innocent with me, Etta Brown! I saw you over there making cow's eyes at Kincaid!"

"Making cow's eyes—" she echoed, only to break off and blink up at him as the significance of his words struck her. "Are you accusing me of *flirting* with Ross Kincaid?" she demanded in wide-eyed disbelief.

"If that's what you want to call it!" he ground out. His hazel eyes were ablaze with jealous fury, and his attractive young countenance was suffused with a dull, angry color.

"I don't want to call it anything of the sort!" snapped Etta, her own gaze full of golden fire. "For heaven's sake, I was only—"

"I saw what you were doing, damn it! And if it wasn't for the fact that I'm bound and determined to stick with this job and keep an eye on *you,* I'd march right over there and tell Kincaid—"

"Why, you . . . you *idiot!* If your brain was in a gnat, he'd fly backwards!" she seethed, her voice rising as her temper did likewise.

"Shut up! Do you want everyone to hear you?" Sam furiously admonished as he sliced a quick worried glance toward the others a short distance away.

"Let them hear! I've certainly nothing to hide! If you weren't always so quick to jump to conclusions, Sam Houstin Rawlins, you'd have let me explain precisely

164

why I was over there talking to Ross Kincaid!"

"All right then—why?" he shot back.

"I'm not going to tell you now!" she retorted with a defiant toss of her strawberry blond head. Sam looked as though he would give anything to get his hands on her. She ignored him and flounced haughtily away, leaving him to glare murderously after her.

Cordi, meanwhile, had taken it upon herself to bring Erik another helping of dessert. He accepted it with an engagingly boyish grin and a twinkling of his expressive, baby-blue eyes.

"You spoil me too much, Miss Brown," he insisted, giving a low chuckle as he eyed the generous portion of cobbler. Cordi's heart fluttered, and she hesitated only a moment before sinking down on the bench beside him.

"It would be easy to spoil a man like you, Mr. Larsen," she responded with a warm smile, one which she would have been delighted to know made the young Swede's pulses quicken. "You are a true gentleman. You're not at all like . . . well, like the other men who have come here because of the boom."

"I am glad you think me different." He grinned again before lifting a spoonful of the cobbler to his mouth.

Cordi watched him, taking pleasure in the way his shining flaxen hair was ruffled by the wind and the way his eyes crinkled at the corners whenever he smiled. Aware of a sharp, inexplicable ache deep inside, one she had never felt before, she finally forced herself to look away. She sat absently rearranging the folds of her pink dimity skirts until Erik spoke again.

"You are different, too, from the women I have

known," he told her with only the glimmer of a smile.

"I am? In what way?" she eagerly questioned.

"In many ways. But all women here are different."

"Oh." She tried, unsuccessfully, to keep the disappointment out of her voice. "I . . . I suppose you've known a lot of women, haven't you, Mr. Larsen?"

"Yes, I have been fortunate in that respect."

"Fortunate?" Cordi echoed, her blue-green eyes growing very round.

"That is to say, I have been privileged to count them as my friends. I have seven sisters in my family, Miss Brown," he informed her with another brief but thoroughly heart-melting smile. "I think maybe this is the reason I appreciate the company of women!"

"And do you appreciate the company of *all* women, Mr. Larsen?" she couldn't resist asking. She swallowed hard when he turned to gaze deeply into her eyes.

"Some more than others, Miss Brown," he replied solemnly. It appeared for a moment that he would say more, but he evidently changed his mind and settled instead for filling his mouth with another bite of the cherry cobbler. Cordi, left with the distinct feeling that he had been right on the verge of declaring that he liked *her* more than other women, had to be content with sitting beside him in silence while he ate.

The dinner break ended soon thereafter, and the men returned to their task of completing the derrick. The women, as always, were left with clearing away the food and doing the dishes. It was a very quiet foursome who set about doing just that—Ruby Mae made a valiant attempt to engage the others in conversation, but since all three sisters were strangely preoccupied, she abandoned her efforts and hummed "Beautiful Dreamer" to herself while she worked.

Dallas arose early the next morning and dressed in her usual Gibson Girl costume of a starched, high-necked white blouse and dark navy broadcloth skirt. She chose to deviate somewhat when it came to her hair, which she braided tightly and wound about her head. Critically examining the resulting effect in the mirror, she mused that it looked like a halo of sorts.

Only angels have halos, she told herself with an inward sigh. *And you're not an angel. Angels don't have wicked dreams about tall, raven-haired drillers, and they certainly don't allow themselves to be very nearly ravished by them!* The memory of that night still burned in her mind . . .

Spinning abruptly about, she hurried from her room and down the stairs. She steered clear of the kitchen and left by way of the front door, happily encountering no one before hitching up the horse to the wagon and setting out for town. Relieved to be able to escape from the house, if only for a while, she felt as though a weight had suddenly been lifted from her shoulders. She smiled to herself and raised her face gratefully to the warmth of the morning sun as she drove to a red brick building on North Beaton Street.

Once there, she climbed the dozen narrow steps leading to the second floor and approached the door marked "Kauffman Photography Studio," just as she had done for the past eight Monday mornings. During that one day each week, she did her best to make sense

167

out of the photographer's imaginative methods of bookkeeping. Jacob Kauffman had pointedly reminded her on several occasions that he was an artist, not an accountant, and as such was more than happy to leave business matters in her capable hands.

"Capable?" Dallas murmured with an indulgent shake of her head as she recalled his words. "Wonder-working would be more like it!" She opened the door, closed it softly behind her, then marched straightaway into the brightly illuminated studio.

Natural light was a necessity to any photographer at that time, so a large skylight had been installed in the roof overhead. The sun's golden rays streamed unrestrainedly through the glass, not only setting the room aglow but heating it so much that the air quickly became heavy and stifling. Dallas wasted no time in throwing open the windows, though she knew full well she'd only have to close them again as soon as the first customer arrived. True to his creative nature, Jacob had declared it impossible to work with all the noise drifting up from the crowded streets below.

"Ah, so you have come already," the photographer remarked in a deep, booming voice as he stepped out of the back room where he kept his impressive array of props. "I implore you, Miss Brown, to have pity on this poor soul and bring order to my life once more! My dear wife is threatening to leave me if I do not learn the difference between a profit and a loss." He heaved a sigh and slowly shook his head for dramatic effect, but Dallas could see the merriment dancing in his brown eyes.

"Then I shall most assuredly do everything in my power to help!" she replied with a soft laugh. In spite of his rather eccentric behavior at times, she liked Jacob Kauffman and enjoyed working for him.

He was a big man, his black hair and beard generously peppered with gray, and he possessed a heart equal in size to his massive frame. The proud father of four sons and two daughters, all of whom attended the local school, he had come with his bride, Maria, to Texas from his native Germany some fifteen years ago. They had only recently settled in Corsicana, however, where Jacob had established one of the town's first permanent photography studios.

"Would that I could afford to pay you for more than one day a week," Jacob said with another sigh. "But that is the way of life, is it not?" he added with a determined optimism. Striding forward, he rearranged the two large white screens—used to reflect the light on to his subjects—on either side of the camera. He next carefully positioned a red velvet settee in front of a draped backdrop painted to resemble an English garden, placed an immense spray of greenery beside it, then stepped back to scrutinize the effect through the lens of his tripod-mounted camera.

Smiling to see the giant bear of a man giving such meticulous care to details, Dallas made her way across the cluttered room to an old rolltop desk and chair near the corner window. She took a seat and immediately began sorting through the overstuffed cigar box full of paperwork Jacob had accumulated the past week. It took only a matter of minutes for her to make two neat stacks out of the confused jumble.

She was doubly pleased to note that Jacob's business was steadily increasing—not only did it signify his eventual prosperity, but he had promised to train her as his assistant when and if the studio became a success. The prospect of acquiring photography skills appealed to her greatly, particularly since she had begun to feel somewhat at loose ends ever since the death of her father.

There were still Cordi and Etta, of course, she told herself with an inward sigh. But, as Ruby Mae had reminded her, they were quickly growing up. In no time at all, they would be leaving home, getting married, and having families of their own. What would she do once they were gone?

She had devoted the past ten years of her life to taking care of her father and her sisters. They had been the center of her world for so long now. Not that she had ever truly neglected her own life; indeed, she'd had plenty of friends and admirers, had received a number of marriage proposals, and had even considered accepting one or two of them just to see what everyone's reaction would be! Still, her heart remained untouched. Even Justin Bishop had never succeeded in releasing the boundless fire and passion and tenderness she knew lay dormant deep within her . . .

Dallas felt a sudden, sharp pang of loneliness. Was she destined to go through life alone, to never know the sort of love she had always dreamt of finding? Would she end up a reclusive old spinster, staying on in that big, empty house until she died?

Mentally scolding herself for indulging in such useless, self-pitying introspection, she frowned and turned her attention back to the work at hand. She had just begun copying a list of figures into the debit column of Jacob's ledger when a loud, insistent knock sounded at the studio door. Glancing hastily about, she saw that the photographer had once again disappeared into the back room.

"I'll get that, Mr. Kauffman!" she called out, already rising to her feet. She quickened her steps as she approached the door, hopeful that it was a customer, and put on her best, professional-looking smile. "Good day to—" she started to proclaim when she swung open the door, only to break off with a sharp intake of breath. The smile froze on her face, and her widening eyes filled with more than a touch of incredulity. "Wha—what are *you* doing here?" she stammered breathlessly.

"Something's come up. I need to talk to you," declared Ross. There was a certain, foreboding grimness about him, and Dallas reflected a bit dazedly that he must have come to town in a hurry, for his blue cotton shirt was still partially unbuttoned, the sleeves rolled up to his elbows, and his boots were caked with mud.

"Now?" she blurted out in disbelief, then drew herself proudly erect and protested in a more even tone of voice, "I happen to be working, Mr. Kincaid, and I hardly think—"

"This won't wait."

Dallas was given no time to argue. A sharp gasp broke from her lips as Ross seized hold of her arm and led her swiftly from the room.

"What do you think you're doing? Let go of me!" She held back when they reached the staircase, but he easily forced her down the wooden steps, overriding her resistance with a steely arm clamped about her waist. He did not release her until they had reached the boardwalk, at which time she rounded on him with all

171

the force of her righteous indignation. She was so angry that she paid no mind to the fact that others might witness their confrontation.

"You listen to me, Rossiter Maverick Kincaid!" she raged in a low voice seething with fury, her hands on her hips and her eyes shooting sparks. "I am sick and tired of your—"

"George Proctor is dead."

Dallas fell abruptly silent while the color drained from her face. *No!* her mind cried. She gazed numbly up at Ross, only to be met with the undeniable evidence of his solemn, tight-lipped expression and the dull glow in his eyes. *Oh, God, it's true,* she thought as the realization sank in. *George is dead. Dear, sweet, beloved George . . .*

"Come on," said Ross as he took her arm again and guided her through the crowd of passersby. Still in shock, she did not resist, instead meekly allowing him to lift her up into the wagon. She sat fighting back tears while he secured the reins of his horse to the back, and she appeared only dimly aware of his presence when he climbed up beside her and set the wagon on a homeward course.

It wasn't until they had traveled several blocks that Dallas finally drew a deep, ragged breath and looked at Ross. Noting the pain in her glistening eyes, he felt a sudden constriction of his heart and tightened his hold upon the reins.

"How . . . how did you find out about . . . George?" she asked, her voice sounding very strained. It seemed impossible that such a thing had happened. Why, only this morning she had been thinking about her godfather and wondering if he might perhaps arrive on

172

the afternoon train. *He can't be gone . . . he can't!*

"I received a telegram from his solicitor this morning."

"From his solicitor?" She hastily dabbed at her eyes with a lace-edged handkerchief and made a valiant effort to compose herself. "But how did he know where—"

"I sent word to George before I left Pennsylvania." He tugged on the reins a bit as the wagon's wheels bounced lightly over the streetcar tracks. The street grew less crowded after that, and Ross allowed the horse to set its own pace while he told Dallas, "He died two days ago. I would have been informed sooner if not for the fact that my folks are in San Antonio right now. The funeral was yesterday."

"Yesterday?" She looked stricken at the news, and Ross was once again conscious of a surge of protectiveness welling up deep within him, of an overwhelming desire to comfort her and erase the sadness that was so clearly written on her beautiful young countenance. Muttering an inward curse, he gave a sharp flick of the reins and reluctantly divulged, "There's more."

Dallas turned to face him, her gaze wide and sparkling with unshed tears. "More?" *What else could there be?* she added silently. George Proctor was dead. She had not only lost a cherished friend, but a trusted adviser as well. Although she had frequently complained about how her father had left George in control of everything, she had always known she could count on him. And now he was gone . . .

"Being the practical and efficient businessman he was, George had a will drawn up before he died," Ross began with a wry half-smile. "He never was the sort who could leave things unsettled. And, by damn, he left things good and settled *this* time!" His sun-kissed brow creased into a frown as he reached up a hand to settle his hat lower upon his head. "The telegram stated that half of his estate will go to his godson, the other half to his goddaughter."

"George left me half of his estate?" Dallas repeated in stunned disbelief. "But what about his family? Surely—"

"He had no family, at least not any blood kin."

"Oh, I . . . I see."

"I don't know if you're aware of it, but George was a very wealthy man. That means you'll be inheriting a sizable fortune."

"I don't care about the money," she murmured with a heavy sigh. Battling a fresh wave of tears, she shifted back around on the wagon seat and stared outward over the sunlit glory of the passing landscape. Her heart was heavy with grief, and she became lost in her sorrowful thoughts for several long moments until Ross's deep-timbered voice drew her back to reality.

"There's something else you should know." He frowned again and waited for her to meet his gaze. "George—"

"Tell me, Mr. Kincaid, why did his solicitor contact *you?*" she suddenly demanded, her eyes narrowing in growing suspicion. "Why didn't he send that telegram to me? After all, George was *my* godfather!"

"Just as he was mine."

Dallas's mouth fell open, and she blinked up at Ross in profound astonishment.

"Are you saying that you . . . that you are—"

"I told you he and my father were old friends," he

indirectly confirmed with a faint, mocking smile.

"Yes, but you never told me you were his godson!" she parried accusingly.

"Would it have made any difference? Hell, you were already prepared to hate me—can you honestly claim it would have made you feel any better about the arrangement if you'd known I only took on this job to humor George?" His mouth tightened into a thin line of displeasure for a moment, then curved into a begrudging smile of irony. "I think the old rascal had it in mind that if you and I were thrown together under such circumstances . . . well, let's just say he was hoping for the best."

"Why, that's ridiculous!" Dallas vehemently disagreed, hot color rising to her face as she caught his meaning. "For your information, George never once mentioned you to me in all these years!" It pained her to realize that her old friend had kept the existence of his godson a secret from her. And yet, she mentally reasoned with herself, why shouldn't he have? There had been no connection between the Kincaids and the Browns—except for George himself, of course—and absolutely no reason to suspect that George had been intent upon playing matchmaker between her and the arrogant rogue who unnerved her by his mere presence! "If such a thing had ever crossed his mind, then why in thunderation didn't he just introduce us?"

"Knowing George, I'm sure he had his reasons. But that doesn't matter now."

"It matters to me!" She impatiently swept a wayward strand of silken, dark red hair from her face. "I don't expect you to understand or care, but I loved George Proctor very much. He was like a second father to me.

And now that he's gone . . ." Her voice trailed away as she swallowed hard and hastily dabbed at her eyes with the handkerchief. She had no idea how much her crying affected Ross; she would have been shocked to know how difficult it was for him to keep from taking her in his arms and kissing her tears away.

Ross's piercing green eyes visibly softened as he stared down at Dallas's bent head. Never had he experienced such a floodtide of emotion. Tenderness stirred his heart while desire fired his blood . . . the highly potent combination of the two sent his usually well-grounded senses reeling. *It might just be that George's little plan worked after all,* he suddenly found himself musing.

"I suppose you can see how this changes everything," she remarked after successfully vanquishing the latest, short-lived round of weeping. She drew herself proudly erect and turned to fix Ross with a coolly purposeful look. In spite of the fact that her eyes were red and the smoothness of her flushed cheeks stained with the evidence of her tears, she had never looked more beautiful—nor more damnably irresistible—to the man beside her.

"Now that George is gone," continued Dallas, "there's no longer any need for you to feel obligated to finish the well. I do indeed take no comfort from the fact that the only reason you agreed to come to Corsicana was out of loyalty to my—to *our* godfather. But I don't want you to waste any more time here!" she feelingly declared, unable to keep the bitterness from her voice. "I'm sure you have more important things to do elsewhere. And quite frankly, I . . . I think this whole episode was a regrettable occurrence. It would have been better for everyone concerned if I had never accepted George's offer to arrange for a driller. Our meeting, Mr. Kincaid, should never have happened!"

Without a word, Ross drew the horse and wagon to a halt in the middle of the road. His tanned, chiseled features appeared prophetically grim, and a light of warning smoldered in his eyes as he rounded on the spirited young redhead who possessed the unenviable ability to send his temper flaring. "Even if I thought you meant that, you little shrew, it wouldn't make any difference!" he ground out.

Dallas's eyes grew round as saucers. Instinctively sliding as far away from him as possible, she gasped when his hand shot out and closed like a vise about her wrist. He yanked her masterfully back, so that her hip and thigh came forcefully up against the denim-clad hardness of his. Her cheeks flamed as she gazed apprehensively up into the angry, ruggedly handsome countenance that was mere inches from hers.

"You see, wildcat, you're stuck with me in more ways than one. Not only am I going to finish drilling that blasted well of yours, but I'm also going to do exactly what George wanted me to do!"

"Wha—what do you mean?"

"Simply that the telegram contained one last bit of information, something of particular interest to us both."

Dallas waited breathlessly for him to finish. In the long seconds that followed, his eyes seemed to burn into hers, and a powerful, invisible current passed between them. She was acutely conscious of being pressed up so close against him on the wagon seat; her skin tingled deliciously beneath the several layers of cotton . . .

"George left half of everything to you, all right, but he named me as trustee," Ross finally revealed. His voice was very low, its wonderfully masculine resonance washing over her, but his next words broke the spell. "In other words, *Miss Brown,* you're looking at the man who now controls your finances."

VII

Dallas stared up at him in horrified disbelief. She scarcely noticed when he relaxed his grip on her wrist and took up the reins again.

"But that can't be!" she cried hoarsely, her thick auburn braids straining at the pins as she shook her head in stubborn denial.

"It can and is," he insisted with another faint, sardonic smile. "George must have figured I was the only one who could handle you." He gave a negligent but practiced flick of the thin leather straps and rapidly put more distance between the wagon and the bustling center of town.

"But what about the trust set up by my father?" asked Dallas, refusing to dignify his last baiting remark with an acknowledgment. "Surely George wouldn't have—"

"The telegram didn't say. We'll find out soon enough. The solicitor's due to arrive here the day after tomorrow. But my guess is that I'm in charge of both accounts." He cast her what she could have sworn was

179

a glance full of mockery and challenge. "In the meantime, I'm going to keep on drilling. And you, my dear Miss Brown, are going to say nothing of this to anyone until we get things straightened out."

"You're enjoying this, aren't you?" she wrathfully accused, her sapphire gaze darkening as she glared up at him. "I'm sure the prospect of being able to order me about is exceedingly appealing to you! You've done nothing but try to . . . to humiliate me and bend me to your will ever since you came here, Ross Kincaid, but I'll be hanged if I'll let you do so ever again! I don't care *what* George's will says—I'll not allow myself or my sisters to be forced into a situation where we're subservient to the likes of you!"

"Subservient?" His eyes danced with pure amusement at the thought. "That's something you'll never be, wildcat."

"Stop calling me that!" she snapped, then bristled anew at the lazy smile she spied tugging at his lips. Drawing herself rigidly erect, she raised her chin and declared in haughty defiance, "Mark my words, Mr. Kincaid. I'm going to do everything in my power to prevent you from gaining control of either my money *or* my life. If there were some way I could age four years in a moment's time, I would gladly do so! But whatever it takes, even if it means marrying someone just for the sake of my inheritance, then I shall do it!" she threatened rashly, hurting inside, and goaded nearly beyond all reason by what she perceived to be his smug confidence in her submission. She did not really think he would take the threat seriously, nor did she believe he would react with anything even remotely resembling jealous fury.

She was mistaken. Without bothering to stop, Ross ground out a savage oath and yanked her back against him with alarming fierceness.

"If you marry any man, it will be *me!*" he decreed harshly, his eyes ablaze with magnificent green fire.

"Y-you?" she stammered, trying desperately to ignore the sudden, wild leaping of her heart. *Don't be a fool!* she furiously chastised herself. *He only said it because he wants to exert that confounded, oh-so-masculine authority of his again; he doesn't care about you at all, except for . . . for wanting to get you into his bed!* Crimsoning from head to toe, she began struggling against the arm that was like a band of iron about her waist. "For your information, Rossiter Maverick Kincaid, I wouldn't marry you if you were the last man on earth!"

"I don't recall having asked you!" he ungallantly shot back.

"Why, you—" Dallas seethed in mingled embarrassment and indignation. Growing visibly enraged, she lunged forward and grabbed hold of the reins. Ross swore and jerked them from her hands. The sorrel mare, snorting loudly in protest, stomped at the ground in confusion before grinding to a halt and backing up against the wagon.

"Easy, girl, easy!" Rising swiftly to his feet, Ross sawed on the reins to curb the horse's rearward flight. The animal calmed somewhat at the sound of his deep, commanding voice. Just when it seemed the situation was approaching a harmless conclusion, however, fate added yet another dash of well-timed mischief.

The only horseless carriage in the entirety of Navarro County suddenly rounded a bend in the road a short distance ahead and came rattling toward them. Cursed from one end of Corsicana to the other, the clamorous, unsightly contraption was notorious for spooking horses. It proceeded to live up to its reputation within seconds, blithely clanging and sputtering until positioned directly alongside the wagon, at which time its engine—racing at a top speed of twenty miles per hour—backfired and coughed out an odorous cloud of black smoke.

In spite of Ross's efforts to control her, the startled mare reared upward, then took off like a bat out of hell.

"Hold on, damn it!" Ross thundered at Dallas as she went toppling back against the seat in an undignified tumble of skirts and petticoats.

Not at all inclined to defy his latest directive—or to take exception with the way he had issued it—she held on for dear life while he fought to halt the horse's wild flight. The wagon bounced and jostled violently over the narrow, rutted road as a choking fog of dust swirled upward from the sunbaked earth to trail behind.

The palomino stallion tied to the back of the wagon whinnied shrilly and strained against its tether in panic. The thin strap of leather finally gave way, leaving the hapless animal to swing about and canter gratefully back toward town as the wagon careened onward at a death-defying pace past houses and derricks and trees.

"Watch out!" screamed Dallas in warning when she looked up and saw that they were about to collide with one of the familiar, red and black delivery wagons belonging to the Corsicana Ice Company. Her breath catching in her throat, she turned her head seconds later to watch in wide-eyed dismay as the driver shook his fist vengefully at them after being forced off the road. She twisted abruptly back around and shouted at Ross, "For heaven's sake, can't you stop this thing?"

"What the hell do you think I'm trying to do?" he growled in furious, tight-lipped response. Born and raised on a ranch, he had been around horses all his life and considered himself to be a highly skilled handler of them, but the accursed animal dragging the wagon pell-mell across the countryside refused to heed either his terse vocal commands or his forceful tugging of the reins.

Dallas's eyes widened in renewed fear when she saw that they were nearing a sharp curve in the road. Instinctively clutching at Ross's arm, she stifled a cry as the wagon went skidding partially off the road. Suddenly, the rear left wheel struck a rock. There was a loud crashing noise as the wheel popped off the axle and bounced down the hill, leaving the wagon to lurch violently in that direction while the axle scraped along the rocky ground. Ross somehow managed to keep the wagon from overturning—it was a tribute to both his strength and ability that he was able to maintain a steady grip on the reins while battling the force of gravity which threatened to pull him over the side.

Straining at the increased weight brought about by the loss of the wheel, the horse began to show signs of tiring. It wasn't long until the exhausted mare, breathing heavily from her exertions, slowed and obeyed Ross's soothing, gently spoken, "Whoa now. That's it. Ease up, girl, ease up."

A much shaken and windblown Dallas meekly allowed herself to be lifted down from the wagon. Her heart was still pounding erratically within her breast, and she could only stand and watch in wide-eyed silence as Ross inspected the damage done to the axle.

"I'll have to ride back to town and get someone out to fix this," he pronounced with a frown. He straightened and retrieved his Stetson from the back floorboard, where it had luckily become caught after being torn from his head by the wind. Knocking the dust from it with a quick slap against his taut, denim-covered thigh, he donned the hat and strode forward to unhitch the horse.

As Dallas began to recover from the benumbing effects of what had just happened, her luminous sapphire gaze bridled with dawning indignation.

"This is all your fault!" she accused her heroic—albeit unwanted—companion in a voice quavering with emotion. She angrily reached up to repair the damage done to her hair, only to give up in disgust when the wind-ravaged auburn locks resisted her efforts to subdue them. Shaking out her skirts with a vengeance, she marched over to where Ross was loosening the harness. "If you hadn't gone and *grabbed* me like you did, none of this would have happened! Now my horse is near death and my wagon is ruined and—"

"I'm liable to grab you again if you don't shut up and let me get this done!" he warned in a low voice edged with simmering ire.

Instead of being intimidated by his threat, Dallas grew thoroughly enraged. Something within her snapped. Seizing his arm, she tried to yank him about to face her; it was like trying to move a man made of stone. She was forced to settle for wedging herself squarely between him and the horse. Hot, bitter tears stung her eyes as she planted her hands on her hips and stormed wrathfully up at him, "Damn you, Ross Kincaid, I have had quite enough of your high-handed, contemptuous, overbearing behavior! I didn't ask you to come into my life and turn it into a shambles, but that's exactly what you've done! Because of you, my sisters are making absolute spectacles of themselves, a dear friend of mine is being denied the pleasure of living under her own roof, my house very nearly caught fire and burned to the ground, my wagon is sitting here with only three wheels, and I'll probably be dismissed from a job I happen to like—and need—very much!"

Pausing to draw in a ragged breath, she swiped angrily at the tears which spilled over from her lashes to course down the flushed smoothness of her cheeks. She was far too upset to notice the way Ross's chiseled features tensed, or the way his green eyes glowed with an intense light that only burned for her.

"Add to all that the fact that you have taunted me and bedeviled me and . . . and virtually *pounced* on me every time we've been alone together," she continued in an upheaval of emotions, "and is it any wonder I can no longer stand the sight of you? And now I find out George has died and that *you* are the man who is supposed to take his place? Dear Lord, if only he hadn't died, if only . . . if only he—" The sentence was left unfinished as a sob welled up in her throat. Though she despised herself for exhibiting such feminine weakness in front of the very man responsible for her present dilemma, she could not staunch the river of tears which suddenly streamed forth. She spun away and buried her face in her hands, her shoulders quaking while she wept in heart-wrenching silence.

Ross felt an odd pain shoot through him as he

watched her cry. Cursing himself for mishandling the whole thing, he reached out for her. She voiced a strangled protest, but he disregarded her resistance and pulled her close. He cradled her tenderly against his chest, his arms enveloping her trembling softness and his bronzed cheek resting on the top of her head.

"Shhh. It's all right, wildcat. It's all right," he murmured softly.

Dallas closed her eyes and let the tears fall. In spite of her grief, she realized that she had never felt so safe and secure as she did now, with Ross Kincaid's strong arms about her, with the comforting sound of his heart beating in her ear, with the feel and warmth of his hard body against hers. Strangely enough, she felt as though she were exactly where she belonged . . .

Finally, when her tears had subsided, she forced herself to stir and draw away. Raising her handkerchief to hastily dry her eyes, she gazed up at Ross with something akin to wonderment, as if truly seeing him for the first time. She had certainly never expected such gentleness and compassion from him, and the way he was looking at her—with a strange, unfathomable gleam in those magnificent green orbs of his—made her tremble anew. A sudden wave of self-consciousness washed over her, and her gaze fell, only to fasten upon the dark stain on the front of his cotton shirt.

"Oh, I . . . I got your shirt all wet," she unnecessarily pointed out to him.

"It'll dry." His mouth curved into a brief but disarming half-smile before he reluctantly decreed, "We'd better get back to town. I've still got work to do, and so do you. We can talk later."

"There's nothing to talk about." She dried the last of

186

her tears and proudly lifted her head. "George is dead. You are now in control of my money. It's all quite simple, really," she remarked with a bitter, humorless little laugh. "Quite, quite simple."

Ross frowned but said nothing. He finished unhitching the horse, then turned back to Dallas with the obvious intention of lifting her up.

"I've decided to wait here, if you don't mind," she coolly proclaimed as she took a step backward. In truth, she was anxious to avoid the close contact that would result from riding on the same horse with him. Her emotions were always thrown into such turmoil whenever he so much as touched her; the intensity of her feelings for him frightened and disturbed her, and she felt too vulnerable at the moment to deal with any further confusion. *Dear God, why did this particular man have the power to affect her as no other man had ever done?*

"I do mind," Ross told her in a low, even tone of voice. Scooping her effortlessly up in his arms, he tossed her onto the now docile animal's bare back. Dallas had done no more than open her mouth to offer a scathing assessment of his actions when he seized hold of the horse's thick red mane and swung up behind her.

"I would rather wait *here!*" she reiterated, two bright spots of angry color staining her cheeks. She was tempted to slide back down to the ground, but told herself that he would no doubt only toss her up again.

"Damn it, woman, can't you stop spitting fire for a while and let down your guard?" he murmured with more than a touch of exasperation. His steely arm slipped about her waist to hold her captive while he took up the reins with his other hand.

Dallas stiffened and remained stubbornly silent as Ross, employing a commanding pressure with his knees, set the tired horse walking slowly back toward town. His deep, vibrant voice sent a tremor coursing down her spine when he spoke softly against her ear a few moments later, "It might not be so bad, you know, having me to run to whenever you need something."

"I have no intention of 'running' to you at all!" she snapped. Painfully aware of the way her hips were pressing so intimately against his taut, powerful thighs, she blushed hotly and tried to inch forward. Ross, however, merely tightened his hold about her and chuckled quietly, "I still say George knew what he was doing."

Silence fell between them as they each became lost in their own reverie. Dallas would have been surprised to learn just how similar in nature and content their thoughts were—thoughts that had a great deal to do with the very closeness she had both dreaded and desired . . .

The relentless Texas sun hung noticeably higher in the cloudless, late-morning sky by the time they joined the commotion of North Beaton Street again. Ross dismounted, expertly looped the reins about the hitching post in front of the building where Dallas worked, then reached back up for her. Her hair was very disheveled, her beautiful face flushed, and her sapphire gaze visibly troubled, but she nevertheless did her best to act calm and collected as she met his penetrating gaze. She drew in her breath sharply when his large, work-hardened hands closed about her waist, and she was dismayed to feel herself swaying toward him as he set her on her feet.

"It might interest you to know that we've already got the rig in place," he told her in a deep, husky voice that belied the matter-of-fact manner of his words. "Swede and I took turns guarding the derrick last night, and we'll continue keeping watch over it until the well's in." His eyes seemed to burn down into hers, and he made no move to let her go.

"I wondered why I never heard you come upstairs last—" she said, only to break off in profound embarrassment when she realized that she was on the verge of revealing something she did not want him to know. She had lain awake in bed for what seemed like hours the night before, listening for the familiar sound of his footsteps and agonizing over the repeatedly wicked turn of her thoughts.

"I'll arrange for the wagon to be fixed and delivered back to your house," Ross continued as though she had never spoken. A faint smile briefly touched his lips. "That blasted horse of mine is probably back at the livery stable by now." His fathomless green gaze flickered over her once more before he turned away and swung agilely back up onto the mare. Tightening his grip on the reins, he offered Dallas a negligent salute with his hat and cautioned her, "Remember what I said about keeping the terms of George's will a secret between us for now."

"But I have to tell Cordi and Etta—" she started to argue.

"You can tell them he's dead, but nothing else." The merest glimmer of amusement danced in his eyes when he added, "You'll just have to trust me about this."

It was on the tip of her tongue to reply that she'd as

189

soon trust a rattlesnake, but she wisely bit back the retort and watched as he rode away. She stared after him, momentarily oblivious to the fact that she was standing in the midst of an ever-passing crowd on the boardwalk of the busiest street in town, with her thick strands of hair streaming in wild disarray down about her face and shoulders and the wrinkled folds of her usually impeccable attire marked by a number of conspicuous smudges.

"What were you and Kincaid doing together?" Justin Bishop startled her by demanding as he suddenly materialized at her side. Guilty color crept up to her cheeks as she wheeled about to face him.

"Justin! I . . . I didn't see you," she murmured weakly. *Hell's bells, he was the very last person she would have chosen to encounter at that particular moment!*

"That's obvious. You were too busy looking at *him,*" he observed with a curt nod in the direction Ross had just gone, "to notice anyone else!" His words were laced with unmistakable displeasure and jealousy, prompting Dallas's brilliant blue eyes to flash defensively.

"I'm sorry, Justin, but I have neither the time nor the inclination to discuss my personal affairs with you right now!" she declared in a tight, low voice. She gathered up her dust-caked cotton skirts in order to return to the photography studio, but Justin's smooth, manicured hand shot out to close upon her arm.

"Why were you with Kincaid?" he demanded again, his attractive features suffused with a dull, angry color. The sunlight set his dark blond hair aglow, but Dallas found herself idly musing that it still lacked the fiery radiance belonging to a certain head of thick, midnight-black hair.

"It's really none of your business, is it?" she indignantly reminded him, casting a pointed glare down at the hand detaining her. He refused to relinquish his hold upon her arm, or his claim upon her affections.

"If I thought for one minute you and that bastard were—" he started to warn, only to be cut off when Dallas furiously wrenched her arm from his grasp.

"You have no right to interrogate me, Justin Bishop!"

"You belong to me, Dallas," he insisted in a dangerously calm manner. His gold-flecked brown eyes glinted down at her with deceptive softness. "You're mine. You're the reason I came back. You're the only reason I was able to get out of this hellhole, the only reason I succeeded in pulling myself up by my bootstraps these past five years. And I'll be damned if I'll let any other man steal what's mine!" Taking a step closer, he peered narrowly down at her while a telltale muscle twitched in the clean-shaven fairness of his cheek. "You will never belong to any man but me. Don't forget that. And don't let Kincaid forget it, either!"

His words struck a chord of fear in her heart. She told herself it was perfectly absurd to be afraid of him—this was *her* Justin, after all, the same young man who had once meant the world to her—and yet she could not dispel the trepidation gnawing at her. Gazing up at him with wide and sparkling eyes, she was even further alarmed to note the raw, covetous look that now smoldered in his hawkish gaze.

The startling events of the morning had left her with a beleaguered spirit as well as strained emotions; otherwise, she would have stood her ground and given the man before her the tongue-lashing of his life. But she could not summon the courage to do so just then.

Murmuring something unintelligible, she whirled about and fled inside the building, racing up the stairs to the welcome sanctuary of Jacob Kauffman's studio. Once there, she hurriedly closed the door behind her and stood leaning back against its comforting sturdiness while struggling to regain her breath.

"Miss Brown? Is that you come back at last?" Jacob called out in his deep, blustery voice. He rounded the corner in the next instant, took one look at her flushed, disheveled appearance, and muttered a German oath that required very little knowledge of the language to decipher its general meaning. "What has happened to you?" He rushed forward and wrapped a burly arm about her shoulders, then led her solicitously over to a chair.

"I'm sorry I disappeared like that, Mr. Kauffman. It's just that I . . . I received some very bad news." The tears sprang readily to her eyes once more, and she was grateful for the kindly photographer's support as she sank down into the chair.

Justin Bishop, meanwhile, stood on the boardwalk outside, debating whether to give chase to Dallas or take himself down to the Double Sixes Saloon. Recalling that his partner was expecting him—and realizing that he probably wouldn't have the opportunity to speak to Dallas alone—he breathed a savage imprecation and reluctantly chose the latter course of action. He shot one last intense, predatory look toward the spot where she had disappeared, then set out for the part of town referred to in polite circles as the "red-light district."

Having spent most of the night gambling and enjoying the company of the prettiest among the even dozen "soiled doves" employed by the management of the Double Sixes, he had finally returned to his room at the Molloy Hotel just before dawn. It was due to his late arisal that he had seen Dallas; he had just been emerging from the hotel when he'd spotted her riding past with the driller.

The memory of it still made his blood boil. Gripped by another violent surge of jealousy, he abruptly bit off the end of a cigar, raised the thin roll of tobacco to his lips, and lit it, all the while cursing himself for losing his edge.

Contrary to what he'd told Dallas, his return to Corsicana owed its origin to the oil boom and *not* to her. He'd lied about that, just as he'd lied about a lot of things. True, it had always been his intent to see her again—if and when he wearied of his high-rolling, hedonistic life-style—but that wasn't what had brought him back. No, he hadn't come back because of anything so noble as love. He had come back because of greed. Greed and a desire to avenge himself on the good folks of Corsicana, the same ones who had reviled and rejected him, the ones who had made his life even more of a misery than the sorry lot fate had dealt him. And the sweetest revenge, he told himself with a malevolent curl of his lip, would be gained by doing exactly what he was doing now.

Of course, he hadn't counted on his feelings for Dallas. Damn, he swore inwardly as his eyes took on a feral gleam, but he would have to be careful not to let her interfere with his plans. His obsession with her was like a fire deep within him, a fire that burned hotter than ever. He knew he would never be satisfied until she was his, body and soul. And he vowed he'd stop at nothing, *nothing* to possess the woman who had haunted his dreams for five long years . . .

Reaching the saloon, nearly deserted at that hour of the morning, Justin flung his cigar to the ground and pushed through the swinging double doors. He was immediately intercepted by a buxom, brassy-haired woman wearing only a thin, rather tattered silk wrapper over her undergarments.

"Ain't no one else up and about yet, honey," she said, smiling seductively while her heavy-lidded blue eyes flashed him an undeniable invitation. She stepped forward and slipped her arm through his. "I know you been takin' up with Darla since you rolled into town, but that don't mean you gotta be such a stranger to the rest of us, does it?" She parted her full, rouged lips ever so slightly, allowing her tongue to moisten them with what she hoped to be tantalizing unhaste.

Justin impatiently shook her off. The image of Dallas's fresh loveliness was still vivid in his mind, and the oversampled charms of the painted harlot before him did not fare well by comparison.

"Tell O'Shea I'm here to see him," he instructed, bestowing a hard slap of dismissal on her ample backside. Rubbing the spot where the blow had landed, she frowned in mingled disappointment and anger, but nonetheless took herself off to do his bidding.

Justin wandered over to the bar, where he drew another cigar from his vest pocket and watched as the woman climbed the stairs to the second floor and disappeared into one of the corner rooms. When she came out onto the landing again a few moments later, she was followed by a tall, beefy man with graying black hair and pockmarked features that could best be described as swarthy. The man known only as O'Shea paused to draw on his tailored black coat, said something which made Justin's would-be "companion" look even more surly, then moved leisurely down the wide carpeted staircase to meet with his young partner.

"You're late," O'Shea complained only halfheartedly as he neared the bar and motioned silently to the bartender to bring them something to drink.

"I had a little business to take care of."

Uncorking the full bottle of whiskey the bartender set before him, the new owner of the Double Sixes poured some of the dark amber liquid into two shot glasses and handed one to Justin. O'Shea's hard blue gaze swept the room after he had downed the whiskey in a single gulp.

"Nice little place I got here, don't you think?" he asked the younger man. He chuckled in evil satisfaction while recalling how he had won the saloon only three nights ago in a game of five-card stud, a game in which the odds had been "adjusted" so that they would be overwhelmingly in his favor.

Justin dutifully allowed his own eyes to travel over the saloon's lush interior, replete as it was with glistening chandeliers, red and gold carpets, a roulette wheel, felt-topped card tables, and a mirror on one wall stretching the length of the polished, brass-railed bar.

"Maybe," he drawled as he finished off his drink and

raised the cigar to his lips, "but it can't measure up to the place I'm going to have by this time next year."

"You mean the one *we're* going to have, don't you?" O'Shea challenged with a dark scowl. "I didn't take you on and teach you everything I know just so you could cut me out whenever it suited you! No, you wet-eared little bastard, once we're done playing this town for all we can get, you and I will be heading back down to New Orleans. There's a place there I've had my eye on for a long time, and I'm damned sure going to get it—with *your* help!"

"Have it your way," growled Justin, capitulating with an ill grace. He knew it was useless to argue with the black-hearted scoundrel who had indeed taught him a wide, profitable variety of scams and tricks over the past few years. But there was no way he'd abandon his own plans for the future. If all went as he hoped, he'd be quit of O'Shea within six months at the outside. "How the hell much longer are we going to stay on here?" he demanded harshly, his fingers clenching about the shot glass in his hand.

"For as long as it takes. Two months, maybe three." The aging confidence man smiled again as he paused to pour them each another drink. "We're making a real killing off the equipment, and the turnaround on the oil's getting better all the time. Who knows—we might even try and get in on this new refinery they're building. The picking's are ripe and easy, my boy," he pronounced with a soft, malignant laugh. "Ripe and easy!"

Justin offered no response. A number of thoughts flashed through his mind as a result of what O'Shea had just said. First of all, there was the equipment business the two of them had set up, a highly lucrative undertaking whereby they arranged for the rigs, steam engines, and other oil field paraphernalia to be stolen and then resold at a price much higher than its true worth . . . then, there was the oil itself, quickly drained off from unguarded storage tanks in the dead of night and spirited away in specially equipped wagons before anyone could become suspicious . . . and lastly, there was the refinery being constructed out on the southwest edge of town, which when completed would no doubt yield a sizable return on any investment made. Just as O'Shea had told him, there was nothing like an oil boom to bring out the "opportunities."

I'll bleed this town dry, he vowed in silence, his dark gaze glinting fiercely and his attractive features becoming a tight, ugly mask of scornful fury. *Yes, by God, before I'm through, I'll be able to bring this whole damned, stinking town to its knees!*

Dallas's face suddenly swam before his eyes again. Something deep within him stirred—whether it was love or merely lust, he didn't care. All that mattered was that she would soon be his. And he had already set the wheels in motion to make certain of it . . .

"Jail?" Dallas repeated in stunned astonishment. Her eyes grew very wide as she faced the three women who had met her at the front door.

"The sheriff and some other men came and took him away less than an hour ago!" Etta breathlessly exclaimed.

"Seems our Mr. Kincaid's charged with stealin' some equipment," drawled Ruby Mae. The calmness of her demeanor seemed out of place in the midst of such excitement.

"Yes, but Eri—Mr. Larsen says it's really *our* equipment!" Cordi hastened to clarify.

"Ours?" echoed Dallas yet again. Her head spinning, she reached up with hands that were not altogether steady and unpinned her hat, then set it and her reticule on the hall table. After somehow managing to complete her work at the photography studio, she had hurried home to inform her sisters of George Proctor's death, never dreaming they would have such startling news of their own to impart. *This day has been an absolute nightmare,* she reflected in numb disbelief. *What else can go wrong?*

"Not only did they arrest Mr. Kincaid, but they hauled away nearly all of the equipment! The sheriff said he was confiscating it as evidence," Etta recalled angrily, "but I don't know why in blue blazes he thought it necessary to do such a thing since the confounded stuff was hardly going anywhere!"

"Mr. Larsen's down at the jail right now, trying to convince the sheriff that he and Mr. Kincaid only took back what rightfully belonged to them—or rather, to us!" added Cordi. "You've got to do something, Dallas!"

Dallas's bright, troubled gaze moved swiftly from one sister to the other. Wondering what in heaven's name she *could* do, she released a long sigh and finally looked to Ruby Mae, who smiled benignly and said, "Come on, honey." She slipped an arm about the younger woman's shoulders. "You and I had best be gettin' ourselves on down to that jailhouse before this whole thing goes even more haywire than it's already gone. If the good Lord's willin' and the creek don't rise, we'll have this straightened out in no time at all!" she proclaimed with her usual, bolstering cheerfulness.

Dallas nodded wordlessly in agreement. Taking up her hat and reticule again, she returned to the front door, only to pause indecisively on the threshold.

"I don't know if now is the right time to tell you this or not," she began, turning back to her sisters, "but . . . I'd rather you heard it from me than from someone else. George Proctor died two days ago."

"George is dead?" gasped Cordi, her face paling.

"When did you find out?" Etta demanded solemnly.

"Today. I . . . I'm sorry, but I'll have to explain it all to you later." She smiled weakly at them before stepping out onto the porch with Ruby Mae and repinning her hat atop her head.

"So George has passed on," murmured Ruby Mae as they moved down the tree-shaded steps. Clouds were beginning to gather and boil in the heat of the late afternoon sky, and the air smelled faintly of rain. "You know, we were once pretty good friends, ol' George and me. You might even say we were more than that."

"You and George Proctor?" Dallas cast a look of wide-eyed surprise upon the sturdily built woman at her side. Ruby Mae chuckled quietly, her expressive brown gaze alive with a combination of amusement, tender reminiscence, and a touch of sadness for what might have been but never was.

"It was a long time ago, even longer than I care to admit. I was awful young then and a mite starry-eyed." She heaved a sigh and smiled softly at Dallas again. "Yes siree, I thought George Proctor just about hung the moon. I'd have probably gone on thinkin' so if not for the fact that another feller caught this fickle eye of mine before anythin' could come of it. 'Course, it wasn't any time at all till another gal came along and laid claim to George's heart for good."

"Oh? But I thought George had never married."

"He didn't."

"Well then why—"

"Because the woman he swore to love till his dyin' day was already promised to someone else." They had reached the edge of the street by now, and Ruby Mae effectively changed the subject by asking with a mild frown of puzzlement, "Where's your wagon?" Sudden color flooded Dallas's face.

"It's a long story," she answered evasively. "But I'm afraid we'll have to walk."

"No we won't. We'll just head on down to my place and fetch my rig. You can tell me that 'long story' of yours on the way!" Looping her arm companionably through Dallas's, she set them on a course along the dusty road, then declared with heartfelt sincerity, "I'm real sorry about George, honey. I know his death must've hit you pretty hard. But he'd not want any of us grievin' for him. One thing about George Proctor—he truly believed in livin' one day at a time. And that's just what we should do."

Especially when every day seems to turn out even worse than the previous one! Dallas added silently, her mind still awhirl as a result of all that had happened within the past eight hours alone. First, she had been practically abducted by Ross Kincaid . . . she had received the terrible news about her beloved god-father . . . she had learned that the same man who had turned her life upside down would now be the man who

200

controlled her finances . . . she had feared for her very life because of an ordeal which had left her bruised all over and her almost new wagon sitting out on the road somewhere minus a wheel . . . and now, *now* she had arrived home to hear that her driller had been arrested and her equipment confiscated because it was allegedly stolen . . .

It was almost too much to bear! But, proudly reminding herself that she was Abner Brown's daughter, she knew she possessed enough backbone to weather it all. And weather it she would, even if it meant letting Ross Kincaid rot in jail as she was so tempted to let him do!

By the time she and Ruby Mae arrived at the jailhouse, Dallas was in a fine temper indeed. She immediately scrambled down from the buggy and went storming inside. Expecting—with more than a touch of vengeful gratification—to find Ross pacing restlessly back and forth in his cell, she was nonplussed to discover him sitting nonchalantly in the front office and playing a friendly game of poker with the sheriff.

"What on earth?" she breathed, drawing up short just inside the doorway. Ruby Mae, arriving on the scene an instant later, moved to stand beside Dallas. Ross and the other man both rose to their feet in the presence of the ladies.

"Good day to you, Miss Brown, Miss Hatfield," drawled the sheriff, a tall, lanky fellow sporting a full head of bright copper hair and a handlebar mustache of only a slightly less brilliant hue. Of indeterminate age, he had served as the foremost enforcer of the law for the past two years, so far outlasting his predecessor by a good eighteen months.

Dallas's eyes flew back to Ross, who favored her with a wordless nod and a bold appraisal that sent the self-accursed rosiness flying to her cheeks. Hastily looking away, she drew herself loftily erect and said to the man wearing the silver, six-point star that was the familiar badge of his profession, "Sheriff Crow, I am here to speak to you about—"

"Beggin' your pardon, Miss Brown, but I know what you're here for," he interrupted with a smile of masculine indulgence, "and I'll be more than happy to release Mr. Kincaid into your custody just as soon as you sign this form right here." He reached down and slid a piece of paper across the surprisingly uncluttered top of his desk. "Shows you just how small a world it is when you arrest a man and then find out he's the same scrawny, ring-tailed rascal who used to pitch horseshoes with you after school back home in Fort Worth."

Unbelievable! Dallas groaned inwardly. Refusing to meet Ross's gaze again, she hesitated only briefly before taking up the pen offered her and inscribing her name in a neat, flowing style that had twice won her the annual teachers' award for handwriting excellence.

"There," she pronounced, straightening again. "Now what about my equipment?"

"I'm afraid I can't do anything about that, ma'am," the sheriff answered regretfully. "The case will probably come before the judge in another week or so. Once things are cleared up, you'll get everything back." He spoke as if already convinced of both Ross's innocence and the trial's outcome, but Dallas took little comfort from his assurances.

"This entire episode is . . . is utterly preposterous!" she indignantly exclaimed. "Why, according to what

Mr. Kincaid's partner told my sister, the equipment was bought and paid for by *me,* stolen off the train, and then recovered!" Finally rounding on a strangely silent Ross, she demanded, "Is that the truth of it or not?"

"Pretty much so," he confirmed in a low voice brimming with wry humor. His green eyes twinkled down at her with maddening unconcern for his predicament.

"What do you mean, 'pretty much so'? What exactly did you *do* to get it back?" she then probed. Her suspicions grew even stronger when she took note of the brief, meaningful look he exchanged with the sheriff.

"Nothing more than any other man in my position would have done," he replied casually. Before Dallas could think of a suitable response to his provoking evasiveness, he sauntered past her and retrieved his hat from a peg on the wall beside the door. He returned the knowing smile Ruby Mae flashed him before remarking without rancor to the man who had miraculously turned out to be an old acquaintance, "It's been a real 'pleasure' meeting up with you again, Crow." His mouth curved into an appreciative grin of irony.

"Sorry it had to be under these circumstances, Kincaid. Let me know if I can help you out in any way." The sheriff stepped forward and shook the hand Ross offered him, then added by way of a friendly warning, "You don't need me to tell you there's someone lookin' to keep you from drillin' that well. Whoever it is, they're liable to do a lot more than just swear out a complaint next time."

"Who *did* file the complaint against Mr. Kincaid?" Dallas queried with a frown.

"I'm not at liberty to say, ma'am. It'll come out at the trial."

Though dissatisfied with his answer, Dallas had no other choice but to leave things as they were for the time being. Once outside, she and Ross paused to face each other on the boardwalk while Ruby Mae hoisted herself back up into the buggy.

"You two go on home," Ross instructed Dallas. "I've got some business to take care of."

"And what business is *that?*" she demanded in tight, clipped tones that left little doubt as to the state of her emotions. She knew it was wrong to blame him for everything, and yet she couldn't seem to help it. Nothing had gone right since he had come to town!

"I'll stop by the livery stable and see if your wagon's ready before I head back" was all he would say. Giving her one last inexplicably disturbing look, he raised the hat to his head, nodded at Ruby Mae, and set off.

For the second time that day, Dallas stood and watched him until he was nearly out of sight.

And try as she would, she could not ignore the way her heart twisted painfully at the thought of him walking out of her life forever . . .

VIII

Dallas was surprised, to say the least, when she arrived downstairs the following morning and discovered that Ross had already managed to replace the confiscated equipment with yet another set. Whirling away from the kitchen window, she hurried out the back door without finishing the remark she had been making to Etta and Ruby Mae.

Since Ross was working alongside Erik and the three crew members they had kept on to get the rig operational, he did not immediately notice Dallas when she came flying down the steps. She might have been out of his sight for the past several hours, but she had certainly not been out of his mind.

Dallas abruptly slowed her steps to a halt and frowned in obvious displeasure when the high heels of her polished, lace-top boots sank into the ground. It was then that she belatedly recalled the cloudburst of the night before. The rare summer storm had left the air smelling fresh and sweet, but it had left the unsuspecting earth so full of moisture that she was forced to pick her way carefully across the backyard in order to keep the entire bottom half of her boots from disappearing into the dark, oozing mud.

Only vaguely familiar with the new technology— new to Corsicana, anyway—of rotary rig drawworks, she eyed the equipment dubiously as she drew closer. Parts of it were easily identifiable; the remainder looked impressive at any rate. Or at least it *would* have, if not for the fact that she had expressly told Ross Kincaid to do no more work on the well! They'd had a brief but spirited discussion of the matter after supper last night. *Damn him,* she swore silently, *he's done it again!*

"Good morning, Miss Brown!" called Erik, doffing his hat and making her a gallant little bow from the derrick floor.

She couldn't help smiling back at the personable young Swede, but her smile quickly faded when her searching gaze encountered the piercing intensity of Ross's. In the process of showing Sam and another young roughneck how to position a section of drill pipe, he made no move to set aside what he was doing and speak to her. Her deep blue eyes bridled with annoyance, for she knew good and well that *he* knew good and well the only reason she had come outside was to talk to him!

Though tempted to open her mouth and summon him to her side in no uncertain terms, she prudently decided against it and watched as he and his partner exchanged a few words she could not quite make out. Then, Erik cast her another smile, bent his head to keep from hitting it on one of the derrick timbers, and strode forward to where she stood in the bright morning sunlight holding the hem of her skirts up out of the mud.

"Tex said I am to tell you what you are seeing, Miss Brown."

"Is that so?" She shot Ross a speaking glare. "Why doesn't *Tex* tell me himself?"

"I do not know," Erik responded with a boyish grin that prompted her to think he did.

She was really in no mood to listen to a discourse on drilling equipment, but she did him the courtesy of remaining still and silent while he patiently explained what everything was for. The gist of it was that there was a hollow column of pipe with an auger bit at the bottom to do the actual boring, a revolving platform with a large, well-oiled drive chain to grip the pipe, and a steam engine and boiler used to maintain sufficient pressure for the pump to flush water through the pipe.

"Thank you, Mr. Larsen. You have been most informative," she told him politely once he had finished. Inwardly, she was still fuming over Ross's arrogant disregard of her orders, but she knew there was little she could do about it. Leveling one last angrily reproachful look at him—to which he responded with a slow, infuriating smile—she spun about and trudged back through the mud to the house.

Ruby Mae and Etta were still sitting at the table, and they raised curious eyes to Dallas when she came charging back inside the kitchen. She muttered something which sounded suspiciously like a curse as she bent to remove her mud-caked boots.

"Almost like a bog out there, ain't it?" Ruby Mae commented dryly. She took another sip of coffee and beamed a warmly maternal smile in Dallas's direction.

"You'n me had better get a move on if we're gonna make it to the church on time."

"It doesn't make much sense to me," said Etta with an expressive frown, "spending the entire day indoors in the company of a bunch of old biddies when you could be out—"

"Careful, honey, or I might just take offense at that," Ruby Mae playfully cautioned.

"I didn't mean *you!* I meant all those other old busybodies who delight in their tea and gossip and their comparisons of which one of them has the most gosh-awful affliction!"

"Oh, Etta, you're just in an ill humor because you and Sam are at odds with each other!" Dallas pronounced with a sigh of sisterly impatience.

"You're a fine one to talk!" retorted the petite blonde. "You've been as touchy as a wet hen around here for nearly a week now! And for your information, Sam and I are *not* at odds with each other!" Assuming a haughty demeanor, she rose to her feet, picked up her cup and plate—Ruby Mae had expressed supreme satisfaction to see her consume a healthy portion of ham and eggs—and carried them to the sink. "As a matter of fact, he's taking me to the social tonight. I plan to get him to propose afterward," she revealed, her lips curving into a secretive, wonderfully calculating little smile.

"Henrietta Brown, you'll do nothing of the sort!" Dallas admonished sharply. The last thing she needed right now was for the little minx to get herself betrothed to Sam Houston Rawlins! "I swear, if I so much as hear about—"

"Maybe you won't hear about it until it's too late!"

With this last bit of defiance, Etta took herself off to spend the day picnicking with some of her friends down at the swimming hole. The remaining occupants of the room exchanged looks of mutual perplexity in her wake.

"I know, Ruby," Dallas murmured with a weary sigh, her gaze visibly troubled as she folded her arms against her chest and crossed to stand beside the table. "I've spoiled her terribly and now I . . . I don't know what to do about her at all."

"I'm not sure there's anythin' to be done." Slowly unbending her stout frame from the chair, the older woman shook her head and added philosophically, "I don't suppose any of us can really help turnin' out the way we do. Lord have mercy, but we'd have a time blamin' everybody else for our mistakes, wouldn't we?"

Dallas's features relaxed into a smile. Determinedly relegating all her troubles to the back of her mind, she hurried to clean the mud from her boots so she and Ruby Mae could be on their way.

Since Cordi had already left for her job at the telephone company, they drove directly to the church in Dallas's wagon—fetched home by Ross just after sundown the night before—and joined the group of women already assembled in the fellowship hall. The sun's rays streamed in through the many windows and filled the large room with soft golden brightness, while the pleasant scent of mint and apple and cinnamon, given off respectively by the tea and hot spiced cider being served, hovered lightly in the air.

Church socials were held frequently, but the one planned for that evening was a significant departure for the congregation; it was the first one to which oil-field workers had been invited. Hand-lettered posters announcing the event had been placed in shop windows all over town, and word had been spread among members of the other churches and fraternal organizations so that anyone who might be interested in attending would know of it.

The greater majority of the workers were single, but a number of the others were men facing a temporary yet possibly lengthy absence from their wives and children. Very few of those who were married had been able to bring their loved ones with them. Single or married, however, the problems facing them were the same—loneliness, boredom, and an unfortunate propensity for the doubly damning vices of drink and "fleshly degradation." As the pastor of Dallas's church had so eloquently put it, it was about time Corsicana's citizens did what they could to "counteract the evil temptations so prevalent in town by providing both religious solace and recreational opportunity." Thus, the church social had been suggested, voted upon, and approved.

Contrary to Etta's disparaging remarks, most of the fifty or so ladies gathered that morning to make decorations for the night's festivities could not be categorized as "old biddies" at all. At least half were Dallas's age or even younger, while a sizable number of the rest were young matrons who had welcomed the respite from housekeeping chores, the exhausting demands of motherhood, or both. Only a small portion of the group had achieved anything approaching a true seniority in years—"biddydom," Etta would have termed it.

Ruby Mae excused herself and moved away to speak

to the pastor's wife, leaving Dallas to seek out her own friends. Since she had attended the same church for the entirety of her life, she was well acquainted with nearly everyone in the room.

"Dallas! Dallas, over here!" a somewhat childish-sounding voice sang out from the far corner. Dallas smiled and raised a hand in greeting, then made her way as quickly as possible through the quietly roaring crowd of females.

"Hello, Marian," she proclaimed with genuine affection as she reached the plump, dark-haired young woman's side. She paused to speak to the three other women seated at the table before turning back to Marian and remarking with a soft laugh, "I had no idea so many of us would actually show up!"

"I know, isn't it terrible? Heavens, it looks like we'll have to share all the good-looking men with half the women in town!" Marian Ridgeway declared with an answering laugh. "Here," she then said, patting the empty chair to her right, "sit down and let's get on with whatever it is we all came to do. Our table's been assigned paper chains. Can you believe it? We got up at the crack of dawn and rushed over here to make paper chains!" She laughed again, and Dallas found herself musing fondly that her old friend had changed little since they had first met some fifteen years ago.

For the next quarter of an hour, they cut strips of colored paper, fashioned them into rings, and pasted the ends together with a gooey mixture of flour and water. It was hardly what one would call fascinating work, but the four of them enjoyed the company of one another and the chance to catch up on the latest news of who had gone where, who had done what, and who had been found out.

Listening to the others, Dallas frequently bent her head to hide a smile. She recalled her sister's scathing assessment of such pursuits, and though she hated to call what she was hearing "gossip," she could not deny that that's exactly what it was! Wrong or right, it was an important ritual to be observed, she told herself with a sigh.

Then, just when she was beginning to believe she would be spared the displeasure of Lorena Appleton's company, she glanced up to find the flirtatious young widow making her appearance at last. She groaned inwardly as she watched Lorena, whose catlike gaze scanned the room until it lit upon the table in the corner, smile triumphantly and make a beeline for her.

"Hellfire and damnation!" Dallas muttered under her breath.

"What? Did you say something, Dallas?" asked Marian, her own smile freezing on her face when she caught sight of the approaching blonde. "Oh, bother! Here comes that blasted Lorena Appleton!"

"Why, Marian Ridgeway!" one of the other ladies at the table gasped in shocked disapproval.

"Well, I don't care!" Marian replied defensively. "She's the biggest troublemaker in town, and I'll be darned if I'll let her spoil everything!"

Lorena was well within earshot by that time, but if she had heard what Marian said, she gave no indication of it. Clad in an expensive, tucked, and ruffled gown of peach-colored organdy, she looked more than a trifle out of place amongst her conservatively attired counterparts.

"Marian, my dear, it's nice to see you looking

212

so . . . *healthy* these days," purred Lorena. She draped an arm over the back of a furiously tight-lipped Marian's chair and smiled at the other women, though the smile did not quite reach her eyes. When she inclined her head to focus her attention solely on Dallas, there was a disturbingly purposeful light emanating from her usually vapid gaze.

"Good morning, Dallas. I thought it might interest you to know that I spoke with that handsome driller of yours yesterday. He and I just happened to run into each other—I was on my way to the dressmaker's and heaven only *knows* where he was going—and we had a nice long talk about . . . oh, about a lot of things!" she related with an airy wave of her hand. Her high-pitched voice carried with surprising strength about the room.

"Why should that be of any interest to me, Lorena?" Dallas responded with deceptive indifference. Though acutely conscious of the dozens of pairs of eyes now fastening upon her, she was determined to keep her composure and not allow the other woman to rile her. Lorena Appleton had taken great pleasure in sparring with her ever since they were children together.

"Because I'm sure you cannot have remained completely immune to the charms of such a man!" replied Lorena, smirking derisively. "But you won't have to worry about resisting him much longer, my dear. You see, Ross—oh, I *beg* your pardon—Mr. Kincaid and I came to an understanding before we parted." She paused here, apparently for effect.

Dallas calmly reached for a square of red paper and began cutting another strip. Dismayed at the way her heart had suddenly taken to pounding, she successfully concealed her intense annoyance at what she had just

213

heard. *Why should it matter to you if Ross Kincaid and Lorena Appleton are on such friendly terms?* her mind's inner voice challenged. *Remember—you don't want him! And after all, a man like him isn't the sort to remain lonely for long.* She tried to ignore the sudden twinge of pain she felt at the thought of him with another woman, particularly a conniving she-wolf like Lorena.

"He's agreed to drill a well for me," Lorena finally announced, knowing it wasn't quite true and yet confident that it soon would be. "Isn't that wonderful news? So when he's finished with that one of yours, he'll be coming on over to my place and—"

"Tell me, Lorena, my *dear,*" Marian broke in at this point, "are you planning to let him stay at your house, too?" Her eyes widened innocently as her mouth curved into an unmistakably taunting little smile. "I mean, you being a widow and all . . . well, you know there's bound to be talk if word gets around that the two of you are living way out there alone together. And word *would* get around, you know. You can be quite certain of that."

The egotistical blonde colored angrily and clenched her teeth, then exercised an amazing amount of restraint and forced the corners of her mouth to turn up. Pointedly ignoring Marian's remark, she turned back to Dallas and said, "By the way, I heard that old beau of yours is back in town. Let's see . . ." her voice trailed away as she pretended to be deep in thought for a moment, "his name was Bishop, wasn't it? Justin Bishop. Yes, that's it!" Her pale-blue eyes glittered with malicious amusement. "The two of you always made such an odd couple, from what I remember. But I *do* hope he's still interested. Maybe you won't have to remain an old maid for the rest of your life after all."

"Better an old maid than a fast widow who will never be able to find another man gullible enough to make her his wife!" Marian muttered loudly enough for everyone at the table to hear.

Dallas stifled a laugh, her eyes dancing merrily as she and Marian exchanged glances. The other ladies were obviously shocked into speechlessness. Lorena, positively livid, fixed both Dallas and her friend with a murderous glare before hissing vengefully, "You won't be so quick to laugh in a few years' time! You just wait and see—I'll be the one who's living like a queen, while the two of you will be ugly, lonely old spinsters!"

"Ugly, maybe, but lonely—I hardly think so," Marian countered solemnly, finding it difficult to keep a straight face as Dallas's eyes continued to sparkle irrepressibly across at her. "After all, we'll still have each other, won't we? And who knows? We may even organize a club for all the other ugly old spinsters in town. We could call ourselves the 'Corsicana Association of Poor Unfortunates Who Refused To Follow The Widow Appleton's Example'!"

Marian erupted into peals of melodious laughter. No longer able to control her own mirth, Dallas followed suit. It wasn't that the situation was so funny, but rather that laughing was an emotional release for her after all that had happened recently. She paid no heed at all to the fact that a good many of the ladies in the room were staring at her and Marian as though they'd taken complete leave of their senses.

Lorena, apparently realizing that she had lost this latest round in her ongoing rivalry with the beautiful redhead she'd always despised and envied, compressed her lips into a tight, thin line of fury and flounced away without another word.

Dallas's soft, delightfully resonant laughter subsided as she turned to watch the viperous young widow leave the room. Her amusement evaporated quite rapidly when her thoughts returned to what Lorena had said about Ross.

"Now, where were we?" Marian asked brightly. "Oh yes, the paper chains. We're making significant progress here, don't you think? Why, at this rate, ladies, we stand a very good chance of being finished . . ."

With her friend's voice fading momentarily out of her consciousness, Dallas became engrossed with the sudden, jarringly vivid image of Ross Kincaid doing to Lorena Appleton what he had done to *her* the night the derrick had been blown up. Her throat constricted, and she experienced a sharp pain in her chest, almost as though someone had taken a knife and plunged it into her heart.

Why? she agonized silently. *Why does it hurt so much to think of him kissing someone else?*

He's nearly thirty years old, she mused, he's bound to have kissed dozens and dozens of women by now! So why should she think there was anything special about the fact that he wanted *her?* To him, she would be just one more conquest . . . one more notch on his gun, as it were. All that talk about the two of them being destined for each other was nothing more than a ploy to soften her up. She'd played right into his hands before, but never again! Never, *ever* again! If Lorena Appleton wanted him so badly, then she could damn well

216

have him!

". . . and then we'll have to hang them from the ceiling, only high enough so the tall men don't have to worry about crashing into them the whole night long!" Dallas became aware of Marian finishing. Forcing her attention back to the present, she smiled faintly at the plump brunette beside her and took up the scissors once more.

The evening began uneventfully enough. Dallas, anxious to check the preparations one last time, left for the church half an hour earlier than the others. Cordi was thrilled that Erik had agreed to attend, and she spent the better part of the afternoon getting ready. Etta, though equally delighted that Sam would be escorting her, found it necessary to expend less than half that amount of time on her own appearance. The end results were the same, however—both young women looked radiantly lovely when they descended the stairs together at half past seven.

"My, my, if you two don't look pure-dee elegant!" pronounced Ruby Mae. Framed in the doorway to the parlor, her generous curves were attired in a new, spruce green calico gown. A black velvet bonnet was tied on her head. "I've heard it said that the prettier a gal is the worse coffee she makes. Well if that's true, then kindly remind me never to try drinkin' any of yours!"

"Do you really like it, Ruby Mae?" asked Cordi as she twirled excitedly about. She had never worn the square-necked dress of pure white muslin before; Dallas had helped her make it nearly a month ago. A sash of blue satin encircled her slender waist, and a matching ribbon was threaded within her carefully pompadoured, light brown hair.

"It's breathtaking, Cordi, and you know it!" Etta remarked with an affectionate grimace. Her own gown, fashioned of palest pink dotted swiss with an under-dress of white lawn, was not quite as new as Cordi's but was every bit as becoming. Its simple, fitted lines set off her still-blossoming curves to perfection, while the way she had arranged her strawberry blond curls—in a braided coronet pinned low on her head—suited her far more than the elaborate style affected by her sister. "Well, I suppose Sam will be here soon. I'm awfully glad Mr. Kincaid agreed to let him quit early today. If all goes as planned," she confided to the other two as her wide golden eyes took on a purposeful gleam, "I will officially be the future Mrs. Sam Houston Rawlins by the time I get home tonight!"

"But I thought you told me Dallas forbade you to—" Cordi started to remind her.

"How in blue blazes can she 'forbid' me to do anything?" retorted the headstrong seventeen-year-old. I'm not a child any longer! I'm of legal age to marry. And that's just what I intend to do!"

"Very well, but what if Sam doesn't propose at all?" Cordi then challenged, her blue-green gaze brimming with sisterly superiority. "Are you going to spend the rest of your life trying to drag that poor boy to the altar?"

"He's not a boy and I won't have to drag him at all!"

"Well I'd like to know how else you'd describe what's been going on! For heaven's sake, Etta, it takes a whole week of planning just for you to be able to get him to—"

"I'd describe *this* as a classic case of the pot calling the kettle black!"

"And just what do you mean by that remark?"

"Only that we've all watched you running around like a chicken with its head cut off ever since Erik Larsen came here! I can't keep count of how many times in a day you change clothes now, and—"

"You're just jealous because *I* haven't found it necessary to employ such devious means to—"

"I think it's about time you and me was leavin', honey!" Ruby Mae finally intervened. She took Cordi by the arm and started leading her firmly toward the front door.

"But I have to get my wrap!"

"I'll fetch it. You go on out onto the porch," the older woman directed, giving her one last gentle but compelling push. Cordi wisely chose not to argue.

Sam called for Etta not long after Ruby Mae and Cordi had gone. Only Ross, Erik, and one of the hands, a stocky young man by the name of Billy Joe, remained at the well site.

"Are you certain you would not like me to stay?" Erik asked one last time, raising his voice to be heard above the noise of the steam engine. "We always drill together, you and I!"

"You know as well as I do that it'll be at least another day, day and half before we stand a chance of hitting anything!" Ross shouted back. Having studied the field's performance beforehand—as any driller worth his salt would do—he knew that most wells had come in around one thousand feet. And with the new rotary drills able to cut through Corsicana's shallow layers of black clay topsoil and strata of soft rock with such ease, it was not uncommon for the drilling to take as little as thirty-six hours. "It won't make much difference one way or the other if you light out for a couple of hours!" he added with a broad grin, his teeth flashing white in the midst of his handsome, grime-coated visage. He straightened from where he had been tightening and oiling the drive chain, and his gaze narrowed in critical scrutiny of the steadily revolving platform that sent the drill bit boring ever deeper into the earth.

"But do you yourself not wish to attend? And what about Billy Joe?"

"Aw hell, Swede," Billy Joe answered for himself as he, too, climbed to his feet beneath the derrick, "I ain't been inside a church in nigh on to ten years, and I don't aim to break the habit now!" His clothes and boots were covered with mud, and his freckled, boyish features were barely recognizable beneath a thick layer of dirt and sweat. "Besides, me and Tex can handle things till you and the others get back!" he insisted with all the supreme confidence of youth.

"He's right! Now get the devil out of here!" Ross thundered good-naturedly. He watched as Swede disappeared inside the house, then squinted idly up toward the calf wheel—a device used to hoist the thirty-foot sections of drill pipe into place—at the top of the derrick.

The sun hovered low upon the western horizon, its fiery brilliance presenting a kaleidoscope of pink and gold and orange. Darkness always came late to a Texas sky during the lazy months of summer, but the advent of nightfall mattered little when a well was being drilled. The search for oil continued round the clock until, boom or bust, the total depth had been reached. If there was one thing Ross had learned in all his years as a driller, it was that "wildcatting" was more a game of chance than skill, and there was only so much a man could do to affect the outcome.

His lips twitched into the ghost of a smile at the thought. He braced a hand negligently against a timber, raised a finger to tip his hat farther back upon his head, and allowed his mind to wander for a moment . . .

The church social would be well under way by now. He could easily imagine Dallas in the midst of all that small-town talk and conviviality and . . . men. *A bunch of randy, homesick young roughnecks.*

His rugged features tightened, while his green eyes darkened to jade and smoldered at the sudden, unpalatable image of her surrounded by a swarm of woman-hungry men gazing avidly upon her captivating beauty, as if they were hawks circling overhead and she the unsuspecting, delectable young chicken being targeted on the ground below. It was enough to make his blood boil, enough to provoke a forceful, almost violent surge of jealousy to blaze through him.

"Hey, Tex, somethin' wrong?" Billy Joe shouted from the opposite side of the platform, concerned at the look of utter savagery that had suddenly appeared on his boss's face.

Ross mentally shook himself and breathed a curse that, as Ruby Mae would no doubt have put it, was "strong enough to sizzle bacon."

"Let's get that blasted pipe ready to go!" he bellowed with a fierce scowl. Billy Joe, accustomed as he already was to the legendary moodiness of drillers, merely

221

shrugged to himself and hastened to obey.

The social was indeed in full swing by that time. More than a hundred oil-field workers had shown up—a very good turnout, considering that the wholesome, church-sponsored event had to compete with the more carnal lure of the saloons and dance halls. It seemed there were a number of young oilmen desirous of meeting the sort of girls who reminded them of what they had left behind.

Clean and scrubbed and smelling of the Bay Rum oil they had used to slick back their hair, the workers had evidently taken considerable pains with their appearance. Whether sporting the only suit in his possession, or a brand-new get-up of denim trousers, cotton work shirt, and a string tie, each of the roughnecks appeared quite eager to get on with the socializing. Boots had been polished to a high sheen, while hats were new or at least dressed up with a band of snakeskin. As one of the church elders had wryly observed, the barber shops, bathhouses, and dry goods stores had obviously made a real killing that day.

The young ladies looked radiant in their best summer frocks. They, too, had gone all out for the occasion; the town had never been such a flurry of sewing and ironing and curling and primping. Now, under the watchful eye of their mothers, the girls welcomed the guests of honor with winsome smiles and polite invitations to enjoy the punch, ice cream, and sandwiches spread upon a long table set up near the doorway.

Although the main activity was centered within the

walls of the fellowship hall—gaily adorned with colorful paper chains and fabric streamers—the windows and doors had all been thrown open to the cool night breeze, which carried the aromatic scent of roses and gardenias from the well-tended plants lining the church buildings. Paper lanterns, dangling from poles, dotted the grounds and added their soft golden glow to the moon's silvery luminescence.

With the lively strains of fiddle music drifting everywhere, the young men and women soon began pairing off to dance. Square dancing was the order of the day, but the musicians occasionally struck up a reel, which gave the couples a better chance to break the ice and get to know one another—all for the sake of good Christian fellowship, of course.

Standing guard over the punch bowl, Dallas smiled to herself and watched Cordi join hands with Erik to promenade about in the movements of the dance. Cordi's blue-green eyes were soft and adoring as she gazed up at the tall young Swede, while Erik, letting down his guard for once, appeared far less than immune to her charms.

If I didn't know any better, I'd say they look suspiciously like two people in love, Dallas found herself musing. She frowned at the thought, not at all certain how she felt about her sister falling head over heels for a driller, even if he was a decent, hardworking young man like Erik Larsen.

Releasing a sigh, she shifted her increasingly troubled gaze to where Etta and Sam were laughing together in the midst of a circle formed by three other young couples. There was no need to wonder how *those* two felt about each other, thought Dallas unhappily. They had formed an attachment some years ago, and no matter how much she had tried to discourage it, the emotional bond between them would not be broken.

It wasn't that Sam was such a terrible person—quite the contrary, she told herself. He could be quite engaging at times, and there was no denying the fact that he truly cared for Etta. But until such time that he showed an inclination to grow up and stop being dependent upon those rich, overdoting parents of his, there could be no possibility of allowing Etta to entertain the ridiculous notion of becoming his wife.

No, Dallas concluded with another sigh, she wanted both Cordi and Etta to make happy, successful marriages. And the only hope she had of achieving such a thing was by standing firm, even if it meant her beloved sisters had to suffer through a temporary case of youthful heartache.

What about yourself, Miss Prim-and-Proper Brown? that devilish little voice in the back of her mind suddenly twittered. *Will you be able to stand firm when it's you who falls in love with the wrong man?*

Her pulses raced and her cheeks flamed as Ross Kincaid's handsome face swam before her eyes. Mentally consigning the face *and* its owner to the devil, she snatched up a cup and ladled fruit punch into it, then set it down on the table with such force that some of the liquid went sloshing over the top to cast a red stain upon the white linen tablecloth.

"Why, Dallas, I'm afraid you've spilled some of the punch!" Lorena Appleton pointed out unnecessarily. She came sashaying up behind Dallas with a scornful little smile plastered on her face and an unmistakable challenge in her narrow, pale-blue eyes. "Oh, and I see you're wearing that sweet blue organdy dress of yours again!" she added, her smile broadening as she raised a hand to administer a negligent but meaningful fluff to the spidery lace ruche trimming the scooped neckline of her exquisite primrose silk gown.

"How astute of you, Lorena—on *both* counts!" Dallas ground out, her own eyes kindling with intense displeasure.

"You know, I can't seem to find that fascinating Mr. Kincaid anywhere," the coquettish young widow revealed with another insincere smile. "Didn't he come with you tonight?"

"No."

"Well, whyever not?"

"Why don't you ask *him* that the next time the two of you have one of your 'nice long talks'!" snapped Dallas.

"I might just do that," Lorena purred with an infuriating smirk that Dallas was sorely tempted to obliterate with the palm of her hand. "After all, he and I will have plenty of opportunity to talk when he comes to work for me, won't we?"

Though it cost her every ounce of self-will to do so, Dallas held her tongue. Her blazing sapphire gaze hurled invisible daggers at Lorena's back as the cattish blonde sailed triumphantly away. She scarcely noticed what she was doing as she grabbed hold of the ladle again and began filling more of the cups.

"I think that ought to do us for a while, honey," Ruby Mae commented with a soft chuckle when she appeared at Dallas's side a few moments later. Following the direction of her friend's amused gaze, Dallas glanced down to note the two dozen glasses of punch resting in neat little rows beside the bowl. She colored in embarrassment and hastily set the ladle aside.

"I'm sorry," she murmured. "It's just that—"

"There ain't no need for you to explain. I saw Lorena over here." Ruby Mae's lively brown eyes shone with kindness and understanding as she smiled again and suggested, "Why don't you go on out there and kick up your heels a bit? Land's sake, you're much too young and pretty to be huggin' the wall with us old maids!"

"Oh, but didn't you know?" Dallas countered with a mock expression of melancholy. "I *am* an old maid!"

"Is that a fact? Well now, if that's so, I must already have one foot in the grave," Ruby Mae responded dryly. She stepped closer to the table and gently but firmly insinuated herself into the younger woman's place behind the punch bowl. "Now off with you! Go dance with some of those young bucks who've been dyin' to ask you!"

Dallas laughed softly and admitted defeat with a good grace. Pressing a quick kiss upon the weathered smoothness of Ruby Mae's cheek, she gathered up her full, flounced skirts and headed toward the opposite side of the dance floor, where the young ladies of the church stood whispering and giggling companionably to one another while waiting to be asked to dance. She smiled and nodded when she saw Marian Ridgeway motioning her over to a group of friends near the outer doorway, and she quickly changed course in order to join them.

Before she had gone far, however, she was surprised to find a man suddenly blocking her path. Her eyes were wide and questioning as they traveled up to his face, and she inhaled sharply when she saw that it was Justin Bishop who stood gazing solemnly down at her.

"Why, Justin! What are you doing here?" Feeling more than a little taken aback by his unexpected appearance, she was also inexplicably relieved that they were surrounded by a crowd of others.

"I'm still a member of this congregation," he reminded her as his features finally relaxed into a faint smile. "Or have you forgotten that, too?" Although he was looking quite dapper in his expensive black suit and high-collared white linen shirt, he did not seem nearly as attractive to Dallas as the roughnecks with their far less elegant attire and traces of oil still under their fingernails.

"No, Justin, I haven't forgotten that. I haven't forgotten anything." Dismayed to feel the two bright spots of color staining her cheeks, she took a deep, steadying breath and forced a smile to her own lips. "I . . . I hope you're enjoying your homecoming. It must have been something of a shock to return after all these years and—"

"The only shock was in finding out how easy it was for you to forget the promise we made to each other!" His voice, laced with reproachful fury, was barely audible above the music filling the hall, but Dallas heard him all too clearly. He stared at her so closely that she felt certain those dark, hawkish eyes of his— the same ones that used to shine with boyish devotion but now glittered with a hard intensity that frightened her—were trying to bore into her very soul.

"Please, Justin, let's not go into that again," she pleaded wearily. "Can't you understand that what's past is past?"

"Then, for old time's sake, will you dance with me?" he startled her by asking with a disarming grin. She peered dubiously up at him, only to see that his change in attitude, though certainly abrupt, appeared to be genuine enough. Not wishing to let him know how uncomfortable she was in his presence now, she gathered the courage to grant his request.

"Of course. For old time's sake." Slipping her hand into his waiting one, she allowed him to place his other arm about her waist and swing her out onto the dance floor. She silently cursed the fact that the fiddlers had chosen that particular moment to play a reel, and she held herself as far away from him as possible, all the while resisting his efforts to draw her closer.

"Relax, Dallas. It won't do you any good to fight against something you can't beat," he murmured huskily.

Her eyes blew back up to his face as she suddenly recalled the time that Ross Kincaid had uttered similar words to her. *Shut up, Dallas,* he had said that night in the barn, *shut up and don't try to fight what's happening to you . . .*

"I heard that driller of yours was arrested yesterday." Justin's voice drew her sharply back to the present. Possessed of the thoroughly unnerving sensation that he had somehow read her mind, she flushed guiltily and stiffened beneath his arm while he continued. "Maybe now you'll realize he's not the sort of man you should have working for you. He's a cocky, unscrupulous troublemaker, and he'll keep causing you trouble until you get rid of him. Besides, like I told you before—you don't need that well."

"And like I told *you,* it isn't your place to decide!"

she retorted with spirit, then gasped as his fingers clenched painfully about hers.

"Oh but it is, damn you, it is!" he insisted in a low, furious tone. His attractive countenance had taken on that same predatory look that had alarmed her before, and his eyes blazed fiercely down into hers. A knot of growing trepidation tightened in her stomach, and she looked anxiously about, only to become aware of the fact that he had maneuvered her close to one of the open doorways leading outside.

"That's enough!" she seethed. Refusing to be intimidated by him, she raised her head proudly and decreed in an emotion-charged undertone that only he could hear, "I don't want to hear any more, do you understand? My life is my own, Justin Bishop. It is no longer any concern of yours. I . . . I'm truly sorry, but that's just the way it has to be. Now, if you don't mind, I think it's time we put an end to this useless and highly unpleasant confrontation!"

She tried to pull away, but he held fast. The next thing she knew, he was twirling her round and round with dizzying speed, until the two of them were outside in the lamplit darkness. There was no one else about at the moment, and Dallas felt panic rising within her.

"What the devil do you think you're doing? Take me back inside at once!" she commanded hotly, still trying to pull free. She realized that, to anyone who might have observed their departure from the fellowship hall, it would no doubt have appeared that she and Justin had merely exited for a cherished moment of privacy.

A loud gasp escaped her lips as she was suddenly yanked back into the shadows around the corner of the building. Wincing as the back of her head connected

229

sharply with the bricks, she made a desperate, belated attempt to scream. Justin acted quickly, silencing her cries for help by clamping a hand roughly across her mouth. His other arm tightened about her until she could scarcely breathe.

"Listen to me, you stupid little bitch!" he whispered hoarsely. The overhang of the roof blocked the moon's rays, but even in the darkness Dallas could make out the menacing, fury-contorted planes of her former sweetheart's face. "I'll soon be able to give you anything you could ever need or want! And when I leave this town behind for good in a few weeks, you'll be coming with me! I won't let Kincaid or any other bastard take what's mine! You belong to me, Dallas! I swear to God, I'll kill you before I'll let any other man have you!"

Her eyes widened in very real terror, and she screamed low in her throat when the hand across her mouth was suddenly replaced by the bruising pressure of Justin's lips. He kissed her with a punishing, brutal passion while his hand closed upon one of her breasts and squeezed hard. She moaned in pain and outrage, hot tears burning against her eyelids as she fought against a forceful wave of nausea.

Doubling her hands into tight fists, she pummeled him wildly about the back and shoulders. Still, he did not release her. She moaned again when his hot, seeking tongue plunged within the softness of her mouth. The invasion provoked her to even greater frenzy, and she did not think twice before ramming her knee upward into the most vulnerable part of his male anatomy, foolishly left unguarded while his obsessive desire raged out of control.

Dallas staggered back against the brick wall when Justin bit out a curse and abruptly released her. She raised a trembling hand to her throat and struggled to regain control of her breathing as she watched him doubling over with the excruciating pain she had inflicted.

In spite of what he had just said and done, she felt a twinge of pity—whether it was for the man who had now fallen to his knees on the ground before her or for the man he used to be, she did not know. Though her mind urged her to run away and leave him there to suffer alone, her heart, stirring with the same compassion she had always shown toward any animal or fellow human being in pain, told her to stay.

"Oh, Justin!" she murmured softly, the tears coursing freely down her beautiful face. Moving forward to kneel on the damp grass beside him, she placed a comforting hand upon his shoulder. "Why did things have to turn out like this between us?" The whispered question was as much for herself as for him, and she realized sadly that the answer did not matter.

None of us can choose where to love, she remembered once hearing. It was true. She couldn't love Justin even if she wanted to, for the simple reason that her heart had to follow its own course. Her glistening eyes widened as the unbidden image of Ross Kincaid supplanted all others yet again. Why on earth was she thinking about him *now?*

"I'm sorry, Dallas," Justin told her quietly. He straightened with obvious difficulty and turned to her with a heavy, ragged sigh. "I lost my head, but I never meant to hurt you." His voice sounded full of remorse . . . and something else she could not recognize. She remained silent as he climbed slowly to his feet and reached down to help her up as well.

Following only a moment's hesitation, she accepted the hand he offered her and rose from the rain-saturated ground. She shook out her skirts, then frowned down at the dark, telltale stain she suddenly glimpsed on the front of her gown. Mentally berating herself for being so careless—there would be little doubt in everyone's mind that *something* had happened while she and Justin Bishop were outside together—she sighed and tugged her hand free of his to at least try and repair the damage done to her hair.

No words passed between them again until after they had emerged from the concealing shadows and paused to face each other in the pale moonlight. The fast-paced fiddle music, swelling to a crescendo, reigned supreme over the other sounds of the gathering and drifted outward into the welcoming coolness of the night air.

"It will never happen again, Dallas," Justin assured her somberly, his dark eyes full of what appeared to be contrition. Inwardly, he cursed himself for letting his emotions get the better of him. It was a failing O'Shea had repeatedly cautioned him about. Reflecting that he'd come too damned close to blowing all his carefully laid plans to hell, he vowed to keep his passions in check until after he'd gotten what he came back to Corsicana for. Then, and only then, would he be free to teach Dallas that she must submit to him, that she must yield to him, body and soul. He would show her what it meant to be loved by a true connoisseur of fleshly delights and erotic pleasures. Yes, he mused as his eyes took on an intense, feral gleam at the thought, he had learned much these past five years, and he would teach her a hundred different ways to please him . . .

"Please, Justin, I'd prefer that we just tried to forget about what happened," replied Dallas, her own gaze clouded with lingering hurt. She knew she would never be able to forget, but she wanted nothing more at that moment than to put an end to the awful, humiliating scene.

He nodded wordlessly and moved closer to her. She instinctively retreated a step, her eyes wide and full of renewed alarm as they anxiously searched his face. Smiling faintly, he leaned forward and brushed her silken brow with his lips, then turned and was gone.

Dallas released a long, pent-up sigh. Pressing her palms to the burning smoothness of her cheeks, she battled the urge to dissolve into a storm of weeping. She was still so utterly distressed and preoccupied as a result of Justin's attack, that she did not notice the four women who had recently arrived on the scene to stand watching her from their vantage point in the open doorway.

"My, my, I do believe that was our Dallas's wayward beau we just saw leaving," Lorena Appleton observed to the others in a voice dripping with sarcasm.

Dallas started and whirled about. Hot color washed over her from head to toe, and her eyes blazed with mingled fury and embarrassment. She opened her mouth to level a well-deserved verbal barrage at the widow, but Lorena cut her off with a throaty laugh of pure, malicious amusement.

"Oh, dear, will you look at *that?* I'm afraid, poor Dallas, that you are an absolute sight! Why, there's mud all over your dress, not to mention the fact that your hair is in a dreadful state!" She turned to her visibly shocked companions and remarked in a loud, conspiratorial tone, "It certainly looks as if she and Justin Bishop are taking right up where they left off, doesn't it?"

"Someday, Lorena," Dallas ground out as her temper flared perilously near the uppermost limits of control, "that spiteful tongue of yours is going to devour itself, and the world will be a better place for it!" Trembling with the force of her anger, she spun about and began marching toward the front of the church where she had left her horse and wagon.

"Dallas! Dallas, wait!" a high-pitched voice called after her.

She immediately recognized it as Marian Ridgeway's. Though tempted to keep going in spite of that fact, she forced herself to stop. Her wide-eyed and breathless friend came hastening up to her side an instant later.

"Dallas, what's wrong? What happened between you and Lorena? I was going outside for some fresh air, and I overheard what you said to her right before you ran away and—"

"I didn't run away!" There was no way she could hope to explain, at least not without telling Marian everything, and that was something she would not do. Uncertain about whether her reluctance to reveal the truth owed its origin to sentimentality over what she and Justin had once shared, or from some other reason, she told herself it really didn't matter. Managing a brief, rather wan smile, she asked, "Please, Marian, will you tell my sisters and Ruby Mae that I've gone home? Tell them not to worry, that I . . . well, that I suddenly developed a headache and went home to lie down."

"But you can't go off alone in the dark like this!" protested Marian in disbelief, the moon and paper lamps casting shadows across her plump, genuinely worried features. "Why, you know there are all sorts of tramps and robbers—"

"I'll be fine!" Dallas impatiently reassured her. She gave the unconvinced young woman a quick hug, then hurried off.

Marian, never one for being able to make spur-of-the-moment decisions, was left in a quandary as to whether or not she should try and stop her friend, or perhaps fetch one of Dallas's sisters to dissuade the stubborn redhead from following such a dangerous course of action. In the end, however, she did neither, instead merely watching as Dallas climbed up into the wagon and quickly drove away into the mild summer night.

IX

Arriving home without incident—and in near record time—in spite of Marian's dire warning, Dallas rushed inside the dark, empty house and up the stairs to her room. She paused only to light a lamp before practically tearing off her dress and yanking the pins from her hair. Anxious to eliminate any and all reminders of what had happened, she stuffed the offending blue organdy gown into a box and slid it beneath her bed. She next snatched up a silver-handled hairbrush and dragged it relentlessly through her tangled auburn locks until her eyes smarted with tears and her scalp felt raw.

What am I punishing myself for? she suddenly wondered, sinking down onto the velvet-cushioned stool before her dressing table. Was it because she had so foolishly underestimated the intensity of Justin Bishop's feelings for her? Or was it perhaps because her own feelings were in such utter turmoil?

She heaved a sigh and sprang to her feet again. Flinging open the doors of her wardrobe, she pulled out a simple red calico shirtwaist and swiftly buttoned it on. Then, tying back her hair with a ribbon and catching up the lamp, she hesitated in the doorway to her room for only a brief moment before returning downstairs.

The kitchen still smelled pleasantly of the beef stew she and Ruby Mae had made for supper, and she couldn't help smiling softly to herself as she recalled how her sisters had almost been too excited to eat any of it. Watching them out on the dance floor tonight had prompted a flood of pride and affection—

Her reverie was interrupted when, upon moving farther into the room, she became aware of the sound of the steam engine chugging away in the backyard. She crossed to the window and peered outward, her eyes widening imperceptibly when they fell upon Ross.

He and Billy Joe, their work illuminated by the light of two kerosene lanterns, stood talking together beneath the derrick, their faces darkened with grime and their clothing covered with mud. Even so, Dallas felt a wild leaping of her pulses as she gazed at the taller of the two men. No amount of dirt could disguise the rugged perfection of his features, nor the virile, hard-muscled litheness of his body.

Acting on sudden impulse, she whirled about and grabbed the coffeepot. She filled it with water, added a generous amount of freshly ground coffee, then set it on the stove and lit a fire under it. Stepping back to the window while she waited for the inevitably strong concoction to boil, she folded her arms across her chest and stared pensively out at the man who, with the sheer forcefulness of his presence, brought a warm rosiness to her cheeks and a sparkle to her eyes.

It wasn't long before she was on her way outside with a tray of coffee and leftover biscuits. She told herself she was merely doing it out of a sense of duty, because no matter what had transpired, the men were after all in *her* employ, but it was a good thing she would not be called upon to swear as much upon a stack of Bibles.

"Mr. Kincaid!" she called out above the engine's roar as she approached the derrick. Ross turned at the sound of her voice, and Dallas felt her knees weaken all of a sudden when he favored her with a slow, thoroughly devastating smile. "I . . . I've brought you some coffee!" she stammered, blushing beneath his scrutiny.

"Thanks!" he shouted back. He motioned to Billy Joe, and they ducked beneath the timbers to step down from the platform.

"This was mighty nice of you, ma'am!" Billy Joe told her with a grin as he gratefully accepted a cup of hot coffee and a biscuit. "I'm so hungry I'm left-handed, and Tex here don't hardly hold with layin' off long enough to do more'n take a piss—" He caught himself, but it was too late. Turning beet-red to the roots of his dirty thatch of straw-covered hair, he noisily cleared his throat and muttered a hasty "beggin' your pardon, ma'am" before taking himself back up to the derrick floor to eat his biscuit. A smile of indulgent humor tugged at Dallas's lips as she watched him leave, but all traces of amusement vanished when she looked up at Ross again.

"Why did you come back so early?" he asked. His piercing green gaze did not fail to catch the shadow which suddenly crossed her face, nor the way her eyes darkened with remembered pain.

"I was feeling a little tired!" Her troubled gaze fell before his as she uttered the half-truth. She could literally feel his eyes on her, and she told herself that it had been a mistake to come outside. For some inexplicable reason, her emotions were in even more of a turmoil than before, and she had the ridiculous but nonetheless unnerving sensation that he knew all about her disastrous encounter with Justin.

"What is it, Dallas?" he then questioned. He rarely called her by her given name. "What happened?"

"Happened? Why, nothing at all!" she insisted with a deceptively casual air. It suddenly occurred to her that she would have liked nothing better than to cast herself upon his broad chest and pour out all her troubles, though why she felt the urge to do such an absurd thing was totally beyond her comprehension . . . well, not *totally,* she admitted to herself. Recalling how he had held her with such comforting strength while she cried tears of grief the day before, she found it difficult indeed to keep from blurting out the whole story.

Ross, as if sensing her inner struggle, did not speak again until after taking a long draw on his coffee. His gaze traveled over her with a strange combination of tenderness, desire, and a possessive familiarity that brought a new rush of color to her cheeks.

"Was Bishop there tonight?" he startled her by demanding. She inhaled sharply, her face paling at the disquieting accuracy of his conjecture.

"I don't see why that should be of any interest to you, Mr. Kincaid!" she retorted evasively, taking refuge in her anger. Anxious to get away, she pivoted about on her booted heel and prepared to hurry back across the muddy yard to the sanctuary of the house. She gasped when her arm was suddenly captured by Ross's strong hand.

"I asked you a question, damn it!"

"And I gave you an answer!"

She wrenched her arm free and started to whirl away again—but she never got the chance. In the next instant, the echoing report of a gunshot shattered the night air.

The following seconds passed in a dizzying haze of fear and confusion for Dallas. Ross, reacting with lightning-quick speed, seized her about the waist and hauled her bodily up to the platform with him. He flung her down behind the protective bulk of the drawworks while he grabbed his shotgun and crouched beside her to return the fire.

Another shot rang out, and there was a loud hiss as steam burst forth from a hole in the boiler. Following the sound of the shots, Ross brought the gun to his shoulder and fired a blast in the direction of the barn. Moving under cover of darkness, however, the unknown assailants had the decided advantage, and they soon retaliated with a deafening burst of gunfire that left several more holes in the boiler and ricocheted off the drawworks where Ross kept Dallas shielded with his own body. The rig slowly ground to a halt as the last of the steam escaped, cutting off power to the circulating pump and leaving a deadly silence to fill the moonlit night.

"The lanterns, Billy Joe!" Ross commanded the young man behind him in a terse undertone. "Douse the light!"

Billy Joe, who had scrambled down on the back side of the platform when the shooting started, had neglected to get his gun. He cursed himself for his stupidity, and though he had every intention of obeying Ross's directive, he obviously didn't realize the importance of it. Deciding to first make an attempt to retrieve his rifle from where he had left it propped up against one of the corner timbers, he cautiously raised himself off the ground and began inching along the derrick floor.

Another volley of shots split the silence. Billy Joe cried out in agony as a bullet lodged itself in his left shoulder. The impact spun him around, and he fell to the ground again, where he lay moaning in pain and clutching at his torn, burning flesh.

Dallas shut her eyes tightly and battled a growing wave of panic while Ross breathed a savage oath above her. She was already feeling stiff and sore from having been thrown so roughly down to the platform and forced to remain in one position for so long, but she dared not move or make a sound.

Dear God, please, please help us! she prayed with heartfelt fervency. Wondering dazedly who the gunmen were and why they had attacked without warning, she was acutely conscious of Ross's every breath. She could feel the tenseness of his body, could feel the way he shifted the gun slightly while his steady, smoldering gaze searched the darkness. Her heart pounded in her ears, and she bit at her lower lip in anguish when Billy Joe moaned again.

The waiting was mercifully short.

The men hiding out near the barn got careless. Two of them, apparently tiring of the situation, exchanged angry words. Though their voices were low and hushed, it was enough for Ross to be able to draw a bead on their location. He quickly took aim and fired. What happened next demonstrated the very reason he chose to use a shotgun instead of a rifle or pistol whenever he was on a job—this wasn't the first time a rig of his had been attacked by a rival gang, and he knew it probably wouldn't be the last.

The buckshot scattered as it blasted through the darkness. There was a harsh, strangled cry of pain, followed immediately thereafter by a string of curses and the unmistakable sound of horse's hooves pounding the earth as someone beat a hasty retreat.

The remaining gunmen—no more than two, thought Ross, judging from the number of shots he'd counted when Billy Joe had drawn their fire—could be heard whispering stridently among themselves before letting loose with another round of bullets. Ross shielded Dallas's body with his again, and she numbly realized that she was just as much afraid for him as for herself . . .

Suddenly, a lone horseman came bearing down upon the unsuspecting assailants. It was Erik, who had heard the distant sound of gunfire while on his way home from the social. Drawing his six-shooter from the holster buckled low upon his hips, he shouted, "Tex!" to identify himself to Ross and galloped straight into the midst of the fray.

The two men on the far side of the barn, taken off guard, swore and turned their guns on the young Swede, but neither of them was able to get off more than a single, woefully inaccurate shot before he brought his booted foot smashing into the face of one, then flung himself off his horse to take the other man hurtling to the ground with him.

Ross wasted little time. Biting out a terse "Stay put!" to Dallas, he went racing across the moonlit yard. He arrived on the scene just as the gunman Erik had kicked was taking aim to fire at the taller of the two combatants furiously rolling and grappling with each other on the ground.

"Drop it!" growled Ross, his shotgun leveled at the back of the man who stood less than ten feet away.

Tightening his grip on the revolver in his hand, the man flung his arm upward and rounded on Ross with the clear intention of shooting. Ross had no choice but to pull the trigger. The shot, concentrated as a result of such proximity, caught the man in the forearm, shattering flesh and bone and very nearly severing his hand. He gave a loud, staccato cry before crumpling to the ground, unconscious but still alive.

At that point, the man's partner in crime wisely chose surrender. Erik hauled him upright and shoved him over to where the other man lay bleeding beside the barn.

"Where is Miss Brown? And Billy Joe?" the young Swede asked anxiously as he moved to Ross's side.

"Over there," Ross answered with a curt nod toward the derrick. "Dallas is all right, but Billy Joe's hit."

"I'll ride to town and fetch the doctor."

"And the sheriff."

Erik nodded solemnly and hurried away to mount up. Ross, keeping his shotgun trained on the uninjured man standing in defeated silence beside the prone body of his less fortunate colleague, turned his head slightly and called out, "Dallas?"

"I'm here with Billy Joe! He's hurt badly, Ross!" she answered, her voice quavering a bit. Upon seeing that the danger had passed, she had climbed unsteadily to her feet and rushed over to help the young roughneck. He was barely conscious, his eyes glazed and his face dangerously ashen beneath the grime. She cradled his head in her lap and pressed a torn strip of petticoat to his wound in an attempt to stop the bleeding. Tears of mingled relief and pity gathered in her eyes, and she murmured in a soft, soothing manner to Billy Joe as she valiantly fought them back.

"Miss Dallas?" he whispered hoarsely during one of his rare moments of lucidness.

"Yes, Billy Joe?"

"Am I . . . am I gonna die, ma'am?"

"Of course not! The doctor will be here soon, and he'll have you right as rain in no time!" She smiled warmly down at him, but his youthful features had become contorted with pain again. Drawing in a ragged breath, she looked to where Ross's tall frame stood outlined against the barn. And suddenly, she felt stronger . . .

After what seemed like an eternity, Erik returned with both the doctor and the sheriff in tow. The doctor, following a quick word with Ross, hurried to tend to Billy Joe first. Dallas assisted him as best she could, and she took a small measure of comfort from the pronouncement that, although the stocky young worker had lost a lot of blood, he stood a good chance of recovering.

In spite of her offer to care for Billy Joe there, the doctor was quite adamant about having him removed at once to the small hospital he had recently established in his home. Ross and Erik were instructed to carefully lift the patient and convey him to the wagon.

Then, after sparing the time for a brief but nonetheless thorough enough examination of the other wounded man by the light of one of the kerosene lanterns, the doctor told the sheriff—with far less compassion than he had displayed toward Billy Joe—that the "cowardly bastard" would also have to be removed to the hospital for treatment.

The doctor and sheriff soon left with their respective charges. Ross and Erik moved back to the drilling site to inspect the damages. Dallas, who had wearily taken herself inside to exchange her bloodstained dress for a clean one, returned outside just as the two men straightened from where they had been discussing the repair of the boiler. The rig would have to remain shut down until the holes were patched, but at least any delay in bringing in the well would be a temporary one. It could easily have been much worse.

"I am glad that you are safe, Miss Brown," Erik told her earnestly as she drew closer. His face was bruised and dirtied a bit, but he was otherwise unharmed.

"And I you, Mr. Larsen. Heaven only knows what would have happened if you had not arrived in time," she remarked with an involuntary shudder. Her eyes moved to Ross, only to widen when they took note of the trickle of blood on his left temple. "Why, you're hurt!" She immediately stepped forward and raised a hand to brush the dark hair away from the source of the blood. Even in the lantern's pale glow, she could see that his head had apparently been creased by a bullet. "You must come inside and let me see to this at once!" she decreed with a stern frown.

"It's nothing," Ross dismissed it with characteristic, masculine nonchalance. His strong hand closed about her wrist and gently but firmly drew it back down, but he did not release it until Dallas's face grew warm and she retreated a step in sudden confusion. Conscious of the way both men were staring at her, she proudly raised her head, fixed Ross with a narrow, stubborn look and insisted, "Nevertheless, you'll have to let me clean and bandage it right away."

"She is right, Tex," Erik threw in his support. "You go on inside. I will see to the horses and keep an eye on things until you are done."

Ross, though reluctant to agree, finally did so because he wanted to speak to Dallas alone for a few minutes. He took her by the arm and led her silently back to the house. Once they were inside the kitchen, she instructed him to have a seat at the table while she hurried across the room to fetch the medical supplies she kept tucked away in the cupboard.

Ross stood and watched her, his gaze hungrily devouring the sight of her slender, supple curves in the plain blue cotton shirtwaist. Her waist-length auburn tresses, tied at the nape of her neck with a ribbon, swayed gently to and fro as she walked, and he longed to bury his face in their fragrant softness before kissing those sweet lips of hers until she begged for mercy.

He had found himself gripped in the throes of a murderous rage when those bastards had been shooting at them—the thought of her being hurt had made his heart twist painfully and his temper flare wildly. Never before had he felt like that. But even then, he had forced himself to keep his head, had vowed to do whatever it took to protect the woman he loved.

The woman he loved.

In that split second of time, Rossiter Maverick

Kincaid knew he had finally "bitten the dust" for good . . .

"I'm afraid this may sting a bit," Dallas cautioned as she returned to the table with a bottle of iodine and a roll of gauze bandaging.

She waited while he bent his tall frame into a chair. Avoiding his eyes, she uncorked the bottle, poured a bit of the alcohol-based antiseptic on to a clean white cloth, then raised it to the spot where the blood was already beginning to clot. She dabbed at the neatly separated edges of flesh, satisfied to find that the wound was no worse than she had originally thought.

"You won't require any stitches, but your head will probably continue to burn for a while," she pronounced quietly. Setting the cloth aside, she took up the bandaging, cut off a strip and folded it, and pressed it to the wound. She quickly wrapped a strip of the gauze about his head and secured it with a knot.

So far, Ross had not spoken a word. Dallas was uncomfortably aware of his eyes on her the whole time, and her hands trembled slightly as she adjusted the bandage. Still refusing to meet his gaze, she started to turn away, only to be detained by the warm pressure of his hand on her arm.

"Dallas."

Her name sounded like an endearment on his lips. She felt her heart turn over in her breast and a sudden, delicious tremor run the length of her spine.

"Dallas, look at me."

Though she tried not to obey, she could no longer prevent her eyes from moving to his face. She caught her breath on a soft gasp when her luminous sapphire gaze encountered the fathomless green intensity of his, for what she saw reflected therein sent her blood racing like liquid fire through her veins.

Slowly, ever so slowly, Ross pulled her to him. She did not resist. Without taking any notice at all of the fact that his clothes were still covered with mud, she allowed him to draw her onto his lap. His powerful arms came up to encircle her, and he cradled her against his hard warmth with infinite tenderness while her head lay nestled securely upon his shoulder.

How long they remained like that, Dallas could not say. Nor could she make herself question why she was so content to rest within the strong circle of his arms. Her eyes swept closed, and she reveled in the sound of his heart beating beneath her cheek. Not since she was a child had she felt so safe and warm and . . . strangely enough, loved. After the night's horrifying ordeal, it was especially heavenly to be held like that, to relax her tired, aching muscles and free her troubled mind of all thought.

Well, not quite *all* thought, she mused with an inward sigh. She couldn't erase one particular, disturbingly vivid memory from her mind. It was of Ross, covering her body with his while shots rang out in a terrible, deafening explosion of sound and bullets flew all about them. He had risked his life to protect her. Any one of those bullets might easily have found a target in him, and he could now be lying seriously wounded or even dead—

Without realizing that she did so, Dallas tensed and caught her breath. Ross lifted a hand to her chin, cupping it with unbelievable gentleness and tilting her head back so that he could gaze directly into her eyes. He was surprised to see the tears glistening in their brilliant blue depths, and he frowned to observe that something was troubling her once more.

"What is it, my love?" he asked softly, the deep-timbred vibrancy of his voice reverberating in the lamplit silence of the room.

My love. His words echoed in her mind, sending a rush of inexplicable warmth through her entire body. She told herself it meant nothing, that he had only said it out of pity, in an attempt to comfort her, but she suddenly realized that she wanted more than anything else in the world for the term of affection he had used to be genuine. Though she didn't understand why, she longed to know that Ross Kincaid had meant those words . . .

She heard him whisper her name. Then, his mouth was claiming hers in a kiss of such sweetly compelling passion that she shivered and felt her head spinning. She clung to him, her lips welcoming the warm caress of his while she instinctively strained upward against him and thrilled to the tightening of his arms about her.

The memory of another kiss suddenly flashed into her mind, the one Justin Bishop had forced on her earlier that same evening. Whereas his had been cruel and punishing, Ross's was both tender and intoxicating, and she felt herself growing increasingly light-headed with an answering desire. It was the first time he had kissed her with such gentle, sensuous persuasion, instead of the impassioned fervency their encounters usually held, and she found herself thinking that it would be difficult indeed to choose which method she preferred—they were both so splendidly, devilishly irresistible in their own right . . .

She moaned softly as the velvety warmth of his

tongue began a slow, evocative dance with hers. He soon elicited another moan of pleasure when his hand made a sweeping caress down across her back to her hips, where his fingers stroked slowly, lovingly over the rounded curve of flesh beneath the layers of cotton.

Suddenly, in the benumbed recesses of her mind, Dallas became aware of the sound of voices. Her eyes flew wide in startlement, and she was about to tear her lips from Ross's, only to realize that he was already reacting to the voices himself. He raised his head and gave her a quick, enigmatic smile, then reluctantly slid her off his lap and set her on her feet. He was just drawing his tall frame up beside her when Cordi came bustling into the kitchen, followed closely by Ruby Mae, Sam, and Etta. The four of them stopped short when they caught sight of Dallas and Ross.

"Dallas! Why, what—what on earth happened to *you?*" breathed Cordi, her eyes growing very round as they traveled over her sister's flushed face and mud-stained dress. Her gaze shifted hastily to Ross, only to note in growing bewilderment that he, too, was covered with mud, and wearing a bandage on his head.

"Why is the rig shut down?" Sam asked before Dallas had a chance to speak. Having become accustomed to the sound of the steam engine chugging away, he noticed the silence and looked to the other man in the room with a frown of puzzlement.

"We ran into a little trouble," answered Ross.

"Trouble?" Ruby Mae echoed with a frown. She hastened to Dallas's side now and slipped an arm about her shoulders. "Lord have mercy, honey, what happened? Marian said you told her you were just feelin' a mite under the weather and comin' home to rest!"

"I . . . I was. I mean, I did," murmured Dallas. She was aware of Ross's eyes on her again, and it was all she could do to keep from giving in to the urge to run upstairs and shut herself away in her room. "I arrived home without incident, but something terrible happened after that." She took a deep breath and revealed, "I was outside with Mr. Kincaid and Billy Joe when someone began shooting at us."

"Shooting at you?" Etta repeated loudly.

"Dear God, are you all right?" demanded Cordi, flying across the room to take hold of her older sister's hand.

"I'm fine," Dallas assured her with a faint smile. "But Billy Joe was hurt badly, as was one of the men who attacked us."

"Who were they?" Sam questioned Ross, his boyish countenance appearing quite grim.

"I don't know yet. But it's a good bet they're the same ones who have been trying to sabotage the well all along." He turned to Dallas and said, "I know it doesn't help much to hear it, but this kind of thing happens all the time in the oil field. You needn't worry—they won't try anything else after tonight."

"How can you be so certain?" she asked. She raised her eyes to his, only to color anew at the way he was looking at her.

"I can't," he replied honestly. Moving to the back door, he paused and added, "But I give you my word I'll do everything in my power to prevent it." Dallas watched as he left and returned outside to find Erik. Sam murmured something to Etta, then followed after him.

"Come on," Ruby Mae said to Dallas once the men

252

had gone. "Let's get you upstairs to bed."

"No, I . . . I couldn't sleep even if I tried," she declared a bit shakily. She drew away and sank back down into the same chair Ross had vacated moments earlier. Unable to prevent her thoughts from returning to the sweet enchantment of his embrace, she felt her head spinning again.

"I'll put on some coffee," offered Cordi. Searching first on the stove and then in the sink, she found the coffeepot Dallas had absently caught up on her way inside to change her dress. She began filling it with water, only to discover that a bullet had pierced the metal clean through. Shuddering in distaste, she let it fall back into the sink with a clatter.

Though Ruby Mae scolded her for doing so, Etta sat down beside Dallas and pressed her for further details about the incident. Dallas related everything she could remember—omitting any mention of what had happened between herself and Ross, of course—then listened with only half an ear as her sisters and Ruby Mae began discussing the events and speculating upon what had prompted the attack. Her thoughts once again drifted to Ross.

What exactly *did* he feel for her? she asked herself, her brows knitting together into a frown of bemusement. More importantly, what did she feel for *him?*

Feeling strangely restless, she sighed and reflected that there could be no denying the strong physical attraction that existed between them. But—was that truly all there was?

My love, he had called her. He had certainly kissed her as though he'd meant it. And she had been far from reticent about kissing him back. Why was it that every time the man touched her she could think of nothing else but him? He had even succeeded in making her forget about the nightmarish ordeal they had endured . . .

"I still say it has nothing whatsoever to do with us, at least who we are, that is," she became aware of Etta theorizing with all the confidence and wisdom of her seventeen years.

"Oh, and I suppose none of the other things that have been happening around here have had anything to do with who we are, either!" retorted Cordi.

"What difference does it make *why* it happened?" Ruby Mae interjected in a low, unusually somber voice. She shook her head slowly and added, "You know, I hate like all get-out to say it, but I'm beginnin' to think you girls would've been better off if that well had never been started."

"That's not true!" Cordi feelingly dissented, unable to bear the thought of never having met Erik.

"No, I . . . I don't think it is," Dallas surprised them—and herself—by agreeing.

She looked up to find three pairs of eyes fastened expectantly upon her, as though their owners were waiting for her to say more. Coloring faintly, she murmured something about suddenly feeling quite tired and left them staring after her in mutual, worried bafflement as she fled upstairs.

X

Etta heaved a long, disgruntled sigh and plopped down onto the chintz-covered sofa.

"We never even got a chance to talk about anything at all last night!" she complained, her golden eyes flashing with lingering resentment at the memory. "Sam insisted upon escorting Ruby Mae and Cordi home, and nothing *I* said about it seemed to matter to him in the least!"

"Oh, Etta," sighed Dallas. She left off pinning on her hat before the hallway mirror and crossed into the parlor to take a seat beside her youngest, and most temperamental, sister. "That's one of the very reasons I am opposed to any sort of commitment between you and Sam. Even if he did make an effort to become more responsible, the two of you would still always be at odds with each other! What kind of marriage could you expect to have if you—"

"Goodness gracious, Dallas, merely because a man and woman have a little difference of opinion every now and then doesn't mean they aren't in love!" the petite, strawberry blonde declared crossly.

"Perhaps not, but with you and Sam it isn't just 'every now and then,' and I fail to see how becoming engaged to him is going to magically infuse your relationship with the sort of peaceful harmony that should exist between a husband and wife."

"Peaceful harmony?" Etta gave an unladylike snort of laughter and swung her legs off the sofa. "Is that what *you* want out of marriage?" she challenged. "Why, the kind of life you're describing would bore me to tears! I want romance and adventure and excitement, not to sit at home and grow old with my knitting!"

"Haven't you ever heard the old saying about the fire that burns highest and brightest? It's said that it will quickly burn itself out, Etta. And that's what will happen between you and Sam if you have nothing else but . . . but passion and raging emotions to build upon!"

"I don't believe that! But even if it turned out to be true, I'd rather be loved wildly and passionately for a short time instead of enduring years and years of 'peaceful harmony'!"

Telling herself in exasperation that it was useless to try and argue with someone who was obviously unwilling to listen to reason, Dallas sighed again and returned to the entrance foyer. Etta, appearing a bit contrite all of a sudden, followed after her.

"I still wish you'd let me come with you."

"I'm not even sure the doctor will allow me to see him," reiterated Dallas. She had worried about Billy Joe all night—among other things—and had announced at breakfast that morning her intention to

ACCEPT YOUR **FREE** GIFT AND EXPERIENCE MORE OF THE PASSION AND ADVENTURE YOU LIKE IN A HISTORICAL ROMANCE

Zebra Romances are the finest novels of their kind and are written with the adult woman in mind. All of our books are written by authors who really know how to weave tales of romantic adventure in the historical settings you love.

Because our readers tell us these books sell out very fast in the stores, Zebra has made arrangements for you to receive at home the four newest titles published each month. You'll never miss a title and home delivery is so convenient. With your first shipment we'll even send you a FREE Zebra Historical Romance as our gift just for trying our home subscription service. No obligation.

BIG SAVINGS AND **FREE** HOME DELIVERY

Each month, the Zebra Home Subscription Service will send you the four newest titles as soon as they are published. (We ship these books to our subscribers even before we send them to the stores.) You may preview them *Free* for 10 days. If you like them as much as we think you will, you'll pay just $3.50 each and *save $1.80 each month* off the cover price. *AND you'll also get FREE HOME DELIVERY.* There is never a charge for shipping, handling or postage and there is no minimum you must buy. If you decide not to keep any shipment, simply return it within 10 days, no questions asked, and owe nothing.

MAIL IN THE COUPON BELOW TODAY

GET FREE GIFT

To get your Free ZEBRA HISTORICAL ROMANCE fill out the coupon below and send it in today. As soon as we receive the coupon, we'll send your first month's books to preview Free for 10 days along with your **FREE NOVEL**.

———— F R E E ————

BOOK CERTIFICATE

ZEBRA HOME SUBSCRIPTION SERVICE, INC.

YES! Please start my subscription to Zebra Historical Romances and send me my free Zebra Novel along with my first month's Romances. I understand that I may preview these four new Zebra Historical Romances Free for 10 days. If I'm not satisfied with them I may return the four books within 10 days and owe nothing. Otherwise I will pay just $3.50 each; a total of $14.00 (a $15.80 value—I save $1.80). Then each month I will receive the 4 newest titles as soon as they come off the press for the same 10 day Free preview and low price. I may return any shipment and I may cancel this arrangement at any time. There is no minimum number of books to buy and there are no shipping, handling or postage charges. Regardless of what I do, the **FREE** book is mine to keep.

Name _____
                        (Please Print)

Address _____ Apt. # _____

City _____ State _____ Zip _____

Telephone ( ) _____

Signature _____
                (if under 18, parent or guardian must sign)

Terms and offer subject to change without notice.

Get a Free
Zebra
Historical
Romance

*a $3.95
value*

visit him. "At least I'll be able to find out how he's doing."

"When will you be back?"

"I don't know—not too late. George's solicitor, a Mr. Howard Willoughby, is supposed to be arriving sometime today." She dreaded the prospect of meeting with the man, but knew she had very little choice. He would want to speak to Ross and her at the same time, no doubt, and she wasn't at all certain she wanted to hear what he had to say. "I'm planning to stop by Ransom's while I'm in town and arrange for some groceries to be delivered. I don't expect Mr. Willoughby to arrive before I return. Even if he comes in on the morning train, he couldn't possibly be here before ten o'clock."

She took up her reticule and headed for the front door, then impulsively turned back and gave her sister a quick hug.

"Please, Etta, let's not quarrel anymore. It seems that's all you and Cordi and I do lately!" Drawing away, she beamed a conciliatory smile down into Etta's youthful, highly expressive countenance. "Maybe this afternoon you and I can see about fitting that new pattern from *Harper's* on you."

"I won't be here this afternoon. I have a job."

"A job?" Dallas echoed in surprise. "What are you talking about?"

"Yesterday," her sister explained quite casually, "I went down to the Collin Street Bakery and applied for employment. I was accepted, so I'll be starting at one o'clock today; an hour later on Fridays. It's only for four hours a day, but the wages are not half bad, and at least they were willing to take me on in spite of my lack of experience."

"But I thought we had decided that you were going to wait until after the summer to find work!"

"We had. But . . . well, things have changed. Cordi's working, so why shouldn't I?" She raised her chin defensively and confessed, "I want to save up as much money as I can, so that when Sam and I are married—"

"Oh, Etta, not again!" groaned Dallas. This time, she did not pause before marching straight outside and down the tree-lined walk to the street. She had hitched her horse to the wagon a short time earlier, and she now climbed up to settle her dark blue skirts about her while she unwound the reins.

The sound of the steam engine reached her ears just as she prepared to drive away. She had seen Ross, Erik, and Sam working on it shortly after sunup that morning, and she suddenly found herself wondering if Ross had ever been to bed at all last night.

Her cheeks flaming at the image her hopelessly incorrigible mind conjured up at *that* particular thought, she leveled a blistering oath at herself and snapped the reins above the horse's back.

When she returned to the house nearly two hours later, it was to discover that Etta had blithely gone on her way somewhere with friends and left Ruby Mae with all the household chores Dallas had charged *her* to complete.

"Oh, Ruby, I told Etta to do that!" Tugging the white straw hat from her head, she hurried into the parlor, where she had glimpsed Ruby Mae bending down to dust the side of the piano. "Where is she? She's supposed to be—"

"Now don't you worry," Ruby Mae prescribed

amiably, her face splitting into a broad grin as she straightened. "I told her it was all right to go ahead and skedaddle."

"Just the same, you shouldn't have to do her work for her," Dallas insisted. She linked a companionable arm through Ruby Mae's and drew the older woman along with her toward the doorway. "You've already done too much around here as it is. We'll never be able to repay you for all your help and kindness."

"Didn't do it for pay!" quipped Ruby Mae, then grew serious and asked, "How's Billy Joe doin'?" Dallas sighed and raised a hand to sweep a wayward tendril of hair from her forehead.

"About as well as can be expected, I suppose. I was only able to look in on him briefly. The doctor's wife appears to be taking very good care of him. She said he'll probably be up and about again in two weeks' time."

"What about that other man, the dim-witted bastard who tried to argue with Mr. Kincaid's shotgun?"

"He'll survive, though they did have to amputate his arm. The sheriff had already been there in an attempt to question him—it seems the man locked up in the jail is refusing to cooperate—but he was still unconscious." They had almost reached the kitchen when a knock sounded at the front door behind them.

Dallas spun about, her eyes growing very round as she realized that it was very likely the solicitor from Fort Worth who stood waiting on her front porch. She had intended to return from town at least half an hour sooner, but the visit to the grocer's had taken longer than she had anticipated.

"Well now, I wonder who that could be?" Ruby Mae

idly mused, half to herself. "I'll be in the kitchen if you need me, honey," she announced, bestowing a final pat upon the younger woman's hand. Dallas nodded, hastily smoothed her skirts, and moved to answer the knock. As soon as she opened the door, she knew without being told that it was indeed the solicitor who stared back at her.

A rather short, bespectacled man of middle age, he was wearing a business suit of black serge and carrying a dark brown leather portfolio under one arm. What little bit of hair he had left was revealed when he swept the bowler from his head. He subjected Dallas to a swift but thorough inspection with his small gray eyes.

"Miss Dallas Harmony Brown?" he inquired solemnly.

"Yes?"

"My name is Howard Willoughby. I believe you are expecting me?"

"Of course, Mr. Willoughby. Please come in." She stepped aside and waited until he had entered, then quietly closed the door. Though her demeanor was that of a poised and self-assured young lady, inwardly she was a mass of nerves.

"Is Mr. Kincaid about as well?" asked Mr. Willoughby with a polite smile, the first one he had allowed himself.

"Yes, he's working in the backyard. If you will please have a seat, I'll tell him you're here." Returning his smile, she led him into the parlor, then took herself off to fetch Ross. She had not spoken to him since the night before, and her trepidation increased as she hurried outside to the derrick.

Ross was in the process of helping Erik and Sam add

a section of drill pipe when he caught sight of Dallas drawing to a halt nearby, and he waited until they had secured it into the coupling before moving forward to speak to her. His eyes glowed warmly as they traveled over her face, and his mouth curved into a smile of such disarming pleasure that she felt herself growing light-headed again.

"Good morning," he proclaimed in a deep, mellow voice.

"George's solicitor, Mr. Willoughby, is inside," she told him, absently noting that he had bathed and donned clean clothing, and that the bandage she had put on his head was missing. He looked even more devastatingly handsome than she remembered—oddly enough, it seemed that was the case each time she saw him again—and there was something different about him, something she could not quite put her finger on but something there all the same . . .

"Well then, I guess we'd better not keep him waiting," Ross drawled lazily. He sauntered over to where Ruby Mae had set a fresh bucket of water, a bar of lye soap, and a couple of towels on a makeshift table in the shade of the house. Dallas could not keep her gaze from following him. He quickly washed his hands, dried them, and turned back to her with an endearingly crooked grin. "That's about as presentable as I get. Shall we go, Miss Brown?"

She eyed him uncertainly for a moment, then preceded him up the back steps and into the house. When they arrived at the parlor, Mr. Willoughby stood up from the sofa and extended a hand to Ross.

"Mr. Rossiter Maverick Kincaid?"

"Just 'Ross'," he amended with a nod and a brief

smile as he shook the other man's hand. Dallas, her skirts rustling softly, moved to take a seat on the sofa. The men waited until she sat down before following suit, the solicitor on the sofa beside her and Ross in a large, overstuffed wing chair opposite them.

"Would you care for some coffee, Mr. Willoughby? Or perhaps some lemonade?" Dallas suddenly remembered to offer.

"No, thank you, Miss Brown. I'm afraid I haven't much time. You see, I've made arrangements to return to Fort Worth on the next train." He settled the portfolio on his lap and withdrew three sets of papers. Handing one set to Dallas and one to Ross, he kept the third for himself.

"I may as well get right to the point," he began. "George Proctor, my friend and my client for the past ten years, was a very wealthy man. As you will note from the list I have provided for your benefit, his holdings were both varied and lucrative. He invested wisely, spent little, and was in general a model of thrift, prudency, and foresight. His will, if I may say so, is a masterpiece, an ironclad work of legal sublimity, and in it he stated quite clearly that his entire estate is to be divided evenly between the two of you, to do with however you see fit."

"Does that mean that I am to have control of my own finances after all?" Dallas asked him with a meaningful glance in Ross's direction. The solicitor frowned and shook his head before replying, "Forgive me, Miss Brown, if I gave you that impression. If you will permit me to clarify—George Proctor, serving in his capacity as trustee, was responsible for safeguarding the inheritance which passed to you and your sisters upon your father's death. Under the original terms of your father's will, you were not to gain total control of said inheritance until the event of your marriage, or twenty-fifth birthday, whichever occurred first."

"I am all too familiar with those terms, Mr. Willoughby!" she remarked, her eyes flashing with a renewed burst of annoyance for the fact that her father had displayed so little faith in her judgment. The man beside her shifted his gaze uncomfortably to Ross and back.

"Yes, well . . . shall we continue? In his will, George Proctor left very clear instructions regarding the aforementioned trusteeship. The position of trustee is now to be assumed by Mr. Kincaid."

"Is my inheritance from George included under this new 'arrangement'?" Dallas asked with a growing edge to her voice.

"Yes, Miss Brown, it is," Mr. Willoughby confirmed. He cast her a weakly apologetic smile before transferring his attention to Ross. "As I mentioned briefly in my telegram to you, Mr. Kincaid, you are hereafter responsible for safeguarding the entirety of Miss Brown's holdings, as well as the ones designated for her sisters. Since George Proctor made no provision for any alteration of the original terms, they will, of course, remain in effect."

"I see" was all Ross said. His gaze traveled back to Dallas, who, upon observing the roguish smile which played about his lips, and what she perceived to be a taunting light in his magnificent green eyes, bristled and rose abruptly to her feet.

"This is absurd, Mr. Willoughby! I am a grown woman, perfectly capable of managing my own

263

finances, and it's high time I was allowed the freedom to do so! Surely there is some way—"

"I'm afraid not, Miss Brown." He and Ross, having drawn themselves upright as well, exchanged a quick look of singularly masculine tolerance that did not go unnoticed by Dallas. "The will is quite explicit on all counts."

"But I hardly know Mr. Kincaid!" she protested, then was dismayed to feel her cheeks flaming. Determinedly avoiding Ross's gaze, which she was certain would only cause her further discomfiture, she pointed out to the solicitor, "He has his own life to conduct. I fail to see how he will be able to spare the time to fulfill his duties in this matter! Besides which, there is a decided disadvantage in the fact that he resides in Pennsylvania. How in heaven's name will I be able to contact him whenever I need to make a withdrawal? Why, it could take weeks just to—"

"Come now, I'm sure you and Mr. Kincaid will be able to work out all the details to your mutual satisfaction," Mr. Willoughby cut her off with a patronizing little smile.

Her color deepened to an angry flush while her eyes sparked with indignation. Ross, his own eyes dancing with wry, appreciative humor as he watched her, mused to himself that Howard Willoughby, learned man of the law that he was, obviously knew nothing at all about dealing with beautiful, redheaded young spitfires who could easily cut most men down to size with a single look.

"But I don't *wish* to work out the details, Mr. Willoughby!" Dallas enunciated in a low, simmering tone. "I *wish* to find a way out of this ridiculous situation!"

The hapless solicitor blanched somewhat beneath the fiery, deep blue vehemence of her gaze, and it took him a moment to think of a response. When he finally offered it, he did so with a nervous chuckle, his eyes darting a silent plea for assistance toward Ross.

"I am still afraid, Miss Brown, that the only way I know of whereby you would be able to extricate yourself from the terms of the trusteeship would be, quite simply, to marry." He paused and chuckled uneasily again before adding with a misguided attempt at levity, "As a matter of fact, it would simplify things greatly if you were to wed Mr. Kincaid! That would solve a great many problems, wouldn't it?"

Dallas, staring at the man as though he had lost his mind, suddenly found herself at a complete loss for words. Ross, on the other hand, suffered no such lapse. He startled the other two occupants of the room by pronouncing in a calm, thoroughly self-possessed manner, "Yes, Mr. Willoughby, I believe it would."

"It would?" the older man echoed, turning to him with a look of wide-eyed bemusement.

"It would," he reconfirmed with a faint, slightly mocking smile and an irrepressible glimmer of amusement in his piercing green gaze.

"*What?*" Dallas finally recovered voice enough to exclaim. Stiffening with visible outrage, she glared at both men and seethed, "How dare you! I do not find your remarks in the least bit funny, and I do not appreciate this situation being treated with such a deplorable lack of . . . of sobriety!"

265

"I'm perfectly sober," Ross replied with maddening nonchalance. He was rewarded with a murderous glare from a pair of blazing sapphire eyes.

"I assure you, Miss Brown, that I meant no offense whatsoever!" Mr. Willoughby hastened to declare. He stuffed his papers back into his portfolio and hurriedly slipped the brown leather case under his arm again. Clutching his bowler in his hand, he gently cleared his throat, gave a quick adjustment to his wire-rimmed spectacles, and said, "I apologize for the fact that I am unable to remain and go over each of the papers with you and Mr. Kincaid, but urgent business awaits me back in Fort Worth. I shall, of course, be in touch, and you may expect a letter from me soon regarding the proposed liquidation of certain of the holdings left to you." Acting on a sudden impulse, he reached out and took one of her hands between both of his for a moment.

"My deepest sympathy on the death of your godfather, Miss Brown, and my sincere apology for creating the impression that I do not understand the dilemma created for you by the terms of his will. But George Proctor, as you well know, was a very kind man, a very shrewd judge of character, and I am convinced that his instructions will result in the most beneficial set of circumstances for everyone concerned."

"Thank you," murmured Dallas. Though not at all in agreement with his convictions, she nonetheless warmed to the genuine benevolence in his eyes. "I . . . I appreciate your coming all this way, Mr. Willoughby."

"Not at all," he responded with another smile. He turned and moved to shake Ross's hand once more.

"Mr. Kincaid, included among the papers I gave you is a document explaining your exact duties as trustee. If you have any questions, any questions at all, please do not hesitate to call upon me. Again, I apologize for the fact that I have been unable to spend more time—"

"I'm sure once Miss Brown and I put our heads together, we'll be able to figure everything out," Ross assured him, his lips twitching almost imperceptibly. He caught Dallas's eye and winked. She felt her face grow warm again, and she abruptly folded her arms across her chest and whirled away to stand near the piano.

Once he had seen Mr. Willoughby on his way, Ross returned to the parlor. Dallas watched in surprise—and more than a touch of misgiving—as he paused to close the seldom used doors. Her eyes were very round and her breathing very erratic when he leisurely swung his tall, hard-muscled frame about to face her.

"We need to talk, Dallas." All traces of amusement had vanished. His handsome face now appeared forbodingly solemn, while his eyes gleamed with a purposeful light that set off a warning signal in her brain.

"Wha—what is there to talk about?" She swallowed hard and hastily looked away. "I would say that Mr. Willoughby made things all too clear!" Bringing the neatly bound collection of papers in her hand slapping downward to the top of the piano, she smiled a bitter, humorless little smile and observed, "It seems I have no choice. First, there was my father, then George, and now you. Yes, indeed, how terribly fortunate that I— poor, weak, *helpless* female that I am—have always had a man to tell me what to do!"

267

Her eyes kindling anew, she balled her hands into fists and planted them on her hips. When she spoke again, it was in a tone that not only brimmed with accusation, but also something suspiciously akin to hurt.

"And *you,* Ross Kincaid, you had the nerve to stand there and make light of the whole situation!"

"I wasn't making light of it," he denied, slowly advancing on her. "I meant everything I said."

"Indeed?" she challenged sarcastically. Desperately trying to ignore the frantic racing of her pulses as he drew closer, she folded her arms tightly across her breasts and retreated a step to the side, farther behind the piano's protective bulk. "You . . . you scarcely said a word the whole time Mr. Willoughby was here!"

"I didn't have much of a chance," he countered with a brief smile of irony.

"Well, you certainly seized the chance when you had it, didn't you? Oh yes, it seems you and Mr. Willoughby share an appreciation of the absurd! Why, that remark about our getting married was—"

"Was on the level."

He stood towering above her now, making her feel small and breathless and very much afraid—but of *herself,* not him! She quickly turned and retreated another step, only to gasp audibly as her back encountered the immovable barrier of the wall.

"What . . . what do you mean?" she stammered.

Ross, his mouth curving into a soft, strangely compelling smile, raised his arms, negligently braced his two large hands on the papered wall on either side of Dallas's beautiful head, and answered, "I mean, wildcat, that Willoughby's suggestion makes a hell of a

268

lot of sense." His unfathomable gaze burned relentlessly down into her wide, bewildered one. "If you were to marry me, then you could gain control of your inheritance."

"Marry you?" Her mouth fell open, and she stared up at him in shocked disbelief.

"That's right. Marry me." There was nothing to indicate he was anything but dead serious.

This couldn't be happening! Dallas thought wildly. Was it possible, was it truly possible that Ross Kincaid was telling her that he loved her and wanted to marry her? She was startled at the way her heart leapt within her breast at the thought, at the way her head started spinning and her entire body began to tremble.

"Are you . . . are you serious?" she faltered weakly.

"I'm serious." He suddenly straightened and dropped his arms back to his sides, then turned away so that his broad back was to her. Dallas could not see the way his eyes darkened and smoldered all of a sudden, nor could she discern how carefully he was choosing each word. "At least we'd be out from under this damned trusteeship. Your money would be your own. And you wouldn't have to come running to me every time you needed something. After a while, whenever you wanted to, you could file for a divorce."

"I'm sorry, but I don't understand," she confessed with a benumbed frown of puzzlement. "Just exactly *what* are you proposing?"

"I guess you could call it a marriage of convenience." He gave a low, sardonic chuckle and turned to face her again. "I'm proposing an equal partnership between us, Miss Dallas Harmony Brown—or at least as equal as anything can be between two such independent, bullheaded people."

"You mean it wouldn't be a real marriage at all? You wouldn't expect me to—"

"I wouldn't expect a blasted thing."

Dallas could feel her heart sinking. Though she didn't know why, she suddenly felt like bursting into tears.

"I see," she murmured in an oddly hollow voice, her eyes falling before his. "And what would you be getting out of such an 'arrangement', Mr. Kincaid? Surely you're not willing to sacrifice your precious freedom without expecting at least something in return?"

"You said it yourself when Willoughby was here— I've got my own life to conduct. Hell, sweetheart, the last thing in the world I need or want is to play father to you and those sisters of yours!"

Dallas colored hotly and unfolded her arms. She forced herself to meet Ross's gaze again, only to feel a sharp, inexplicable twinge of pain when she looked at his faintly smiling features.

"Let me make sure I understand you correctly. You're suggesting that you and I enter into this marriage of convenience—a business arrangement, actually—for the express purpose of giving you your freedom and me my inheritance?"

"That pretty well covers it."

"And you are prepared to give me your word that our relationship would entail nothing more?"

"I give you my word it will never be anything other than what you want it to be."

"Forgive me, Mr. Kincaid, if I find it a bit difficult to swallow that!" She went charging forward to confront him, her eyes narrowing combatantly up into his while her breasts rose and fell rapidly beneath the white cotton of her blouse. "How can you possibly expect me to believe our marriage would be in name only when you have, at every available opportunity, forced your attentions on me? Why, the very first night you were here, as I recall, you threatened to . . . to continue *bedeviling* me until I—"

"Whatever else I may be," he broke in to declare with a deep frown, "I'm a man of my word. And if I tell you I'll not force you to share my bed, then by damn I'll not do it!"

"In other words, Mr. Kincaid, I'll just have to trust you—is that it?"

"What other choice do you have? Either you marry me, or you'll have to put up with things the way they are for the next four years. Quite frankly, my dear Miss Brown, if you're looking to get rid of me, then the best way to do it is to marry me."

"Well now, that makes a whole *hell* of a lot of sense!" she retorted with biting sarcasm.

"More than you know," murmured Ross. He lifted his hands to her shoulders and forced her to remain when she would have stormed away. "Damn it, woman, it's the best solution all the way around!"

"I can't believe I'm actually standing here discussing this with you!" breathed Dallas, her eyes wide and sparkling with mingled confusion and incredulity. "Why, this whole thing is . . . is positively ludicrous! I could never think of marrying you or any other man merely for the sake of money!"

"It's as good a reason as any. And it isn't as though you'll be tying yourself to someone you don't love for the rest of your life. You can call it quits anytime you want."

She stared speechlessly up at him. With only the

271

ghost of a smile, he released her and sauntered over to open the doors. He paused to look back at her briefly, and she could have sworn his eyes were filled with tender amusement.

"Think over what I said. I'll be back in an hour for your answer."

"*An hour?* How can I possibly make a decision like this in an hour's time?" She grew visibly suspicious again. "Why are you in such a hurry to—"

"I've got a well to bring in." With that, he left the room. Dallas heard him deliver his parting shot from the hallway. "Who knows, wildcat? Things may turn out better than you think."

She moved on unsteady legs to the sofa and sank gratefully down upon one of its chintz-covered cushions. Her mind was in utter chaos, and a number of conflicting emotions played across her face as she closed her eyes against a sudden onslaught of tears.

It was preposterous, of course, she told herself. There was no way she could even consider accepting his startling, contemptible proposal.

She tried not to think of how she had felt upon learning he wanted to marry her for purely selfish reasons—well, perhaps not purely selfish, since he had claimed to be making the offer for her sake as much as for his own. Still, it was far from flattering to have a man ask one to be his wife because he has a burning desire to get one out of his life!

A sob rose in her throat when she recalled how, only the night before, he had cradled her lovingly on his lap and kissed her with such an irresistible combination of tenderness and passion. She thought about all the other times he had kissed her, about that night in the barn when she had very nearly been swept away for the first time in her life—

"A marriage of convenience," she murmured aloud, dashing impatiently at her hot, bitter tears.

What other alternative do you have? that inner voice of hers challenged. It was all too true. The only other suitor for her "affections" was Justin Bishop, and there was no way she could ever be prevailed upon to marry him! No, she reflected with a sudden, involuntary shiver, even if there had been any doubt in her mind beforehand, what had happened between them at the church social was enough to convince her that she could never care for Justin again.

At least we'd be out from under this damned trusteeship, Ross's words rang in her ears. Other things he had said returned to haunt her as well . . . *if you're looking to get rid of me, then the best way to do it is to marry me . . . I wouldn't expect a blasted thing . . . you can call it quits anytime you want . . .*

"Damn you, Ross Kincaid! Damn you to hell!" she whispered brokenly. She leapt up from the sofa and whirled to take a stance at the window. Blinded by her tears, she stared unseeingly outward while her fingers clenched about the lace curtains.

So there it was. Either she took him up on his offer, or she would be forced to maintain contact with him for the next four years. She would have to yield to his decisions regarding all financial matters. She would have to ask his permission before she could withdraw so much as a single, blasted dime! It would be just like it was before with George, only this time she'd have to be dealing with Ross Kincaid.

Just supposing she *did* accept. From what Mr.

273

Willoughby had said, she would be very wealthy indeed when she gained control of everything George had left her. She would finally be independent, and she could give Cordi and Etta the kind of life she had always wanted them to have. The three of them could even travel. Yes, they could get away from Corsicana, at least for a while, and perhaps then Etta would forget about Sam and Cordi would meet some nice, suitable young man with a steady income and a desire to settle in one place—Corsicana, preferably.

Dear Lord, I must be losing my mind! she thought, aghast when she realized that she was actually leaning toward saying "yes" to Ross's proposal.

What could be the harm in it? she proceeded to ask herself the very next instant. It would be only temporary, wouldn't it? And there would be no need for a scandalous divorce, since an annulment would suffice. No one need ever know. It could remain a secret between her and her "husband." She would eventually tell Cordi and Etta the truth, of course, but not until after the inheritance was safely in her control and Ross Kincaid was safely out of her life for good.

Out of her life for good. There were those words again. Why, oh why didn't the thoughts that went with them give her any pleasure?

Heaving a ragged sigh, she withdrew her handkerchief and resolutely dried her tears. She smoothed her skirts and paused a moment to collect herself, then swept from the parlor to resume the chores Etta was supposed to have already completed.

She was later to reflect that the hour Ross Kincaid

had given her to make her decision was without a doubt the shortest one she had ever known . . . and the hour following *that* one was the longest.

Before she could change her mind, or her dress, she and Ross were sitting closely beside each other in the wagon and on their way to the church. Ruby Mae had fortunately chosen not to pry when Dallas had announced, as calmly as possible under the circumstances, that she and Mr. Kincaid were going into town to take care of an urgent matter of business.

It was a "matter of business" all right, Dallas thought guiltily as she realized that what she was about to do constituted an outright deception. She would be standing before a preacher and repeating vows that she had no intention of keeping . . .

"It will be over with before you know it," Ross assured her with a remarkably unconcerned grin. Giving a negligent flick of the reins, he urged the horse to an even brisker pace.

"I doubt that very seriously, Mr. Kincaid," she replied unhappily. She was feeling more uncertain of her decision with each passing moment, and the temptation to have Ross stop the wagon and take her right back home was so strong that her head ached with the strain of battling it.

"Don't you think it's about time you started calling me by my first name?"

"No, *Mr. Kincaid,* I do not!"

"Have it your way. But I'll be damned if you'll ever be 'Miss Brown' to me again."

Though it was on the tip of her tongue to tell him she would be more than happy to see him "damned," she compressed her lips into a thin, angry line and rewarded him with a speaking glare, then deliberately turned her attention on the passing countryside.

They arrived at the church shortly before noon. Dallas gathered up her skirts and scrambled down from the wagon before Ross could reach her side. Holding herself stiffly erect, she led the way down a stone-paved walk across the lawn from the church itself. Ross followed unhurriedly after her, his mouth curving into a crooked smile of appreciative humor for the situation and his eyes glowing as they fastened upon her gently swaying hips.

The parsonage, a charming little cottage set amidst sun-drenched flowers and surrounded by a white picket fence, had originally been built to house the church's first pastor—a "confirmed" bachelor who had run away with the mayor's daughter. It was now inhabited by the present minister, his wife, and their two young children, all of whom materialized in the open doorway in response to Dallas's loud, determined knock.

"Why, Miss Brown! What a pleasant surprise!" the pastor and his wife proclaimed in unison. They were an oddly matched but well-suited pair, the Reverend Kennicott a dark, thin man with rather pinched but kindly features and Mrs. Kennicott a plump, fair-complexioned pixie of a woman who reached no higher than her husband's shoulder.

"I'm sorry to disturb you and your family, Reverend," apologized Dallas, flushing uncomfortably beneath their smiling scrutiny, "but I . . . I must speak to you about something."

"Of course, of course!" Turning to his wife, he quickly bid her to take the children back to the kitchen,

276

which she did after bestowing another friendly smile upon their unexpected guest. He swung the door wide, dutifully preparing to welcome a member of his flock into the house in spite of the fact that he had just been sitting down to his dinner, when his gaze happened to fall upon the tall, raven-haired man who suddenly rounded a curve in the walk and came to stand behind Dallas. The pastor's eyes widened in mild surprise, and he looked expectantly back to the young woman he had known for several years.

"This is Mr. Kincaid, Reverend Kennicott," she informed him as the accursed, telltale rosiness stained her cheeks. "He and I . . . well, we would like you to perform a marriage ceremony."

"A marriage ceremony?" He blinked across at her in almost comical bafflement for a moment, then suddenly remembered his manners and extended a hand in greeting to Ross. "How do you do, Mr. Kincaid?"

"Reverend," Ross said with a nod and a brief smile. He took a possessive grip on Dallas's arm, and the minister did not fail to notice the odd manner in which she stiffened at the contact.

"Isn't this a bit sudden, Miss Brown?" he felt obliged to ask, sensing that something was not quite right. He didn't recall ever having seen this Mr. Kincaid before, and he told himself it wasn't at all like Dallas Brown to behave with such impulsiveness. From what he'd been able to glean about her character during their long acquaintanceship, she was a sensible, highly principled young woman—perhaps a trifle too headstrong at times, but still worthy of veneration.

"Yes, I'm afraid it is," she conceded with a troubled frown. "But we, Mr. Kincaid and I, that is . . . well, you see we—" She broke off in momentary confusion and searched for the right words. It occurred to her that she could always tell the truth. *Pardon me, Reverend Kennicott, but Mr. Kincaid and I want you to bind us in holy wedlock that won't be holy at all, in order that he may have his freedom and I may have my money.* Groaning inwardly, she was about to make another attempt to explain, when Ross took over for her.

"You know how these things are, Reverend. Sometimes it hits like a bolt of lightning." His green eyes twinkled irrepressibly while his mouth curved into a disarming, quizzical smile. Dallas blushed fierily, unaware that in doing so she only served to lend credence to Ross's words.

"Yes. I suppose it does," Reverend Kennicott murmured with a frown of ministerial disapproval. Too often did the flesh triumph over the spirit, he told himself. But, if Dallas Brown and this man were so determined to let their emotions overpower their better judgment, then at least he could put God's sanction on their impulsive union. "Please wait for me in the church," he instructed them solemnly. "I'll join you there in a moment. We'll need a witness, of course."

"Oh, but—is that absolutely necessary?" asked Dallas.

"Well," the pastor replied with another frown, "the marriage would be legal enough without one, but it *is* a practiced formality."

"We'd prefer not to practice it, if you don't mind," she insisted, then was relieved when, after eyeing her dubiously, he nodded his reluctant answer.

As soon as Dallas and Ross left the parsonage to set out across the lawn, she jerked her arm free of his grasp and stormed indignantly, "I can just imagine what he thought when you made that ridiculous statement about a 'bolt of lightning'! Why, you made it sound as though . . . as though you and I couldn't keep our hands off each other!"

"We haven't done a very good job of it so far," Ross observed with a low, unrepentant chuckle. Dallas's eyes flew to his face in sudden, visible alarm, and he smiled mockingly again before reassuring her, "Don't worry, wildcat. I gave you my word, didn't I?"

"So help me, Ross Kincaid," she ground out threateningly, "if I thought for one moment you meant to break your promise, I'd—"

"We made a deal, didn't we?" he reminded her with a faint, strangely enigmatic smile. "You stick to your end of the bargain, and I'll stick to mine." She eyed him warily for a number of seconds longer, before murmuring something he could not quite make out and continuing on her way.

Reaching the church, they stepped inside to the cool semidarkness of the sanctuary. There was no one else in sight. The carved wooden pews, the uncushioned hardness of which had caused many a youngster and grownup alike to squirm in discomfort, stretched in neat rows all the way down to the altar. Sunlight streamed softly through the stained glass windows set high in the whitewashed walls, up near the beamed ceiling that boasted of a brass chandelier, while an only slightly off-key pipe organ rested in one corner of the room beside the pulpit.

Dallas's trepidation increased tenfold. Again, she was tempted to flee, but she forced herself to stay. *You're not going to turn tail and run!* she rigorously commanded herself. *You've made your decision. Think of Cordi and Etta, think of how wonderful it will be to be truly independent for the first time in your life . . . think of anything but Ross Kincaid!*

She wisely chose not to venture another look at him before sweeping down the center aisle to the altar, where she stood with her hands clasped tightly together in an effort to still their trembling. She could hear his footsteps behind her as his boots connected softly with the polished wooden floor, and she was painfully aware of the moment when he came to stand at her side. Catching her breath, she was afraid he was going to say something to her, something that would make her take flight for sure, but it was Reverend Kennicott's voice that sounded in her ears.

"Shall we begin?"

The pastor strode across the platform, took his place on the opposite side of the altar, and made a swift adjustment to the fit of his loose black sack coat. Clutching a rather tattered Bible in one hand and a small, equally worn book of rituals in the other, he fixed both Dallas and Ross with a stern look, then asked, "Are you certain this is what you want?"

Dallas, swallowing a sudden lump in her throat, tried not to give any outward evidence of the guilt and panic rising within her. Reflecting that what she was doing was ethically and morally wrong, she nonetheless sought to rationalize it to herself with the comforting thought that her sin would be only a temporary one. *A temporary sin?* her mind's inner voice taunted.

"Yes, Reverend Kennicott," she answered, dismayed to hear the tremulous note that crept into her voice.

"Let's get on with it," decreed Ross.

"Very well. If you'll please join hands," the pastor reluctantly directed.

The ceremony itself passed in a blur for Dallas. She was scarcely aware of repeating the vows the minister spoke first, nor was she totally cognizant of that single, fateful moment in time when he pronounced that she and Ross were man and wife. There was, however, certainly nothing "otherworldly" about the kiss Ross pressed upon her unsuspecting lips immediately afterward.

She inhaled sharply when she felt his strong arms slipping about her, and she raised wide, startled eyes to his. He merely smiled softly down at her and claimed her mouth with his own before she could utter so much as a breathless protest.

The kiss was both gentle and demanding, and Dallas felt it clear down to her toes. Just when she found herself wishing that it would go on forever, it ended. Ross released her and smiled down at her again. She gaped up at him in dazed confusion, but her confusion quickly turned to indignation.

"Why, you—" she started to lash out, only to break off when he seized her arm in a firm, meaningful grip.

"Careful, *Mrs. Kincaid,*" he warned in a resonant undertone as he bent his head close to her ear. "You don't want the reverend here to think he made a mistake, do you?" She colored angrily and shot him a look that conveyed, quite successfully, her present feelings.

"I hope the two of you will be very happy together," the pastor declared earnestly. He shook the bridegroom's hand once more, accepting with a wordless nod of acknowledgment the money Ross gave him. His eyes widened in shocked disbelief when he glanced down at the coin and discovered that it was a twenty-dollar gold piece. "I . . . I'm afraid, Mr. Kincaid, that you have given me far too much!" Indeed, he told himself with just a touch of regret for having spoken up, it was more than he made in an entire month of Sundays!

"You earned it," Ross casually dismissed the other man's protest.

"Reverend Kennicott," Dallas suddenly remembered to appeal, "I would appreciate it if you would keep what happened here today solely in your confidence for the time being."

"You want me to keep your marriage to Mr. Kincaid a secret?" he responded with a puzzled frown. "I don't understand."

"Please, Reverend. It's only for a little while. I . . . well, I haven't had an opportunity to speak to my sisters, and I would prefer if no one else knew just yet."

"I'm sorry, Mis—Mrs. Kincaid, but the law compels me to enter your marriage into the record books at the courthouse. I will, of course, say nothing to anyone myself." He sighed and shook his head. "I doubt very seriously if it will remain a secret for long. It never ceases to amaze me, the way nearly everyone in the congregation learns about everything so quickly." His features relaxing into a smile at last, he took Dallas's hand and said, "Whatever the cause for your impulsiveness, I hope that you and your new husband will make a good life for yourselves. Remain true to each other in all things, and your blessings will be many."

Dallas felt sudden tears gathering in her eyes, and

she nodded mutely before following the pastor's instruction to sign the book of church records. She watched as Ross inscribed his name beside hers, then allowed him to lead her from the church. Emerging into the hot, glaring sunshine, they didn't speak as they returned to the wagon. It wasn't until after they were settled beside each other again that Ross finally broke the silence.

"I do believe," he drawled lazily as he took up the reins, "that it's customary at this point for the happy couple to go on a honeymoon." His green eyes were alive with devilment, and he smiled roguishly before adding, "Sorry, Mrs. Kincaid, but like I said before, I've got a well to bring in."

"Don't call me that!" she snapped, her own gaze full of fire. "And don't you dare, don't you *dare* say anything else about our being married! We agreed that no one else would know about this!"

"Did we?" He snapped the reins and the horse began pulling the wagon away from the church.

"Why, you . . . you know very well we did!" she sputtered.

"I didn't," he denied in an infuriatingly offhanded manner. Dallas gasped and rounded on him in blazing fury.

"You most certainly *did!* Damn you, Ross Kincaid, I—"

"Even if I had, what difference does it make now? You heard what the reverend said. It'll be all over town soon."

Dear Lord, he was right! she realized numbly. There was no way it could remain a secret once the pastor had made his entry in the books. The news would travel throughout the courthouse, then be carried forth to find its way into every blasted nook and cranny in Corsicana! Everyone would know that Miss Dallas Harmony Brown had married her driller—a man she had met only a week ago, the same man who had been living under her roof—and they would also know that she had done so in a hurried, furtive manner, without benefit of the fine, fancy wedding girls who had nothing to hide enjoyed. *How could I have been so stupid?*

Dallas sat back against the green leather seat with a look of utter dismay written on her face. Ross fought back the powerful urge to gather her in his arms. Tightening his hold upon the reins, he mused to himself with an inward smile of mingled tenderness and satisfaction that his darling bride was in for a hell of a lot more surprises . . .

XI

My wedding night.

Dallas's mouth curved into a bitter little smile at the thought. Releasing a long sigh into the silent darkness of her bedroom, she turned on her side and drew the covers up to where the high, buttoned collar of her white lawn nightgown ended in a fluff of lace just beneath her chin.

She closed her eyes and listened to the soft, steady sound of Ruby Mae's breathing. Her thoughts soon began to wander back and forth from the present to the recent past . . .

She was married now. She was married to Ross Kincaid, of all people. And her new husband was at that very moment outside in her backyard, drilling a well she no longer wanted and making her absolutely miserable in spite of—*or because of*—his absence!

It had been extremely trying for her to behave normally all afternoon. She still wondered if Ruby Mae had suspected anything, but at least she knew Cordi and Etta hadn't. Etta had been bubbling over with the excitement of her first day at work, and Cordi had been preoccupied with matters of her own heart. Erik Larsen, it seemed, had received a letter from Pennsylvania. Cordi had brought it home with her and delivered it to him personally, and she had been quite distressed at the thought that it might have come from some Yankee woman in love with *her* Erik . . .

Facing Ross again had been even more difficult than she could have imagined. Once they had returned from town, he had disappeared outside, and she had not seen him again until much later in the day, when she and her sisters had taken supper outside to the men.

Those penetrating green eyes of his had never left her. Thinking about how he had looked at her—as though he wanted to do a whole lot more than just look—still unnerved her. She had never felt exactly comfortable in his presence, but now, with the memory of the marriage ceremony constantly burning in her mind, things had worsened so much that she could scarcely come within fifty yards of him without feeling a certain inexplicable tingle course throughout her entire body!

How on earth was she ever going to be able to go through with this ridiculous little charade of theirs? And what was going to happen when their marriage was exposed for what it really was—a cold, mercenary, heartless arrangement that she had entered into of her own free will?

Heartless? She tried to ignore the sharp twinge of pain she experienced at the thought.

Sighing again, she mused that she would have to tell her sisters and Ruby Mae first thing in the morning. Even if no one else knew that her marriage to Ross

Kincaid was a false one, she had to tell *them* the truth. It would be impossible for her to practice that sort of deception with the people she loved, the people who knew her better than anyone. How could she go about feigning happiness as a newlywed when the truth of the matter was that her "husband" didn't love her at all?

Why does it hurt so much to think of that?

Justin Bishop's face suddenly swam before her eyes, and a slight tremor of fear shook her. It wasn't difficult to imagine what his reaction to the news of her marriage would be . . .

Next came the unbidden image of Lorena Appleton. Strangely enough, however, thinking of Lorena brought her pleasure for a change—she could envision quite clearly the way the simpering, spiteful young widow's face would look when she learned that the man she had been pursuing with such shameful audacity had up and married her most detested adversary . . .

Her thoughts, as always, came full circle back to Ross himself.

"Dear God, what have I done?" Dallas whispered into the softness of her pillow. "What have I done?"

Her new husband, meanwhile, was suffering no qualms whatsoever about *his* actions.

Standing outside beneath an endless, starlit sky, Ross smiled to himself and braced a hand against one of the roughhewn timbers of the derrick. Swede and Sam, in the midst of a well-deserved respite from their labors as well, enjoyed the last of the coffee Ruby Mae had brought them while they talked together near the flickering light of the lanterns. All three men were armed, their bodies casting long shadows on the ground as the sound of the steam engine filled the cool night air and the rotary drill bored ever deeper into the earth.

I give you my word that it will never be anything other than what you want it to be. Another soft, thoroughly unrepentant smile played about Ross's lips as he recalled how he had uttered those words to Dallas that morning in the parlor. He had meant them, all right, but not quite the way she had taken them . . .

If I tell you I'll not force you to share my bed, then by damn I'll not do it. His eyes filled with a vibrant glow at the memory of that particular statement, and his handsome features tightened as a near painful blaze of desire for the woman he loved shot through him. He had been speaking the truth then as well. But he had every intention of claiming his beautiful young bride— and soon. There was no doubt in his mind that he would be able to overcome any resistance when the time came; his confidence stemmed from the undeniable fact that neither he nor Dallas had been able to resist the remarkably powerful attraction that had been there from the very first. And it had been growing stronger ever since, he thought, battling another fierce wave of desire.

Whenever you wanted to, you could file for a divorce. That, too, had been no lie. Hell, she could file all she wanted to, he told himself with an inward chuckle. But it would never get any farther than that. She was his, and he'd never, *never* let her go.

He felt no guilt for having purposely misled her about the reasons for their marriage. He loved her more than he had ever believed possible, and he was firmly convinced that she cared for him as well. Musing wryly that she just needed a little more time and "persuasion" before she was ready to admit it, he vowed to woo her with a vengeance . . .

His mouth curved slightly upward again as he gave silent thanks to Howard Willoughby for that unintentionally brilliant remark about marriage solving all their problems. Although the idea had crossed his mind more than once—quite often, as a matter of fact, in the hours following the realization of his love for her—it had taken Willoughby's visit to give him the necessary means to accelerate his plans. George's will had indeed been a masterpiece.

How could you have known, you old devil? Ross silently asked his godfather, gazing heavenward as he gave a soft, mellow chuckle.

"Do you think we will bring her in before morning, Tex?" Erik suddenly called out, as usual having to raise his voice to be heard above the engine's chugging. Ross straightened and unhurriedly swung his tall, hard-muscled frame about to face his partner.

"I'd say just after sunup!" he predicted with a crooked grin.

"Isn't it about time we started getting those storage tanks ready?" Sam questioned eagerly. It seemed he had found his calling at last.

"No hurry!" Ross assured him. "Once we've made the strike, we'll have to cap the well and set up a flow line first!"

"Damn, but I wish Billy Joe could've been here!" Sam then offered with a rueful shake of his head. "I bet he hates like hell having to miss all the excitement!"

"I think he has had enough excitement to last for a good long while!" Erik pointed out, exchanging a silent look of understanding with Ross.

Thinking of Billy Joe immediately brought to mind the visit the sheriff had paid them that afternoon. The news he had brought was less than encouraging—the man sitting behind bars down at the jailhouse was still refusing to cooperate, and the one recovering from the amputation of his arm over at the doctor's house would be unable to make any kind of statement for at least another day or two.

The investigation would continue, of course, Sheriff Crow had assured them, but there were little to no leads in the case. Anyone at all might have set up the attack. Anyone at all . . .

The long night wore on.

Sometime before dawn, Dallas, tossing and turning restlessly in her bed, finally heaved a sigh of complete exasperation and slid from beneath the covers while Ruby Mae slept on. Flinging her wrapper about her shoulders, she eased open the door and slipped quietly from the room.

She stood alone in the darkened hallway, trying to decide what to do next. Though tempted to travel downstairs for something to eat—she had managed scarcely a bite at supper—she told herself with a frown that it was highly possible she would encounter Ross again if she ventured into the kitchen.

"That's the last thing I need right now!" she muttered. No, she mused with yet another sigh, she needed to go someplace where she could be alone with her thoughts, where she could try and make some sense out of the turbulence of her thoughts—not to mention her wildly chaotic emotions. There had to be *some* place in the entirety of that big old house where she could find uninterrupted solitude for a while.

The perfect place suddenly flashed into her mind. *The attic.* It was the same hideaway to which she had fled when something had upset her as a child. Cordi and Etta never went up there—they were afraid of mice—and it was the one place, aside from the bathroom, where she would not have to worry about being disturbed by any of the house's other inhabitants.

Dallas cast one last troubled look toward the staircase, then spun about and began padding barefoot down the hallway. Drawing her wrapper more closely about her, she crept past Cordi's room, which was occupied at the moment by both of her peacefully slumbering sisters . . . past Etta's room, which was where the gallant young Swede slept when he was not outside drilling . . . then past her late father's room up near the stairs leading to the attic, the room she had assigned to Ross Kincaid . . .

She drew to a sudden halt and turned back. Though she fought against it, a strong, mysterious impulse prompted her to reach out and take hold of the brass doorknob, turn it, and begin pushing the door cautiously open. Her heart pounded in her ears as the hinges creaked ever so softly.

She told herself that what she was doing was utterly childish and contemptible, that there was no excuse for . . . for *prying,* and yet she could not seem to dispossess herself of this powerful, inexplicable curiosity to see how different—if at all—the room appeared now that Ross's personal effects were in it. Heaven help her, but she wanted to see *his* things, wanted to touch the pillow where *his* head rested . . .

There was no harm in it, she breathlessly reasoned with herself, and it was perfectly safe, of course, since he was outside working on the rig and would probably remain there the whole night long. Besides, one quick look was all she wanted, and then she would be on her way again.

He would be leaving Corsicana for good soon. She might very well never see him again. Dear God, she thought as hot, bitter tears stung her eyes, was it so much to ask that she be allowed this one brief glimpse into the life of the man she had married?

The door was open now, and she tiptoed stealthily into the room. It was virtually pitch-black inside; the little bit of moonlight that would normally find its way in from around the edges of the single window shade was being denied that privilege by virtue of a woolen blanket, tucked in atop the curtain rod, which draped almost all the way to the floor.

Dallas frowned to herself in puzzlement, but she quietly closed the door behind her. Following the details of her memory, she made her way across the room to where she knew a lamp rested on a table beside the bed. When she reached the table, however, she discovered to her dismay that the lamp was not there.

It was then that she finally listened to her outraged conscience and decided to abandon the whole, ridiculous scheme. What on earth had she been thinking of to do such a thing? It wasn't like her to be so snoopy, *or* impulsive, and she felt a twinge of mingled shame and embarrassment for the way she had let herself be tempted into such disgraceful behavior.

"Damnation!" she swore aloud. There she was, in Ross Kincaid's room, sneaking about in the darkness as though she were some . . . some . . .

A warm hand suddenly came into contact with hers.

292

She started in very real fright and suffered a sharp intake of breath, her eyes flying wide with the awful realization that *someone was lying in the bed!*

Whirling about in panic, she started to run, only to gasp again when the hand shot out to close about her wrist.

"Dallas?" It was Ross's voice, slightly hoarse and groggy with sleep.

"Let me go!" she cried in breathless alarm, her face flaming in the darkness. She tugged frantically at her wrist, but he held fast.

"Come here," he commanded in a low, devastatingly vibrant tone of voice.

"No!" Though she tried to keep her own voice to a whisper, it rose shrilly. *Dear Lord, what he must think of her—creeping into his room in the middle of the night!* With an inward groan of awful, intensifying dismay, she brought her other hand up and tried to pry his fingers loose, while at the same time pulling at her wrist with all her might.

A soft cry broke from her lips as she was abruptly yanked forward. Before she quite knew what was happening, Ross seized her about the waist and tumbled her down onto the bed. Her legs flew up in the air as she went rolling over him to land on her back upon the feather mattress, where she lay shocked and struggling for breath while he brought his own body down upon hers.

Her arms were stretched above her head and imprisoned there by his hands. The wrapper she had so carelessly flung about her shoulders had fallen off, leaving her clad only in her delicate, white lawn nightgown, the lower portion of which was now

293

tangled immodestly up about the silken paleness of her thighs. She could feel the warm hardness of Ross's bare legs against her exposed limbs, and her eyes widened in shock when it occurred to her that the rest of him was no doubt every bit as unadorned. Her suspicions were confirmed when he shifted his weight a bit.

"Get—get off me!" she gasped out, acutely conscious of the fact that his virile, naked body was pressing intimately down upon her thinly covered softness. She writhed beneath him in a futile attempt to escape—but as she soon learned, her actions only made matters worse.

Ross groaned softly before his mouth came crashing down upon hers in a fierce, urgent kiss that quite literally took her breath away. His hands released her arms and traveled quickly downward to roam over her trembling curves with such bold impatience that she felt her head spinning riotously.

Totally unprepared for such an impassioned assault of her body as well as her senses, Dallas could at first only cling weakly to the man who was setting her blood afire. She moaned low in her throat when his hot, velvety tongue plunged within the moist cavern of her mouth and virtually ravished its sweetness.

Then, in one swift motion, he eased himself off her a bit, grasped the hem of her nightgown, and jerked it upward. She gasped to feel the rush of cool air upon her skin, but she could not bring herself to protest as he continued kissing her with such wild, intoxicating fervency. The next thing she knew, he was smoothing the nightgown up past her hips to her breasts, where his hands were tempted to linger but did not. He tore his lips from hers for one brief moment, tugged the thin, lacy garment over her head, and tossed it heedlessly to the floor below.

She was completely naked now—a fact of which she was made startlingly aware when he claimed her lips once more and covered her quivering woman's body with his warm, hard, undeniably masculine one. Gasping against his mouth as bare flesh met bare flesh, she felt a delicious tremor run the length of her spine. Her arms entwined about his neck, and she returned his kiss with a rapidly increasing ardency that both delighted and inflamed him.

Gone now was all trace of the cool, prim-and-proper Miss Brown she usually made such a concerted effort to be, and in her place was the passionate, hot-blooded woman Ross had always sensed lay just beneath the surface. Her smoldering desires, long dormant and long denied, had been waiting only to be awakened by the right man.

Heaven help her, but she could no longer fight against what had been happening to her ever since Ross Kincaid came into her life!

She could no longer deny that *this* man—the impossibly handsome, maddeningly arrogant, devilishly irresistible rogue who had stirred up her emotions like no one else had ever done—was the man she had been waiting for. Suddenly, nothing else mattered. The world receded, leaving only Ross and the rapturous spell of enchantment he was weaving so adroitly about her . . .

"Dallas! Dallas!" he whispered huskily as his mouth finally relinquished hers and began to travel hungrily across the flushed smoothness of her face. She moaned softly, then murmured his name as well while her hands, growing bolder, appreciatively explored the broad, hard-muscled planes of his back and shoulders.

She stifled a cry when his lips trailed a fiery path downward along the slender, graceful column of her neck, to the sensitive spot in the hollow of her white throat where her pulse beat so wildly . . . and downward still. His hands curled tightly about her hips while his mouth first pressed a warm, urgent spray of kisses over the rose-tipped fullness of her breasts, then fastened about one of the silken globes and drew the delicate peak greedily within. His tongue flicked erotically back and forth across the nipple as his lips suckled.

Shivering with passion, Dallas instinctively arched her back. Her fingers clutched at his bronzed, sinewy arms for support as he lovingly teased and taunted at her naked breast, then moved to do the same to the other one. His strong, questing fingers caressed her buttocks, kneading and stroking their delectable roundness, before one hand suddenly glided over the curve of her hip and down across her firm abdomen to the downy triangle of dark red curls nestled between her thighs.

A loud gasp broke from her lips when he touched her there. Her beautiful head tossed restlessly to and fro as her lustrous auburn tresses fanned out across the pillow, and she felt her thighs opening to him as his warm fingers paid tender, provocative tribute to her femininity. She felt her passions spiraling out of control, and she was afraid she would faint with the sheer pleasure of it all, with the fierce longing and near painful ecstasy he was creating within her . . .

Just when she was certain she could bear no more,

his lips left her breasts and his fingers ceased their exquisite torment of her moist, pink flesh. She blinked up at him in the darkness, dazedly wondering why he had stopped. The question in her mind was answered quickly—and most effectively—when he raised up a bit, positioned himself above her, and eased his throbbing hardness into the soft, honeyed passage of her womanhood.

Dallas could not prevent a breathless cry of pain from escaping her lips. There was a sudden fullness and burning between her legs, but it quickly gave way to other, eminently more pleasurable feelings as Ross began a slow rotation of his hips. She felt her tensed muscles relaxing, and she instinctively followed his movements, her hands curling upon his powerful shoulders while her breath mingled with his.

Her languor did not last for long. Soon, she was on fire again, and a deep, unfamiliar yearning rose within her. She clasped Ross tightly to her as his thrusts accelerated and grew more demanding. There was no time to wonder what was happening to her, no time to ask herself if it was normal to feel this terrible yet exquisite ache that seized her in its grip and threatened to make her faint dead away . . .

The splendid agony was soon over with. Dallas, only dimly aware of the moment when Ross caught his breath and tensed, felt a rush of warmth deep within her. Soaring higher and higher, she reached the very pinnacle of fulfillment seconds later, collapsing weakly back upon the bed as an amazing completeness she had never known filled her entire being.

Ross slowly rolled to his back upon the bed, his arms gathering her close against him in the darkness. He cradled her head upon his shoulder as her naked curves fitted perfectly to the length of his hard body. Her eyes swept closed. Listening to the rapid beating of his heart, she sighed and let herself bask in the warm afterglow of their lovemaking.

She was feeling much too contented at the moment to think about what she had just done. There would be time enough later for sorting things out, time enough later for deciding exactly how she was going to deal with everything . . .

"Ross?" she finally whispered, some minutes later.

There was no answer.

She lifted her head and peered up at him, but could not tell if he was looking at her or not. She decided to try again.

"Ross?"

When he offered no reply this time, she raised up on one elbow and lifted her other hand tentatively to his face. She traced a light finger across the rugged smoothness of his cheek, but still he did not respond. Frowning to herself, she leaned her head very close to his, only to hear the soft, steady breathing that usually signaled unconsciousness. Her suspicions were confirmed when she discovered that his eyes were closed.

He . . . he had actually fallen asleep!

She no sooner started to grow indignant when it occurred to her that this was probably the first time—or second, given the fact that she had awakened him when she had come into the room—that he had allowed himself the luxury of sleep in the past two days. He was no doubt exhausted, which would certainly explain why he had been unable to remain awake in spite of her presence in his bed.

Dallas sighed again and returned her head to its resting place upon his shoulder. She told herself that she would have to leave soon. Indeed, no matter how pleasant it was to lie there with her body pressed against the warmth of another human being's— especially *this* human being's—she must try and be reasonable about the situation. After all, Ruby Mae would notice her absence eventually and would become worried. Besides that, there was a good chance that Erik would come to wake Ross when it was time for him to return outside.

"Just a few more minutes," she murmured aloud. Releasing another sigh, she closed her eyes and snuggled closer to her new husband's lithe hardness . . .

She awoke with a start.

Her eyes flew wide and flickered rapidly over the unfamiliar, dimly lit surroundings. It took a moment for her sleep-drugged mind to be able to assimilate what it was being told, but when she finally did realize where she was, she sat bolt upright in the bed. The sheet fell away, leaving her to stare down at her naked breasts in shocked disbelief before yanking it upward again. Her widened gaze traveled hastily to the empty space in the bed beside her, and she crimsoned as the events of the night suddenly came flooding back.

Dear Lord, she had let Ross Kincaid make love to her! Not only that, but he probably believed she had come into his room wanting him to do just that!

Groaning aloud, she dropped her head into her hands, her long, tangled locks falling like a shimmering red curtain about her. She was so distressed at the

299

realization of what she had done, that she did not immediately notice the fact that the sun's rays were already warming the blanket draped across the window and creating a soft golden glow that bathed the room in a sort of eerie, subdued light.

"Oh my gosh—Ruby Mae!" she gasped as a sudden thought struck her. Her eyes finally cut to the window, and the color drained from her face. She sprang from the bed and hurried to jerk the blanket downward, only to discover that it was indeed already morning. About to turn away again, she idly noted that the shade had apparently become stuck, for the fringed edge of it rested crookedly across the glass a few inches from the top. *So that was why he—*

She ended the thought with a well-chosen curse and whirled to snatch up her nightgown and wrapper from where they rested together in a discarded heap on the floor. Blushing fierily once more as she recalled, with shocking clarity, the way Ross had stormed her maidenly defenses (heaven help her, but what defense *could* she have had in the face of such a masterful, wildly inflaming passion?), she looked back to the bed. She drew in her breath as her eyes fell upon the small, telltale bloodstain in the center of the white cotton sheet.

Another groan of utter dismay escaped her lips. Trembling with the force of the volatile, conflicting emotions that warred together in her breast, she somehow managed to slip the nightgown over her head, draw on her wrapper and yank the belt so tight it hurt, and make her way to the door. She did her best not to wonder how long Ross had been absent from the bed—*nor* to think about the possibility that Erik might

300

have come inside the room to rouse him.

Easing the door open, she leaned cautiously outward, her gaze scanning the hallway for any sign of life. Satisfied that there was no one else about, she closed the door behind her and scurried quickly down the narrow corridor to her room. It came as no real surprise to find that Ruby Mae had already risen, but she nonetheless frowned to herself in consternation. How on earth was she going to explain away her disappearance?

Wasting little time in gathering up clean white undergarments, black cotton stockings, a red gingham shirtwaist, and her brown leather high-top boots, she flew to the bathroom and locked herself inside.

She quickly bathed and dressed—all the while endeavoring, none too successfully, to keep her traitorous body from remembering how it had been thoroughly kissed, stroked, and caressed by one Rossiter Maverick Kincaid—then twisted her hair into a tight chignon and pinned it low on her neck. Pausing to draw a deep, steadying breath, she flung open the door and moved with a furiously pounding heart down the stairs.

"Why, there you are, honey!" Ruby Mae greeted her with a broad smile when Dallas bravely entered the kitchen moments later. "I was startin' to get a mite worried about you. Where'd you disappear to this hour of the mornin'?"

"I couldn't sleep, so I . . . I went for a walk." Consoling herself with the thought that it wasn't a complete lie, she quickly averted her face and crossed to the stove, where she took up the new coffeepot to pour herself a cup of the desperately needed brew. Ruby

Mae had apparently been awake only a short time, she mused, since the coffee was steaming hot.

"Well now, what are the two of *you* doin' up so bright and early?" Dallas suddenly heard the older woman query in a voice brimming with amusement. She turned to see Cordi and Etta shuffling wearily into the room, still clad in their nightclothes.

"Cordi kept me awake half the night with her fidgeting," complained Etta with a reproachful scowl at her sandy-haired sister. "I finally said to heck with it and got up!"

"Well, I didn't do it on purpose, you know!" Cordi shot back indignantly. She threw herself into a chair beside Ruby Mae and heaved a long, slightly ragged sigh. Her blue-green eyes were visibly troubled. "It's just that I couldn't get . . . certain things out of my mind."

"What she means to say is that she's mooning over Erik Larsen!" Etta was ungracious enough to remark.

"I'm not 'mooning' over him at all!" Cordi fixed the seventeen-year-old with a quelling glare, then looked to the stout, maternal woman who reached over and patted her hand in a sympathetic manner.

"I hate to say it, Cordi, honey, but it wouldn't do to go settin' your hopes too high where Mr. Larsen's concerned," Ruby Mae advised gently. "From what I've seen of these drillers, they ain't exactly what you'd call the marryin' kind."

Across the room, Dallas colored and very nearly choked on the sip of coffee she had just taken. Hastily bringing her hand upward as some of the hot liquid spilled, she whirled about to the sink and lowered the dripping cup into it. She stood coughing in an effort to regain her breath, her tear-filled eyes moving with a will of their own to peer through the window. Before her searching gaze could light upon Ross, however, Cordi demanded her attention by declaring, "Erik isn't like the other drillers, and you may as well know that I . . . well, I have every intention of becoming his wife!"

"Cordelia Brown, you'll do no such thing!" protested Dallas, rounding on her with a sternly admonishing frown. *Good heavens, it was bad enough that Etta was trying so hard to get herself betrothed to the wrong man—now here was Cordi, blithely announcing that she was planning to do the same!* "You are very much mistaken if you think I'm going to stand by and watch while you get your heart broken by—"

"Don't you understand?" the other woman cried as she rose abruptly to her feet. Tears swam in her eyes, and there was a look of genuine desolation on her attractive young countenance when she proclaimed, "I love Erik Larsen! I don't know how I shall bear it if he goes away! Can't any of you understand what it means to be in love?"

A heavy silence hung in the room. Dallas felt a dull flush rising to her face again, and her eyes fell uncomfortably before her sister's. Ruby Mae and Etta exchanged quick, equally guilty looks. Finally, Etta sighed and murmured, "I'm sorry, Cordi. I *do* know how you feel."

"So do I," averred Ruby Mae. A faint smile tugged at her lips when she added, "It may have been awhile, but there was a time when I felt like I'd shrivel up and die if a certain beau of mine didn't marry me. He didn't. And I didn't. But all the same, nothin' hurts like bein' in love."

Cordi, still fighting back tears, sank down into the chair again and despondently folded her arms together atop the linen-covered table. Dallas hastened forward to slip an arm about her shoulders.

"I . . . I didn't realize things had become that serious between the two of you, Cordi," she confessed, gazing solemnly down at the slender young woman who had always been very sensitive and impressionable. "Has Mr. Larsen asked you to marry him?" She held her breath in anticipation, then expelled it softly when the answer came.

"No," admitted Cordi, "but I'm hoping that he will soon. I know he cares for me, I know he does! The other night, at the social, he never left my side. And at one point during our conversation, he actually introduced the subject of marriage!"

"What did he say?"

"Well," she revealed with obvious reluctance, "he said that in Sweden, a man doesn't . . . well, he doesn't ask a girl to marry him until he has a home of his own to take her to."

"Oh," Etta murmured from across the table. "Then I suppose that really does settle the matter, doesn't it?"

"It doesn't settle anything at all!" Cordi vehemently denied, her turquoise eyes flashing. "I don't care anything about having a home—I only care about having Erik!"

"Yes, I know," sighed Dallas. Though she silently applauded the young Swede's character and common sense, she remained firm in her opinion that he was not the right sort of husband for her beloved sister. "But he is, after all, a driller. What kind of life would it be, gallivanting all over the countryside with him, living in

304

cheap hotels and boardinghouses in one wild boom-town after another? No, Cordi, that isn't what I want for you."

"But it's what *I* want! Why, nothing else would matter as long as the two of us were together!"

Dallas felt her temper flaring. She was close to exhaustion because of lack of sleep, her nerves were already strained to the limit as a result of her "encounter" with the husband no one knew about yet, and she was plagued by an embarrassing soreness in places she hadn't even known existed before now!

"Why the devil is it that *everyone* in this family," she demanded in a burst of emotion as the color rode high on her cheeks and her brilliant sapphire gaze snapped fierily, "has suddenly taken it into their heads to fall in love with men who do *not* love them back and who do *not* wish to commit to anything more than a brief, momentary . . . *dalliance?*"

While Ruby Mae stared up at her young friend in speechless astonishment, Cordi and Etta both leapt to their feet with the light of battle in their eyes.

"How dare you!" exclaimed Cordi. "What a perfectly disgusting thing to say!"

"Sam does *so* love me back!" stormed Etta. "And what's more, he—"

She was not given an opportunity to finish, for at that moment all four occupants in the kitchen heard a loud whoop of exultation from young Sam Houston Rawlins in the backyard. The shout was immediately followed by an unmistakable "She's going to blow, Tex!" from Erik and a "Douse the fire, damn it!" from Ross.

"What on earth—" breathed Dallas. She spun about

305

and rushed to the back door, wrenched it open, then flew outside with the others close on her heels.

They came to an abrupt halt in the yard just beyond the steps when they heard a loud rumble and felt a slight, foreboding tremor of the earth. In the next instant, their wide, startled eyes were met with the sight of an ever-increasing column of Texas crude gushing forcefully upward from the derrick to reach as high as the top of the eighty-foot wooden tower.

The wind, a strong southwesterly blow that was common in the heat of Corsicana summers, whipped the spray of crude in the direction of the barn. The smelly, thick black oil rained downward, falling on not only the derrick and the men scrambling furiously about beneath its timbers, but also the surrounding yard, the rear portion of the house, and the four women who gazed upon the exciting, strangely spellbinding scene before them in breathless silence.

"Let's get her capped!" Ross shouted to Erik above the roar. Anxious to tame the gusher, he and his partner hurried to get the wellhead in place. While he knew that to some, particularly oil promoters who delighted in such an obvious, dramatic show of success, it looked impressive to allow the blow to continue for quite some time, he himself considered such tactics both stupid and wasteful.

Sam, meanwhile, who had already been forewarned about the dangers of letting the fire burn once the strike came—if anyone in town had ever needed proof as to the flammability of crude, there was a perfect example to be found in what had happened four years ago with that first well down by the tracks of the Cotton Belt Railroad—wasted little time in following Ross's orders to douse the flames with the several buckets of water resting beside the boiler for just such a purpose. Once that deed was accomplished, he raced back to the derrick to help the other men.

"Lord have mercy!" Ruby Mae finally exclaimed as she shook her head in wonderment and brought a hand up to try and shield her face from the downpour of oil. "We must be plumb loco to be standin' out here in this!"

"I don't care!" Etta retorted with a laugh of youthful exuberance while she briefly examined the slick black substance coating her own hands and clothing. "Isn't it wonderful? Why, just look at Sam over there! I've never seen him work so hard in his life!"

Standing beside Etta, Cordi said nothing. She seemed scarcely aware of the fact that she was turning darker by the second. Her initial happiness at the strike had quickly given way to renewed despair at the realization that Erik Larsen would now be leaving town.

Dallas, flanked by Ruby Mae on one side and Etta on the other, was silent and preoccupied as well, her troubled thoughts remarkably similar to Cordi's—except that they were centered on the raven-haired driller whose handsome face and tall, muscular frame were at that moment nearly as black as his hair.

There will be no reason for him to stay any longer, she reflected, surprised at the way her spirits abruptly plummeted. *I may very well never see him again. Unless, of course, what happened last night changes everything . . .*

But why should it? she then asked herself angrily. He had made it quite clear that he didn't want a wife, that he had only married her to free the two of them from a

307

difficult situation. He didn't love her. Simply because they had made love didn't mean he cared for her. No, she thought as her heart twisted painfully and her face flamed beneath the coating of oil, it didn't mean anything, other than the fact that he could finally add her to his list of conquests . . .

Why should that thought distress her so much? After all, it wasn't as if they had actually fallen in love with each other—was it? Their marriage would never be anything more than a sham—would it?

Sometimes it hits like a bolt of lightning. Ross's words, spoken half in jest to Reverend Kennicott the day before, rang in her ears once more . . .

"Stand back!" Ross suddenly thundered at the women.

Dallas's eyes flew up to see that he and the others were now attempting to set the cap in place. Their actions caused the powerful surge of oil to begin shooting outward and spraying wildly over everything within twenty feet.

Ruby Mae grabbed Dallas's arm and pulled her hastily back around the side of the house. Etta did the same with Cordi, and the four of them stood there, covered with oil and clinging to one another, while the men fought to bring the well under control.

Finally, the cap was set. Ross, Erik, and Sam, breathing heavily from their exertions, climbed slowly down from the platform to take a well-deserved break before assembling the flow line—the pipe through which the crude would travel to collect in the wooden storage tank a short distance from the derrick—and cleaning up the oil.

Dallas moved dazedly along with her sisters and

Ruby Mae as they returned to the backyard. Etta immediately hurried over to speak with Sam, while Cordi visibly hesitated before crossing the petroleum-soaked ground to where Erik stood between Sam and Ross, surveying the mess.

Unable to prevent her gaze from seeking out Ross's, Dallas was startled to see the way he was grinning at her as she approached the derrick. Even more startling, however, were the words he uttered to her in clear, deep-timbred tones that could easily be heard by everyone present.

"Well, Mrs. Kincaid, your well's in."

XII

"Mrs. Kincaid?" Cordi was the first to echo, though every other member of the group—with the noticeable exception of Erik—turned upon Dallas with a look of stunned disbelief.

"Dallas? Why did he call you that?" Etta's youthful brow creased into a frown as her golden gaze shifted rapidly from her oldest sister, to Ross, and back again.

Dallas crimsoned beneath the thin layer of oil and shot Ross a murderous glare. Opening her mouth to offer an explanation, she was dismayed to find the necessary words eluding her. She could only stare back at her sisters in helpless confusion while battling the temptation to do her "husband" bodily harm.

"Are you two really married?" Sam piped up, his face splitting into a boyish grin.

"Well, my love," Ross drawled to Dallas, "would you like to tell them—or would you prefer that I be the one to do it?" His eyes gleamed with irrepressible humor, and he flashed her a slow, rakishly challenging smile that did little to help the near explosive state of

311

her temper.

"Tell us *what,* for heaven's sakes?" Etta demanded in growing impatience.

"Mr. Kincaid and I . . . were married yesterday," Dallas reluctantly disclosed. She was embarrassingly conscious of everyone's eyes upon her, and she silently cursed Ross Kincaid for forcing her into the announcement. She had wanted to tell her sisters in her own way, when the time was right, but *he,* damn him, she thought as she sliced him a particularly dagger-filled look, had robbed her of that privilege, just as he had robbed her of—no, he hadn't robbed her of *that,* she was honest enough to admit, her cheeks burning at the memory of their lovemaking.

"Married?" gasped Cordi and Etta in unison.

"Married?" seconded Ruby Mae. Her black-smudged brow cleared in the next instant as her mouth curved into a broad, delighted smile. "Well, bust my buttons! Congratulations, honey!" she told Dallas as she caught the younger woman up in a warmly affectionate hug.

"No! Wait! It . . . it isn't what you think!" Dallas protested breathlessly. She drew away and hastened to set the facts straight. "We didn't get married for the reasons people usually get married!"

"We didn't?" Ross quipped sardonically. He merely smiled when she favored him with another indication of her fierce displeasure.

"No, we did *not!*" she seethed, trying desperately not to think about what they had done together just a few hours earlier.

"Then what were your reasons for getting married?" Cordi sharply demanded. Recalling what had been said

312

in the kitchen about marriage and drillers, she eyed her auburn-haired sister resentfully.

"It was a business arrangement!" insisted Dallas, a defensive expression crossing her beautiful yet presently oil-coated features. She cast a quick look in turn at Sam and Erik, but she dared not look at Ross again. Taking a deep breath, she told her sisters in a quiet, deliberate manner, "I'll be more than happy to explain it to you later. For now, however, I suggest we go inside and see what we can do about removing this blasted oil!"

"Come on, girls," said Ruby Mae. She took both Cordi and Etta by the arm, then paused to smile at the men. "I'm glad you made a strike. It's an all-fired miracle you did it, what with everythin' you ran up against!"

"I'll talk to you later, Sam!" Etta called to her beloved as she was led away by the large, sturdily built woman. Cordi felt tears welling up in her eyes when Erik smiled at her and nodded a good-bye.

"And I will talk to *you* later as well!" Dallas ground out to Ross, her eyes shooting their brilliant sapphire sparks. She wheeled about and went trudging furiously back across the slick backyard to the house.

Once the four women had disappeared inside, the three men exchanged looks of mingled amusement and satisfaction, then returned to their work. Sam was assigned to start sorting pipe, while Erik and Ross stepped back up to the platform to make another inspection of the wellhead.

"I do not mean to pry, Tex," the young Swede told Ross in a low voice that would not reach Sam's ears, "but I was under the impression that you and Miss

Brown . . . that is, I naturally believed the two of you were—" He broke off in obvious embarrassment. It had been no small shock for him when, upon entering Ross's room to awaken his partner at the appointed hour early that morning, he had discovered the presence of another body in the bed—and a woman's body, at that! He gave silent thanks for the fact that he had not actually seen anything of Dallas's "person"; with the little bit of light spilling into the room from the hallway, he had scarcely been able to make out the outline of her curvaceous form beneath the covers . . .

"We were and are," Ross assured him with an endearingly crooked grin, his green eyes alight with merriment and his heart soaring with the certainty of a lifetime spent sharing a bed with the spirited, passionate redhead he loved.

"I was very happy when you told me of your marriage. Miss Brown is a fine, beautiful woman," Erik earnestly declared. "But to be honest, my friend, it seems that there is a serious misunderstanding between you."

"Not for long" was all Ross said in response, though he smiled again and clapped the other man companionably on the back.

Once again, Dallas was relieved to get away from the house.

She, her sisters, and Ruby Mae had spent the entire morning scrubbing the oil first from themselves, then from the bathtub and floors, and lastly from the exterior of the house. It had been thoroughly unpleasant, tedious work, and it was still not yet completed. Cordi had been only too happy to hurry off to her job at the telephone office, and now it was Etta's turn to escape. Dallas, remembering that she had planned to pay a visit to the bank that day, offered to drive her youngest sister to the bakery.

The sun blazed almost directly overhead in the cloud-dotted sky when they finally set off in the wagon. Etta, who had already declared that her skin felt raw from the scouring she had subjected it to, heaved a sigh and squirmed a bit uncomfortably on the green leather seat.

"I thought I'd never get all that horrible stuff out of my hair!" she complained.

"Keep in mind, Etta, that all that 'horrible stuff' will probably make us a great deal of money," Dallas remarked dryly.

"Yes, and we all know how fond you are of money, don't we?"

"And what exactly do you mean by *that?"*

"You married Mr. Kincaid because of it, didn't you? I still can't believe my own sister would do such a thing!"

"I thought you understood," Dallas replied coolly, though she was in truth stung by Etta's condemnation. "As I explained to you earlier, Mr. Kincaid and I entered into this agreement—"

"That's precisely what I'm talking about! Marriage isn't supposed to be something you treat like a business transaction!" Etta loftily declared. "I don't care what you and Mr. Kincaid agreed to, it was wrong of you to marry each other for anything but love!" She settled back upon the seat in a stiffly indignant manner, prompting Dallas to sigh in exasperation and tighten her grip on the reins.

"Perhaps someday, when you're older, you'll be able to understand."

"If you think another four years of age are going to make me like *you,* then you are sadly mistaken!"

Dallas's eyes kindled with reproach, but she bit back the angry retort she was tempted to offer her sister. A tension-filled silence fell between them after that. Rolling swiftly past green, fertile landscape punctuated by the tall wooden towers that were a constant reminder of Corsicana's newfound prosperity, they soon arrived in the midst of the city's bustling commercial district.

Dallas drew the wagon to a halt in front of the First National Bank—known as "The Old Reliable" among the permanent residents—and turned to a still frowning Etta with a conciliatory smile.

"Would you like to come inside with me?"

"No, thank you."

"Oh, Etta, there's no reason for you to behave this way, and there's no reason for the two of us to be quarreling!"

"I'm not behaving *any* way!" the young strawberry blonde snapped, her golden eyes flashing anew. "I simply do not wish to go inside with you!"

"Very well then," murmured Dallas as she secured the reins and climbed down from the wagon. "But you're going to get a trifle warm while you're sitting out here in the hot sun—sulking." She disregarded the icy glare leveled at her, gathered up her blue cotton skirts, and sailed into the bank.

Emerging again nearly a quarter of an hour later, she suppressed a smile when she took note of the way Etta was vigorously fanning her hot, flushed face with a folded section of newspaper. She was preparing to rejoin her stubborn, temperamental sister in the wagon when a hand suddenly closed painfully about her arm and jerked her about.

"Is it true?" snarled Justin, his fury-twisted features mere inches from her own visibly alarmed ones.

"Justin! Let—let go of me!" She tried to pull free, then gasped when his punishing fingers merely tightened upon her soft flesh.

"Is it true? Are you married to Kincaid?" His dark eyes blazed menacingly down into hers.

"Yes! Yes, it's true, but—"

"Damn you! You've probably been that bastard's whore all along, haven't you?"

"Justin Bishop, you take your hands off her!" cried Etta, recovering from her own shock and jumping to her sister's defense. "Do as I say, or I swear I'll scream and bring the whole town running!"

Dallas gasped when she was abruptly released. She staggered back against the wagon, her eyes wide and frightened as she continued to gaze speechlessly up at the fair-haired man before her. Numbly realizing that he had already heard the news of her marriage, she told herself that his reaction had apparently been every bit as violent as she had feared.

"Kincaid may have married you, but he'll not keep you!" he vowed, his low tone one of deadly calm. His words struck a sudden, terrible dread in Dallas's heart.

"What do you mean?" she demanded breathessly as the color drained from her face. "Oh, Justin, please don't—"

"You'll regret this, damn you!" he ground out. "I'll

317

make you pay! I'll make you all pay!"

He shot her one last savage, vengeful look, then spun about and was gone. Dallas clutched weakly at the side of the wagon for support, her heart pounding furiously and her whole body trembling.

"Why, he—he *threatened* you!" Etta gasped in shocked disbelief.

"I know," murmured Dallas. Finally regaining her composure, she climbed into the wagon and took up the reins with hands that were not quite steady. "Please, Etta," she said, suddenly turning to the young woman beside her with a look of heartfelt appeal, "I don't want anyone else to know about what just happened!"

"But he said such horrible things to you, and—"

"It will only make matters worse if you tell anyone! Now please, Etta, give me your word that you'll keep quiet about this!" She placed an anxious hand upon the girl's arm, and Etta frowned to see the tears sparkling in her older sister's eyes.

"Why did he say those things, Dallas?" she asked in genuine concern. "What's been going on between the two of you?"

"I . . . I can't explain it to you now." She sat back and lifted the reins again. "Please, just believe me when I say it's for the best that no one else know."

"Well, I don't see how! Besides, I think Mr. Kincaid should hear about what happened. After all, you *are* his wife, even if—"

"*No!*" Dallas practically screamed. Her face reddened, and she hastily lowered her voice before insisting, "This is really none of Mr. Kincaid's affair! Now please, Etta, promise me you won't tell anyone!"

Etta, though still far from convinced about the wisdom of such silence, nonetheless gave a reluctant nod of agreement. Dallas breathed an audible sigh of relief. She was glad for the fact that Etta did not press a discussion of the matter as they continued on their way down the crowded main street. Once she had dropped her sister off in front of the bakery, she headed the wagon back to the house on the outskirts of the city.

Justin's words returned to haunt her several times throughout the day, but she determinedly pushed them to the back of her mind each time and went on with her work. By the time twilight began to steal slowly over the countryside, she and Ruby Mae had removed the last vestiges of oil from the house.

She made no attempt to speak to Ross. Purposely avoiding his eyes throughout the day, she had found her emotions alternating between indignation and embarrassment—and a certain, warm pleasure—as her thoughts alternated between the memory of how he had so arrogantly forced her into an announcement of their marriage, and the memory of how he had so passionately claimed possession of her as his bride . . .

His temporary bride, she amended in silence, then felt her heart grow inexplicably heavy once more.

That evening's meal, the first shared by all of the house's inhabitants—plus Sam—in nearly a week, yielded Dallas yet another surprise from Ross. It was during the main course of baked chicken and rice that he calmly announced his intention to drill another oil well on her property.

"Another *what?*" she demanded, her eyes growing enormous within the delicate oval of her face as they flew to the man seated at the opposite end of the table.

Ross smiled mockingly back at her.

"What's the matter, Mrs. Kincaid? Don't you like the idea of being independently wealthy?"

"I thought I already was—or at least I *will* be, once you have contacted Mr. Willoughby!" she retorted with a meaningful narrowing of her eyes. "But even if that were not the cause, I still wouldn't want another well drilled!"

"Why not?" Cordi was quick to ask. "I think it's a splendid idea!" She cast a warm smile at Erik, who responded in kind.

"Far from it!" Dallas adamantly dissented. "Why, look at all the misfortune that *this* well brought down upon us! No, thank you very much, but I would rather not be dynamited or arrested or . . . or shot at ever again!"

"You weren't the one arrested," Etta obligingly reminded her. She was rewarded for her efforts with a glare of sisterly reproval.

"I bet there won't be any more trouble now that we've shown everyone we're not going to knuckle under!" Sam opined with an emphatic nod.

"Well, I have to say one thing," Ruby Mae interjected at this point, her brown eyes twinkling at both Ross and Erik. "Life has sure picked up around here since you two pulled into town!"

"Thank you, Miss Hatfield," Ross told her with a soft chuckle. His irrepressibly roguish gaze traveled back to Dallas. "The well we brought in today looks to be better than most of the others in the field. It goes against my grain to let all that potential remain untapped."

320

"Well it certainly won't go against mine!" she shot back.

"I don't know what you're getting so upset about," remarked Etta. "It isn't as though this is going to go on forever!"

Maybe not, but it's beginning to seem like it! Dallas silently retorted. She was indeed quite disturbed at the prospect of Ross Kincaid living under her roof for another week. Though she hadn't been at all certain about her feelings regarding his departure from Corsicana, she dreaded the thought of being thrown into contact with him for so much as another day!

"I do not wish to discuss this any further, Mr. Kincaid," she told Ross in a deceptively self-collected manner. "I simply will not allow another well to be drilled on my property!"

"Don't you think you're being more than a little unreasonable about this?" challenged Cordi. "You've always told us to consider something quite carefully before making a decision. Why then are you refusing to do the same?"

"I think she's still upset over what Justin Bishop told her—" Etta started to theorize, only to break off guiltily as Dallas rounded on her with eyes ablaze.

"Henrietta Brown, you promised!"

"Promised what?" Cordi didn't mind probing.

"I may as well tell them the rest!" Etta said to her oldest sister with a defensive toss of her reddish-blond curls. Dallas's hand shot out to close upon the girl's arm.

"Don't you dare!" she warned in a low, simmering tone. "You gave me your—"

"I know I did, but it isn't right," cried Etta, jerking her arm free. "I know I promised, but it isn't right that my own sister gets accosted on the street and nothing is done about it!" Her bright, defiant gaze encompassed everyone at the table as she disclosed in an excited rush, "Justin Bishop grabbed Dallas when she came out of the bank today, and he threatened her! I was sitting right there in the wagon, and I heard him insult her and say all sorts of terrible things to her, and then he told her that she was going to regret marrying Mr. Kincaid and that he was going to make her pay!"

"Lord have mercy!" Ruby Mae whispered in horror.

"Oh, Dallas!" breathed Cordi.

Dallas sat with eyes downcast, her cheeks flaming and her lips compressed into a tight, thin line. She was furious with Etta, and she was afraid to look at Ross.

"Why that no-account son of a—" Sam ground out, breaking off when he saw that Ross was slowly drawing his tall frame upward. "Bishop hangs out down at the Double Sixes!" he eagerly supplied, jumping to his feet as well. His excited gaze moved to Swede, who also stood and faced Ross with a somber, expectant look.

"Wha—what are you doing? Where are you going?" Dallas breathlessly demanded, rising on unsteady legs as she finally raised her eyes to Ross's face. She caught her breath at the look of grim purposefulness on his handsome face. His green eyes glowed with a dangerous light, and she felt her throat constrict in growing dread.

"It might be better if you was to cool off and wait awhile," Ruby Mae quietly offered Ross. "If the three of you go on down there to that saloon, you're liable to find yourselves outnumbered."

322

"You mean you—you're planning to go *fight?*" Cordi stammered, her eyes flying to Erik in dawning dismay. He said nothing in response, merely staring down at her and looking every bit as grim as his partner.

"Of course they are, you idiot!" Etta impatiently established.

"No they're not!" Dallas contended in a voice charged with emotion. Her flashing, deep blue eyes snapped back to Ross as she demanded, "You must stop this nonsense at once! This is none of your concern, Ross Kincaid, and I'll not have you tearing off to avenge my 'honor' against nothing more than a few angry words spoken by an old—"

"You're my wife," he stated in a low, level tone that made it clear he would brook no further interference.

She knew it was useless to argue. She'd seen it too many times before—a bullheaded, thoroughly enraged Texas male going off to beat the devil out of someone who had dared to insult his woman. Only, she wasn't Ross Kincaid's woman! She was his wife all right, but not truly *his!*

Oh, but you are, that dreaded inner voice of hers took perverse pleasure in attesting. *After last night, you are more his than you've ever been any man's.*

"But you might get hurt!" Cordi tearfully remonstrated. She placed an insistent, imploring hand on Erik's arm, but he merely shook his head regretfully and said, "I am sorry, Miss Cordi, but this is something that must be done." He took her hand and gently but firmly carried it back to her side, then turned to follow Ross, who was already on his way to the door.

"Give 'em hell, Sam!" Etta enthusiastically told the

endearing young firebrand who was, as usual, eager to charge into the fray. He flashed her a grin before tugging on his hat and leaving the house with the two other soon-to-be combatants.

Dallas, angry and heartsore and worried all at the same time, muttered an extremely unladylike curse and flung her napkin to the table. She knew she would be waiting up to see whether or not her "husband" came back in one piece, and she knew it was going to be a long wait . . .

A short time later, on the other side of town, Ross Kincaid pushed through the bright red swinging doors of the Double Sixes Saloon. Erik Larsen and Sam Houston Rawlins were close on his heels.

The most popular establishment in Corsicana was enjoying its usual brisk business that night. Brimming with every kind, shape, and size of man—and a number of painted women—the room was filled with smoke and laughter and the strong smell of spirits.

Justin Bishop was sharing a companionable drink with O'Shea at the far end of the long, brass-railed bar when Ross's searching gaze picked him out of the boisterous crowd of revelers.

His green eyes narrowing and smoldering with the most intense, bloodthirsty fury he had ever known, Ross nonetheless kept his head and waited for the other man to make the first move. He didn't have to wait long—Justin caught sight of him seconds later.

The fair-haired con man stiffened while his dark, hawkish gaze glittered with hatred. He exchanged a quick word with O'Shea, and the message traveled swiftly through the crowd. As if by prior arrangement, the area immediately surrounding the bar cleared and the music suddenly dropped to a more subdued level.

"I knew you'd show up sooner or later, Kincaid!" sneered Justin, raising his cigar to his lips with deceptive nonchalance.

"You and I have business to settle, Bishop," Ross ground out.

At a wordless nod from O'Shea, a dozen men stepped into position behind Justin. Erik and Sam edged closer to Ross, who merely smiled faintly and said, "You big sons of bitches line up, and you little sons of bitches bunch up, because I'm damn well going to have a 'talk' with your friend!"

Justin Bishop gave a soft, evil laugh and tossed his cigar to the floor of the saloon.

Listening to the clock chime twelve, Dallas released a long sigh and crossed wearily to the stove to put on yet another pot of coffee.

"If we drink any more of that stuff, honey, we'll be up for days!" Ruby Mae commented with a quiet chuckle.

"Maybe we ought to go look for them!" suggested Cordi. Jumping up from her seat at the table, she flew to peer anxiously out the back window for at least the hundredth time since the men had gone.

"Now how in blue blazes could we do *that?*" Etta parried with a deep frown. "It's the middle of the night, and they could be anywhere out there!"

"They'll be along soon," Ruby Mae assured the sandy-haired young woman who kept envisioning all sorts of terrible things happening to her reluctant Nordic beau.

"But what if they don't come home at all? What if

they're lying in a dark, deserted alley somewhere? What if—"

"For heaven's sake, Cordi, that's enough!" Dallas chided sharply. She was nearly as tense as her sister, but she had no intention of allowing her imagination to run away with her. No, if something was going to happen to Ross—*and* Sam and Erik, of course—then it was going to happen and there was nothing on God's green earth she could do about it! She tried to ignore the dull ache in her heart, an ache that was only growing worse as the night wore on.

Finally, at ten minutes past midnight, they heard the distinct sound of masculine voices in the backyard. Dallas was the first to reach the door, and she flung it open to reveal two bruised and bloodied, and smiling, faces that looked vaguely familiar.

"Dear Lord!" she gasped, then took an instinctive step backward.

"It's them!" Cordi joyfully proclaimed, only to gasp in shock as well when Ross and Erik stepped inside into the warm light of the kitchen. The unmistakable aroma of whiskey hung about them.

"Where's Sam?" Etta demanded right away.

"We took him home," Ross told her. He smiled wryly again before adding, "The last I saw of him, he was grinning like a possum and singing his heart out while his mother lit into him for coming home drunk."

"Why, you—you and Mr. Kincaid have been drinking, too, haven't you?" Cordi asked Erik in wide-eyed astonishment.

"I am afraid so, Miss Cordi," the young Swede admitted with a sheepish grin. "But I am not so drunk that I cannot walk!" he boasted proudly.

"Come on over here and set yourselves down while we have a look at those cuts!" Ruby Mae commanded the men in her characteristically bossy fashion. Neither of them chose to argue.

"What happened? Did you find Justin Bishop?" Etta questioned while Dallas and Ruby Mae hurried to fetch the necessary medicine and bandages.

"We found him," Ross answered with a fierce scowl of remembrance. "He was at the Double Sixes, just like Sam thought he'd be."

"And the black-hearted scoundrel is there still," supplied Erik, chuckling in satisfaction. "Or I should say, what is left of the black-hearted scoundrel!"

"Good heavens, don't tell me you killed him?" This came from Cordi, who paled and raised a trembling hand to her throat. She was profoundly relieved when Erik shook his head and replied, "No, we did not. But Tex, he—" the sentence was left hanging for a moment while he searched for the right words, "—he 'beat the man into bad health.' I believe that is the expression?"

"That's it, all right," Ruby Mae verified dryly, setting to work on the young Swede's wounds. Dallas took up an iodine-soaked cloth and applied it with a certain vengeful relish to the bloodied ruggedness of her husband's cheek.

"That hurts like hell you know," Ross informed her in a low, vibrant tone.

"Good!" she retorted, her eyes flashing resentfully. "It's no more than you deserve for behaving like a . . . a rattlebrained barbarian!" Her stomach did a strange little flip-flop when he smiled rakishly up at her and, green eyes twinkling, murmured in a voice barely above a whisper, "You might just find out you like being the wife of a barbarian."

"How many were you up against?" it suddenly occurred to Etta to inquire. "I bet Sam was able to hold his own, wasn't he?"

"He was and did," Ross confirmed with a quiet chuckle.

"In the beginning, we were outnumbered by four to one," revealed Erik. He paused to cast Cordi a reassuring smile. "But it was not long until the others in the saloon joined in on the fight. That is usually the case," he added, drawing on the vast experience he had gained in oil towns, and as Ross Kincaid's partner, throughout the past several years.

"Come here, Cordi," Ruby Mae instructed. Smiling as the younger woman came forward with a puzzled frown, she pressed the bottle of iodine and the roll of bandages into Cordi's surprised hands. "There! You take over and see to Mr. Larsen. It's time me and Etta were takin' ourselves on up to bed."

"But I don't want to go to bed yet!" protested Etta. "I want to stay and hear more—"

"Land's sakes, honey, just humor an old woman and help me up them stairs!"

"You're the farthest thing from an 'old woman' I've ever seen!" countered Etta, nonetheless moving to join her near the doorway. "And I doubt very seriously if you'll need any help climbing stairs before you're a hundred and one!"

Ruby Mae bid Dallas, Cordi, Ross, and Erik a good night, then led the youngest Brown sister from the room with a whispered, conspiratorial remark in Etta's ear about the two of them not wanting to be a "fifth wheel on the wagon."

Cordi, though wrinkling her nose in distaste at the sight of blood on her beloved's face, took a deep breath and charged resolutely ahead to tend to his injuries. Like Ross, he had sustained a split lip, bloodied nose, sore knuckles, and a general pounding about the head.

Unlike Cordi, whose touch was light and gentle, Dallas continued to minister to *her* patient with a vengeance. She was burning mad at him for endangering his life, as well as those of Erik and Sam, all because of what she told herself was truly nothing more than an insignificant outburst by a hurt, jealous man. Justin had no right to be jealous, she mused indignantly, just as Ross Kincaid had no right to be possessive!

"If you're through scourging me, I'd like to have a word with you—alone," Ross told her quietly, his face impassive and his eyes gleaming with an unfathomable light.

"I'm not 'scourging' you and we have nothing to talk about!" she parried in a simmering undertone. She directed a hasty glance at the opposite end of the table, only to observe that Cordi and Erik were deep in their own conversation. "And even if we did, it can easily wait until morning!" Giving one last vigorous swipe of the cloth across his bronzed forehead, she frowned down into his faintly bruised and swollen, but still devastatingly handsome, features and pronounced with a noticeable lack of conviction, "I'm afraid that's the best I can do!"

Ross drew himself slowly upright as Dallas presented her back to him and began gathering up the soiled cloths and unused bandages on the table with tense, angry movements. She gasped to feel the warmth of his strong hand closing about her arm.

"What do you think you're doing?" she demanded in a furious whisper, at the same time painfully aware of the way her whole body tingled at the contact.

"We're going to have that talk, Mrs. Kincaid."

"We most certainly are *not!* Why, I'm not about to go off and leave my sister here alone with—"

"That's exactly what you're going to do!" Giving her no further opportunity to argue, he escorted her firmly from the kitchen and down the darkened hallway. She offered no resistance until they were inside the parlor, whereupon she pulled free from his grasp and hurried to light the lamp. Hearing him close—and lock—the doors behind her, she felt her face color and her pulses quicken. Surely he wasn't planning to try and do *that* to her right there in the parlor, was he? she asked herself in growing alarm.

"I want to know what's been going on between you and Justin Bishop," decreed Ross, his deep voice reverberating in the silence of the room. He began advancing on her with slow, measured steps as she retreated instinctively to the other side of the sofa.

"I've told you before—my personal life is none of your business!" she answered in a proudly defiant manner that belied her inner disquietude.

"Damn it, woman, do we have to go through all that again?"

"Only if you persist in . . . in barging into matters that do not concern you!" Swallowing a sudden lump in her throat, she watched in breathless anticipation as he rounded the corner of the sofa and finally arrived to stand towering ominously above her.

"Today wasn't the first time Bishop threatened you,

was it?" His sun-bronzed features tightened when he noted the dull, telltale flush which crept up to her face, and his eyes sparked with a renewed fury directed at the man he'd already had the great pleasure of trouncing with his bare fists. "He did something to you that night at the social, didn't he?" When she did not answer, his hands shot out to grip her upper arms. She drew in her breath sharply while he once again demanded, "Didn't he?" His smoldering gaze bored down into hers.

"Yes! Yes, damn you, yes!" cried Dallas, her eyes sparkling with sudden tears. "But what difference does it make now? He . . . he didn't hurt me, and I've simply tried to forget the things he said!"

"What *things?*" Ross ground out. His fingers clenched with near bruising force about her arms.

"He told me that he . . . he loved me and would not accept the fact that I no longer cared for him!" She purposely omitted any mention of how Justin had threatened to kill her before he'd let any other man have her, or of how he had forced that cruel, frightening kiss upon her. "That's why he acted the way he did today, because he found out about our marriage!"

"Nothing excuses the way he acted. But he'll not come near you again, not if he values his life!"

Dallas felt a tremor of fear as she glimpsed the savagery in his gaze. *He is still little better than a stranger to me,* she thought numbly. It was true. What did she really know of this man? Only that he was capable of infuriating her like no one else, that he could be both tender and strong, and that he alone could make her feel things she would never have believed it possible to feel . . .

331

"You're to tell me if that bastard so much as looks at you again, understand?" commanded Ross, shaking her slightly for emphasis.

"No, I do *not* understand!" she hotly dissented. "I am under no obligation to tell you anything, Ross Kincaid, and you have no right to—"

"I have every right, damn it!"

"Why? Because we're married? Well, the sort of marriage you and I have entitles you to no 'privileges' whatsoever!" Her voice was laced with both anger and bitterness, and her brilliant, deep blue eyes blazed with pain as well as defiance. "If you by any chance think that what happened last night changes anything, then you are very, very much mistaken! I didn't come into your room for . . . for *that!*" she declared, her cheeks burning. "It was a terrible mistake, a mistake that will most definitely never be repeated!"

"What makes you so sure of that?" he challenged quietly.

Dallas's eyes grew very round as she drew in her breath upon a gasp. Trying desperately to ignore the sudden fire that coursed through her veins, she raised her chin and demanded with as much bravado as she could muster, "Is that a threat, Mr. Kincaid? Because if it is, I—"

"It's not a threat, wildcat," Ross cut her off, his voice dropping to a low, slightly husky tone while his magnificent eyes glowed alarmingly. The merest hint of a smile played about his lips, and his powerful arms were already slipping purposefully about her when he vowed, "It's a promise."

"No!" She brought her hands up to push at the granite-hard expanse of his chest, but it was too late.

His arms easily held her captive. She battled the familiar weakness descending upon her as best she could, only to feel all her defenses crumbling. *Heaven help her, but there was no way she could fight them both . . .*

With a low moan of surrender, she swayed toward him, reveling in the feel of his hard, muscular body pressed intimately against her trembling softness. Her eyes swept closed when his lips, warm and demanding and oh-so-sensuously persuasive, conquered hers in a kiss that, once again, quite literally took her breath away.

The embrace ignited her passions, passions that Ross had so masterfully awakened and tutored the night before, and she found herself yearning for more—*much, much more.* He was apparently of the same mind, for in the next moment he scooped her up in his arms and bore her around to the other side of the sofa. Swiftly lowering her to the chintz-covered cushions, he covered her body with the wonderfully virile length of his and kissed her with such an impassioned urgency that she felt desire coursing through her like wildfire.

"Oh Ross, Ross!" she gasped out when his mouth, finally relinquishing its fierce, intoxicating possession of hers, began to sear its way downward to where his hands were impatiently liberating the dainty pearl buttons on the front of her bodice from their corresponding loops.

Her fingers curled tightly upon the hard, cotton-clad smoothness of his shoulders as she felt her senses reeling. She gasped again when, sweeping apart the unfastened edges of her white lawn blouse, Ross's hands delved beneath the low, beribboned neckline of her chemise and lovingly claimed the twin perfection of her breasts.

His fingers stroked across the satiny, rose-tipped fullness which swelled above her corset. Seconds later, his warm lips joined in, rendering her practically mindless as they fastened about one of the exquisitely formed globes. She stifled a moan when he drew the delectable peak within the warmth of his mouth, his lips suckling as greedily as any babe's while his hot, velvety tongue teased at the sensitive pink nipple.

Dallas's head tossed restlessly to and fro upon the flowered chintz, and her fingers threaded almost convulsively within the ebony thickness of Ross's hair. The lamp cast a soft golden glow upon the two lovers, and the forbidden sweetness of the moment served to heighten their already blazing passions . . .

While one of his hands remained beneath her breast to lift it farther upward into the moist caress of his mouth, his other hand moved to tangle within the gathered fullness of her skirts and petticoats. He swiftly tugged the folds of dark blue broadcloth and white cambric upward, thereby exposing her shapely, black-stockinged limbs. Her hips and thighs were encased in a pair of white, open-leg drawers, which provided him with unintentional, yet highly convenient, access to her womanly secrets.

Ross seized full advantage of the "handiness" of such attire. His warm fingers wasted little time in traveling to the garment's opening, then disappearing within the delicate, hemmed edges to close gently upon the beckoning triangle of soft auburn curls.

Another sharp gasp broke from Dallas's lips, and she

arched instinctively upward when she felt his fingers seeking, and finding, the tiny flower of womanhood nestled between her slender thighs. He caressed her velvety softness with a slow, tantalizing expertise while his mouth scorched a path back up from her breasts to claim her parted lips demandingly once more.

She returned his kiss with such an innocent, captivating boldness that he felt his own desire flaring dangerously toward the uppermost limits of masculine endurance. With a low groan, he drank even more deeply of her sweetness, and their lovemaking rapidly intensified to the point that neither of them could bear any more of the exquisite torment.

Finally, after making a swift adjustment to the fastening of his denim trousers, Ross slid his two large hands beneath Dallas's bottom and lifted her for his pleasure—and hers. She cried out softly as his manhood sheathed expertly within her honeyed warmth, and she clung weakly to him as they soared together to what she had earlier recalled was the nearest thing to heaven on earth . . .

Her breathless cry of fulfillment was lost against his mouth. He tensed above her an instant later, his lips releasing hers at last when he gave a soft groan that signaled his own satisfaction. They slowly returned to earth, their breathing erratic and their eyes aglow with a lingering wonderment at what they had just shared.

The next thing Dallas knew, Ross was tenderly wrapping his arms about her and shifting his tall frame so that she was lying beside him on the sofa. Their bodies were pressed closely together, so closely that their hearts seemed to be beating as one. They felt no need for words at the present. Content to bask in the warm afterglow of their wild, tempestuous loving, they lay in each other's arms, the only inhabitants of a special world created by their union.

The sound of a knock abruptly shattered the spell.

"Dallas? Dallas, are you in there?" It was Cordi's voice, calling out softly from the other side of the locked doors.

"Dear Lord!" gasped Dallas, starting in guilty alarm. Resisting her husband's efforts to keep her exactly where she was, she scrambled up from the sofa and frantically began to set her clothing to rights. Ross's gaze filled with wicked amusement as he watched her.

"She'll go away if we don't answer," he murmured with an undeniably wolfish grin. Dallas blushed hotly and shot him a quelling look as she continued with her efforts to button her bodice.

"Dallas? Dallas, can you hear me?" Cordi demanded a trifle louder, punctuating her words with another knock.

"Yes, I—just a moment, please!" she called back unsteadily.

Ross, finally accepting the inevitability of the situation, muttered a good-natured oath beneath his breath and pulled himself leisurely upright. He refastened his trousers and raked a negligent hand through his thick black hair, then smiled to himself as his eyes moved back to where Dallas stood before the gilt-framed wall mirror near the doorway.

She had managed to reclaim the former orderliness of her clothes, but her hair was still in a noticeable state of dishevelment. Working feverishly to tame the wayward auburn tresses, she yanked the pins out one at a time, stabbed them back into place, and heaved a loud sigh of exasperation when she saw that it was a hopeless case indeed.

"Dal*las!*" Cordi's voice had taken on a discernible edge of impatience by now.

"I'm coming!" Dallas virtually shouted as she whirled away from the mirror. She caught her breath when her wide luminous gaze met and locked with the piercing green intensity of Ross's one last time.

"There's going to come a time, wildcat," he promised softly, the look on his handsome face sending a new rush of color to her cheeks, "when there are no wells to be drilled and no interruptions."

Although tempted to ask him exactly what he meant by that remark, she did not. She eyed him with a certain wary confusion for a moment longer, before hurrying across to unlock and open the doors. A noticeably vexed Cordi swept into the lamplit room.

"What on earth took you so long? I was beginning to think you were never going to let me in!" she blurted out, then suddenly became aware of Ross's presence. "Oh, I . . . I thought perhaps you had already gone up to bed, Mr. Kincaid!"

"My 'discussion' with your sister took longer than she planned," said Ross. Flashing both young women an equable smile, he sauntered from the parlor and back down the hallway to the kitchen.

XIII

The next morning found Dallas on her way to town again. Ruby Mae accompanied her for a change—a very pleasant change, she mused, since her friend neither interrogated her nor judged her . . . nor created utter havoc with her emotions.

Pulling up in front of the store identified by a big red-and-white sign stating "Ransom Grocery" above the doorway, Dallas secured the wagon's brake and gathered up her skirts to alight. Ruby Mae climbed down on the other side and frowned up toward the overcast sky. The air was already hot and sticky, and she told herself there'd be rain for sure before morning was done.

"I'll meet you back here in half an hour, honey. Any longer than that, and we're liable to find ourselves tryin' to outrun a storm."

"Are you sure you wouldn't rather I went with you? I really don't mind," Dallas reiterated with a smile as she stepped up to join her on the boardwalk.

"I got myself too many piddlin' things to take care

of," Ruby Mae declined the offer with a shake of her head. "Now you go on and do whatever you need to do. I'll bring myself back in a little while."

Dallas, watching for a moment as the other woman set out for the feed store, turned back to the grocer's and strolled inside. The cool, dimly lit interior of the store was crowded with a vast array of food in boxes, barrels, crates, and bins. Although it was scarcely nine o'clock in the morning, a dozen women were already sweeping purposefully down its narrow aisles, their hand-held shopping baskets overflowing with the "few items" they had popped in to buy.

Knowing exactly where to find the cherries she needed, Dallas headed straightaway toward the far corner of the store. She was still annoyed with herself for having forgotten her promise to Fanny Woodward regarding the extra pies, but she wasted little time on self-recrimination as she paused before the neat, colorful rows of fresh fruit and quickly selected the cherries. Once that was done, she moved back to the counter, only to hear a familiar voice call her name.

"Dallas!" Marian Ridgeway's plump, dark-haired frame filled the doorway, her face wreathed in smiles at the sight of her friend. She bustled excitedly forward as Dallas smiled in response and stepped away from the counter.

"Hello, Marian. What brings you to town so early?"

"Why in heaven's name didn't you *tell* me?" whispered Marian, grabbing Dallas's arm and pulling her insistently toward a more secluded area of the store.

"Tell you what?" Dallas responded with a puzzled frown, then suddenly remembered—*her marriage*. She groaned inwardly while reflecting that the secret was out. Indeed, Justin had known about it yesterday . . .

"Dallas Brown, you know very well 'what'! Why didn't you tell me what you were planning, and with that handsome driller of yours, of all people?" the other woman demanded in a hushed voice full of good-natured reproach. "Christopher Columbus! My very best friend in all the world goes and gets herself married and doesn't even bother to let me know! No, *I* had to find out from Lila Beth Franklin, and you know how I *despise* Lila Beth Franklin! Now why on earth didn't you tell me yourself?"

"It was . . . rather sudden, I'm afraid," murmured Dallas, her eyes falling guiltily before her friend's as the hot color stained her cheeks.

"A whirlwind romance!" Marian breathed dreamily. She clasped her hands together and brought them up against her ample bosom while her mouth curved into a smile of mingled triumph and delight. "I knew it, I just knew it!"

"No, Marian, it isn't quite what you think—" Dallas started to explain, breaking off when she realized that she didn't know *how*. But even if she did, she then thought, she wouldn't do so. She didn't want Marian, and certainly not the whole town, to know that her marriage was not what it should be. Hellfire and damnation, she told herself defensively, she still had her pride!

"Well then, why don't you walk on down to the Opera House with me and tell me just what the dickens it is?" her friend suggested with a pleasant trill of laughter.

"No, I can't!" she protested hastily, dreading the

341

prospect of further questions. "I have to meet Ruby Mae in half an hour and—"

"Oh pooh, we'll be back in plenty of time!" Marian waved aside her objections. "It can't possibly take more than ten minutes. I've simply got to purchase some tickets. Mother and I are planning to attend tonight's performance of *The Mikado,* and I'm anxious to make certain we get decent seats for a change! I'll wait for you outside while you pay for those," she announced, gesturing airily toward the basket of cherries Dallas was clutching. "Do hurry! I'm just dying to hear all about that new husband of yours!"

Dallas knew she had little choice. She and Marian were soon strolling down the boardwalk on their way to the Merchants' Opera House, an ornate, three-story building that was inarguably the finest such facility between Fort Worth and Houston.

"I can't say I'm not a little disappointed," Marian remarked with a dramatic sigh as they were passing the millinery shop. Two dimples suddenly appeared in the plump smoothness of her cheeks, and her eyes sparkled with her usual good humor. "I had always counted on attending you at your wedding—I knew you'd be the first, you see—and I had expected you to return the favor for me!"

"I'm sorry, Marian, truly I am. But . . . well, to be perfectly honest, nothing has turned out quite the way I expected!" confessed Dallas, her own gaze troubled. *Not quite the way I expected,* her own words echoed throughout her brain. The vivid memory of last night's wildly rapturous encounter in the parlor returned to haunt her again. Her thoughts and emotions had been in absolute chaos . . .

"Of course not! After all, who can predict when they're going to fall in love? But I really do understand, you know—about your not wanting a big wedding and all that, I mean. I think I'd rather have a small, intimate ceremony myself when the time comes." She smiled rather mysteriously before adding, "And the time might just come sooner than anyone thinks!"

"Why, Marian!" Dallas turned to her in surprise. "Have you been seeing someone?"

"You might say that!" the other woman retorted playfully, then confided in a rush of starry-eyed excitement, "Oh, Dallas, I met him at the social! His name is Jack Stone and he's from Oklahoma and he has the most beautiful smile you've ever seen! He must be at least a head taller than me and he has curly brown hair and blue eyes, and he's a bit on the thin side, but he's young and ever so charming and, best of all—he *likes* me!"

"How could he help it?" Dallas countered with a soft, affectionate laugh. Not only was she genuinely interested in hearing all about her friend's new beau, she was also very relieved that the conversation had drifted away from the subject of her marriage. "I suppose he's one of the oil-field workers?"

"Yes, but he won't be much longer. He told me he's planning to return to Oklahoma and farm once he saves up enough money." Sighing happily, Marian linked her arm through Dallas's and observed with a philosophical air, "Who would have believed it? You, married to a driller, and me, married to a farmer. Not that I'm counting my chickens before they hatch, mind you! It's just that I *do* have a certain feeling about Mr. Stone. But of course you know exactly what I'm talking about, don't you? I suppose you felt the same way when you first met your husband!"

"No, not really," Dallas replied uneasily, another dull flush rising to her face. She *had* felt something, but she could just see herself trying to explain to the woman beside her that what she had felt was nothing more than . . . than pure animal magnetism!

Nothing more? her mind's voice begged to differ.

Suddenly growing conscious of the quizzical look Marian had turned upon her, she cleared her throat gently and steered the talk away from herself again.

"Well, I certainly hope you'll keep me informed as to your 'progress' with the charming Mr. Stone. If he's only half as nice as you appear to find him, then I sincerely hope you are able to convince him that you would make an excellent farmer's wife!" she teased, her eyes dancing with fond amusement.

Reaching the Opera House at last, they took their place at the end of the line which had already formed in front of the ticket window. The satiric operettas of Gilbert and Sullivan usually drew a full house, recalled Dallas, and it appeared that this one would be no exception. Wandering away from Marian for a moment, she absently scrutinized the copy of the program cover featured on a placard announcing *The Mikado*'s week-long engagement.

"Well, well," she heard Lorena Appleton drawling behind her, "as I live and breathe, if it isn't Dallas Brown—the 'blushing bride' herself!" The young widow's voice was laced with even more venom than usual.

"Good morning, Lorena," Dallas proclaimed in precise, measured tones as she pivoted slowly about.

Her deep blue eyes glowed with a certain, pleasurable anticipation for what was to come, and she could not resist flashing the woman a triumphantly challenging smile. "It's *Mrs. Kincaid* now."

"Yes, so I heard!" Lorena ground out, her own eyes glittering viperously. "I must say, the news came as a bit of a surprise. Why, the last I remember, you were swearing up and down that you cared nothing for the man!"

"Love does have a way of changing things, doesn't it?" sighed Dallas, feigning a dreamy-eyed look for effect. She was satisfied to observe the other woman's lips compressing into a tight, thin line of spleenish disgruntlement.

"I suppose, however, that I should congratulate you on the 'timeliness' of your wedding," Lorena then sneered. "Was there perhaps a particular reason for the way you and Mr. Kincaid went *sneaking* to Reverend Kennicott? That is to say, I do hope the two of you won't be forced to take an 'extended trip' in a few months' time!" Her contemptuously spoken words were heavy with meaning, but Dallas merely smiled again.

"Not at all, though I do expect we will enjoy a long, leisurely honeymoon once my husband completes his work here," she lied, enjoying every minute of it. "Oh, I *do* hope you realize that Ross won't be able to drill that well for you after all? He and I discussed the matter at great length, and we agreed that he simply won't be able to spare the time. I'm terribly sorry, but I'm quite sure you won't have any trouble finding another man to take his place!"

Lorena grew livid at that. In fact, she looked very

much like she would dearly love to strike Dallas. Whether or not she would have acted upon the impulse was never known, for Marian chose that opportune moment to join them in front of the placard.

"Why, Lorena Appleton, don't tell me you're here buying tickets, too?" Dallas's friend queried sarcastically.

"Why shouldn't I be?" snapped the spiteful blonde, her pale-blue eyes blazing at the interruption.

"No reason at all. It's simply that I thought you always had an escort for these things," Marian answered with deceptive innocence.

"Unlike you!" Lorena cattily retorted.

"Yes, of course," said Marian, smiling sweetly. She made a great show of stealing a furtive glance about them before declaring in a loud whisper, "But I'm sure that if you take yourself on down to the Double Sixes, you'll be able to locate an escort in no time at all. As a matter of fact, I've no doubt there are a few men who are actually *deserving* of your companionship!"

"Is that so? Well, I doubt if you could get any of them to even look at you, Marian Ridgeway!"

"Oh, haven't you heard?" Her eyes were glimmering with devilment as she and Dallas exchanged a quick look. "It doesn't look like I'll be qualified to organize that group of spinsters after all. You see, Lorena, it seems there are some men who find well-rounded 'old maids' attractive!" Marian finished with a complacent grin.

Lorena, whom no one had ever accused of possessing either a quick mind or an extensive vocabulary, could think of nothing to say. Forced to settle for shooting both young women the most scathing glare her rather lackluster eyes could manage, she spun about in a huff and flounced away.

"Someday that pasty-faced shrew is going to get her comeuppance," Marian predicted as she watched Lorena disappear around the corner of the building, "and I hope to goodness I'm there to see it!"

"You won't be," murmured Dallas. She smiled warmly at her friend and added, "You'll be living on a farm in Oklahoma, remember?" Marian giggled and linked their arms companionably together again.

"Come along, Mrs. Kincaid. You and I still have an awful lot to talk about!" She happened to glance up at the dark, ominous sky as they strolled back out to the boardwalk. "I hope Ruby Mae shows up sooner than she's supposed to, for I do believe it's going to rain."

The first drops began to fall shortly after those highly prophetic words had been uttered. The two young women scurried back to the grocer's, where Marian said a hasty good-bye and hurried off to where she had left her own horse and buggy parked in front of the courthouse. A breathless Ruby Mae returned to scramble up into the wagon beside Dallas almost immediately thereafter.

Although the "almost new" spring wagon boasted of a sturdy canvas top, they were still soaking wet by the time they pulled up in front of the house. Sam, who had been standing in the barn doorway watching it rain, came dashing gallantly across the yard in the downpour to take control of the horse. Rewarded for his generosity with expressions of profound gratitude from the women, he merely grinned and told them it was the least he could do since he'd be staying for supper again.

The summer rainstorm lasted less than an hour and ended almost as suddenly as it had begun, but it left the air smelling fresh and the earth looking renewed. Dallas and Ruby Mae worked throughout the remainder of the morning and most of the afternoon to bake the two dozen pies that would be delivered to the Molloy Hotel the next morning.

Ross, Erik, and Sam, meanwhile, spent the better part of the day "rigging down" and staking the location for the new well Ross still fully intended to drill in spite of his wife's objections.

Cordi and Etta were, as usual, too busy with their own pursuits to be of much help with the housework or cooking, even though Cordi had been given the day off and Etta didn't have to report to her job at the bakery until after dinner. Instead of becoming annoyed with her sisters, Dallas was glad for the fact that they were out from underfoot—and away from two of the men working in the backyard.

Sheriff Crow rode up to the house later that same afternoon. Catching sight of Ross near the barn, the lawman dismounted and moved forward with long, easy strides to speak to him.

"Howdy, Kincaid," he drawled affably. "Glad to see you got your well in."

"Thanks." Ross smiled and gave a nod of greeting as he shook the other man's hand. "What brings you out here?"

"I thought you might like to know I finally had a talk with that one-armed bastard over at the hospital. He wouldn't say who put him up to the attack, but that's not too damned surprising, is it?" He shook his copper-maned head and gave a short, humorless laugh. "The

348

other one's still holding out, too. I figure they've been promised a hell of a lot of money to keep their mouths shut."

"Either that, or they're afraid they'll be killed," Ross offered grimly. "How big of an outfit do you think they're with?"

"Hard to say. But these attacks are starting to get too damned common around here. There's been a lot of oil getting siphoned off lately—seems like that's on the increase, too. And I heard tell someone's trying to buy up a lot of the property out near where the refinery's going in. Something's going on all right, but I'll be hanged if I've been able to figure out who's behind it!"

"I've been doing a little investigating on my own," Ross suddenly revealed.

"You found out anything?"

"Some. I'll let you know when and if the pieces hang together."

"You do that. By the way, the judge is due to get back the middle of next week. Just between you and me and the fence post," the sheriff remarked with a crooked grin, "I expect the case to be thrown out on a 'technicality,' if you get my meaning. Since the charges aren't exactly on the up-and-up, I kind of doubt if the complainant's going to show up in a court of law."

"I've got the same doubts," said Ross, his green eyes narrowing imperceptibly while his mouth twitched into a faint smile of irony.

The following day dawned bright and clear, and Dallas rose early to get the pies down to the hotel. It occurred to her while she was dressing that, once she gained control of her inheritance, she would no longer need to bake pies for extra money—or do any more bookkeeping for Jacob Kauffman. While she certainly wouldn't mind giving up the baking, she *would* mind giving up her job with the photographer.

"Well then, I won't give it up!" she murmured decisively to her reflection as she stood before the bathroom mirror. Regardless of the recent, and highly substantial, change in her financial prospects, she still intended to hold Mr. Kauffman to his promise to train her as his assistant. The life of the idle rich did not appeal to her in the least; she could not imagine herself sitting around in a big fine mansion somewhere, being waited on hand and foot. No, she mused with a vibrant sparkle in her eyes, there was a whole world waiting out there, a world full of interesting places and fascinating people. Wealthy or not, she'd never be content to sit back and let life pass her by!

Isn't that exactly what you've been doing for the past twenty-one years? that damnably sagacious inner voice of hers charged. *Yes, and you probably would have kept on doing it if Ross Kincaid hadn't come along and stirred everything up!*

"Oh, shut up!" she muttered crossly, then whirled about and hurried from the bathroom. When she stepped into the kitchen a few minutes later, she discovered that Ruby Mae had not only already prepared breakfast for the men, but had washed the dishes as well.

"Ruby Mae Hatfield," Dallas scolded affectionately as she frowned and planted her hands on her hips, "when I asked you to come and stay with us for a while, I did *not* intend for you to spend all your time cooking

350

and cleaning and—"

"I know you didn't, honey, but I'll be dadburned if I'm the sort who can sit twiddlin' my thumbs when there's somethin' to be done! Besides," she added with a broad grin and a twinkle of her lively brown eyes, "it's been kind of nice havin' so many folks to do for. Usually when I work from dawn till dark thirty, it's only for myself. Bein' down here with you girls has made me feel younger than I've felt in years!"

"Well," sighed Dallas, "I suppose it would do me no good to try and argue with you anyway, would it?"

"No good at all," the older woman replied complacently.

Pausing only to drink a cup of coffee, Dallas carefully stacked several of the boxes of pies and conveyed them outside. She had stolen a quick look out the window in the hallway before heading into the kitchen, and had been pleased to note that someone had been thoughtful enough to hitch up the horse and wagon and leave them waiting in front of the house. Naturally assuming that the "someone" had been Ruby Mae, she tossed a smile over her shoulder at the woman who followed her down the walk carrying an equal number of the pies.

"Thank you, Ruby Mae. Not only do I appreciate your help with the pies, but it was so kind of you to bring the horse and wagon around, too."

"I'll take credit for the first," Ruby Mae declared with a soft chuckle, "but I'm afraid you'll have to thank that husband of yours for the second." Dallas's eyes widened in surprise.

"You mean Ross—" she started to question.

"He did." The tall, big-boned woman set the boxes

351

on the backseat, then turned to her with a strangely cryptic little smile. "You know, he and I had a little talk after breakfast."

"A . . . a little talk?" stammered Dallas, her beautiful face paling a bit beneath the light smattering of freckles while her heart took to pounding in sudden apprehension. "What about?"

"Oh, nothin' in particular," Ruby Mae murmured with frustrating evasiveness, then commented, "I don't think you know it yet, honey, but he's a good man—a right smart one, too. Why, if Ross Kincaid was to tell me a rooster could pull a railroad train, I'd buy myself a ticket!"

"I didn't realize you had developed such a high opinion of Mr. Kincaid!" Dallas responded with a certain edge to her voice. "He's only been here a week." *It seems more like a year!* she grumbled silently. "And how on earth can you know so much about a man you've scarcely spoken to? I seriously doubt if the two of you have exchanged more than a dozen words the whole time he's been here!"

She suddenly realized that she was protesting a bit too long and loudly for someone who professed to care nothing about the man one way or the other, and she hastily sought to change the subject.

"Are you sure you wouldn't like to come along?" she asked, gathering up her skirts and hoisting herself up into the wagon with an easy, natural feminine grace.

"No, thanks," Ruby Mae declined with another brief smile. Her eyes scrutinized the younger woman closely for several moments longer, and her weathered brow creased into a faint, pensive frown before she said, "I'm plannin' to go on back down to my place for a while and check on my stock, maybe air out the house a bit."

"I'm sorry, Ruby Mae," Dallas apologized with a troubled sigh. "When all of this started, I truly believed it was only going to be for a few days. I had no idea—"

"Now you stop worryin' about that, you hear? Land's sakes, honey, I'm havin' the time of my life!"

Warmed by the gratitude and affection shining in Dallas's eyes, Ruby Mae stood and watched as her young friend drove away. Then, shaking her head slowly at a sudden thought, she turned and ambled back inside.

Dallas had not yet returned when a telegram arrived at the house an hour later. Its recipient was Ross, who—after accepting the typewritten message from the breathless, heavily perspiring young man who had bicycled all the way from the other side of town to deliver it—quickly scanned its contents and then crumpled it in his hand with a muttered curse.

"It is bad news?" Erik questioned with a frown of genuine concern. He straightened from where they had been re-examining a prospective drilling sight down the hill from the barn.

"It sure as hell isn't good," Ross confirmed in a low, tight voice, his eyes glittering with intense displeasure. "I'll have to be away for a few days. There's trouble at the ranch."

"What sort of trouble?"

"Our foreman's been arrested on charges of rustling. The telegram's from him." He whipped the hat from his head and swore again before telling his partner, "This is a devil of a time for me to be going off and leaving you with everything, but it can't be helped."

"I will handle it," the young Swede confidently

353

assured him. "You know you can trust me to take care of things until you get back. But how will you be able to go when the sheriff has said you must not leave town before the trial?"

"I'll stop by and square things with him beforehand. As long as I give him my word to return before that judge shows up, I doubt if he'll stand in my way." He and Erik began striding purposefully back up the sun-drenched rise in the land. "We'll have to hold off on the other well for now. And I don't suppose I need to tell you to keep an eye out for Bishop."

"Do you believe he will try something while you are gone?"

"I don't think so, but it's hard to predict what an oily, four-flushing bastard like that will take it into his head to do." His rugged, handsome countenance tightened while his eyes gleamed with a particularly fierce light. "But it's me he'll be after." The thought which had already taken seed in his mind evolved into an outright decision now, and he announced quietly, "I'll be taking Dallas with me."

"I think that would be for the best," Erik readily concurred. "Because of what Bishop might decide to do, if for no other reason. But there is another reason," he then remarked with a sudden, lopsided smile, his sky-blue eyes twinkling companionably across at the man beside him, "is there not?" Ross's features relaxed into a wry smile, and his gaze was alight with roguish amusement as he cast his friend a lazily challenging look.

"Maybe you ought to quit worrying about my love life and concentrate on your own."

"Mine?" echoed Erik, a faint color suffusing his

charming Scandinavian visage. He shook his head regretfully. "No, Tex, I am too poor to think of marriage. You are a driller the same as I, but you are a wealthy man and have always been one. How can I ever hope to be able to build a home and—"

"Damn it, man, there are some things a hell of a lot more important than a house! Besides, I don't think you stand a snowball's chance in hell of leaving Corsicana without a wife," Ross told him with a low, mellow chuckle and a hearty clap on the back.

When Dallas returned home shortly thereafter, it was only to be met with the startling news that Ross was leaving town.

"But why—where is he going?" she breathlessly demanded of Ruby Mae as she peeled the white straw hat from her auburn tresses and lowered it to the hall table. *Dear Lord,* she thought while her heart twisted painfully, *the time has finally come . . .*

"Fort Worth. He asked me to pass along that he's plannin' to talk to you about it just as soon as he gets back."

"Back? You mean he's already *gone?*"

"Only into town," Ruby Mae explained with a laugh. "He lit out on horseback ten, maybe fifteen minutes ago. I heard him say somethin' about payin' a visit to the telegraph office and the jailhouse."

"Oh, I . . . I see." Dallas heaved an inward sigh of relief and sought to regain control of her strangely erratic breathing. More than a trifle perplexed by the awful emptiness she had felt during those few seconds when she had believed Ross to be gone forever, she raised a trembling hand to tuck a wayward strand of hair into place and swept into the parlor to sink

355

gratefully down upon the sofa.

That was exactly where Ross found her. Following his usual custom, he sauntered into the house—without bothering to knock—by way of the back door and was directed to the parlor by the always helpful Ruby Mae, who had just returned to the kitchen for another glass of lemonade.

"You didn't happen to see Justin Bishop while you were in town today, did you?" he demanded by way of announcing his presence.

Dallas started at the sound of his deep voice and twisted abruptly about on the sofa to face him. Her wide, luminous eyes bridled with indignation at the tone of mistrust underscoring his words. Rising to her feet, she stiffened angrily and cast him a speaking glare.

"Of course not! Why, how dare you accuse me of—"

"I'm not accusing you of a blasted thing," he declared with maddening affability as he came forward to stand smiling softly down into her flushed, stormy countenance. His eyes glowed with such warmth that she felt her color deepening and her knees weakening. "But you wouldn't have told me of your own free will, would you? You see, wildcat, I know you better than you think."

"You don't know me at all!" she hotly denied.

"Don't I?" challenged Ross, his penetrating green gaze flickering over her with bold, meaningful familiarity. Dallas caught her breath upon a gasp and, as usual, sought refuge in her anger.

"If you have something you wish to discuss with me, *Mr. Kincaid,* then you'd better get on with it!" She resumed her place upon the sofa, where she sat with her back rigidly erect and her flashing eyes stubbornly focused on a spot just beyond Ross's head.

He merely smiled again and tossed his hat onto the cushion beside her. She watched in surprised puzzlement as he moved over to the chair and leisurely bent his tall, muscular frame down into it. He then proceeded to stretch his long, denim-clad legs out before him, crossing one booted foot over the other, and locked his hands negligently together behind his head. Though he gave the appearance of being totally at ease, Dallas had the distinct feeling that he could spring into action quicker than she could blink an eye . . .

"I suppose Ruby Mae told you about the telegram," he began.

"Telegram?" she echoed with a frown of bewilderment. Ruby Mae had said nothing about a telegram.

"There's been some trouble at my family's ranch," Ross explained patiently. "The foreman's an old friend of mine. My parents are in San Antonio at the moment, and J.D. sent word to me because he doesn't want them to know what's going on yet. Yesterday, he was arrested on a charge of cattle rustling. It's a serious charge, serious enough to get him hanged if he's found guilty."

"So that's why you're going to Fort Worth," she murmured, half to herself.

"Correction, Mrs. Kincaid—that's why *we're* going to Fort Worth."

Dallas's eyes grew round as saucers, and she stared across at him in stunned disbelief. A tenderly mocking smile played about Ross's lips as he drew his lithe hardness upright again and began sauntering toward her.

"Surely you wouldn't think of passing up this golden opportunity to be alone with me for a few days, would you, my love?"

"Why you—you're out of your mind if you think I have any intention whatsoever of going with you!" she vehemently declared, snapping to her feet once more.

"Maybe," he allowed with a quiet chuckle. "But there's a method to my madness."

He was towering over her now, making her feel small and breathless and—*damn it!*—so acutely conscious of the absolute maleness of him that she felt her head spinning and her pulses racing. Struck with yet another shockingly vivid memory of what the two of them had done together in that very same room the night before last, she inhaled sharply and felt every square inch of her body tingling while she turned beet-red from head to toe.

"I am *not* going with you, Ross Kincaid!" she reiterated, defying herself as well as him.

"I'm afraid you have no choice," he calmly insisted, "because I'm sure as hell not going to leave you behind. Not only am I concerned that Bishop might try to take advantage of my absence, but I think you and I should pay a visit to Willoughby together."

"You're planning to speak to him about . . . about our marriage?" Her eyes widened again, and she momentarily forgot about everything else but the pressing matter of her inheritance, though she experienced no real joy at the thought of resolving the problem. "Do you think he will be able to organize the necessary papers on such short notice?"

"I have every confidence in his abilities," Ross assured her, his voice brimming with ironic humor.

358

"But, surely you can settle things without me? I mean, I don't see why my presence would be required to—"

"Whether or not Willoughby requires your presence doesn't matter—*I* require it." His eyes were filled with that fierce, dictatorial light she had already come to know so well. "You're coming with me, Dallas. Now you can do so of your own free will, or you'll do so over my shoulder. Either way, you *will* go with me," he masterfully decreed.

"Damn you, Ross Kincaid, you can't force me to go with you! Why, if you so much as lay a hand on me, I . . . I'll have you back in jail so fast it will make your head swim!" she threatened impetuously, her eyes blazing their brilliant, deep blue fire and her whole body quaking with the force of her outrage.

"In case you've forgotten, my beautiful little spitfire, you and I are married," he reminded her as his mouth turned up into another faint, sardonic smile. "And unless my memory fails me, it isn't against the law in this grand and glorious state of Texas for a husband to do anything he damn well pleases with his wife."

"Why, you . . . you . . ." she sputtered in helpless fury, so incensed she could not find an appropriately scathing epithet to fling at his handsome head. Her hands curled into fists at her sides, and it was all she could do to keep from flying at him in a veritable storm of emotions.

"We'll be leaving in an hour," Ross told her in a low, level tone. "Swede will look after things while we're gone, and Ruby Mae's agreed to stay on here with your sisters. I've just come back from speaking with Sheriff Crow. As long as we're back in town by Tuesday, there

359

won't be any problem with the judge."

"I can't possibly be ready to go in an hour's time!" Dallas protested breathlessly, though she knew she was waging a hopeless battle. She told herself it would be just like the arrogant, green-eyed rogue before her to make good on his threat to carry her bodily from the house!

"You can and will. Our train pulls out at noon." His features relaxed into another brief, disarming grin when he added, "This should prove to be an interesting trip."

"It might be 'interesting', but you are very much mistaken if you think for one moment that I'm going to let it be anything *else!*" she retorted acidly, folding her arms tightly across her swelling bosom.

"Is that a threat, Mrs. Kincaid?" parried Ross, posing the same question she had posed to him there in the parlor two nights ago. His eyes darkened to a deep-hued jade, and his warm, chiseled lips curved into an undeniably challenging smile. "Because if it is, there's something you ought to know about me."

He left the matter hanging while he slowly bent and retrieved his hat. Then, straightening to his full, ultimately superior height once more, he stared intently down into his bride's sparkling sapphire gaze and finished in a voice that was scarcely above a whisper, "I never let a threat go unanswered. And answering your threat, wildcat, is going to give us *both* the utmost pleasure."

Another wave of hot color washed over her as she drew in her breath upon a soft gasp and hastily uncrossed her arms. She could only blink up at him in mingled trepidation and excitement, her heart leaping

360

wildly and all of her senses aflame.

Ross, subjecting her to one last long, unfathomable look from those magnificent green orbs of his, turned and strolled unhurriedly from the room. Staring dazedly after him, Dallas sank back down upon the sofa and pondered all that he had said . . .

In the end, she was forced to admit that she did indeed have little choice. An hour didn't allow her much time in which to pack her things and say her good-byes to everyone, but she nonetheless managed to do it all, though she mentally cursed Ross Kincaid throughout nearly every one of those sixty minutes.

When it was time to leave, Ruby Mae did not even try to conceal her pleasure at the fact that the "newlyweds" were going away together—even if it was on business—and she embraced Dallas warmly while charging her to "quit tryin' to tie down a bobcat with a piece of string." Drawing away with a deep frown of bafflement creasing her silken brow, Dallas was about to ask the older woman exactly what she meant by that peculiar remark, but was not given the opportunity, for Etta caught her up in a tight, sisterly hug and then was immediately replaced by Cordi.

Her eyes filled with tears as she sat in the wagon beside Ross and stole a glance up at the white, gable-roofed house again. She had been away from home only once before, when she had gone to visit her aunt— in Fort Worth, of all places—during the summer preceding her last year in school. Her father had thought it would do her good to get away from the familiar faces and sights of Corsicana, and most especially away from Justin Bishop.

"Good-bye, Dallas! See you Tuesday!" her sisters

361

called out to her from the front porch. She forced a smile to her lips and lifted a hand in farewell. A strangely prophetic feeling came over her as she stared at the group assembled there. On one side of Ruby Mae, Cordi stood smiling across the yard at Erik—who was riding along to the train depot so that he could bring the wagon back—while an equally beaming Sam and Etta stood together on the other side . . .

Ross gave a snap of the reins, and Dallas twisted about to hold onto the back of the seat as the wagon rolled away from her derrick-shadowed property. Only when the house was no more than a tiny speck in the distance did she shift dispiritedly around again and release a slightly ragged sigh.

This can't be happening, she thought numbly. She told herself she must be dreaming, that she couldn't possibly be on her way to Fort Worth with Ross Kincaid. But it was all too true, she realized, her troubled gaze wandering over the passing landscape once more. *Dear Lord, what am I going to do now?* she desperately prayed as she felt panic rising within her.

They had soon reached the station. Erik, bidding them a safe journey, shook Ross's hand and nodded politely down at Dallas before driving away. The two of them were left alone on the platform, their small amount of baggage resting beside the brick depot office while the train's engine hissed loudly and coughed out another dense cloud of steam. Ross stepped up to the ticket window, while Dallas remained where she was and eyed the train with a pensive frown.

"Well now, if it ain't the new Mrs. Kincaid!" Mason Parnell pronounced with a broad, self-satisfied smile when he caught sight of her waiting behind Ross. She groaned inwardly and rolled her eyes heavenward before pivoting reluctantly about to speak to the depot agent.

"Hello, Mason."

"I heard tell you went and got yourself married!" he chuckled, his eyes brimming with insolent humor. "Boy howdy, the whole town's talkin' about how you ended up marryin' the same feller who drilled the well your pa was so dead set against havin'!"

Dallas colored and tried her best to ignore the devilishly bantering look Ross cast her.

"Yes sirree," Mason continued in the true spirit of smalltown busybodies as he took Ross's money and began counting it out, "I expect folks'll be jawin' over it for a long time to come, 'specially since you two went and got yourselves hitched so secret-like and all. 'Course, it ain't nearly as big a news as the time when Homer Pullen's daughter up and ran off with that acrobat feller from the circus that came through here a few years back." Shooting a glance up at Ross now, he grinned knowingly and speculated, "I reckon you two are finally goin' away on your honeymoon!"

"You might say that," Ross drawled with a faint, noncommittal smile.

"And then again you might *not!*" Dallas blurted out behind him, only to realize how childish her words sounded. She spun about on the wooden planks, presenting her back to the two men and holding herself stiffly erect. Mason Parnell's grin widened.

"You know, Mr. Kincaid, I'm a married man myself," he confided with an air of masculine camaraderie. "And it's been my experience that if you don't lay down the law in the very beginnin', you're settin' yourself up for a whole lot of trouble later on, if you catch my meanin'." He slid the tickets across the counter and added with a nod toward Dallas, "Take that wife of yours there. She's a mighty pretty gal, and I doubt if there's a better cook on the face of the earth, but she's high-spirited. She'll need a firm hand, Mr. Kincaid. Yes sirree, a right firm hand!"

"I'll keep that in mind," Ross promised with a deceptively straight face as he took the tickets and moved back to Dallas's side. He was not at all surprised when she refused to let him take her arm, but he remained characteristically undaunted and did so anyway. Then, pausing to catch up their bags with his other hand, he led her forward to board the train.

XIV

The train ride was of a mercifully short duration. Some three hours after leaving Corsicana, Dallas found herself sitting beside Ross in yet another wagon and heading west out of Fort Worth. Her fascinated gaze was frequently drawn back to the city's impressive skyline, which was dominated by the Renaissance-revival style spires of the massive red granite courthouse towering four stories above the commotion that was Main Street.

Known more familiarly as Cowtown, the seat of Tarrant County had first sprung to life on the untamed, Indian-controlled prairie as a frontier fort nearly fifty years ago. Through sheer tenacity, and more than a little luck, it had managed to survive and flourish, and had by now evolved into a major business center for livestock, banking, and railroads. The cattle trails, once the economic lifeblood of the area, had shriveled up and blown away with the dust, though the wild, bawdy way of life they had brought to the area could still be evidenced in a deservedly infamous prolifera-

365

tion of saloons and brothels known as Hell's Half Acre. The rest of the city, however, had embraced progress with an almost religious zeal, and it was for this reason that Fort Worth could boast of being a major force in Texas's increasingly bright future.

To Dallas, who was seeing it for the first time in more than five years, the city appeared a good deal larger than she had remembered. But then, she mused as her lips compressed into a tight, thin line of displeasure, Ross had been in such an all-fired hurry to get to the ranch that she had been able to catch only a passing glimpse of its tall brick buildings and crowded streets.

"I naturally assumed our first order of business would be to pay a visit to your friend in jail," she remarked with a discernible edge to her voice. "And I was hoping we would stop by Mr. Willoughby's office before leaving town!"

"I sent word to Willoughby to come out to the ranch tomorrow," Ross informed her casually, his gaze making a broad, leisurely sweep over the gently rolling countryside. "As for J.D.—I plan to do some checking around before I talk to him. I might be able to learn something from the other hands that will prove helpful in clearing him."

Silence fell between them again after that. They had spoken little to each other on the train, too. Dallas reflected in still simmering anger that it was just as well, since she was in no mood to make idle conversation with the man who had forced her to leave her home and family, and who no doubt had every intention of getting her into his bed again at the first available opportunity!

She mentally cursed herself once more for having

been so weak-willed (weak-*fleshed* would be more like it, she amended wrathfully) as to let Ross Kincaid make love to her—not once, but *twice!* What made her actions particularly despicable, she thought with an inward sigh, was the fact that there was no love involved. She would have been able to forgive herself, at least a little, if she had been swept away by true affection instead of mere passion. Her marriage was supposed to be a business arrangement. So why in thunderation did she feel so utterly wretched at the thought that it meant nothing more than that to her husband? Wasn't it just possible that she herself hoped it would turn out to be so much more?

The question remained unanswered, for the moment anyway, as the tall cedar gateposts of the Kincaid ranch rose up before her eyes. A large wooden shingle hanging from the top announced the name of the vast, long-established spread to friend and visitors alike— "The Bar K"—while the house Dallas glimpsed in the near distance, standing guard at the end of a well-traveled drive, attested to the prosperity of the Bar K's owners.

Flanked by the usual collection of ranch structures—barns, sheds, corrals, and the like—the house itself was anything but usual. It was more of a mansion than a ranch house, and was much grander than anything Dallas would have expected to find even if she had been aware of the Kincaids' considerable wealth.

The massive, three-storied white building was surmounted by a peaked Gothic roof. There was a colonnaded porch, complete with arches and spool-turned balusters, surrounding all four sides of the house, as well as two second-story balconies that featured arches, Doric columns, and balusters. A small third-floor balcony was neatly tucked into the roofline. Roses bloomed all about, while a thick, neatly trimmed array of green shrubbery punctuated the immediate grounds. Huge oak trees shaded the house, yard, and outbuildings, and Dallas smiled to herself to note the circle of peach trees resting within a square section of white picket fence near the house.

"Well, this is it. Welcome to the Bar K, Mrs. Kincaid," Ross said as he drew the wagon to a halt just beyond the front porch.

"It's a very large ranch, isn't it?" murmured Dallas, still gazing about her in wonderment. She'd had no idea that Ross's home would be like this! When he had mentioned that he had grown up on a ranch near Fort Worth, she had envisioned something like the few ranches around Corsicana, which were successful enough but could not begin to compare with what she saw before her now.

"Yes, it is," he confirmed in a low voice brimming with laughter.

She sat waiting as if in a daze while he came around to help her down from the wagon, and she was a bit startled when she felt his strong hands closing about her waist. He swung her up and around in one lithe motion, then lowered her slowly to the ground while his piercing green eyes bored down into the wide, glistening sapphire depths of hers. His fingers retained their possessive encirclement of her waist for several moments longer, and she trembled as a pleasant warmth spread throughout her entire body.

"Well, bless my soul, if it isn't that young devil, Ross

Kincaid himself!" a woman suddenly exclaimed from where she had just emerged onto the front porch. Ross reluctantly let go of his wife and turned to face the Bar K's housekeeper.

"Hello, Bessie," he told her with a crooked smile. Taking Dallas's arm, he began leading her up the front steps.

"Why didn't you tell us you were coming?" Bessie demanded in a voice full of mingled pleasure and reproval. She was about the same height as Dallas, though a good thirty or perhaps even forty years older, and her light gray hair was twisted into a severe chignon that did little to help soften the angularity of her dark-complexioned features. But her eyes were shining with kindness as well as curiosity when she looked to Dallas, and she smiled warmly at the two young people who came to stand before her. "I'm afraid your folks aren't back yet," she hastened to inform Ross. "They've been down in San Antonio with your sister, waiting for the birth of their first grandchild. You did know Emmeline was going to have a baby, didn't you?"

"I heard about it a while back," he affirmed with a brief nod, then cast a sudden, thoroughly disarming smile at Dallas before announcing in a mellow tone laced with amusement, "Bessie, this is my wife."

"Your wife?" the woman repeated in obvious stupefaction.

"Dallas, this is Bessie McPherson," Ross went on as though his getting married was an everyday occurrence. "She's been with the Bar K for as long as I can remember—even longer than that, if you believe her stories about how she once fought off a whole band of

369

Comanches with nothing more than a frying pan!"

"I . . . I'm very pleased to make your acquaintance, Miss McPherson," murmured Dallas, her cheeks flaming and her eyes momentarily clouding with uncertainty. She didn't know why but it had non-plussed her to hear Ross introduce her as his wife. Telling herself that she was probably just feeling another twinge of guilt for the fact that her marriage was not what it seemed, she managed a weak smile. "I'm sorry we've come unannounced. I hope it won't be too much of an inconvenience to—"

"Inconvenience? Why, no, child, it's the most wonderful thing that's happened around here in years!" Bessie McPherson breathlessly proclaimed, giving a laugh of pure delight. Without further preamble, she caught Dallas up in an exuberant hug, then did the same to Ross. "How could you have gone and gotten yourself married without even bothering to let us know?" she scolded him halfheartedly when she drew away again. "Why, your ma's going to be the happiest woman alive when she finds out about this! And I wouldn't put it past your pa to throw the biggest shindig this county's ever seen!"

"I gather you think they're going to be pleased," Ross observed wryly, his green eyes alight with merry humor.

"Pleased? Why, you know as well as I do, Rossiter Maverick Kincaid, that they'd just about given up all hope of seeing you married! Yes indeed, if it weren't for Emmeline's condition, I've no doubt at all they'd hightail it up here on the next train!"

Ross gave a low chuckle and took Dallas's arm again. She peered narrowly up at him as Bessie's words rang in her ears. It seemed her "husband" was every bit the wild, womanizing rogue she had judged him to be that first day!

The thought was anything but comforting.

"I expect you're tired after coming all this way. I heard you've been over in Corsicana for a while," Bessie chattered amiably while they moved inside the house. Her full, black cotton skirts and stiff petticoats rustled softly as she bustled through the doorway. She flashed an apologetic smile back at Dallas and explained, "I'm afraid the place is a bit deserted right now. Most of the hands are out on the range, or working elsewhere for the summer, since things are kind of slow around here right now. The cook, Mrs. Greely, won't be back until tomorrow—she's visiting her daughter over in Weatherford—and I've had most of the rooms closed off while the Kincaids have been away."

Dallas, quickly digesting all this information, reached up and took off her hat as she started to precede her husband across the threshold. A sharp gasp broke from her lips when she was suddenly swept up in his arms.

"What do you think you're doing?" she demanded, her face crimsoning when she saw how the housekeeper was beaming indulgently upon them. "Will you please put me down?" she forced herself to ask Ross, though her tone was strained and her eyes blazed deep blue fire into the mischievously glowing viridescence of his.

"I'm following a time-honored custom, Mrs. Kincaid," he declared, refusing to set her on her feet again until they were well within the confines of the entrance foyer. Dallas, resisting the urge to jerk away, threw him one last blistering look before she took a step backward and turned her stormy gaze upon her surroundings.

The interior of the house was at the same time both luxurious and unostentatious, with the most striking feature being the extensive use of wood. The foyer in which she stood featured a faux leather wainscoting that followed the stairway to the second floor, a coffered stairway casement with panels of richly hued oak, and three variations of twist-turned balusters, as well as a carved and turned newel post. The floors were of polished pine, and the walls were papered in a light, elegant floral design in cream and rose and gold.

As Dallas was soon to learn, the rest of the house was every bit as pleasing to the eye. There was a fireplace in each room—with a multipaned, beveled ornamental mirror above each mantel—and the color scheme varied from one spacious chamber to the next. The furniture was an intriguing mixture of styles, mostly running toward a fashionably ornate description, while the paintings were of an equally diversified nature—some were classical in nature, while others followed an appropriately western theme. Leaded glass chandeliers hung from the center of the high, beamed ceilings, and the bathrooms were outfitted in exquisite detail with pure brass faucets, wood and porcelain water closets, and huge claw-foot tubs.

"Bessie will show you up to our room," decreed Ross. He was already replacing the hat atop his thick, midnight-black hair when Dallas's eyes flew back to his handsome face in surprise.

"Where are you going?" she demanded with a slight frown.

"I thought I'd ride out and have a word with the

hands. Then I'll go see J.D. I should be back before dark." He suddenly caught her about the waist, bent his head, and pressed a quick but nonetheless breathtaking kiss upon her parted lips. Releasing her again, he smiled unrepentantly down into her flushed, wide-eyed countenance and took himself back outside. She stared after him, struggling to regain the composure his kiss had stolen, while Bessie McPherson laughed softly and shook her head.

"He really is a devil, isn't he? I hope you'll tell me just how it was the two of you came to be married. But first things first," the housekeeper pronounced with a sigh. Turning about, she began leading the way up the staircase. "This isn't the original house, of course. I expect Ross told you what happened to the first one?" It was more of a question than a statement.

"No," replied Dallas. *As a matter of fact,* she added silently, *Ross told me very little about anything!*

"Well, it burned to the ground nearly eight years ago. That was such an awful, awful night," recalled Bessie, shaking her head. "Most of the children still lived at home then. Ross—he's the oldest, you know—was away at that college up North. We managed to get everyone out in time, though none of us were left with anything but the clothes on our back. Mr. Kincaid swore he'd build his wife an even finer and bigger house than before. That's exactly what he did, all right."

"Does my—does Ross get home often?" asked Dallas. She followed the older woman up to the second-floor landing, then frowned in mild puzzlement when they started climbing yet another flight of stairs.

"Not more than once a year, usually. I sure do hope you're planning to stay until his folks get back. They'd be heartsick if they missed seeing him—or you, for that matter," Bessie added with another chuckle.

"I . . . I'm afraid we have to return to Corsicana by Tuesday."

"Oh, I'm sorry to hear that. Is that where you're from?"

"Yes. I live there with my two younger sisters."

"I guess now that you've gone and married yourself a driller, you'll have to get used to living in Pennsylvania."

"Pennsylvania?" Dallas echoed in bemusement. "Why would I—" she started to ask, only to break off when it dawned on her that the woman was referring to the fact that Ross had spent the past several years working in the oil fields up there.

"Unless, of course," the housekeeper went on as though Dallas hadn't spoken, "that boom there in Corsicana I've been hearing about turns out to be as big a thing as everyone around here hopes it will. Why, it goes without saying that nothing would please Ross's folks more than to have him living so close for a change!"

Much to Dallas's relief, she saw that they had reached the third floor by now. Bessie showed her into the topmost bedroom, the one which boasted of the small, roofline balcony she had glimpsed in front of the house earlier.

"This one was decorated with Ross in mind," the housekeeper disclosed with a soft smile as she swung open the door. "His ma used his favorite color—sort of a royal blue, I guess you'd call it."

"Why, it's lovely!" Dallas remarked in genuine admiration when she stepped inside. Her eyes made a swift examination of the room's furnishings—a massive, four-poster bed with an untrimmed canopy of deep blue silk and a matching coverlet, a double wardrobe which reached nearly to the ceiling, a mirrored chest of drawers, a wing chair upholstered in a dark wine leather, draperies of cream-colored velvet, and a large oval wool rug sporting a circular combination of blue, wine, and cream. A doorway leading to the bathroom could be seen on the papered wall opposite the windows.

"I'll leave you to rest up. If you want anything, I'll be down in the kitchen. At least you and Ross will only have to tolerate my cooking for this one night!" Bessie remarked with another smile, then grew serious for a moment as she suddenly took the younger woman's hand between the two of hers.

"I'm real happy for you, Dallas. I don't claim to be impartial, but it's my opinion that you've married yourself one of the best. And I always said that the woman who someday managed to get Ross Kincaid to the altar would have to be mighty special, mighty special indeed. Now," she said, giving Dallas's hand a final pat before turning to leave, "I hope you'll come on down and have a cup of coffee with me in a little while. It strikes me that the two of us have an awful lot to talk about!"

Returning Bessie's infectious smile, Dallas watched as the housekeeper left the room and went rustling softly back down the staircase. She then released a long, pent-up sigh, closed the door, and leaned heavily back against it. Her eyes kindled with sudden displeasure as they traveled about the room again.

Our room, Ross had said. He was obviously expecting them to share it. Well, she'd soon set him straight on that particular score! He may have been able to persuade her to come to Fort Worth with him, but he would most assuredly *not* meet with success if he thought he'd persuade her to do anything else.

Pushing away from the door, she wandered over to the window and peered outward. Her face grew warm as her gaze suddenly fell upon her tall, devilishly handsome husband. He was leading a horse from one of the barns, and she saw that there were three men following after him. He swung up into the saddle in one lithe motion, exchanged some further words with the men, then reined about and rode away, heading southward across the open pastureland beneath the blazing sun.

Dallas turned slowly away from the window. Unconsciously raising a hand to rest upon the spot where her heart pounded with such alarming irregularity in her breast, she moved to the chair and sank down into it.

It seemed so strange to be there in Ross Kincaid's home—in *his* bedroom, no less. He had seemed different somehow ever since they'd left Corsicana, she mused with another sigh. Why, even she herself seemed different . . .

"But nothing's changed at all!" she hastily murmured aloud in denial.

She and Ross would sleep in separate bedrooms that night and every other night, Mr. Willoughby would pay them a visit the following day and set all the financial matters in order, Ross would complete his own business on behalf of his friend, and they would return to Corsicana on Tuesday. Yes indeed, she told herself firmly, everything would go exactly as planned, and she would soon be home, living her own life and leaving Ross to live his. There would be a certain stigma attached to being a divorced woman, of course, but she wouldn't mind too much. Better that, she reasoned, than being forced to continue her stormy association with Ross Kincaid for four more years!

And better that than never to have known what it meant to be a woman, that dreaded inner voice of hers piped up, then added more fuel to the fire with, *At least your marriage was real enough for you to experience the sort of earth-shattering passion some women only dream about.*

Shocked and dismayed at her own thoughts, Dallas jumped up from the chair. Her inner turmoil only increased when she looked at the canopied four-poster. Silently cursing Ross, herself, *and* the bed, she marched angrily across to the bathroom door and wrenched it open.

She was much more in control of her emotions when she ventured downstairs a short time later. Having washed her face, repinned her hair, and smoothed her travel-creased skirts, she felt a good deal better. She easily located the kitchen by way of the delicious smells it sent wafting through the house. Lifting her head determinedly, she pushed open the swing-hinged door and peered inside. Bessie McPherson greeted her with a warm smile of welcome.

"Come on in and have a seat! I can put on a fresh pot of coffee, or I've got some lemonade made up if you'd rather have that," the housekeeper offered.

"Lemonade sounds best," Dallas admitted with a smile of her own. She took a seat at the flour-dusted worktable while Bessie hurried to fetch the pitcher from the oak icebox next to the sink. The kitchen was not appreciably larger than the one at home, mused Dallas idly, but the Kincaids' kitchen was obviously used for the sole purpose of preparing food, while the one at home had of necessity always doubled as a dining room.

"It is a bit warm in here for coffee, isn't it?" the older woman remarked with a pleasant chuckle. She filled two glasses with the half-sweet, half-tart liquid and handed one to Dallas across the width of the table. "I've survived a lot of summers in these parts, but you never know what it's going to be like from one year to the next. I do believe this will turn out to be one of the real scorchers, though. Why, here it is only June, and I swear it's already hot enough to wither a fence post."

Dallas smiled to herself at that, for it was the same expression she had heard her father use many times. Taking a long, grateful drink of the lemonade, she glanced toward the tall, open windows which stretched all the way around the other end of the room.

"There's a very nice breeze, though." Her eyes moved back to where Bessie had resumed the bread baking. "Is there something I can help with, Miss McPherson? I feel rather at loose ends, I'm afraid," she confessed a bit self-consciously. She told herself her awkwardness stemmed from the fact that she had no right to be there. The other woman believed her to be Ross's loving bride, but she wasn't. He didn't love her, and he hadn't really brought her home to be welcomed into the bosom of his family. She was in truth nothing more than an outsider . . .

"First off, it's 'Bessie', and secondly, you're a brand-new bride and shouldn't have to worry about cooking and such just yet! Which brings me back to the question of how you and Ross came to meet. It wasn't all that long ago, was it?" she asked with a kindly, knowing smile as she continued kneading the dough.

"No, it wasn't," Dallas verified uncomfortably, her gaze dropping to the glass in her hands.

"I didn't think so. The two of you still have every bit of that 'bloom' about you! It's easy to see he's crazy about you. But then, he'd have to be pretty well smitten to marry you. If there was ever a man who fought tooth and nail against getting tied down, that man was Ross Kincaid!"

"I gathered that he's always been quite popular with the ladies," Dallas murmured with a touch of bitterness.

"That he has. Why, there were girls all over the county chasing after him! But he didn't pay as much attention to them as you would have thought. No, Ross has always been what you'd call the choosy type," Bessie concluded with another soft laugh. She paused for a moment and placed one of the newly formed loaves into a pan. When she spoke again, it was with a more serious demeanor. "I don't mean to be prying, Dallas, but you seem a bit worried about something. I hope I haven't said anything that—"

"Oh no, Bessie, not at all," Dallas hastened to assure her. "I . . . I'm still a little tired, that's all." She forced a deceptively bright smile to her lips and suggested, "Why don't you tell me something about yourself?"

"There's not much to tell. I grew up on a farm in Georgia a long time ago. Ross's pa and I are distant cousins. He married Ross's ma and came to Texas back in '66. They wrote me a few years later and said they could use the help if I wanted to come. Seeing as how I had never married and didn't have any family of my own to care for, I decided to take them up on the offer. I've been here ever since." She broke into another grin when she added, "That husband of yours was nothing more than a gleam in his pa's eyes when I came out here. I don't mind telling you that Ross has always been my favorite."

"Yes, I can see that," Dallas murmured quietly. Seized by a sudden, powerful desire to know more about the man she had married, she smiled again and asked, "Was he this overbearing as a child?"

"Almost!" Bessie answered with a laugh, her eyes twinkling at the memory. "He was always stubborn and independent, but such a charmer that he could usually talk his way out of any trouble with me or his ma! His pa was not a lenient man, though, so I suppose it all evened out in the end." She finished kneading the other lump of dough and dusted some of the flour from her hands.

"He grew up in the saddle, of course, and he started riding the range with the men when he was only twelve. His pa taught him to shoot and hunt and rope long before that, while his ma made sure he got to school during the week and to church every Sunday. Life wasn't easy back then, but it was good," she concluded, carrying the pans over to the oven. Once she had popped them inside, she turned back to Dallas and said, "I don't know about you, but I could do with a bit of fresh air! Since that new husband of yours went off and 'deserted' you for the afternoon, how would you like for me to show you around?"

"Thank you, Bessie, I'd like that very much," Dallas accepted with genuine pleasure. She took one last sip of the lemonade, then stood and accompanied the other woman outside.

Dallas had learned a great deal about her husband and his family by the time he returned from Fort Worth that evening. Most of the information Bessie Mc-Pherson had been so willing to impart concerned Ross's childhood there at the ranch, although the devoted housekeeper *had* made mention of a few details relating to his life for the past ten years—for instance, he had attended that college up North because it was the same one his father and grandfather had attended, he had refused to return home after graduation and take up ranching or the law or some other "worthy profession" in spite of his father's insistence that he do so, he had very nearly been killed in a well blowout not too long after becoming a driller, and he had continually worried both his parents during the long periods when they received no word from him.

As a matter of fact, Dallas mused with a complacent smile as she stepped into the bathtub and eased her naked curves down into the water's comforting warmth, she no doubt possessed certain bits of knowledge about Ross Kincaid that he would much rather she did not!

She leaned back against the smooth white porcelain of the tub for several minutes, content to relax and allow the tiredness of her muscles to be soothed away. Feeling considerably refreshed, she took up the cake of soap and scrubbed every inch of her glistening satiny form, then decided to wash the journey's dust from her hair as well.

When she unlocked the door and emerged into the bedroom again a short time later, she was attired in nothing more than a thin cotton wrapper. She rubbed vigorously at her long, wet tresses with a towel as she went padding barefoot across the wooden floor, and it wasn't until she had reached the bed that she looked up and saw Ross watching her from the leather wing chair. She instinctively gasped and clutched the towel to her thinly covered bosom.

"What the devil are you doing in here?" she demanded indignantly, her eyes flashing. Her wet hair streamed wildly about her face and shoulders, giving her a particularly vulnerable look which Ross found enchanting.

"Waiting for you. This *is* our room, isn't it?" he challenged with a mocking smile as he leisurely drew himself upright. His gaze darkened and smoldered as it raked over her damp, lavender-scented loveliness, but he made no move to approach her.

"No it isn't!" she hotly denied. "Now get out!"

His only response was to raise his hands and begin unbuttoning his shirt. Dallas's eyes widened in alarm, and her fingers tightened about the soft cotton towel she held clasped to her breasts.

"Wha—what do you think you're doing?" she now demanded, her voice a good deal more tremulous than she would have wished.

"Exactly what it looks like." He drew off his shirt and sat back down in the chair to remove his boots.

"Why are you getting undressed?" Her eyes were full of growing suspicion and alarm, and though her instincts told her to flee, her body refused to obey.

"I'm going to take a bath," he announced casually. His eyes, however, were alive with devilment. He set the boots aside, quickly peeled off his socks, and stood again while his hands moved to the front of his trousers.

"Not in *my* bathroom you're not!" Her outrage was tempered with relief—and a nagging sense of disappointment which she refused to acknowledge.

"What's mine is yours, my love, but there's no need to get selfish," he quipped. His mouth curved into a wicked grin as he finished unfastening his trousers and began sliding them downward over his lean, hard-muscled hips. Dallas crimsoned and spun about.

"Damn you, Ross Kincaid, it was never agreed upon that we would be sharing a room! I don't care about appearances—let Bessie or anyone else think what they please! Either you move your things elsewhere, or I'll do so myself!" she furiously threatened.

"I'd strongly advise against such action, wildcat," he drawled as he began heading, naked, toward the bathroom. "But just in case you feel compelled to disregard my advice, be forewarned that I'll do whatever's necessary to 'resolve' the situation." He spoke this last in a low, vibrant tone close to her ear, and she was dismayed to feel a warm shiver dancing down her spine.

She closed her eyes tightly when he brushed past her, but a sudden, mischievous impulse prompted them to flutter briefly open again. They were treated with a tantalizing glimpse of the bronzed, powerfully muscled expanse of her husband's back and shoulders . . . the lean, perfectly formed roundness of his buttocks . . .

the tapered hardness of his thighs . . .

"I'd ask you to scrub my back, sweetheart, but Bessie's waiting for us downstairs," he drawled without even turning his head. His voice was brimming with undeniable amusement, and Dallas could almost *feel* him smiling that infuriating, self-satisfied smile of his.

"You can go straight to hell, Ross Kincaid!" she shot back, whirling about with a vengeance as her cheeks burned anew.

She stood there fairly quaking with anger for several long moments, until she heard Ross's deep-timbred voice drifting outward from the bathroom. He had broken into a low but nonetheless hearty chorus of "Sweet Betsy From Pike," certain lyrics of which were hardly suitable for a proper young lady's ears.

Dallas leveled a murderous look at the door, though her intended victim was safely on the other side, and virtually tore off her wrapper. She yanked on her undergarments, then hurriedly donned a square-necked, embroidered gown of robin's egg blue muslin. There was little she could do with the heavy auburn locks cascading so damply about her, so she created a single long braid and coiled it low upon the nape of her neck, securing it with an extra number of pins.

Stealing one last glance toward the room where her husband was still alternately splashing and vocalizing, she swept from the bedroom and down the stairs. She explained away her lone appearance in the dining room moments later by telling Bessie quite truthfully that Ross was not yet dressed. The housekeeper seemed to accept the explanation, for she chuckled and said that Ross had nearly always been late getting to the supper table as a boy, too.

It wasn't too much longer, however, when the perpetual latecomer in question arrived to take his place at the opposite end of the table from his bride. He bent his tall, splendidly virile frame into the chair, then cast Dallas an unsettling look from eyes that were aglow with an intense, tenderly predacious light.

His appearance was equally disquieting. For the first time since Dallas had known him, he was attired in something other than denim trousers, cowboy boots, and a simple cotton shirt. Tonight, he wore an impeccably tailored suit of black serge, a fitted shirt of white linen with a black string tie, and a pair of boots that, although undeniably western in flavor, were elaborately stitched and fashioned of rich, dark brown leather. Dallas told herself that he had never looked more handsome—or more dangerous.

Bessie, waving aside the younger woman's offer to help, bustled cheerfully off to the kitchen to fetch the first course of the special meal she had prepared. The merest hint of a smile played about Ross's lips as his gaze once again traveled the length of the elegantly set, chandelier-brightened table to where his wife sat with her back stiffly erect.

"It might interest you to know that the charges against J.D. are probably going to be dropped by this time tomorrow," he disclosed while absently fingering the crystal goblet beside his plate. Dallas's eyes widened at him in surprise.

"Dropped? But I thought—"

"The situation did look pretty bad, at first," said Ross, anticipating her question. "After questioning the hands, I rode into town and spoke with the sheriff. Strangely enough, he and I had reached the same conclusion—the whole damned thing was nothing more than a setup. Someone planted that stock on Bar K property, then arranged to have J.D. caught with the evidence. It's an old practice," he explained quietly, "left over from the days of the open range. Back then, however, it was usually settled without benefit of the law."

"But why would anyone do such a thing?" Dallas asked in stunned disbelief. She shuddered to think that an innocent man might have been hanged as a result of someone else's treachery.

"I don't know. But I'm sure as hell going to find out," Ross vowed grimly, his eyes gleaming with a fierce, vengeful light as his fingers suddenly clenched about the goblet's delicate stem.

"I don't understand," Dallas murmured with a frown of bemusement. "If the sheriff is as convinced as you are that his prisoner is innocent, then why hasn't he released him yet?"

"Because he's been trying to find the man who turned J.D. in. It seems the 'key witness' has suddenly disappeared," he revealed with a faint, sardonic smile. "My guess is that the bastard lit out once he'd done the dirty work for whoever it was that framed J.D."

"What makes you so certain the man who gave testimony against your friend isn't the same one who devised this villainous little scheme?"

"Call it instinct." He smiled again, but this time it was with wry humor. "So, Mrs. Kincaid, it appears our journey may have been unnecessary after all."

"You're forgetting about Mr. Willoughby." She was about to elaborate, but Bessie finally reappeared, bearing a tray laden with two bowls of split-pea soup and a chilled bottle of wine.

"Sorry it took me so long. I guess you could say I'm more than a little out of practice at this!" the housekeeper laughingly remarked. "I'm a good cook, mind you, but Mrs. Greely doesn't let me try my hand at it too much anymore."

"It smells delicious, Bessie," Dallas hastened to assure her.

"I just hope it tastes better than it looks," teased Ross, his sun-kissed brow creasing into a mock scowl as he stuck his spoon into the thick green liquid.

"You never did want to eat anything green, did you?" Bessie recalled fondly, chuckling again. "Well, it won't kill you to make an exception just this once!" She finished pouring the wine, then announced, "I'll be back in a little while with the meat and potatoes. At least I know *that* will get eaten." Casting a narrow, meaningful look at the man whom she remembered being hardheaded even as a child, she left the newlyweds alone once more.

"About Mr. Willoughby," Dallas began anew after sampling the soup and finding it every bit as palatable as she had expected. She had little appetite, however. Dining alone with Ross only served to make her feel more uncomfortable than ever. No matter how much she pretended to be perfectly calm and collected, she was in reality a mass of raw nerves! She couldn't forget the way he had looked at her upstairs a short time ago . . . nor how she had looked at *him*. More than anything else, she wished she were safely back at home, surrounded by her sisters and Ruby Mae and—

"What about him?" Ross's deep voice, brimming with amusement, broke in on her increasingly frantic reverie. She blushed and gently cleared her throat.

"Exactly when is he supposed to come calling tomorrow?" she managed to ask with admirable composure.

"He won't be coming."

"He—he won't?" she faltered in bewilderment, her eyebrows knitting together into a frown. Smiling softly, Ross leaned back in his chair and negligently swirled the wine round in his glass.

"No. He won't." His vibrant green eyes held an unmistakable challenge.

"Well, why not? I thought you said he—"

"I stopped by his office while I was in town today," he broke in to divulge with seeming nonchalance. "We were able to take care of everything then."

"But I thought my presence was required!" she reminded him sharply, her eyes kindling as her temper flared. "That was the very reason—no, the *only* reason I agreed to come with you!"

"Was it?" he retorted with maddening complacency. His rugged, thoroughly masculine features appeared even darker and more striking than usual above the snowy whiteness of his collar, and there was a certain, inexplicable air of intent about him that set off a warning bell in Dallas's brain.

"You know very well it was! So why in blue blazes did you pay a visit to him without me?" she demanded in a furious undertone, remembering that Bessie was on the other side of the door behind Ross.

"Because, my dearest bride," he replied, straightening in his chair and lowering his almost empty glass back to the table, "I decided it would be best if I handled the business with Willoughby alone."

"That's all well and good, Ross Kincaid, but it was not *your* decision to make!" she stormed. She snatched the napkin from her lap and flung it wrathfully down beside her plate. "How dare you do such a thing! I am every bit as involved in this matter as you, and you had no right, no *right* to leave me out of the discussion with Mr. Willoughby! Why, there were several things I wanted to talk over with him, not only about *my* inheritance but also about *our* divorce!"

She was startled to observe the slow, eminently satisfied smile that rose to her husband's lips, but she was positively thunderstruck by the words those same lips uttered.

"There isn't going to be a divorce."

XV

"What?" breathed Dallas, staring at him as though he had suddenly taken complete leave of his senses. "What do you mean 'there isn't going to be a divorce'? Of course there's going to be a divorce!"

"No, wildcat," Ross disputed with a slight shake of his head. His expression was now forebodingly solemn, while his eyes gleamed with an intense, determined light. "There will be no divorce."

Her emotions were thrown into utter chaos by his words. Although thoroughly outraged at the realization that he intended to break his promise, she could not deny that she also felt a strange, heady exhilaration . . .

"I guess maybe it was a little too hot for soup," Bessie observed, blissfully unaware that she had chosen such an inopportune moment to reappear. She came bustling into the dining room with the main course, which she served up with a pointedly jubilant little smile for each of the silent newlyweds before taking herself off to the kitchen again.

"It looks like Bessie's outdone herself tonight," Ross commented dryly as he eyed the pot roast and vegetables the woman had heaped on his plate. Dallas, however, was in no mood to talk about the house-keeper's culinary triumphs.

"Is this some cruel jest of yours, perhaps?" she accusingly demanded. "Because if it is, I do not find it in the least bit humorous!" The color rode high on her cheeks, and she waged a visible battle to maintain control over her flaring temper. "We agreed that this arrangement of ours would be temporary, remember? We also agreed that I would seek a divorce just as soon as all of the legalities concerning the trusteeship were out of the way. Since you have already taken the liberty of speaking to Mr. Willoughby, I'm sure it will only be a matter of time until all of the documents pertaining to this matter have been filed. Therefore," she concluded with a narrow, fiery glance in his direction, "it is no longer necessary for us to continue with this . . . this contemptible charade! I fully intend to pay a visit to Mr. Willoughby myself and—"

"You'd be wasting your time." A glimmer of mocking amusement danced in his magnificent green eyes once more. "I've already made it clear to him that divorce is out of the question. So, Mrs. Kincaid, you might as well get used to the fact that you're stuck with me—for life."

"But why?" she demanded in furious confusion, her head spinning. *This can't be happening!* she thought dazedly. "Why are you doing this? You . . . you don't want to stay married to me, so why—"

"For the simple reason that I hold what's mine," he told her, knowing damned well it was not that simple at all. "You belong to me now, Dallas. Neither one of us counted on things working out this way, but they have. As far as I'm concerned, the original terms of our agreement ceased to matter the night you came to my room." He did not add that he still thanked God for the fact that she *had* come—aside from leaving him with the warm, delectable memory of holding her in his arms, that night had also convinced him once and for all of her true feelings.

"I've already told you I didn't come to your room for *that!*" Blushing fierily, she threw him a murderous glare and declared, "What happend that night changes nothing! You made it perfectly clear to me before we got married that you had no desire to take on the responsibility of a wife! Your freedom is the most precious thing in the world to you, isn't it? Well then, you may have it, for I still intend to divorce you as soon as possible!"

"You're my wife," he countered in a low, disturbingly vibrant tone. "In every sense of the word. And I have no intention of letting you go."

"To hell with your intentions!" she seethed, feeling angry and betrayed . . . and terribly sick at heart. For one fleeting moment, she had believed that Ross Kincaid wanted to keep their marriage intact because he had come to care for her. But such was not the case. No, she mused bitterly, their marriage was still a farce, only worse now. He wasn't claiming to love her, but merely to *own* her because he had made love to her. Whether this sudden change in plans stemmed from a misplaced sense of duty or a burst of masculine pride, the fact still remained that he was refusing to honor his part of the bargain.

She rose abruptly to her feet, then watched as he drew himself upright as well. They stood there at opposite ends of the table, facing each other like two combatants instead of husband and wife—or perhaps, thought Ross as an appreciative smile of irony tugged at his lips, the comparison was really an analogy—while Dallas struggled with her temper and Ross struggled with his desire.

"If you think for one moment that I am going to let you get away with this," Dallas feelingly expounded, "then I am afraid that *you,* Mr. Kincaid, have greatly underestimated my intelligence as well as my determination! After all, Howard Willoughby is certainly not the only lawyer in Fort Worth, and I am quite sure I will be able to find someone willing to help me obtain a divorce!"

"On what grounds?" parried Ross.

"Wha—what?" she stammered, her eyes widening in bemusement again.

"You'll be required to list a specific reason for wanting to rid yourself of me." Another slow, affectionately taunting smile lit his handsome visage as he folded his arms across his broad chest. His gaze raked over her with a significant boldness. "Assuming you're inclined to tell the truth, then you won't be able to claim that I beat you, or that I failed to perform my husbandly duties, or even that I was untrue. No, my love," he concluded, frowning slightly, "I'm afraid I've been guilty of none of those things, nor of any other misdeed serious enough to warrant a dissolution of our marriage."

The color drained from Dallas's face as the truth of his words sank in. *Damn him, he was right!* She couldn't very well stand before a judge and admit that she had only entered into the marriage for purely mercenary reasons, that she had never intended to remain true to her wedding vows, or that she had allowed everyone but her family to think that her relationship with Ross Kincaid was everything it should be. Worst of all, she couldn't deny that their union, though founded on selfish calculation and purposeful deceit, had been consummated—*on their wedding night,* she recalled with an inward groan—and thus rendered perfectly valid in the eyes of the law ...

"Sit down, Mrs. Kincaid," Ross commanded with a smile of maddening equanimity. "You can rant and rave at me all you like after supper."

His words, combined with his deceptively cavalier attitude about the matter, made Dallas see red. She grew visibly enraged, her beautiful countenance flooding with hot, angry color while her eyes fired a barrage of brilliant sapphire sparks at the man who had done nothing but bedevil and inflame and humiliate her from the very first. Something deep within her snapped.

"Oh, how I hate you!" she ground out, so infuriated she could scarcely speak. "You are without a doubt the most detestable, arrogant—" Breaking off as an almost painful surge of tears threatened to overwhelm her, she cast him one last fiercely belligerent look, then whipped about and went storming from the room in a furious, rustling swirl of muslin and lace.

Ross frowned after her for a moment, before his brow cleared once more and another slow, purposeful smile touched his lips.

"Good night, Bessie!" he proclaimed, his deep voice

easily reaching the kitchen. His gaze, darkening and smoldering as he strode from the dining room, traveled up the staircase with a foreboding intensity.

A much surprised Bessie McPherson came rushing out of the kitchen just in time to see Ross's tall frame disappearing through the doorway. Her widened eyes flew back to the table, where she noted the untouched food and the chairs that had obviously been vacated in a hurry. She shook her head and chuckled softly to herself, marveling at the passionate impetuosity of youth while giving thanks for the fact that she was well past such things. Tossing a glance overhead, she said a quick prayer for the two young people, for she had already guessed they were having a bit of difficulty adjusting to their wedded bliss.

"Don't they all?" Bessie mused aloud. Heaving a sigh, she began gathering up the dishes.

Dallas, meanwhile, was at that very moment safely—or so she believed—ensconced within the confines of the third-floor bedroom, where a lamp had been left burning in anticipation of the coming nightfall. After pausing to lock the door, she had flung herself facedown upon the canopied four-poster and was now in the process of giving vent to her anger and misery. She raised her head and gasped in alarm when a loud, insistent knock sounded unexpectedly at the door.

"Open the door, Dallas." There was no mistaking that low, wonderfully resonant voice.

"No!" She drew herself into a sitting position on the bed and dashed impatiently at the tears coursing down the flushed smoothness of her cheeks. "Damn you, Ross Kincaid, leave me alone!" she cried, her own voice rising shrilly.

"Either you open this blasted door, or I'll break it down," he warned in a tone that left little doubt as to the sincerity of his threat.

"Go away! I . . . I never want to see you again!" she countered with a rather watery vehemence. She collapsed back down upon the blue silk comforter and buried her face in her hands.

Suddenly, there was a loud crash.

A breathless cry broke from Dallas's lips as she jerked herself upright again. Her glistening eyes filled with mingled startlement and alarm when they fell upon her husband, who stood framed ominously in the open doorway.

She scrambled off the bed in a flash, hastily smoothing her skirts down about her. An involuntary shiver ran the length of her spine when her wide, luminous gaze was drawn back to encounter the glowing, fiery green steadiness of Ross's.

"Why, you—how dare you!" she raged with admirable spirit, though her whole body trembled with fear . . . and an excitement she dared not acknowledge. "Get out of here at once!"

"No, wildcat," he refused with a faint, dangerously enigmatic little smile. "You and I have some unfinished business to settle." Closing the door he had just forced open, he sauntered across to the wing chair and took a seat. Dallas blinked at him in astonishment when he began calmly removing his boots.

"What are you doing?" Initially expecting him to pounce on her, she was unnerved by his nonchalance.

"Once again, my love, I think my actions speak for themselves," he drawled with lazy good humor. Setting

397

his boots neatly beside the chair, he peeled off his socks and rose to his feet. He next shrugged out of his jacket, slipped the tie from about his neck, and tossed them heedlessly across the chair. When his hands moved to the buttons of his shirt, he smiled roguishly and said, "It might interest you to know that I fully intend for this time to be unlike the others. No wells to drill, no interruptions—remember? We've the whole night, Mrs. Kincaid. I intend to make use of every minute of it," he vowed, taking off his shirt and baring the bronzed, hard-muscled expanse of his upper body to his bride's mesmerized gaze.

Dallas, her cheeks burning and her legs weakening, swallowed hard and finally sprang to life once more. She whirled about and flew to the door, only to cry out sharply when Ross caught her about the waist and pulled her forcibly back against him.

"It's too late for that," he murmured close to her ear. "You're mine, Dallas, and I'm damn well going to make sure you never forget it!"

"Let go of me, you bastard!" she shot back, squirming furiously within his grasp. "Take your hands off me or I'll scream! I'll scream so loud everyone on the ranch will hear me!"

"Go ahead," he retorted with a low chuckle as he easily held her captive. "No one will dare to interfere. Hell, sweetheart, even Bessie wouldn't dream of denying me the right to make love to my own wife!"

"But it *isn't* love!" Dallas hotly dissented, her struggles intensifying in spite of their futility. "It's nothing more than simple lust and—"

"There's nothing 'simple' about what we feel for each other," insisted Ross, "just as there's nothing wrong with a strong, healthy desire for wanting to do what we're about to do!"

Another gasp was forced from her lips as he suddenly spun her about and flung her facedown over his shoulder. She beat at his powerful, naked back with her fists, but her blows appeared to have little—if any—effect, for his arms merely tightened about her knees as he bore her relentlessly toward the massive four-poster.

"Put me down, damn you!" She squirmed and started to kick, only to give a small, indignant shriek when he brought his large hand up against the conveniently placed roundness of her buttocks in a forceful, stinging whack.

She had no sooner raised her fists to retaliate when she suddenly found herself being tumbled backward through the air to land upon the silk-covered bed. She lay there for the moment, stunned and gasping for breath, while Ross swiftly unfastened his trousers, drew them off, and flung them aside.

Although she turned a fiery red, Dallas could not force her shocked and fascinated gaze away from the tall, undeniably masculine rogue who stood beside the bed wearing nothing but a smile. She had never viewed a man's naked body before, yet she sensed that Ross's was far superior to most.

His powerful shoulders, sinewy arms, and broad, softly matted chest tapered down into a trim waist and lean-muscled hips, which in turn beckoned her widened eyes downward to a pair of granite-hard thighs and long, perfectly formed legs. To Dallas, however, the most alarming feature of his magnificent form was the one she had certainly been made aware of before now—with highly pleasurable results—but which she had never actually seen. Her attention was ultimately drawn to, and held by, the thatch of curly, midnight-black hair where the evidence of her husband's virility grew even harder beneath her innocent observation.

"Now, Mrs. Kincaid, it's time to return the favor," he decreed in a low, slightly husky tone. She colored guiltily as her eyes flew back up to his. What she saw reflected therein prompted her to retreat hastily to the other side of the bed.

"You keep away from me, Ross Kincaid! I . . . I'm not going to let you do this to me!" she faltered breathlessly. "I don't care what you say, our marriage was a terrible mistake, a mistake which should be rectified without further delay!"

"You're right," he startled her by agreeing. Perched rather precariously on the edge of the bed, she blinked up at him in bewilderment.

"I . . . I am?"

"Our marriage was a mistake in that I never should have allowed you to keep me at a distance after that night in my room," he clarified. "As you say, the mistake should be rectified without further delay—*and it will be!*"

Dallas inhaled sharply. She looked anxiously about for any means of escape, her eyes growing very round when they lit upon the double French doors leading out onto the balcony. It occurred to her that, if she could only make her way outside, she would be able to climb down onto the second-story roof and thence to the ground below. Then, she would ride like the very devil and never look back!

Even if her plan had not been so foolhardy, she still would not have been given the opportunity to put it into action—Ross had grown impatient by now. Without another word, he dropped to his knees upon the bed, his hand shooting out to entangle within the fullness of her muslin skirts. She slid from atop the silk comforter and tugged at the delicate cotton folds with all her might, but to no avail. Finally, in an act of desperation, she yanked on the imprisoned fabric, succeeding only in ripping a goodly portion of the gathered skirt from the bodice.

"Now see what you've done!" she stormed, her eyes blazing reproachfully at him.

"I'm going to do a hell of a lot more than that if you don't stop fighting me," he threatened with an unrepentant scowl. "Damn it, woman, you know you want this as much as I do!"

"I *what?*" seethed Dallas. Drawing herself rigidly erect, she declared with proud, angry defiance, "The only thing worse than your insolence, Ross Kincaid, is the size of your . . . your—"

"Yes?" he challenged pointedly, his mouth curving into a brief yet thoroughly wicked grin.

"Your *ego!*" she finished wrathfully as a wave of embarrassment washed over her. She cursed herself for being unable to prevent her eyes from straying to his exposed manhood once more.

Ross, apparently tiring of the game, gave a sudden, forceful jerk and brought her tumbling unceremoniously back down to the bed. Landing on her stomach, she lay sprawled across the sumptuous blue silk with her skirts and petticoats up about her knees. She was given no time to flee this time, for Ross immediately straddled her and began unlooping the buttons on the back of her tight-fitting bodice with a swift dexterity borne of much practice.

"No!" she protested feebly. Her twisting and squirming, she soon realized, only made things worse. Almost before she knew what was happening, her dress and petticoats were being tugged impatiently downward, leaving behind the thin barrier provided by her chemise and drawers.

Dallas, taking advantage of the momentary freedom afforded her when Ross moved aside to strip the loosened clothing from her body, scrambled to her knees with the intention of climbing down from the bed and bolting for the door. Her plans were once again thwarted, however, as Ross looped a hand in the waistband of her drawers. She gasped in mingled shock and outrage when he suddenly seized hold of the undergarment with both hands and yanked it downward, baring her lovely backside to his searing gaze.

"No, damn you, no!" she cried again, her voice edged with rising panic now.

Ross said nothing in response. He caught her about the waist as she made yet another desperate attempt to escape. Quickly liberating her shapely limbs from the tangled folds of her beribboned, white muslin drawers, he transferred his attention to her chemise, which reached to just above the middle of her silken thighs. Though she did her best under the present circumstances, she could not prevent him from stripping the chemise from her as well.

She was as naked as he now, a fact which most assuredly did not go unnoticed by either of them.

Ross, swiftly forcing his beautiful captive back upon

the bed, imprisoned her wrists with his hands and stretched them above her head, while one of his powerful legs easily subdued both of hers. Her struggles gradually lessened.

Dallas, her breasts rising and falling rapidly as she sought to catch her breath, blushed rosily from head to toe as Ross's scorching gaze traveled hungrily over her supple, lamplit curves. She was both frightened and strangely thrilled by the look on his handsome face, and she trembled beneath his intense, undeniably appreciative scrutiny.

"You're even more beautiful than I imagined," he pronounced in that low, vibrant tone that never failed to send a delicious tremor coursing through her.

"Will you please let me—me go now?" she faltered weakly, her eyes falling self-consciously before his. Heaven help her, but she knew in that moment that she had neither the strength nor the inclination to fight him any longer . . .

"Never," murmured Ross. With that, he lowered his head and claimed her lips in a tender yet demanding kiss that would have destroyed any lingering resistance. She shivered with the first stirrings of passion, her lips parting beneath his and her naked breasts tingling as they brushed against his softly matted chest.

His warm, velvety tongue explored the willing sweetness of her mouth, prompting her to give a soft sigh of surrender and return his rapidly deepening kiss. Her wrists were released soon thereafter, and she brought her arms down to entwine about the corded muscles of his neck while his strong arms slipped possessively about her quivering softness and gathered her close.

He suddenly rolled to his back upon the quietly rustling blue silk so that Dallas was atop him. His hands moved to her braided chignon, where he expertly tugged the pins free and untwisted the strands of lustrous auburn hair. Still slightly damp, her long tresses spilled down about them both like a glorious, dark red mantle.

Ross's warm fingers trailed an imaginary, fiery path downward, across the graceful curve of her back, over the satiny roundness of her buttocks, then back up along her sides to where her full breasts were pressed against his chest. His hands lovingly stroked the pale, rose-tipped globes while Dallas gasped softly and felt his hardness making itself known against her thighs.

She moaned low in her throat when his lips finally relinquished hers and wandered over the flushed smoothness of her face, across to her ear, where his teeth gently nipped at the silken lobe and his tongue dipped provocatively within the sensitive cavern. At the same time, his hands were leaving her breasts and gliding back down to fasten about her shapely hips. His strong fingers curled about them in a firm grip. Then, he was urging her body farther upward atop his so that his mouth could worship at her beautiful breasts.

"Oh!" gasped Dallas, her eyes sweeping closed and her hands tightening upon the bronzed hardness of her husband's shoulders. Liquid fire raced through her veins as Ross's lips first pressed a warm, compelling spray of kisses across her breasts, then claimed possession of one of them. His mouth closed about the rosy peak and sucked gently upon it, while his hot tongue swirled about the delectable pink flesh in tantalizingly slow circles before flicking lightly, tauntingly back and forth across the pert nipple.

Dallas felt her senses reeling and her own desire spiraling wildly upward. She instinctively arched her back and strained upward, shivering and gasping in delight as Ross worked his highly evocative magic. Everything else ceased to matter to her, everything but this enchanting, near painful ecstasy that only he could create within her.

After performing the same exquisite torment on her other breast, Ross's lips seared their way back up to capture hers while he eased her soft, womanly form back down the hard, lithely muscled length of his. His steely arms wrapped tightly about her, and he rolled her to her back once more, careful not to hurt her with the weight of his body upon hers.

Her eyelids fluttered open, and she moaned softly in protest when he suddenly broke the kiss. She gasped with pleasure, however, when his mouth began a thorough exploration of her delectable curves. His sensuously persuasive lips and tongue soon wreaked utter havoc with her emotions as he made it clear that he intended to kiss and tease at virtually every square inch of her body.

She closed her eyes again and clutched weakly at his arms for support while her head swam dizzily and she struggled to control her erratic breathing. Gasp after gasp broke from her lips as he kissed and gently lapped at her breasts again, and she stifled a cry a few moments later when she felt his hot tongue snaking erotically into her navel, before trailing a moist, fiery path lower still . . .

Then, just when she was certain he meant to bring the exquisite, almost unbearable agony to its inevitable conclusion, he startled her by raising himself off her again. She gazed up at him in mingled bewilderment and frustration as he knelt on the bed beside her.

"Not yet, my love," he murmured, his mouth curving into a tender, warmly irresistible smile while his eyes gleamed vibrantly down into hers.

Dallas colored hotly, but said nothing. Her thoughts were in a highly chaotic state, and she could not seem to make herself do anything other than lie there and meekly wait for whatever was to come. *Dear Lord, he was right,* she thought dazedly, *I want this every bit as much as he does!*

The next thing she knew, she was being turned gently upon her stomach. Ross swept her thick, titian locks out of the way and bent to press a captivating succession of kisses across the satiny smoothness of her back. His mouth then followed the entrancing curve of her spine, traveled lovingly across her buttocks and the backs of her thighs, all the way downward from the sensitive indentation behind her knees to her trim ankles, before returning to linger at the pale, alluring fullness of her bottom.

Dallas gasped loudly, her arms tightening almost convulsively about the pillow beneath her head. Her skin tingled deliciously. Blushing all over, she felt the cheeks of her derriere growing as warm and rosy as their more familiar counterparts. Her hips moved restlessly beneath the tender onslaught of his kisses, and she crimsoned anew when she felt his teeth gently nipping and his tongue flicking at the trim roundness of her shapely, undeniably feminine behind.

She was nearly mindless with yearning by the time he urged her to her knees upon the bed. A frown of renewed bewilderment creased her brow, and she turned her head to look questioningly back at him, for he was still kneeling behind her.

How could he take her when he had yet to turn her around? she wondered, hoping that he would do so *soon*. She could not take much more . . . she would surely go mad with longing if he did not put an end to the sweet torment!

The answer to her unspoken question proved equally satisfying to them both.

Ross pulled her back against him, and she inhaled sharply when her bare bottom came into contact with his hot, rigid manhood. He held her about the waist with one arm while his other hand moved to the downy triangle of auburn hair between her quivering thighs. His warm, breathtakingly skillful fingers stroked her moist, velvety flesh with such a gentle mastery that she trembled violently and felt every fiber of her being come alive with passion.

The sheer forcefulness of the sensations he was arousing within her caused her to grasp helplessly at his arm, and she was unable to prevent a series of soft moans from escaping her lips while her thighs spread wider and she strained back against him. Her bottom wriggled upon his masculine hardness, unintentionally but quite effectively driving him to the very limit of human tolerance as well.

Ross, although a lover of incredible stamina, was after all only flesh and blood. His rugged features tightened, and he gave a low groan before seizing his bride about the waist with both hands and quickly pressing her forward onto her knees once more.

Much to Dallas's amazement and delight, she felt

him kneeling behind her and positioning his manhood at the entrance to her feminine passage. She cried out softly as, with one powerful thrust, he sheathed himself within her honeyed warmth.

He pulled her back against him, his fingers curling tightly about her hips as they instinctively matched the amorous rhythm of his. She could have sworn he touched her very womb, so deep within her did she feel his throbbing hardness. His hands moved upward to close upon her breasts, prompting her to gasp anew and arch backward into the perfectly corresponding hollow of his kneeling, hard-muscled body.

Dallas felt herself growing faint as Ross's thrusts intensified. Her limbs seemed too weak to hold her any longer, and she was certain she would have pitched forward onto the bed if not for his arms about her. Her heart pounded in her ears, and the room swam before her eyes before her eyelids fluttered closed once more. Although she had experienced passion before, it had never been quite this powerful or all-consuming. Desire burned hotly throughout her entire body, and she felt as though her very soul were soaring up toward the heavens . . .

A soft, breathless scream broke from her lips when the fire deep within her exploded into a thousand tiny sparks. She collapsed back against Ross, only to feel his whole body tense. There was a sudden rush of warmth inside her, and then he, too, expelled a long breath and relaxed. His hands slid back down to her hips. Reluctantly withdrawing from her, he lowered her tenderly to the bed and stretched out beside her. He pulled her back against him, cradling her head with his right arm while he kept his left one flung possessively across her languid softness.

Dallas was too overwhelmed by what had just taken place to do anything more than release a sigh and snuggle contentedly against her husband's hard, unmistakably virile warmth. She would never have believed it possible to feel what she had just felt, just as she never would have believed it possible to share such wild ecstasy with a man she had continually professed to despise.

But how can I despise him when I so desperately yearn for his embrace, when I tremble beneath his gaze and surrender at his very touch?

He had vowed to make sure she never forgot she was his. Well, there was certainly no danger of that now! she mused with another faint sigh, her eyes shining softly in mingled wonderment and confusion. Even with her limited knowledge of such things, she realized that he had concentrated on her pleasure instead of his own. A sudden, strange tenderness welled up deep within her at the thought. Scarcely aware that she was doing so, she lifted a hand and began tracing a light, repetitive pattern across his broad chest while her sparkling sapphire gaze fastened upon the lamp still burning across the room.

Ross smiled softly down at the woman in his arms. *My beautiful, redheaded spitfire,* he thought, his gaze reflecting all the love in his heart as it flickered over her naked curves with bold possessiveness. Their love-making had proven even more pleasurable and satisfying than he had anticipated. Indeed, he reflected as the gleam in his magnificent green eyes deepened, he had never wanted to please a woman as much as he had wanted to please her, and he felt his passion stirring anew as he recalled the way she had responded to him with such an enchanting mixture of fire and innocence.

Although he was once again tempted to throw all caution to the winds and declare his love for her then and there, he did not. He told himself that she wasn't ready yet, that she still needed more time—not only to adjust to their marriage, but also to learn to trust him. But, he mused as another smile rose to his lips, since they were getting to know each other in bed as well as out of it, he could afford to be patient . . .

As if awakening from a trance, Dallas suddenly pushed his arm aside and drew herself up into a sitting position. Her mass of shimmering auburn hair cascaded down about her naked body in glorious disarray while her face took on a noticeably troubled look. Ross seized her arm in a firm but gentle grip and asked softly, "What is it, my love?"

"Please," she murmured as her cheeks flamed and her eyes dropped self-consciously to the bed, "just let me go!"

"Not until you tell me what's wrong," he decreed with a slight frown.

"I don't know!" she replied honestly, still refusing to meet his gaze. Painfully conscious of the fact that she was sitting there without a single stitch of clothing on—*his* lack of attire was also very much on her mind—she reached down and brought the edge of the comforter up over her, then told herself with an inward, bitter little smile that it was a trifle late for maidenly modesty. Finally, she drew a ragged breath and reluctantly confessed, "I was thinking about what you said, that there would be no . . . no divorce, and it occurred to me that you haven't mentioned anything about our

410

living arrangements."

"Living arrangements?" Ross echoed with another frown. He released her arm and turned over on his side. Propping himself up on one elbow, he lay there revealed in all his masculine splendor, totally unashamed and at ease with his nakedness. Dallas's face burned anew, for she was once again unable to prevent her eyes from straying to him. "We'll be living together, of course."

"But that's impossible!" Her eyes grew very round as they flew to his. "Why, I . . . I have no intention of leaving my home and going with you to Pennsylvania!"

"Who the hell said anything about Pennsylvania?" he retorted with a low, mellow chuckle, his own gaze full of loving amusement.

"That's where you've been working for the past ten years, isn't it? I naturally assumed you would be returning there once you had finished—"

"You assumed wrong, wildcat," he told her, his mouth curving into a disarming smile. "I've had it in mind for a while now to ride along with the boom in Corsicana. Even if George hadn't contacted me about drilling your well, Swede and I would have made our way down eventually. The oil industry's just beginning to take shape here in Texas, and I, for one, intend to be right smack-dab in the middle of things."

"Then you . . . you're planning to continue living in my house?" she asked, wondering how she was ever going to be able to explain things to Cordi and Etta. She had sworn up and down that her relationship with Ross Kincaid was nothing more than a business arrangement—what would they think when they discovered she had actually *given* herself to him?

411

Imagining their reaction, she groaned inwardly and flushed with embarrassment. To make matters worse, her eyes still refused to stay away from her husband's bare-skinned magnificence.

"Of course." He rolled to his back again and shifted his muscular frame slightly upward in the bed. Then, reclining negligently back against the pillow he had pulled from beneath the blue silk and placed against the bed's massive headboard, he flashed Dallas a crooked grin that made her heart flutter. "You didn't really think I was going to move out, did you?"

"I didn't know what to think!" It was all too true, she realized, her deep blue gaze clouding with anxiety. She felt terribly confused and unsettled . . .

"Well you do now," murmured Ross, his voice underscored by a disturbing resonance once more. She caught her breath and stared at him with eyes that were very wide and luminous. "You're mine, Dallas," he reiterated, all traces of amusement gone now. "You've been mine from the first time I saw you standing there on that station platform, looking so damned young and beautiful, your eyes full of fire and your whole, desirable body stiff with proud defiance. You belonged to me even then. We both knew it."

"That's not true!" she breathlessly denied with an emphatic shake of her auburn-maned head.

"Yes it is." A faint, wry smile briefly touched his lips. "Hell, I don't think we ever had a chance. You can't fight against the kind of thing that's between us, wildcat."

As if to prove his point, he reached out and took hold of her wrist. Her skin literally burned at the contact, and she was dismayed to feel the hot, telltale color staining her cheeks. His hand slid lightly upward upon her arm, sending an involuntary shiver dancing down her spine. She swallowed hard and stole another look at his face, only to see that his eyes were smoldering with renewed desire.

Good heavens, surely he didn't mean to make love to her again so soon? she wondered, her pulses racing.

Seized by a sudden, inexplicable feeling of alarm, she wrenched her arm free and sprang from the bed. It wasn't that she feared him, but rather that she feared herself. She knew she could not resist him, knew that he had only to touch her to render her completely and shamefully powerless. But she wanted more than he was willing to give! She wanted him to love her as much as she—

Dear God! she exclaimed inwardly as the truth hit her at last. *She was in love with Ross Kincaid!*

Thunderstruck, she drew to an abrupt halt before the bathroom door. Ross was upon her in an instant, scooping her triumphantly up in his strong arms and bearing her back to the bed. He tossed her down to the mattress, then covered her body with his own while his lips descended upon hers.

Dallas, although still feeling stunned by her new-found discovery, moaned in surrender and returned his kiss with an answering fire that delighted him. Over and over in the benumbed depths of her mind ran the thought that she loved him.

She didn't know how or when or why, but she had fallen in love with this tall, green-eyed rogue who held her in his arms . . .

XVI

Dallas stretched long and lazily beneath the covers. Her lips curved into a smile of drowsy contentment as she rolled onto her side and hugged the pillow close to her naked breasts. She released a sigh while her gaze, after traveling leisurely about her surroundings, came to rest upon the half-open window. The rays of the newly risen sun warmed the sparkling panes of glass and filled the room with a soft golden glow.

Ross had left her only a quarter of an hour ago. Announcing his intention to ride around to some of the neighboring ranches and see if he could gather any more information relating to J.D.'s arrest, he had dropped one last kiss upon her bare shoulder and reluctantly taken himself off.

"Oh, Ross," Dallas whispered with another faint, rather wistful sigh. Once again recalling the wickedly erotic splendor they had shared last night, she blushed and felt her skin tingling deliciously at the memory.

She had behaved with shocking abandon, and yet her love had freed her to respond more boldly than ever before. Ross had taken her to dizzying new heights of passion—in all, they had made love three more times after their first tempestuous encounter. *And each time,* she mused while her cheeks pinkened anew, *he had taught her things no respectable woman would ever dream of learning!*

"You should be ashamed of yourself, Mrs. Kincaid," she murmured with a mock scowl of self-reproach, then laughed softly and rolled to her back again. Her amusement soon vanished, however, when her thoughts returned to the dilemma facing her as a result of last night's startling revelation.

She loved Ross Kincaid. There was no longer any doubt or ambiguity when it came to her feelings for him. She loved him with all her heart and knew that she would love him forever. Things that had been puzzling her ever since he had come into her life were made vividly clear to her at long last—she now understood why she had been unable to resist him, just as she now understood why his proposal of a marriage of convenience had caused her so much pain. She had loved him even then.

Hugging the secret knowledge close, she was at once joyful and disconsolate. For, although she was pleased to have finally realized the truth of her feelings for her husband, she did not have any assurance whatsoever that he returned her love. He had said that he wanted her—but never that he loved her.

Drawing a long, somewhat ragged breath, Dallas sat up in the bed and wrapped her bare arms about her bent, silk-covered knees. She tried to console herself with the thought that at least Ross had declared his intention to remain married to her. Even if his decision had indeed been prompted by pride or duty, she reflected, there was nothing to prevent him from falling in love with her, was there? He could grow to love her, couldn't he? Such occurrences couldn't be all that uncommon. As a matter of fact, she had heard of more than one instance where a marriage had been based on nothing more than friendship and a mutual respect for each other.

Hell's bells, we already share a lot more than that! she thought, only to feel warm all over again as another vivid recollection of the previous night's intimacy drifted back into her mind. She and Ross Kincaid had certainly progressed far beyond mere friendship.

It suddenly occurred to her that perhaps she could *make* him fall in love with her. Why not? she asked herself as the idle notion began to take seed and blossom into a full-blown idea. Other women seemed perfectly capable of doing such a thing, so why couldn't she?

She had never tried to make any man fall in love with her before now. She wasn't even sure she knew *how.* Heaven help her, she mused with a heavy sigh, but she wanted more than anything else in the world to win Ross's heart . . .

Then do it! her mind's voice urged insistently. For once, she was willing to obey.

"I shall," vowed Dallas, her brilliant blue eyes aglow with determination. "I'll make you love me, Ross Kincaid, if it's the last thing I do!" Tossing the pillow aside, she flung back the covers and bounced resolutely from the bed.

After taking a bath, she dressed in her usual informal attire of white lawn shirtwaist and dark blue cotton skirt—once again foregoing the hot, torturous restraint of a corset—and hurried downstairs to find Bessie.

She turned her steps toward the kitchen first, but there was no sign of the housekeeper. After making a quick but thorough search of all the ground-floor rooms, she decided to look outside. She had no sooner stepped onto the white-columned front porch, when she heard someone call her name.

"Dallas! Good morning!"

Dallas, raising a hand to shade her eyes from the morning sun, smiled when her eyes fell upon the slender, gray-haired woman who stood with a bucket in hand within the circle of peach trees.

"Good morning, Bessie!" she called back warmly. Gathering up her skirts, she quickly descended the steps and moved across the yard to the white picket fence.

Throughout the next several hours, while she insisted upon helping the older woman with the many chores about the house, she pressed her for more information about Ross. Bessie, of course, was only too willing to comply, even going so far as to show her several photographs of the large Kincaid brood. She elaborated a bit on the personality traits and current marital or employment status of each member, providing Dallas with even more clues about Ross's family life.

The cook, Mrs. Greely, arrived back at the ranch in the early afternoon. She and Bessie, Dallas soon discovered, were total opposites in disposition as well as appearance. Iris Greely was a short, plump brunette with a perenially frowning expression and an abrupt, almost surly manner of speaking that would have made it impossible to carry on a lengthy conversation even if Dallas had been inclined to do so. Mrs. Greely did not seem in the least bit pleased to hear the news of Ross's marriage, nor did she offer the bride anything other than a terse "I've got work to do" before disappearing into the kitchen.

Thus, when Bessie left to pay what she said would be a "short visit to a sick friend," Dallas found herself wandering rather aimlessly about the house. She had ample time in which to think about Ross and their marriage—and about her determination to win his love—but she was unable to come up with any definite plans. After all, she thought with a rather dispirited sigh, she was a complete novice when it came to purposely ensnaring men. Her brow cleared and her mouth turned up into a soft smile of irony when she mused that perhaps she should ask Lorena Appleton for some pointers . . .

Her thoughts drifting homeward, she wondered about Cordi and Etta and how they were getting along without her. She had no doubt that they were managing quite well, if for no other reason than the fact that Ruby Mae was there to keep them in line. Of course, Ruby Mae would be returning to her own home soon, for there was no longer any reason for her to remain—the danger of a scandal had ceased to exist when Miss Dallas Brown had up and married "her driller."

If someone had told me a week ago that I would become the wife of Ross Kincaid, and actually fall in love with him, I would have promptly told that person that he or she was as crazy as a loon! she reflected. Fate had undoubtedly played a trick on her, and yet she had no complaint to offer regarding the outcome—other than the fact that she must now worry about whether or not her husband would ever return her affection.

Dallas glanced up toward the ceiling, though her thoughts extended all the way to heaven, and smiled to herself once more. She could easily envision her father and godfather congratulating themselves on their individual roles in her present circumstances—Abner Brown had sired her and was largely responsible for the woman she had become, while George Proctor had sent Ross Kincaid into her life . . .

Much later that afternoon, while she was strolling about the front yard with Bessie after one of those brief summer rain showers that were all too rare, she observed Ross riding down the drive toward them. Her heart took to pounding quite erratically, and she was certain Bessie could see the warm flush stealing over her. She watched, wide-eyed and breathless, while he drew his mount to a halt a short distance away and swung lithely down from the saddle.

"How would you like to go for a ride, Mrs. Kincaid?" he asked Dallas, his own eyes alight with an irrepressible twinkle as he sauntered forward to stand towering above her.

"Why, I . . . I'd love to, but I'm afraid I don't have anything suitable to wear," she stammered in mingled delight and perplexity.

"Bessie can find you something, can't you, Bessie?" He turned to grin roguishly down at the woman who, by her own account, was like a second mother to him.

"I'm sure of it!" Bessie replied with a chuckle. She and Dallas hastened back up the porch steps and inside the house. When Dallas emerged alone a few minutes later, she was clad in a fitted white cotton blouse and three-quarter-length, split riding skirt of buttersoft calfskin. The ensemble, which belonged to one of Ross's younger sisters, was a trifle too snug, but Ross offered no criticism of her appearance as he took her arm and led her back across the yard to where he had two fresh horses waiting.

Dallas had ridden little. She was, however, determined to enjoy the outing with her husband, and so she said nothing to him about her lack of equestrian skills. He lifted her up into the saddle, then mounted beside her and remarked, "I thought I'd show you a bit more of the Bar K while we've got the chance. We'll be heading back to Corsicana tomorrow morning."

"Tomorrow morning? But I thought we weren't going to leave until Tuesday!" She was disappointed at the news, for she had looked forward to being alone with him for the next few days. Although she would never have believed it, coming to the ranch had provided the two of them with a much-needed idyll. She smiled inwardly as she recalled Mason Parnell's remark about their trip being a belated honeymoon . . .

"There's nothing more to be done here right now. J.D.'s been released—he's already back out on the range. I still haven't found out who set him up, but I've got some friends working on it." He smiled crookedly across at her and resettled his hat upon his dark head. "I can't say I'm sorry we didn't make the last train out today. I'd have us stay on a few days longer if not for the fact that I'm anxious to get that second well in."

"I thought perhaps you had decided to postpone it."

"Why would I do that?" His smile deepened, and his

eyes danced with indulgent humor. "No, my love, as I've told you before, I never give up on something I've set my mind to."

With that, he reined about and set off across the open pasture just as she had seen him do the day before. Following only a moment's hesitation, she urged her own mount forward, quickly reaching the spot where he had slowed and waited for her to catch up. The two of them rode side by side, with the sun peeking out from behind the clouds every now and then to turn the land before them into a patchwork of green and gold and brown.

Dallas soon became more at ease in the saddle. She took pleasure in the warm caress of the wind against her face, as well as in the various sights and sounds of the countryside. Most of all, she enjoyed being with Ross.

He spoke little, only doing so to point out a landmark or make an occasional comment about the cattle they saw grazing on the rolling, sparsely tree-dotted range, but she nonetheless reveled in the long periods of silence between them, for she had never experienced such a feeling of easy camaraderie with him. Their relationship had always been so stormy and passionate! she reflected with a sigh. This new, added dimension to it was particularly gratifying—for the first time since Ross Kincaid had arrived to turn her world upside down, she was discovering what it felt like to be his companion as well as his lover.

They finally reined to a halt beneath a canopy of huge oak and cottonwood trees bordering what Ross told her was the Clear Fork of the Trinity River. The river, less than twenty-five feet wide at that point, set up a gentle roar as it flowed past the base of an imposing bluff whose face had been eroded away by a combination of time and the elements of nature to reveal alternating layers of white chalk and reddish-brown clay.

Dallas looked to Ross, expecting him to dismount, but he merely shifted a bit in the saddle and lowered a hand to the saddlehorn, where he maintained a negligent grip on the reins while his other hand moved up to tilt the tan, snakeskin-banded Stetson farther back upon his head. Meeting his wife's questioning gaze, he smiled and disclosed in a voice brimming with wry amusement, "You know, Mrs. Kincaid, I'd like nothing more than to make love to you right here beside the river, but being that it's late in the day, in the middle of summer, *and* near water, we'd run the risk of getting snakebit."

Dallas colored and started to retort that she had not expected him to do anything of the kind, but she held her tongue and settled for throwing him a narrow, playfully reproachful look that elicited a low chuckle from him in response. Her eyes were drawn back to the slow-moving waterway, and she raised a hand to sweep a stray tendril of hair from her forehead as she asked in a teasing manner, "Does your family own the river as well?" From what she had seen thus far, the Kincaids appeared to hold at least half of the entire county in their possession!

"In a way," drawled Ross, another ghost of a smile touching his lips. "It's always been the main source of water for our stock. My father was fortunate enough to be able to buy up some of the best range land in these parts. The war took its toll on everyone in Fort Worth.

Most ranchers had cleared out by the time my folks arrived."

"Bessie told me they came here from Georgia."

"They did. And they had a hell of a lot to learn about raising cattle," he remarked as his mouth twisted into an ironic grin.

"Bessie also told me that your father . . . well, that he doesn't exactly approve of your being a driller." She watched as his features tightened for a moment, then relaxed.

"That's one way of putting it." His eyes darkened in remembrance of more than one heated discussion on the subject. "But I've never let someone's disapproval stop me from doing what I want."

"So I've noticed," she murmured with a pointed widening of her eyes. Ross chuckled again and raised the hat back to his head, easing it down with a leisurely tug on the front of the stiffened felt brim.

"What the devil *else* has Bessie told you?" he demanded in mock annoyance.

"Oh, a good many things," Dallas answered evasively, her mouth curving into a secretive little smile. She was rewarded for her impudence when he suddenly leaned over and caught her about the waist, lifting her half out of the saddle while his lips crashed down upon hers in a fiercely demanding kiss that provoked a surge of hot, raging desire within them both. Their horses, peacefully grazing at the sweet grass along the river's edge, merely snorted in mild protest.

By the time she was released and her bottom slid back down into the smooth, curved leather of the saddle, Dallas was flushed and shaken. She gripped the saddlehorn with both hands, battling to regain control of her breathing while Ross promised in a low, devastatingly vibrant tone, "Later, my love. *Later*."

They were soon heading back to the house. The sun, breaking free of the clouds at last, hung low on the western horizon by the time Ross dismounted in front of the barn and moved to lift Dallas down as well. His eyes burned up into hers, and she trembled at the way his hands lingered upon her waist for several long moments after he lowered her to the ground and turned back to unsaddle the horses. She stood on shaky legs when he released her, her heart hammering in her breast and her face becomingly flushed once more.

She soon discovered, much to her dismay, that the afternoon's ride had left her with an embarrassing soreness. Unaccustomed to spending so much time on horseback, she was unable to walk without feeling a dull ache in her legs and buttocks. She made a valiant attempt to conceal her disconcerting condition from her husband, but he could not fail to notice the fact that she was experiencing difficulty in making her way from the barn to the house. His handsome face split into a broad, knowing grin.

"A hot bath's the best remedy," he called out, his deep voice easily carrying the message across the yard to her, "followed by a rubdown with liniment!" His eyes gleamed with a wickedly mischievous light when he added, "I'll be happy to oblige!"

Her face flamed, and she groaned inwardly, musing that not only was everyone within earshot now privy to the knowledge of her highly personal affliction, but also to the equally intimate details of her relationship with Ross. Vowing to make him pay for his devilment, she continued on her way with as much dignity as possible under the circumstances and soon disappeared inside the house.

She wasted little time in following his advice about the bath. Within minutes after entering their bedroom, she was peeling off her clothes and easing her painfully reproachful muscles down into a tub of steaming hot water. Hearing the sound of the outer door being opened and closed a few seconds later, she sat up with a soft gasp. Her luminous sapphire gaze flew to the bathroom door, which she had closed out of an instinctive modesty. She waited, wide-eyed and breathless and listening . . . but nothing happened. There was only silence on the other side of the door.

Releasing a long, pent-up sigh, she frowned to herself and settled back against the massive porcelain tub once more. She closed her eyes and felt the tension leaving her body.

The door opened slowly. By the time Dallas became aware of a rush of cool air and sat up with another sharp intake of breath, Ross was already kneeling beside the tub. He was clad only in a pair of trousers. She stared at him in surprise for a moment, then hastily folded her arms across her naked breasts and brought her knees upward.

"What are you doing?" she asked in a voice that was not quite steady.

"I thought I'd give you a hand," he replied, his rugged features strangely inscrutable. Without another word, he took up the sponge and the cake of soap from a small shelf beside the tub.

"I . . . I can manage quite well by myself, thank you," she insisted as she sank lower in the water. "So will you please get out and . . . and leave me to it?"

"If you're sure that's the way you want it."

"It is!" she declared emphatically. She knew it made no sense whatsoever, but she suddenly felt awkward and shy, sitting there without a stitch on while he had the decided advantage of a pair of trousers!

"All right," he startled her by agreeing without so much as a single argument. He allowed the sponge and the soap to slip from his hands and fall into the water. Relief and disappointment warred together within Dallas's breast as she watched him rise to his feet again. Her eyes traveled back up to his face, and she felt her pulses leaping anew when she glimpsed the wickedly purposeful light in his magnificent green gaze.

"Ross?" she questioned, eyeing him suspiciously. "Ross, what are you—" She broke off when she realized that he was unfastening his trousers. Her eyes grew round as saucers while her beautiful face paled a bit.

"Water's a precious commodity on a ranch, my love," he offered casually, drawing his trousers off now and flinging them to the far corner of the warmly lit bathroom. Dallas swallowed hard and was only dimly aware of him adding, "We might as well make that bath of yours serve double duty."

"But I thought—you said you were going to get out!"

"Did I?" he quipped. It was obvious that he was not the least bit contrite about the falsehood.

He stepped into the opposite end of the long, clawfoot tub from where his wife sat all scrunched up in an effort to shield herself from his amused yet smoldering gaze. Water was sent splashing everywhere when he lowered his tall, muscular frame into the soapy warmth, and Dallas gasped in protest as he reached for her.

"Stop it!" she squealed when his hands closed about her arms. "For heaven's sake, Ross Kincaid, this is a bathtub, not a . . . a bed! Now will you please let go of me and—"

"Shut up, Mrs. Kincaid," he commanded huskily. Pulling her forward between his bent knees, he silenced her in the best way he knew how.

Dallas melted against him. Her arms came up about his neck, and she trembled as her breasts made delicious contact with the immovable force of his broad chest. Her supple curves were fitted intimately atop his lithe hardness, and she moaned softly as the warm water swirled about them and their kiss rapidly deepened.

His hands glided beneath the water to fasten upon the satiny roundness of her hips—the soreness was driven completely from her mind now—while his mouth lovingly ravished the sweetness of hers. She caught her breath when she felt his hot, undeniably aroused manhood pressing against her belly, and she shivered as her own desire flared.

Then, he suddenly released her and drew himself upright to step from the water. She blinked up at him in stunned bewilderment, only to gasp in delight when he lifted her in his strong arms and lowered her swiftly to the braided cotton rug on the floor beside the tub.

They proceeded to make wildly passionate love on that rug, proving to Dallas in an effective and highly satisfying manner that, while a bed or a sofa are quite nice, there are other places that will serve just as well . . .

Much later, after they had dined on Mrs. Greely's roasted chicken and sat outside on the front porch for a while with Bessie McPherson, Ross and Dallas returned to the private, enchanted world they had created for themselves in the third-floor bedroom. The two of them lay entwined beneath the silk canopy of the four-poster, content for the moment to do nothing more than talk quietly and think of what the future held in store for them.

"Someday, when I finally decide to give up on drilling—or when it decides to give up on me—I'd like to come back here and start my own ranch," confided Ross. Dallas inhaled rather tremulously as his deep-timbred voice washed over her in the darkness. She smoothed an appreciative hand across the bronzed, muscular hardness of his chest.

"That will no doubt please your father greatly," she murmured with a soft sigh.

"And what about you?" he challenged, his voice now holding a discernible note of amusement while his fingers trailed lightly over her bare arm. "Will it please you to find yourself the wife of a rancher instead of the best damned driller in Texas?"

"I have no doubt that you will always be the best at whatever you do!" she retorted saucily. "And as for being the wife of a rancher, I must admit that the idea appeals to me, if for no other reason than the fact that it would mean we could have a real home."

"I suppose that's important to you, isn't it?"

"Yes," she admitted. Settling her pliant, captivating softness more closely against him, she released a rather wistful sigh and said, "I want no more than most other women want—a home, a family, the simple pleasures

429

to be found in such things." She peered up at him, wishing she could see his face more clearly. "You . . . you do want children, don't you?" she asked a bit tentatively.

"At least a dozen."

"*A dozen?*" gasped Dallas, then felt a low chuckle rumbling up from his chest. "You devil!" she charged with wifely affection. "I was trying to engage you in a serious discussion of the matter, Ross Kincaid! After all, if we're going to continue being together like this, then it's highly possible—"

"There's no 'if' about it, wildcat, and the possibility of your being with child has already occurred to me." His hand glided knowingly downward to her abdomen. She caught her breath upon a soft gasp and shivered warmly as his strong fingers gently explored her silken smoothness. "There may very well be another Kincaid taking shape here right now," he remarked, punctuating his words with a feathery teasing of her svelte, quivering flesh.

"And would you be pleased if there were?" she asked in a small, breathless voice.

"Yes—and no," he answered honestly, his hand leaving off its exquisite torment and returning to its former resting place upon her arm. "Given the choice, I'd rather we had some time together first."

Dallas was both encouraged and perplexed by his reply. Her spirits soared as a result of hearing that he wanted to be with her. His behavior toward her that day had certainly prompted her hopes to rise, making her believe more than ever that she really *could* win his love. The mention of children, however, had planted yet another seed of doubt in the fertile depths

430

of her mind.

Perhaps that's the true reason he refused to consider a divorce. Her heart twisted sharply at the thought. She told herself that it wasn't so, that he hadn't decided to keep their marriage intact simply because he feared she might be carrying his child, but the awful suspicion refused to be vanquished. It had been painful enough to think that he had changed his mind because of the fateful night when he had taken her maidenhood, but it caused her even more anguish to think that his decision had not really had anything to do with *her* at all . . .

Her uncheering reverie was interrupted when Ross suddenly swept her atop him. Entangling a hand within her mass of lustrous auburn curls, he urged her head downward so that his lips could taste of hers in a sweetly inflaming kiss. A low moan rose in her throat as she gave herself up to his embrace. Once again, she forgot about everything else—there was only Ross, only this wonderful, sensual madness she felt whenever he took her in his arms. Her heart swelled with love while passion fired her blood.

Moments later, when he made it clear that he intended to roll so that she was beneath him, Dallas stopped him. He stared up at her in mild bemusement, his eyebrows dancing together as his mouth twisted into a faint, quizzical smile.

"Dallas?" he murmured in a low, vibrant tone, her name like a caress on his lips.

"Shhh," she whispered. Although she blushed fiercly in the darkness, she pushed herself up into a sitting position atop him, so that she straddled his body with her shapely limbs, her knees on either side of his lean-muscled hips. She then leaned forward to press her mouth upon his once more, her long, silken tresses cascading down about them both.

Emboldened by her love for Ross, and wanting desperately to please him, she took the initiative in their lovemaking for the first time. He was apparently delighted with his wife's boldness, for he gave a low groan and kissed her with such a breathtaking vehemence that she felt positively singed from head to toe. His fingers curled about her slender waist as her own fingers tightened upon his shoulders.

She finally tore her lips from his and set them to wandering across his bronzed hardness. Pressing a half dozen soft, provocative kisses along the rugged column of his neck, she followed an imaginary path downward, where she trailed her hands seductively all about the magnificent breadth of his muscular, lightly matted chest before bending her lips to tease and nibble at his burning flesh.

Warming to her task, she slid her body farther downward upon his, her mouth and hands still working their loving enchantment while Ross clenched his teeth against the surge of near painful desire she was creating in him. He was not at all accustomed to being a passive participant when it came to such things, and he wasn't sure how much more of the delectable torture he could stand, but he forced himself to control his own passion—for as long as humanly possible, he mused with another low groan.

Guided only by instinct and a desire to please the man she loved, Dallas suffered a moment of uncertainty, but she forged resolutely ahead in the next instant, her hair streaming wildly across her husband's body while her lips traveled ever lower. She lingered at his navel for a moment and, just as he had done to her the night before, sent the warm moistness of her tongue snaking tauntingly down into it. Satisfied to hear his sharp intake of breath, she then lifted her head and reached a hand out to touch the rigid instrument of his masculinity. Her fingers closed rather tentatively about it, and she gasped to feel its throbbing hardness moving within her grasp. Following another brief hesitation, and shocked at her own daring, she bent her lips to it . . .

Ross could bear no more. With a low, hoarse growl, he seized his beautiful bride about the waist and drew her flushed and startled curves sliding abruptly back up the muscular length of his taut frame. She gave a soft, breathless cry when she felt his mouth closing about one of her breasts. His lips suckled as greedily as any babe's while his hot, velvety tongue flicked across the rose-tipped peak with tantalizing strokes that prompted another sharp gasp from Dallas. Her fingers threaded tightly within the raven thickness of his hair, and she strained farther upward against him, the satiny fullness of her breasts positioned perfectly for his moist caress.

His hands moved to take the firm mounds of her bottom in a possessive grip, and she trembled as she felt his virile maleness burning beneath her. Her pulses leapt and her head spun dizzily when, pulling her downward between his knees, the triangle of auburn hair at the apex of her thighs made boldly intimate contact with him. She stifled another cry as he tutored her hips into a slow, circular motion that brought the sensitive pearl of her femininity rubbing against his hardness. Clinging weakly to him now, she was certain she would be driven to the very brink of insanity with the familiar yearning building to a fever pitch deep within her.

Mercifully, the torment ended soon thereafter. Ross lifted her hips one last time and brought her masterfully down upon his throbbing manhood. Dallas nearly fainted when she felt him sheathing perfectly within her honeyed passage. She gasped again and again as she rode atop him, meeting his demanding thrusts with an equal passion while her fingers curled almost convulsively upon his shoulders and her titian locks fanned about her in glorious disarray.

The final blending of their bodies gifted them with the most heavenly fulfillment possible in an earthly guise. Ross tensed and groaned low in his throat, while Dallas softly screamed her pleasure and collapsed weakly back down upon him, gasping for breath.

Neither one of them spoke as they lay together in the sweet aftermath of their passion—there was no need for words between them. He cradled her tenderly within the warm circle of his arms, his chin resting atop her head. She heaved a sigh of total contentment and snuggled even closer. All doubts and worries were relegated to the back of her mind, and her heart sang as she mused dreamily that Ross Kincaid had once again made it *quite* clear that she belonged to him . . .

After bidding Bessie McPherson an affectionate farewell—and promising the insistent housekeeper that they would return again soon—they drove away from the Bar K and headed back into Fort Worth to catch the morning train.

Dallas was sorry to leave the ranch, not only because of what she and Ross had shared there, but also because she had experienced another vague feeling of uneasiness at the thought of returning home. She determinedly set it aside, however, and vowed to enjoy the trip home with her husband. Inwardly marveling at how a mere forty-eight hours had made such a startling difference in their relationship, she sighed and settled herself even closer to him in the wagon.

"I'm going to catch all hell for not staying until my folks get back," he predicated wryly, giving an easy flick of the reins.

"I wish I could have met them." She smiled and added, "Though from what I learned from Bessie, I feel that I already know them."

"Is that so? Well, Bessie talks too much," he pronounced with a lazy grin.

"She does not!" retorted Dallas, springing to the other woman's defense. "She was very kind to me, and I was very interested in hearing everything she had to say about you and your family." Sitting back against the leather cushion again, she raised a hand to sweep an ever-rebellious tendril of dark red hair from her forehead. She had pinned a small white straw hat sporting a banded ribbon of black grosgrain atop her carefully pompadoured tresses, and she was wearing a simple tailored suit of pale-blue cotton that set off her slender curves to perfection. "As a matter of fact, I found it all quite fascinating!"

"I'm glad to hear it." And he was—only not in the way Dallas thought. It pleased him to know that she had been so curious about him. He smiled to himself, and his eyes gleamed in secret triumph as he reflected upon the events of the past two days . . .

Arriving back in Corsicana just before noon, they found Erik and Cordi waiting for them at the station. Dallas could tell the moment she looked at her sister's face that something had happened—there was a particular glow about her, as well as a new, animated sparkle in her turquoise eyes.

"Oh, Dallas, I'm so glad you're back!" said Cordi, embracing her warmly while the two men went to collect the baggage. "I took the rest of the day off so I could come down here with Erik! You'll never believe all that's been going on while you've been away! One of the sheriff's deputies got shot by some man caught stealing oil, and Marian Ridgeway's gotten herself engaged to a roughneck she's only known a few days, and Sam had a terrible quarrel with his parents and is staying at our house for a while!" she enumerated in an excited rush, then dropped her voice to a more confidential level before adding, "And Erik finally admitted that he loves me!"

"He *what?*" Dallas echoed in less than delighted surprise. "Oh Cordi, you haven't—"

"He didn't propose marriage, if that's what you're worried about!" Cordi hastened to assure her with a sigh of lingering disappointment. Her pretty young features brightened again in the next moment as she went on to reveal, "But he said he *would* have if he had been in a position to do so! He still has this absurd notion that he can't take a wife until he's built a home, but I am going to do everything in my power to change his mind!" she finished, her eyes shining with a stubborn determination Dallas knew all too well.

"I'm relieved to know that Mr. Larsen, at least, has

436

kept a clear head about things!"

"Oh, Dallas, when are you going to realize—" Cordi started to protest, breaking off as Ross and Erik returned to collect them.

Ruby Mae and Etta were awaiting their return on the front porch. As soon as Ross guided the wagon to a halt before the house, Etta came flying down the walk to greet her oldest sister with a sincere "welcome back" and an affectionate hug.

"But—what are you doing here?" Dallas asked when she drew away and gazed down into Etta's smiling face. "I thought you'd be at work by now."

"Didn't Cordi tell you? I got fired!" confessed Etta, not sounding in the least bit upset about it.

"Fired?" Dallas echoed, wondering what other surprises were in store for her. *Was it possible she had been gone only two days?*

"Yes, but it was my own fault," the petite seventeen-year-old readily admitted. "I went round this morning and told them I wasn't coming in today."

"Why did you do that?" Dallas was almost afraid to ask.

"Because Sam's still fuming over a fight he had with his folks and I thought I should stay here!" Etta replied with a defiant toss of her strawberry blond curls. "Can you believe it? They actually told him that either he gave up 'disgracing' them by working as a roughneck, or they'd cut him off without a cent!"

"I can believe it," sighed Dallas. "I can believe just about anything after this past week!" She turned and started up the walk to where Ruby Mae stood waiting patiently to welcome her home. Ross unhitched the horse and led it into the barn while Erik lifted the bags and strolled toward the house with Cordi. Etta took herself around to the backyard to tell Sam the news of the homecoming.

"I'm right glad to see you again, honey!" proclaimed Ruby Mae, catching Dallas up in a warmly maternal embrace. The older woman's face was wreathed in smiles as she then held her at arm's length and commented teasingly, "Somethin' tells me that trip of yours turned out a lot better than you thought it would!" Dallas's eyes widened, and she blushed rosily beneath her friend's knowing scrutiny.

"Why, how did you—" she started to question as Cordi and Erik moved past them into the house.

"A body'd have to be blind not to see that you're happy as a bride!" laughed Ruby Mae. "Come to think of it, that's exactly what you are! So then," she said, taking Dallas's arm, "let's you and me go on inside and have ourselves a cup of my good strong coffee while you tell me all about your trip. I want to hear everythin'—everythin' you think is fit for an old maid's ears, that is!" she added with another chuckle.

There's a great deal that isn't, Dallas mused with an inward smile, her eyes aglow with deliciously wicked memories as she stepped through the doorway.

XVII

Ross and Erik disappeared for the remainder of the afternoon. After announcing that they were going into town to round up more equipment and hire another derrick crew, Ross had flashed his wife a roguish grin, pressed a hard kiss upon her lips right in front of the entire Brown household, and left her to explain things to her startled sisters. The task had proven anything but easy . . .

"Why, he—he *kissed* you!" gasped Cordi, her eyes very wide and full of incredulity.

"What in blue blazes was that all about?" Etta demanded with an indignant frown. "Since when do you allow Ross Kincaid to kiss you like that—to kiss you at *all?*"

"If the two of you will please sit down, I'll try and explain," Dallas murmured with a heavy sigh. She had known this moment was coming, but she hadn't counted on it being expedited by Ross. Recalling how he had forced her to announce their marriage, she told herself with an inward smile of irony that perhaps it was only fitting that he had now made it necessary for her to confront her sisters with the truth of their relationship.

She watched as Cordi and Etta took a seat at the kitchen table, then crossed from the back door to do the same. Suddenly wishing that Ruby Mae hadn't already gone back to her own house, she squared her shoulders and forged resolutely ahead.

"As you know, I married Ross Kincaid so that I would be able to gain control of everything George left me, as well as the estate left to all three of us by our father. It was supposed to be nothing more than a business arrangement, and we—Mr. Kincaid and I— had agreed that it would be terminated by divorce just as soon as the legalities concerning the trusteeship were out of the way. It was for that reason that I accompanied him to Fort Worth."

"What do you mean 'it was supposed to be'?" Etta questioned, her golden eyes narrowing in growing suspicion.

"Only that things didn't . . . well, they didn't turn out quite the way I had expected," Dallas reluctantly admitted. A dull, telltale flush rose to her cheeks, and her eyes fell guiltily before her sisters'.

"What are you saying?" asked Cordi, her gaze widening in naive bafflement. "Has something gone wrong between you and—"

"Oh, Cordi!" Etta groaned in exasperation. "Don't you know *anything* about men and women?"

"Of course I do! But what has that got to do with Dallas and—" She broke off as realization finally sank in. Inhaling sharply, she grew very red and turned a look of shocked disbelief on her older sister. "Dallas

Harmony Brown! Why, how *could* you?" she demanded in a breathless, undeniably accusing tone of voice.

"You hypocrite!" Etta now fumed, rising abruptly to her feet and fixing Dallas with a resentful glare. "You've been going around here spouting all sorts of blasted poppycock about 'unsuitable' marriages, and warning us against letting our emotions run away with us, and insisting that we can't possibly be in love with men *you* don't approve of!"

"Yes, and you stood right here in this very room the other day and told me that drillers were not the sort to make a commitment and that my life would be nothing but a misery even if I *did* get Erik Larsen to marry me!" Cordi chimed in.

"I know. I'm afraid I've said and done all those things," Dallas conceded with another sigh. She felt stung by her beloved sisters' words, and yet she knew she deserved every bit of their anger and reproof. Her sparkling, visibly troubled gaze encompassed both of them as she sought to explain. "I honestly intended for the alliance to be in name only, but several things occurred to alter the circumstances of my marriage."

"And I can just imagine what those things were!" Etta retorted impatiently.

"Oh, Etta, stop it!" Cordi sharply admonished, then looked back to Dallas with a puzzled frown. "But I thought you didn't even like Mr. Kincaid! The two of you always seemed to be at odds with each other. I don't understand how you could . . . could *be* with a man you quarreled with all the time!" she finished with another faint blush.

"It's really not so hard to understand," replied

441

Dallas, smiling ruefully. "The truth is, I fell in love with my husband. But I didn't realize it until we went away together. Not only that, but I also discovered that he no longer had any intention of dissolving our marriage. So it's just as well that I changed my way of thinking, isn't it?" There was an underlying tension in her voice at this point, due to a sudden, renewed twinge of uncertainty about the status of Ross's affections, but it fortunately went unnoticed by her sisters.

"It's just so difficult to think of you as being married—truly married, that is," murmured Cordi. "I was beginning to think you really would remain a spinster for the rest of your life. And now here you are, married to Ross Kincaid, of all people!"

"It's difficult for me to believe, too," Dallas confided with another brief smile.

"Does this mean that you'll be going with him when he leaves Corsicana?" This came from Etta, who resumed her seat and gazed at Dallas with a frown of genuine concern now. Her anger was forgotten as it occurred to her that she might soon be saying good-bye to the woman who had been both sister and mother for the past ten years. "We . . . we might not see you again for a long time."

"Ross said that he wants to remain here for now and continue drilling. After that, I don't know." Reaching across the table, she covered Etta's hand with her own and smiled brightly. "Even if I do have to leave you, you can be certain that I shall find a way to see that you're looked after properly!"

"But we're old enough to look after ourselves!" protested Cordi. "Goodness gracious, Dallas, when are you ever going to realize that we're not children any longer? We're grown women, just like you, and it's . . . well, it's highly possible that we'll be married ourselves by the time Ross and Erik are ready to move on again!"

"Perhaps, but you're not married *yet*," Dallas pointedly reminded her, "and I hate to think that either of you would rush into something as serious as marriage simply because—"

"You're the only one who's been rushing into anything around here!" snapped Etta, her easily provoked temper flaring once more. She drew her hand away while declaring with a good deal of feeling, "I've been in love with Sam for years, and Cordi certainly hasn't gone sneaking off to wed Erik! When *we* get married, it will be for love and love alone!"

"I'm well aware of that, Etta, just as I'm aware of the fact that neither Sam nor Mr. Larsen appear to have any intention of embracing matrimony for quite some time to come! I love you and Cordi too much to—" The sentence was left unfinished as something deep inside prevented her from going any further. For the first time in her life, she knew what it meant to be in love. How then could she lecture Etta and Cordi about not getting too deeply involved when she herself had done that very thing?

None of us can choose where to love, she remembered thinking the night of the church social, when she had stood gazing down at Justin Bishop after fending off his cruel embrace. She knew from her own experience that it was true. And if it had proven true for her, how could she possibly expect it to be any different for her sisters?

If they were truly in love, she reflected with an inner

sigh of capitulation, then the only thing she could do was pray that they would find the same kind of happiness she had found with Ross. Her happiness only lacked one thing to make it complete, but, Lord willing, it would not remain that way much longer . . .

The hot, sweltering afternoon faded into a blessedly mild summer night.

After supper, all three couples adjourned to the parlor, where Cordi regaled everyone with a succession of lively tunes. Sam showed Etta how to perform a new dance step he had learned recently—he lied about exactly where he'd gained such knowledge, realizing that Etta would never believe he'd only been *dancing* with that girl down at the saloon—while Erik was perfectly content to sit beside Cordi at the piano and watch her fingers flying over the keys.

Ross drew Dallas down to the sofa. They spoke briefly about what he and Swede had accomplished that day, then talked of the worsening troubles which plagued the town. Finally, he told her that he had stopped by to speak with the sheriff, who had found in him a willing recruit for the new patrols being set up to keep watch over the field at night.

"You'll be riding out every night?" Dallas asked, dismay written on her beautiful countenance.

"Only when I'm not drilling," Ross answered with a soft chuckle. His green eyes twinkled down at her in loving amusement. "You can't get rid of me that easily, my love."

"Do you have to go tonight?"

"No. Tomorrow night."

"Oh. Well, I . . . I suppose you have to do your part," she murmured, trying unsuccessfully to keep the disappointment from her voice. "Something's got to be done about these awful crimes taking place." She heaved a sigh, her brows knitting together into a worried frown. "I certainly hope Sheriff Crow's deputy is going to recover."

"He is," Ross assured her as his own features took on a dangerous grimness, "though he won't be of much use for at least a month. If we can persuade enough men to join in on the patrols, we might be able to catch the bastards and put them behind bars for good—or maybe send a few of them to hell a little sooner than they'd counted on."

Dallas shuddered and settled back against the comforting strength of his arm. Her thoughts began to wander as her gaze moved from Cordi and Erik at the piano, back to where Sam and Etta were laughing like two children over his efforts to guide her in the dance. It was a pleasant, strangely moving scene, and Dallas was surprised to feel sudden tears gathering in her eyes.

"Come on." Ross's deep voice startled her a bit.

"What?" She hastily blinked back her tears and turned to face him with a look of bemusement. "What did you say?"

"We're going upstairs, Mrs. Kincaid," he decreed, his mouth curving into a devastating smile.

"But we . . . we can't go yet!" she protested lamely. Her heart was all aflutter at the look in his eyes, and she was afraid she would disgrace herself by melting against him then and there. "I can't leave my sisters down here alone with Sam and—"

"They'll be perfectly safe." He stood and drew her firmly up beside him. "Hell, sweetheart, I'd trust Swede with *my* sister," he remarked wryly, "and I find it highly

445

unlikely that young Rawlins over there will try anything he hasn't tried before." Dallas blushed and made one last halfhearted attempt to reason with him.

"That's all well and good, Ross Kincaid, but it's still quite early, and I wouldn't want them to think—"

"I don't give a damn what they think," he insisted, casting her a thoroughly wicked grin. "We're married, remember?" Wasting no more time, he turned and proclaimed to the other occupants of the room, "My wife and I bid you good night."

Sam and Erik merely smiled knowingly and returned the benediction. Cordi and Etta, their eyes first flying to their sister, colored faintly and exchanged a pointed look of understanding before murmuring their own good nights.

Dallas suffered a moment of embarrassment before Ross led her out of the parlor and up the stairs. Stepping inside her room mere seconds later, she moved to light the lamp while he closed the door. She was assailed by a sudden feeling of shyness as a result of being alone with him in such familiar surroundings, and her hands shook a bit when she reached up to start unpinning her hair.

"I'll do that," offered Ross. Leisurely crossing the room to where she stood before her mirrored dressing table, he urged her down onto the small, velvet-cushioned bench and smiled softly at her reflection. He said not a word as his fingers went to work. Dallas watched him, her eyes glowing with love and her face flushed with ever-blossoming passion.

In an amazingly short amount of time, Ross had freed the lustrous auburn tresses and sent them tumbling down about her shoulders. She shivered in delight and caught her breath upon a soft gasp when his warm fingers brushed her hair aside and he bent to press a tantalizing little kiss upon the back of her neck.

"Oh, Ross!" she breathed, every square inch of her skin tingling. "Why is that even the most simple things you do to me have such a . . . a potent effect?"

"Because, wildcat," he murmured in a low, splendidly vibrant tone as he drew her upright once more and turned her about to face him, "we are perfectly—and most permanently—mated."

Sweeping her up in his powerful arms, he carried her to the bed and lowered her gently to its welcoming softness. His gaze darkened and smoldered as he began removing his clothes.

"You've no idea how many times I lay in that damned bed down the hall and visualized you lying here just like you are now. Well," he amended with another rakishly meaningful grin as his eyes flickered over her still clothed form, "not exactly like you are now."

"I . . . I heard you walking past my door sometimes," Dallas told him in a small, increasingly breathless voice. Her pulses leapt crazily when he peeled off his shirt and took a seat on the bed close beside her to dispense with his boots.

"If not for the fact that Ruby Mae was keeping guard, I might have done a hell of a lot more than just walk past." Setting the boots aside, he stood again and started on his trousers.

Dallas's sparkling sapphire gaze widened, and she caught her lower lip between her teeth when her husband was finally revealed in all his masculine glory. She took a deep, rather tremulous breath as he tossed

447

the denim trousers across the footboard of the bed and turned back to her with a decidedly purposeful gleam in his magnificent green eyes.

"Now, Mrs. Kincaid, I'm going to do something I've wanted to do from the first moment we met," he declared with a slow, enigmatic smile.

"And what is that, Mr. Kincaid?" she asked, her eyes issuing him a silent challenge.

He did not offer a reply, but instead allowed his hands to do the talking for him—and Dallas was thoroughly enraptured by the language they spoke.

With infinite care and gentleness, Ross methodically stripped her bare. His warm, adoring lips paid tribute to each portion of her silken body as it was exposed. By the time he had finished and she lay completely naked beneath his burning gaze, they were both aflame with desire. He plunged within her velvety warmth in the first near violent gesture of the night, while she welcomed him with a hoarse cry and a passion to match his. Together, they rode the powerful waves of ecstasy, until at last finding release and floating back to earth in the sweet afterglow that always followed.

Dallas, her heart swelling with love and her body totally satiated, lay within her husband's arms and stared across at the lamp which still flickered beside the bed. She smiled to herself as she mused that, while she loved Ruby Mae Hatfield dearly, she was so very glad that Ross was the one who now shared her bed . . .

The next morning dawned brilliantly clear. Leaving Ross and his derrick crew hard at work at the new drilling site down the hill from the barn, Dallas drove the wagon into town to pay a visit to Jacob Kauffman. She dropped Cordi off at the telephone company's office first, then took Etta—who had risen at a decently early hour for a change—to the Kiber and Cobb Confectionary, where the incorrigible youngest Brown sister hoped to persuade the manager of the establishment to offer her employment.

Finally reaching her own destination, Dallas hurried up the outer staircase of the red brick building and went inside. She found the burly photographer readying his equipment for the day in the large, sunlit room he used as a studio.

"Mr. Kauffman?"

"Miss Brown!" exclaimed Jacob, his normally gruff features breaking into a smile of genuine pleasure when he pivoted about to face her. "So you have come back!"

"I have indeed," she affirmed with a soft laugh. Her eyes sparkled warmly up at him as he stepped forward and took her hand in an affectionate clasp between the two of his.

"When your sister told me the reason you would not be coming to work yesterday, I was very surprised. I told myself, *Miss Brown is not like the other young ladies of the town who think of nothing but catching a husband. She is not one to marry in haste.* But that is what you have done, have you not?" he scolded with a mock, teasing scowl, then smiled again. "I wish you much happiness in your marriage. And I hope your new husband will agree to let you work for me. I have not yet learned to make sense of my books, and I still have hopes that I can someday hire you as a full-time assistant."

"I would like that very much," Dallas replied

earnestly. She did not add that she had no idea how much longer she would be living in Corsicana, for there was no sense in worrying about something that might not come to pass for months or even years. For the first time since the beginning of the oil boom, she found herself praying that it would continue.

She and Jacob spoke for several minutes longer. After promising him that she would return the following morning and work for as long as necessary to bring his accounts into order once more, she took her leave and moved back down the steps to the board-walk. She frowned at the visible cloud of dust which was borne aloft by the hot, capricious wind. Reflecting that she might as well run a few errands before returning home, she gathered up her skirts and set off in the direction of the grocer's.

"Oh, Dal-las!" someone called out behind her in an irritatingly singsong manner.

Dallas stopped short and rolled her eyes heavenward at the sound of Lorena Appleton's all too familiar voice. *Just what I needed!* she mused in displeasure. Though tempted to ignore the viperous young widow altogether, she forced herself to turn and await Lorena's approach.

"To tell the truth, I wasn't at all sure you'd care to speak to me, now that your husband's gone and made a liar out of you!" Lorena remarked with a grating trill of laughter as she came to stand before Dallas. Her pale-blue eyes were full of malicious triumph, and she smiled cattily. "Dear me, how very distressed you must have been to discover you hold so little influence over Ross Kincaid!"

"What are you talking about *this* time, Lorena?"

450

asked Dallas, her voice edged with mingled impatience and annoyance. She was well aware of the fact that the other woman went out of her way to provoke a quarrel between them every time they met—and bringing Ross's name into the conversation, she thought with an angry frown, was the surest way to do so.

"You mean you don't know? He hasn't told you?" Lorena countered, feigning wide-eyed innocence.

"Told me what?"

"Why, that he's going to drill my well!"

"What?" Dallas blurted out in stunned disbelief. "What do you mean he's going to drill your well?"

"Exactly what I said, of course!" the spiteful blonde retorted smugly. "He and I spoke about it at some length only yesterday. It was such a fortunate occurrence, our running into each other like that again! Anyway, he asked me if I was still planning to have a well drilled, and I told him yes, and then he said he'd be glad to take on the job just as soon as he had finished—"

"Are you quite certain you didn't imagine all this, Lorena?" Dallas accused bluntly, her eyes kindling with suspicion. "I can't believe Ross would do such a thing without telling me about it first. And he's made no mention of you at all!"

"Well, perhaps that's because he didn't want you to know," she suggested as her lips curled into another derisive smile. "It's possible that he never would have told you, you know. I'm quite sure he had his reasons. Whatever the case, the fact remains that your husband will soon be working for me! And you can rest assured that he will be very well treated while he is at my place throughout all those days—*and* nights!"

Her words were followed by a very pregnant pause, during which time she watched with malevolent satisfaction as several conflicting emotions played across Dallas's face. Finally, she rubbed salt into the wound with, "Why, if Ross Kincaid were *my* husband, he'd never even think of spending time with another woman—especially one as young and beautiful as myself—even if it were supposedly for business purposes. I'd have more control over him if he were mine. But then," she added with a haughty uplifting of her chin, "in order for any woman to wield that kind of power over a man, she has to possess a certain knowledge of how to please him. You might as well be prepared for the worst when it comes to your marriage, Dallas, for I fear that husband of yours is too much of a man to be satisfied with what little *you* know. Yes indeed," she concluded, heaving a dramatic sigh, "he's bound to look elsewhere for certain 'comforts' eventually, and I'm not at all sure I'd have the strength to turn him away should he come knocking at my door."

"Though my opinion of you has never been high, Lorena Appleton," Dallas ground out, her eyes ablaze, "I wouldn't have believed you capable of such a blatantly immoral, contemptible declaration such as the one you have just made. However, since you *have* made it," she went on to warn in a low tone laced with white-hot fury, "I must tell you that, while I am not the least bit concerned about my husband's fidelity, I will not hesitate to tear every hair from your head if you so much as bat an eyelash at him!"

Lorena's face paled and her eyes widened in alarm. In that moment, she had no doubt whatsoever that Dallas would make good on her threat.

"Why, you . . . you . . ." she sputtered with a sudden, comical incapacity for speech.

Dallas, subjecting the brazen young widow to one last menacing glare, swept abruptly past her and back down the boardwalk to where she had left the horse and wagon. She was so angry, she forgot about everything else but getting home, where she intended to confront Ross with the information Lorena had just passed along to her with such malevolent satisfaction. Catching up the reins, she snapped them together and drove away at a particularly brisk pace, prompting a number of the other drivers to swear roundly while hastening to remove their vehicles from her path.

By the time she reached the house, she was in a fine temper indeed. She tried to reason with herself, tried to play devil's advocate and view the situation from Ross's perspective, but her efforts at calm introspection failed. She was deeply hurt to realize that he had kept the details of his arrangement with Lorena a secret from her—it pained her even more to think of him being with the voluptuous widow for several days and nights on end.

It wasn't so much that she didn't trust *him,* she reflected miserably, but rather that she didn't trust Lorena. And yet, how could she place any faith at all in a man who had never even told her he loved her? *Dear Lord, if only she could be sure of his love.*

She told herself it was ridiculous to get all worked up over the matter—after all, simply because he had agreed to drill a well for Lorena Appleton didn't mean he would ever succumb to her wiles—but the doubts and fears refused to be quelled.

Jealousy, feeding on her insecurity, had seized her in

453

its powerful grip and now provoked her to a single-minded rashness. Securing the reins and alighting from the wagon with stiff, angry movements, she recalled how Ross had looked at Lorena when the she-wolf had boldly presented herself there at the house the week before. From what she had observed then, there was no question that he found the flirtatious blonde attractive . . .

She set off toward the spot where the new derrick was being constructed. Her fury-quickened steps led her across the backyard and down the hill in a matter of seconds. Upon nearing the center of activity, her fiery gaze conducted a hasty search, only to narrow when it fell upon her husband. He stood with his back to her, talking with Erik and punctuating his words every now and then with a slight frown.

"Ross!" Dallas hailed him from a short distance away, finding it necessary to raise her voice to a shout in order to be heard above the pounding and sawing.

He turned, caught sight of her, and smiled a disarmingly tender greeting. Pausing to offer one last opinion to his partner, he moved toward Dallas with long, easy strides, tugging the hat from his head so that his hair gleamed a rich-hued sable in the bright sunlight.

"To what do I owe this pleasure, Mrs. Kincaid?" he asked in a lazily bantering manner.

"I've just seen Lorena Appleton!" she informed him tersely. "She was positively *overflowing* with all sorts of information!" Studying his reaction closely, she observed the way his eyes suddenly filled with an unfathomable light.

"I think we'd better talk about this inside," he

decreed quietly. It was obvious that he did not need to ask what had set her off.

He took her arm and led her silently back up the hill to the house. Dallas, holding herself stiffly erect as she moved along with him, wrenched her arm from his grasp as soon as they stepped into the kitchen.

"Is it true?" she demanded, rounding on him with a vengeance now. "Did you agree to drill a well for her?"

"I did," Ross confirmed in a low, even tone, his handsome visage strangely impassive.

"But . . . but why?" she asked in hurt, angry bewilderment.

"Because I'm a driller."

"I know that! What I want to know is why you felt compelled to offer your services to *her?*"

"She asked me if I wanted to take on the job several days ago," he informed her with maddening calm. "I told her I'd consider it, which is exactly what I did. Swede and I will be through here by the end of the week."

"Why didn't you tell me you were planning to go to work for Lorena?" She folded her arms tightly across her heaving bosom and peered resentfully up at him.

"I didn't make up my mind until yesterday," he answered, still treating the situation with a studied nonchalance that only added fuel to the fire. A faint, mocking smile played about his lips when he added, "The Widow Appleton can be very persuasive."

Dallas's eyes hurled invisible daggers at his head while her cheeks flamed with wrathful indignation. Battling the urge to do him bodily harm, she uncrossed her arms and curled her hands into tight fists at her sides.

"Is that why you didn't tell me about your conversation with her—because she *persuaded* you to keep it from me?" she seethed, her voice edged with biting sarcasm. "And was it due to that same *persuasiveness* that you decided to enter her employ?"

"If I'm going to stay on here in Corsicana, I'll have to take on other jobs," explained Ross, his eyes twinkling with devilish humor. "I didn't tell you about my agreement with the fair Mrs. Appleton because I suspected you'd be less than thrilled at the news." He paused and smiled unrepentantly. "I would have told you eventually." In truth, he had been hoping to provoke his beautiful, high-spirited bride to jealousy.

"The *fair* Mrs. Apple—" Dallas started to echo, only to break off and feelingly reproach, "How could you do this to me? How could you do this to *us?*"

She knew she was being irrational, knew she was probably attaching far too much significance to the matter, and yet she couldn't seem to help it. Her usually well-ordered emotions had been in absolute turmoil ever since the tall, raven-haired rogue she loved had come into her life. Plagued by an awful sense of betrayal, she fought back the hot tears gathering in her eyes and recklessly proclaimed, "I forbid you to do it, Ross Kincaid! I absolutely forbid you to go over there and—"

"What the devil do you mean, 'you forbid it'?" demanded Ross, his amusement fading fast.

"I am your wife, and I . . . I will not allow you to make a fool of me in front of the whole town!"

"And just how the hell would I be doing that?" A tight-lipped expression crossed the rugged perfection of his features, and his eyes gleamed dully. While he had been satisfied to observe the evidence of her jealousy, he was *not* pleased with the domineering attitude she had suddenly assumed toward him.

"By going anywhere near Lorena Appleton! You can rest assured there would be plenty of talk about the two of you, and I won't have people gossiping about my husband and that . . . that *jezebel!*" She lifted her head proudly and gazed up at him with wide, glistening eyes that reflected both pain and indignation. "If you do this, you may as well forget about what you and I have together!" she warned. "I'll be damned if I'll let you sleep in my bed each night after you've been over there with her!"

"Do you really trust me so little?" He suddenly seized her arms in an angry, forceful grip. "Do you honestly believe me to be incapable of keeping my hands off all women in general?"

"Well, aren't you?" Dallas retorted bitterly, then gasped as he pulled her up hard against him.

"No, damn you!" Ross ground out. "*You,* my dearest little shrew, happen to be the only one enjoying that particular honor! And right now," he then threatened with deadly calm, "I'm tempted to turn you over my knee and apply my hand to your backside until you beg for mercy." Dallas inwardly blanched at the savage gleam in his eyes, but she tossed her head in defiance and bravely countered with, "You do, Ross Kincaid, and it will be the last time you ever lay a finger on me!"

"Will it?"

Too late, she remembered what he had once said about never allowing a threat to go unanswered. Her eyes grew round as saucers while very real alarm shot through her. She struggled within his grasp, but to no avail. He easily drew her along with him to the table where he wasted little time in taking a seat on one of the chairs and yanking her facedown across his knees. She gasped to feel him tossing her skirts up about her waist and exposing her white, lace-trimmed drawers. Her face burned as it suddenly occurred to her that Etta might return from town at any moment and witness her humiliation.

"Let me go!" she cried hotly, frantically trying to push herself off his lap. Ross easily held her captive with his strong arm clamped across her back, and he seemed oblivious to her futile struggles as he lifted his other arm and brought his large hand down upon her writhing bottom with carefully controlled force. She gasped in mingled pain and outrage. "Why, you—stop it! Let go of me!"

"I once told you I'd never let you run roughshod over me, Dallas," he reminded her in a low, deceptively level tone.

"Damn you, Ross, let me go!" she demanded, her words ending on a breathless shriek as his hand slapped against her thinly covered flesh once more. *This couldn't be happening! Why, she hadn't been spanked since she was eight years old!*

Ross, apparently not in the least bit swayed by the fact that she was no longer a child, spanked her several more times after that, until her bottom felt as though it were on fire and her beautiful, stormy countenance was flushed a deep red.

Then, he stood and hurled her upright with him. His smoldering gaze softened a bit when he saw the tears swimming in her brilliantly blue eyes, but he would not allow himself to weaken in his resolve. Though he loved her with all his heart, he was determined to hold the upper hand in their marriage.

"I won't go back on my word to Mrs. Appleton," he stated grimly. Dallas, refusing to look at him, remained furiously silent and unyielding within his grasp. "But I won't go back on my word to you, either—and I'm telling you here and now that I have no intention of getting involved with her or any other woman. You're all I can handle." This last he spoke with a faint, appreciatively sardonic smile while a discernible note of wry amusement could be heard in his deep-timbred voice. Since Dallas stubbornly refused to meet his gaze, however, she failed to see the way his eyes glowed with mingled tenderness and desire.

Ross finally released her. Settling the hat upon his head once more, he headed back outside, his boots connecting softly with the bare wooden floor. It wasn't until she heard the door close behind him that Dallas released a long, ragged sigh and sank down into the chair he had just vacated. She winced as her still smarting backside made contact with the uncushioned seat. Shifting gingerly about, she muttered a very unladylike curse, folded her arms atop the table, and brought her forehead down to rest upon them while the tears coursed freely down her face.

"Dallas? Dallas, where are you?" It was Etta's voice, calling to her from the front entrance foyer.

Her head came up with a jerk as her eyes filled with dismay. Springing to her feet, she withdrew the handkerchief from the pocket of her skirt and swiped hastily at her tears. She smoothed a trembling hand over her hair, then drew a deep, steadying breath and forced a smile to her lips.

"I was able to catch a ride back with—" Etta was explaining when she arrived in the doorway and caught sight of Dallas. She frowned as she took note of the unmistakable redness about the other woman's eyes. "What's happened now?" she demanded, her concern tempered with a touch of sisterly exasperation.

"Nothing. Nothing at all."

"That's not true," Etta insisted. "You've been crying."

"Women in love cry easily!" Dallas retorted flippantly.

"*I* don't!"

"Did you get the job, Etta?" Dallas then asked, pointedly changing the subject. She crossed to the stove and bent to light it so that she could begin preparations for the noon meal. Her movements were somewhat stiff and mechanical, for her troubled thoughts were still focused on the turbulent confrontation with Ross.

"No." Heaving a disgruntled sigh, Etta marched to to the sink and filled a glass with water. She strained to catch a glimpse of Sam, but the new drilling site was too far down the hill to be visible from the kitchen window. "They said it was due to my lack of experience, but I think it was because I'm a woman," she disclosed with a deep frown. "There aren't any 'dadburned females' working at the soda fountains in this town, but I was hoping to be the first!"

"I suppose you'll just have to keep trying."

"I suppose," the petite blonde agreed with another sigh, then grew characteristically animated once more. "Oh, I forgot to tell you—I heard some very unpleasant

460

news on my way home. I can only hope it isn't true!"

"What?" asked Dallas, her emotions still in too much of an uproar for her to be able to pay more than vague attention to her sister's words. Etta's next remark, however, shook her out of her preoccupation.

"Lorena Appleton's going all over town saying that Ross is going to drill a well for her! You can imagine my reaction upon hearing that *my* sister's husband is planning to go to work for that pasty-faced witch! I'll bet Cordi's heard by now, too. Working down at the telephone company like she does, she always hears the best gossip before any of the rest of us. Anyway, is it true? Are Ross and Erik really going to—"

"Please, Etta," murmured Dallas weakly. "I . . . I . . ." A sob welled up in her throat, and she could do nothing more than mutter an unintelligible excuse as she suddenly went rushing from the kitchen to seek the much-needed privacy of her bedroom.

XVIII

Dallas released a disconsolate sigh as her gaze drifted back to the lace-curtained window once more. *Ross was out there somewhere . . .*

Unlike the previous night, she had remained downstairs in the parlor to provide suitable chaperonage for her sisters, who, although secretly wishing her elsewhere, were once again delighting in the attentions of Erik and Sam. Etta and her practically lifelong beau were sitting on the front porch swing at the moment, while Cordi and the conscientious young Swede were engaged in a quiet discussion close—but not too close—beside each other on the sofa.

Ross had ridden off less than an hour ago to take part in the second nightly patrol of the oil field. The first night's vigilance had proven a success in that no one had been injured; but neither had anyone been apprehended.

Recalling how she had refused to speak to her husband before he'd gone, Dallas silently berated herself once more and leapt up from the chair to follow the direction of her troubled gaze. She wandered over to the window, where she stood distractedly fingering the curtains as she stared out into the warm, moonlit darkness.

He could be in danger right now, her mind's inner voice told her, *and you let him go off without so much as a word.*

It was all too true, she mused unhappily. Still fuming over his humiliating treatment of her, she had scarcely even glanced his way when she and Etta had taken food and coffee out to the men at noon and then again at six o'clock that evening. Surprisingly enough, he had not forced the issue, but had kept his distance as though he understood her sorely wounded pride needed time to heal.

He had tried to kiss her when saying good-bye, but she had obstinately turned her head aside so that his lips brushed her cheek instead of her mouth. She experienced a sharp pang of remorse for her childish behavior now, particularly when she recalled how he had smiled softly down at her before leaving. Watching him ride away from her vantage point at the same window where she now stood, she had felt terribly heartsore, and she had found herself wanting to call him back . . .

"Dallas, why don't you go on up to bed?" suggested Cordi. "Honestly, you don't look at all well and I think the extra rest would do you a world of good."

"Thank you," Dallas murmured with a faint smile of irony, "but I don't think I should retire until you and Etta have done so." She did not add that she also hated the prospect of being alone while waiting for Ross to come home. Turning away from the window, she trailed a hand lightly across the back of the sofa as she meandered over to the piano.

"For heaven's sake!" Cordi sighed, a mild frown of exasperation creasing her brow at the thought that she was being treated like a child again. "When are you going to realize—"

"Your sister is right," Erik quietly intervened. He smiled tenderly at his much-surprised beloved before telling her, "It is only because she cares for you that she stays."

Cordi, her blue-green eyes gazing adoringly up at the young Swede, nodded in acquiescence and obediently refrained from any further attempt to get rid of their chaperone. Musing that her sister would never have given in so easily if *she* had been the one to make such a statement, Dallas shook her head in amused wonderment and raised a hand to the ivory keys. She absently fingered them for a few moments, then lifted her other hand and began to play in earnest while her mind was drawn irrevocably back to thoughts of Ross.

It was nearly midnight by the time the three women, and one of the men, took themselves up to bed. Erik returned outside to the drilling site, insisting that Sam get some sleep while he himself took first watch. They were determined that the newly erected derrick would not meet the fate of the original one built upon the first site. Although they did not anticipate any real trouble, Ross had warned them to remain alert.

Certain she would never be able to sleep, Dallas nonetheless changed into her sheer lawn nightgown and got into bed. She turned out the lamp and lay there alone in the darkness, her nerves feeling strained to the limit and a knot tightening in the very pit of her stomach.

"Oh, Ross!" she sighed aloud. She knew it was possible he would not return until dawn, and she told herself that there was no sense in tormenting herself with thoughts of all the horrible fates that could befall him. No matter how desperately she tried, however, she couldn't help thinking about the injured deputy again. A sudden, terrible vision of Ross, lying wounded in the darkness somewhere, flashed into her mind.

"No!" she whispered in horror, her throat constricting painfully. If she had ever doubted how much she loved him, she could doubt it no longer. Her anger had long since fled, and her fears for her husband's safety had driven everything else—including Lorena Appleton—from her mind. The only thing that truly mattered was Ross.

Dear Lord, please keep him safe! she prayed fervently. Releasing another long, pent-up sigh, she rolled onto her side and hugged the comforting softness of her pillow close to her trembling body . . .

Lying happily ensconced in that dreamworld that exists between sleep and consciousness, Dallas was not at all certain if what she felt was real.

She slowly became aware of the soft moans rising from her own throat, and of the delicious tremor coursing through her like wildfire. Other sensations followed—the feeling of cool air against her feverish skin, the soft fabric of her nightgown tickling upward across her quivering form, the faint creaking of the bedsprings beneath the weight of another body on the feather mattress beside her, and the highly pleasurable touch of a pair of warm lips pursuing a bold, fiery path along the satiny curve of her naked hip to the entrancing hollow of her waist as she lay on her side, still clutching the pillow to her breasts.

This was no dream!

"Ross?" she gasped, her eyes suddenly flying very wide. Her body tensed in startlement at the realization that someone really *was* baring her body and kissing it with such shocking familiarity.

"Damn it, woman, who else would it be?" As always, there was no mistaking that deep, wonderfully masculine voice.

"Oh, Ross, you're back!" Swiftly rolling over, she threw her arms about his neck. "Thank God you're safe!"

"Of course I'm safe," he responded with a low chuckle, his own arms gathering her close against his naked, hard-muscled frame. "Why wouldn't I be?"

"Because you were in danger out there tonight!" She tilted her head back and studied his face in the semidarkness of the room. The sun's rays were just beginning to set the window shade aglow as the new day dawned. "I was afraid something might happen to you," explained Dallas, "and then I . . . I never could have told you how sorry I am for the way I behaved!"

"I'm glad to know that's the only thing about my death that would have bothered you," Ross murmured sardonically, his eyes twinkling down at her.

"That's not what I meant!" she hastened to protest. "Of course I'd be sorry for others reasons, too!"

"Such as?" he challenged softly. Before she could reply, he settled back upon the bed and drew her down beside him so that the hills and valleys of her body fitted perfectly into his and her long hair fanned about them both. She was acutely conscious of the way her thinly covered breasts were pressing against his hard warmth.

"Oh, Ross," she sighed again as she smoothed an appreciative hand across his broad chest, "why do we always seem to be at odds with each other?"

"I suppose, my love, because our tempers are as well matched as the rest of us. And maybe because we care more than either of us is willing to let on."

She caught her breath at his words. *Was it possible that this was his way of saying that he loved her?* The thought prompted her heart to pound erratically while her eyes filled with a hopeful light.

"Do you really . . . think so?" she queried in a small, tremulous voice.

"I do," confirmed Ross, smiling to himself as his hand glided back down to where her nightgown was still caught up about her waist.

A soft gasp escaped Dallas's lips when his strong fingers curled possessively about the bare, undeniably feminine roundness of her bottom. She suddenly recalled, with discomfiting clarity, the spanking he had given her. She also remembered how she had vowed in anger that he would never lay another finger on her. *So much for threats,* she mused with a rosy blush.

"You know, Mrs. Kincaid, you have an adorable backside," he pronounced, the vibrant note in his deep-timbred voice sending a delicious shiver dancing down her spine.

"I suppose you've seen a good many of them, haven't you?" she retorted saucily. He gave another low chuckle.

"A few."

"Well, those days are in the past, Ross Kincaid," she decreed with wifely severity, then demanded, *"Aren't they?"*

"My word on it," he agreed without hesitation, his voice now brimming with irrepressible humor. "Your backside's the only one I'll look at for the next fifty years."

"Only fifty?" teased Dallas, raising up on one elbow to cast him an archly challenging look.

"I figure by that time I'll be ready for a change." Rewarded for his devilish raillery with a murderous glare, he merely grinned and drew her head back down to rest upon his chest.

Neither of them spoke again for several long moments, during which time she was content to let Ross hold her and he was content to let his fingers caress her silken flesh. The love between them, though unspoken, was a very tangible thing. Dallas's heart soared at the renewed camaraderie they shared, and she pressed herself even closer against him.

"Did you encounter any trouble while on patrol?" she asked, breaking the silence at last. Her thoughts had suddenly returned to the reason she had lain awake for hours before drifting into blissful unconsciousness.

"Some" was all Ross would say. Then, apparently desirous of doing a good deal more than he was already doing, he urged her onto her back and quickly stripped the nightgown from her alluring curves. She trembled with impassioned delight when he covered her naked body with his own.

"Will it always be like this with us?" she wondered aloud, inhaling sharply as one of his hands closed upon the rose-tipped fullness of her breast.

"No." His reply threw her into a quandary, from which he rescued her in the next instant by smiling tenderly and explaining in a low, resonant tone that sent a warm flush stealing over her, "It will only get better."

His lips claimed hers in a deep, fiercely possessive kiss that rapidly ranned the flames of an ever-smoldering passion, a passion which was never far from the surface. And soon, very soon, the magnificent rogue and his redheaded spitfire were as one . . .

Glancing down at the watch pinned to the white cotton of her shirtwaist above her left breast, Dallas frowned pensively and rose from her seat at the desk in Jacob Kauffman's studio. She wandered over to one of the windows and opened it a bit more, then stood gazing down upon the crowded street below for a moment.

For what she mused was probably the hundredth time that morning, she thought about Ross. He had accompanied her into town a short time earlier and was now at the courthouse, where he would no doubt remain for the better part of the morning. It was because of the inordinate amount of time away from his work, and not because of any concern over the outcome of the case, she recalled with a fondly indulgent smile, that he had complained about the scheduling of his appearance before the judge.

Turning away with a sigh, she crossed back to the desk and sat down to resume her work. The photographer was still in the outer room, where he had been fielding a barrage of questions and instructions from a wealthy young matron for the past ten minutes. The woman was anxious to make certain he understood exactly what she wanted in the way of a portrait of her three little darlings, and she was leery about trusting his judgment.

A faint smile touched Dallas's lips as she heard the booming tones of Jacob's voice echoing throughout the entire studio. He had lost more than one customer as a result of his gruff manner.

Finally, the matron left. Jacob came stomping back into the skylight-brightened room where Dallas sat doing her best to make sense of his sadly infrequent ledger entries. It was obvious to her that the recent negotiations had left him in a foul humor.

"These women!" he grumbled, his black brows drawing together into a ferocious scowl. "They want me to forget I am an artist!" He muttered an oath and marched forward to begin rearranging the props.

Dallas said nothing. She kept her attention focused on the task before her while she waited for Jacob's temper to cool, which she knew from experience usually calmed as quickly as it had flared. Sure enough, it was only a matter of minutes until she heard a deep, quiet laugh rumbling up from his chest.

"Alas, I cannot afford to be an artist!" he proclaimed with a dramatic sigh. His dark eyes twinkled merrily across at Dallas as he turned to face her. "Maybe someday you will think of this when you are—"

He was interrupted by the sound of a knock at the outer door. Casting his eyes heavenward in anticipation of another difficult interview, he took himself off to answer it before Dallas could make a move to do so.

He was gone only a few moments. When he returned, however, it was immediately apparent to her that something was amiss.

"Mr. Kauffman?" she questioned solicitously, rising to her feet as she noted the grim set to his features. He held a piece of paper in his hand, and he frowned down at it before informing her,

"The teacher at my Peter's school sends word that he is injured."

"Injured?" echoed Dallas, her eyes filling with worriment. "Oh no, I . . . I hope it's not serious!"

"The message does not say. I must go at once," he declared calmly, though his voice shook a little.

"Of course! Don't worry about the studio. I'll handle everything until you return!" she hastened to assure him. He nodded curtly and hurried from the room.

Dallas sank back down upon the chair. Her eyes swept closed, and she uttered a silent prayer for the welfare of Jacob's son. She didn't remember much about the six-year-old boy she had seen only once, other than the fact that he resembled his mother more than his father and was terribly shy.

She released another long sigh and resumed her work, though she found it difficult to concentrate as thoughts of the injured boy continually intruded. The photographer had been gone only five minutes at the most when she heard the unmistakable sound of the outer door opening and closing.

"Mr. Kauffman?" Dallas called out. She told herself with a frown that it was impossible for him to have traveled to the school and back in such a short amount of time since the school was clear on the other side of town. Receiving no reply, she rose to her feet and headed toward the other room to investigate. She stopped short when a man suddenly stepped into the studio to block her path. A sharp gasp broke from her lips while her eyes widened in alarm. *"Justin!"*

"Hello, Dallas," Justin Bishop proclaimed softly, his mouth curling into a sneer and his dark, hawkish gaze raking over her with sinister boldness.

"Wha—what are you doing here?" she demanded, trying desperately to control the fear gripping her heart. She raised a hand to her throat and could feel the color draining from her face.

"Did you really think I'd stay away?" he challenged scornfully. "You and I have some unfinished business, remember?" Wasting no time, he began advancing upon her, his attractive features now an ugly mask of vengeful rage.

"No, Justin!" She backed away in growing panic, her gaze moving frantically about the studio. *Dear God, what was she going to do? There had to be some way to make him see reason!* "Mr. Kauffman will be—" she started to warn, only to be cut off with a soft, malevolent laugh.

"We both know he won't be coming back for a while, don't we?" Justin challenged with a significant cocking of his eyebrow. "No, Dallas, it will be much too late by the time he returns."

"Why, you—you sent him that message!" she accused, her bright gaze filling with horror as the truth dawned on her.

He merely smiled again, his dark eyes filling with a predatory gleam while he continued to close the gap between them. Dallas sensed he would not be swayed by either pleas or threats. Retreating on terror-weakened legs, she looked hastily about once more. *Scream, damn you, scream!* the instinct for survival prodded her. She waited too late to obey.

Just as she opened her mouth and drew in a deep breath, Justin shot across the remaining distance. He reached her before she could utter a sound. Clamping one hand across her mouth with bruising force, his other arm seized her about the waist and tightened like a band of steel, very nearly cutting off her breath when he yanked her brutally against him.

Dallas screamed low in her throat and struggled with all her might, but Justin Bishop's blackhearted purpose gifted him with an almost supernatural strength. He dragged her with surprising ease to the small equipment room. Once inside, he flung her to the hard wooden floor and slammed the door behind him.

There was a window cut high in the outer wall, but it had not been opened in years, and Dallas knew there was little hope of anyone hearing her screams. She climbed to her feet and faced the man who now seemed like a stranger to her—an evil, menacing stranger whom she knew to be capable of the worst kind of treachery.

"You can't do this, Justin," she told him, still refusing to surrender to the waves of panic which threatened to send her reeling.

"Oh, but I can!" he parried derisively. "You're mine, damn you! Kincaid may have had you first, but you belong to *me!* I'm going to do what I should have done long ago. I was a fool for leaving you untouched!" He started moving toward her again now, his eyes glittering with a horrifyingly obsessive lust. "I'll make you beg for it, you little bitch! I'll bury myself so deep

474

inside you, you'll forget all about Kincaid!"

"My husband will kill you!"

"He'll never know," insisted Justin with another sneer. "If you tell him, he'll be the one to die! I've got a lot of 'friends' in this town, Dallas. It wouldn't be all that difficult to arrange his death!"

"No!" she cried hoarsely. "Please, Justin, if you ever cared for me at all, you'll—"

"Shut up!" he growled, lunging for her at last. She fought him like a veritable tigress, her hands curling into fists and pummeling him wildly about the head. Struggling to push past him and get to the door, she found her efforts thwarted when, after slamming her up against the wall, he grabbed her wrists. She cried out in pain as he wrenched her arms savagely behind her back.

"No, damn you, no!" she screamed in furious defiance. She squirmed helplessly against him while he brought his lips crashing down upon hers. A sudden wave of nausea rose in her throat, and she jerked her head aside. Gripping both of her wrists with one hand, Justin lifted his other hand to take her chin in a cruel grip. His mouth ground upon hers until she tasted blood.

Please God, please help me! she pleaded in near mindless desperation.

Her prayer was answered in the very next moment. Yanking one of her wrists free, she flung her arm outward—and her hand came up against one of Jacob's metal flash pans resting atop a table in the corner. She did not think twice before acting upon her discovery of the weapon she needed. Her fingers curled about the wooden handle, and she brought the sharp-edged piece of equipment forcefully up against the side of Justin's head.

Suddenly, she was free. She watched as Justin went staggering dizzily back against the wall. Stunned by the blow, he raised a hand to the spot where blood oozed from the wound she had inflicted.

Seizing advantage of her attacker's temporary debilitation, she sprang to the door and jerked it open. She raced across the studio and into the outer room, where her flight was arrested when she encountered difficulty unlocking the main entry door. Throwing a frantic glance over her shoulder, she finally wrested the door open and stumbled down the stairs to the boardwalk.

Ross! Her first impulse was to tell him what Justin had done. Gathering up her skirts, she set off in the direction of the courthouse, making her way as quickly as possible through the crowd of men and women going about their usual business on a Wednesday morning.

If you tell him, he'll be the one to die! Justin's words suddenly returned to haunt her. Her eyes filled with renewed horror, and she drew to an abrupt halt on the boardwalk.

No! her mind cried as her heart hammered painfully in her chest. *No, I . . . I can't let him know! I can't ever let him know!*

Hot, bitter tears stung against her eyelids, and she felt a sob welling up in her throat. She turned and looked back toward the redbrick building she had just left. A loud gasp broke from her lips as she saw Justin stepping out from the foot of the staircase. He held a handkerchief to the cut on his head, and his dark, piercing gaze searched the immediate area for a moment before he spun about and strode away in the opposite direction from where Dallas stood watching him.

Feeling light-headed with relief for the fact that he had not seen her, she released an audible, ragged sigh and leaned weakly back against the side of the wood-sided structure which housed a dry goods store. She struggled to regain control of her breathing while her stomach churned at the terrible memory of Justin's attack.

Finally, giving silent thanks for her escape, she drew herself resolutely upright and headed back to the photography studio. Once upstairs, she locked the door and sank down into a chair to await Jacob Kauffman's return.

Oh, Ross! her heart cried out to him. She buried her face in her hands as the aftereffects of the frightening, emotionally draining ordeal took hold and her tears refused to be quelled any longer . . .

The incident, fading somewhat as a result of time and Jacob's consoling presence, seemed little more than a terrible nightmare by the time Dallas returned home that afternoon. She had not told the photographer the whole truth, of course—merely that a former friend of hers had played a cruel joke on them both and had been severely reprimanded for it. Jacob had been furious at first, but then had calmed somewhat and said that, since no real harm had been done, they might as well put it from their minds. He had then added with a chuckle that poor little Peter, quite startled to see his father at school, would probably be talking about it for days.

Gathering courage, and assuming what she believed to be a perfectly normal demeanor, Dallas finally went outside to speak to Ross an hour after returning from town. She discovered that he himself had come home shortly before noon. True to Sheriff Crow's predictions, the case against him had been thrown out of court due to lack of evidence.

Ross, though preoccupied with the drilling he, Erik, and Sam had started earlier that day, did not fail to notice that his wife appeared a bit more subdued than usual. He questioned her about it, but she merely smiled and said with a deceptive airiness that she was tired from poring over the photographer's thoroughly disorganized books all day. Apparently satisfied with her answer, he pressed a sweetly compelling kiss upon her lips and took himself back to work.

Dallas's heart swelled with love as she watched him resume his place on the derrick floor. She caught her breath at the sudden, unbidden memory of Justin's assault, and she told herself once more that she was doing the right thing in not telling Ross. A fresh rush of tears gathered in the brilliant sapphire depths of her eyes as she turned away and walked back up the hill . . .

The next two days passed in a whirl of activity for the entire household.

The men continued drilling around the clock, while the women kept busy with their own work. As usual, most of the cooking and other domestic chores fell to Dallas, though Etta did provide an increasingly helpful hand when her efforts at finding another job proved fruitless. Cordi, too, lent her assistance whenever she wasn't away at her job.

Dallas saw far too little of her husband. The two of them managed to share a few moments together during meal breaks, but that was usually the only time they were able to speak. Although Ross did come to bed late at night, it was of necessity for the sole purpose of catching a few hours' sleep. Dallas would snuggle gratefully close to his hard, familiar warmth before returning to her own slumber. Her dreams were often troubled by visions of Justin Bishop, but each morning found her putting them determinedly from her mind.

The second well was "brought in" not long after sunrise on Friday. This time, however, none of the women felt compelled to get themselves drenched in oil, so they remained inside and watched the momentous event from their vantage point at an upstairs window inside the house.

Dallas viewed the completion of the well with mixed feelings. Though she naturally shared in her husband's sense of accomplishment, she couldn't help thinking about the fact that he would now be going over to Lorena Appleton's to begin his next project. To her, it wasn't a matter of trust, but of pride. Lorena had issued a challenge she could not ignore, and she told herself she'd be hanged if she'd let that spiteful witch get away with anything, especially when it came to the man she loved. If she heard one word, *one word* about Lorena playing up to Ross, she would not hesitate to carry out the threat she had made! She smiled inwardly at the thought of Lorena Appleton without hair.

On Saturday morning, Dallas followed her usual custom of stacking the boxes of pies she had made the day before. Cordi and Etta sat at the kitchen table, following their usual custom of eating a late breakfast.

"Would either of you care to come along?" asked Dallas, favoring them with a brief smile.

"No, thanks," Etta was the first to decline. "Sam will be coming in soon. We're supposed to go on an all-day picnic." She cast a frown toward the window and murmured, "It looks a bit like rain, but maybe the clouds will blow over by the time we leave."

"Erik has promised to take me later," revealed Cordi. Her face literally beamed with pleasure, and she giggled before adding, "He said Ross ordered him to do so!"

"Ross is very good at giving orders," Dallas noted dryly, her own eyes sparkling with amusement. "Well then, I'd best be getting these pies down to the hotel. Will the two of you at least help me carry them out to the wagon?"

Driving away from the house a few minutes later, Dallas tossed a glance toward the spot where she knew her husband to be working. Only the top portion of the derrick was visible from the road. Her mouth turned up into a mischievous little smile as it suddenly occurred to her that with Erik and Sam and her sisters gone for the day she and Ross would be completely alone at the house.

Perhaps, Rossiter Maverick Kincaid, she told him silently, *you and I will be able to make very good use of our privacy!* Then, blushing at the utter wickedness of her thoughts, she gave a vigorous flick of the reins and guided the wagon toward town.

XIX

Ruby Mae Hatfield quickened her steps along the boardwalk on that busy Saturday morning and smiled broadly at the woman who had just stepped outside from the lobby entrance of the Molloy Hotel.

"Mornin', Fanny!" she called as she drew nearer. Fanny Woodward turned hopefully at the sound of the familiar voice, but her face fell when she saw that Ruby Mae was alone.

"Oh, Ruby Mae, I was hoping Dallas was with you!"

"Dallas?" Ruby Mae echoed with a puzzled frown. "You mean she ain't showed up yet?"

"No," answered the Molloy's head cook, "and to tell the truth, I'm beginning to get more than a little concerned. She's never late with those pies, and she should have been here an hour ago!"

"That don't sound like Dallas at all," murmured Ruby Mae, her brow creasing into another frown while her expressive brown eyes filled with worriment. She had been over to the house only yesterday and had stayed to help Dallas with her baking.

481

"I know it doesn't. She would have sent word if she been unable to deliver the order, I just know she wou have! Our customers are starting to raise an absolu ruckus. They've gotten to where they demand tho pies of hers every Saturday," sighed Fanny. "I came o here in the hopes of catching sight of her or one of h sisters. Maybe one of them took ill, or—"

"Now don't you worry none. I'm sure there's reason for her not bein' here on time," the older woma sought to reassure her. "Just the same, I think I'll dri on out to her house and find out what's goin' on."

"Oh, would you?" Fanny responded, her fa brightening. "I'd appreciate it so much, Ruby Mae

"Either me or Dallas will talk to you late dependin' on what's happened." Smiling briefly at t cook once more, Ruby Mae set off at a brisk pace where she had left her horse and buggy tied up.

She pulled up before the Browns' house a short tin later. Hurrying around to the back door, she knock first and, receiving no answer, went inside.

"Dallas? Dallas, are you here?" she called out loud, ringing tones so that her voice easily carrie upstairs as well. Again, there was no answer.

Truly concerned now, Ruby Mae wheeled about ar returned outside to hasten down the grassy incli behind the barn. She spied Ross bending down examine a bolt in one of the metal bands of the stora; tank.

"Ross!"

He immediately straightened and turned to face he His mouth curved into a smile of welcome, but t smile faded when he viewed the unmistakable conce

ritten on the woman's normally blithesome counte-
ance.

"What is it?" he demanded, striding forward to take
er arm in a steadying grasp.

"How long ago did Dallas leave?" Ruby Mae asked
reathlessly, her eyes very wide and her face flushed.

"Why?" His handsome features tightened as a
udden dread gripped his heart.

"Because she never showed up at the hotel. I just
alked to Fanny Woodward, and she's been waitin'
own there for Dallas to bring them pies for more than
a hour! Now, I didn't see no sign of her on my way
ack out here, and I don't figure she would've taken
erself off somewhere else before deliverin' those pies.
Maybe Cordi or Etta—"

"They're with Sam and Swede."

"Lord have mercy, then where could she *be*?"

Ross muttered an oath and whipped the hat from his
ead. He cautioned himself against jumping to
onclusions, and yet he couldn't shake the suspicion
king seed within him. Like Ruby Mae, he knew it
asn't like Dallas to be late for anything, just as he
new she would never have treated her responsibility
o lightly. No, though he hated to admit it, something
as very wrong.

"Stay here," he instructed Ruby Mae grimly. She
urned to watch as he strode quickly up the hill and
isappeared into the barn. Minutes later, he had
addled his horse and was mounting up. He reined
wiftly about and urged the sleek chestnut stallion to a
allop along the dusty road leading into town.

One name rose in his mind as he thought of Dallas.

Justin Bishop. His green eyes filled with a fierc[e] vengeful light while his face became a mask of savag[e] fury. He cursed himself for having underestimated h[is] adversary, and though he prayed there was anoth[er] explanation for his wife's disappearance, he sensed th[at] Bishop was involved.

Dallas. He loved her, loved her more than life itsel[f] and he swore he'd kill anyone who dared to touch he[r]. His heart twisted painfully at the thought of her i[n] danger. Sternly commanding himself to keep a cle[ar] head, he refused to acknowledge any visions of her i[n] Bishop's clutches, refused to think of what might b[e] happening to her at that very moment.

Dallas, he repeated silently. Her name reverberate[d] throughout his entire being.

Still hoping his instincts would be proven wron[g] Ross set a course for the Double Sixes Saloon. H[e] arrived there in a matter of minutes, bursting throug[h] the double half-doors and striding purposefully acros[s] to the bar.

"Where's Bishop?" he demanded tersely. The ba[r] tender took one look at his face and blanche[d]. Swallowing hard, the man decided to answer with th[e] truth.

"He ain't here. Him and O'Shea lit out at first lig[ht] this mornin'!"

"Where to?" Ross's eyes darkened, and the savag[e] gleam in their magnificent green depths intensified. H[is] worst fears had been realized—it was no me[re] coincidence that Justin Bishop had disappeared th[e] same time as Dallas.

"Don't know. O'Shea sold out last night. Said h[e] wasn't never comin' back. Bishop didn't seem too happ[y] be goin', but he went," the bartender went on to sclose.

Ross nodded wordlessly and left. Every muscle in his ody grew taut while his mind raced to formulate a an of action.

Dallas cried out as she was thrust roughly into an npty, airless room. She staggered forward and fell to r hands and knees on the dust-caked floor, wincing pain while the door slammed shut behind her.

Her long, tangled auburn locks streamed wildly out her, and her clothing was torn and disheveled as result of her struggles with the men who had abducted r earlier that same day. Climbing hastily to her feet, e flew to the single, boarded-up window and peered ut through the cracks in the weathered planks. She uld see nothing more than the overgrown, heat-riveled foliage which surrounded the deserted cabin.

Drawing in a ragged breath, she swung away from e window and desperately searched for any possible enue of escape. Her gaze traveled all about the hot, mly lit room, but she found nothing. There was only e door.

She fought back tears of rising panic as she folded r trembling arms across her chest and returned to the indow, where the sun's rays penetrated just enough to st several long slivers of light upon the floor. Her ad spun while she frantically wondered about the entity of her two captors and their motivation for ducting her.

Ross! her heart cried out to him as a sob welled up ep in her throat.

Surely she would have been missed by now. Sure
Fanny Woodward had grown worried and would ha
sent word—but no, there was no assurance that Fan
would do that. It might be hours yet before anyo
realized she had disappeared.

Recalling the awful moment when she had seen tho
men on horseback blocking the road in front of h
Dallas shuddered involuntarily and turned to le
back against the log wall for support.

She had fought them with every ounce of streng
she possessed, but there had been little she could
against the two of them. They had both dismount
and approached her without a word. Though she h
tried to drive past them, one man had taken control
her horse while the other ruffian, a coarse-featur
giant of a man, had dragged her from the wagon a
easily overpowered her struggles.

With her hands bound and a gag tied painfu
across her mouth, she had been tossed up onto one
the horses. The big man had mounted behind her a
clamped a burly arm about her waist. Spirited aw
across the sun-drenched countryside at a breakne
speed, she had lost all track of time, as well as any se
of distance. She had no idea how far from Corsica
the cabin lay—nor for what purpose she had be
brought there.

"Ross! Oh, Ross!" she whispered in anguish, closi
her eyes tightly against another wave of panic. "De
God, please let him find me! Please!"

She gasped and started in alarm when the do
suddenly burst open. A man she had never seen befo
stood framed in the doorway. Wearing an expensi

486

ilored black suit and red satin vest, he looked very
fferent from the two ragtag villains who had
dnapped her. A tall, beefy man with graying black
ir and a swarthy, pockmarked face, he smiled across
Dallas in scornful amusement as he strolled inside
e room. His gaze raked insolently over her.

"It's easy to see why Bishop lost his head. You, my
ar Mrs. Kincaid, very nearly cost us the entire
eration," he remarked, his smile fading into a tight
owl of displeasure.

"Bishop?" echoed Dallas, her eyes growing very
de. *Justin!* she thought in benumbed horror. *Justin
as the one who had arranged this!* Raising her head
oudly, she demanded, "Who are you? And where is
stin Bishop?"

"The name's O'Shea. As for Bishop, I'm afraid you
on't be seeing him until tonight."

"Tonight?" she repeated once more as his words
ruck sudden fear in her heart.

"Yes, Mrs. Kincaid—tonight," confirmed O'Shea,
s lips curling into a sneer while his eyes glittered with
dangerous light. "You'll be staying here until then.
n sorry I couldn't offer you more agreeable ac-
mmodations, but at least these are only temporary."

"You can't keep me here like this!" Dallas bravely
fied. "I don't know who you are, Mr. O'Shea, nor
w you came to be involved in Justin Bishop's
eacherous little scheme, but surely you must realize
at my husband will be looking for me! He *will* find
e," she declared with a good deal more conviction
an she actually felt, "and when he discovers that
stin Bishop is responsible for my abduction, he'll

487

stop at nothing to—"

"Your husband will do nothing," the hard-edg[ed]
confidence man insisted, "for the simple reason t[h]
he'll never have the chance." With that foreboding
enigmatic statement, he turned to leave. He paused
the doorway and cast her one last faint, mocking smi[le]
"By the way, Bishop's not the one who mastermind[ed]
this 'treacherous little scheme,' as you charmingly p[ut]
it—I am."

"You?" She stared at him in stunned bewilderme[nt]
"But why? What have I—"

"Later, Mrs. Kincaid," he dispassionately promise[d]
"Later." He closed the door softly behind him on [his]
way out. There was a rattle immediately afterwa[rd]
when he shot the bolt on the other side.

Dallas sprang forward seconds after O'Shea h[ad]
gone and knelt down to peer through the keyho[le]
below the rusty doorknob. She caught a glimpse of t[he]
two men who had brought her there, and she watch[ed]
as they exchanged a few words with O'Shea before o[ne]
of them moved back outside with him. The larger of t[he]
two remained in the outer room, guarding the prisor[er]
from his seat at an old table strewn with bottles a[nd]
torn packages of food.

Releasing a heavy sigh, Dallas straightened a[nd]
whirled away from the door. She began paci[ng]
distractedly back and forth, her thoughts in utter cha[os]
as she sought to come up with a plan. There must [be]
some way to escape! she told herself, fighting ba[ck]
despair.

"Oh, Ross," she sighed, then added silently, *Whe[re]
are you now?* The question seemed to taunt her as [it]
echoed throughout the turbulence of her mi[nd]

Crossing to the window again, she sank wearily down upon the floor . . .

A command post had been set up at the Browns' house. With the aid of the sheriff, word had spread quickly and scores of men had volunteered to join in the search. By the time afternoon began to fade into twilight, a good many of the buildings in town had been combed and the quest had expanded to include the outer fringes of the oil field.

Ross, meanwhile, was investigating every lead that came his way. He was convinced that he would eventually find someone who knew the whereabouts of Justin Bishop and his partner—just as he was convinced that, in finding Bishop, he would find Dallas. Erik and Sam remained at his side, not only because they were anxious to help, but also because they were afraid of what he might do to the men he was interrogating.

Ruby Mae stayed at the house with Cordi and Etta, who were naturally quite distraught at their sister's disappearance. Dozens of townfolk stopped by to offer assistance or simply a word of comfort, and several ladies were thoughtful enough to bring food as well. As Ruby Mae commented, "What with so many prayers and well wishes bein' spoke on Dallas's behalf, there ain't no way the good Lord can let anythin' happen to her." Just as they had done for years, Etta and Cordi drew strength from the older woman's presence.

Although it seemed that everyone in Corsicana had heard of Dallas's abduction by then, there was at least one young man who had not.

Billy Joe, released from the hospital a scant quarter of an hour earlier, sauntered into the Double Sixes Saloon and ordered the rare extravagance—for him anyway—of whiskey. It would be his first taste of strong spirits since the night he had been shot, and he told himself it might as well be a damn good one.

"Thanks," he said to the bartender, then downed the shot of fiery amber liquid in a single gulp. His eyes watered while his boyish, freckled countenance grew beet red.

Coughing loudly after the whiskey had burned itself all the way down to his stomach, he grinned at no one in particular and turned about to lazily scrutinize the scene before him. He found himself thinking that the place looked oddly deserted for that time of day, and he eased his stocky, still rather stiff frame back around to ask the bartender, "Where the hell is everyone?"

"Ain't you heard?" the bartender responded with a frown of disbelief.

"Heard what?"

"Half the town's out lookin' for a local gal that's turned up missin'!"

"What's her name?" Billy Joe then asked with only mild interest.

"Kincaid. Used to be Brown. She's married to that driller who went at it with Bishop and O'Shea in here a few days back. Matter of fact," the bartender added as he glanced surreptitiously about and leaned an elbow on the polished surface of the bar, "there's some talk that Bishop's the one who took her, since him and O'Shea turned up missin' at the same damned time she did!"

Billy Joe gaped at the man in astonishment. *Miss*

490

Dallas, his mind confirmed the awful truth. Growing enraged at the thought of her in danger, he wheeled about and strode outside, anxious to get over to the house and see for himself what was going on.

He had not traveled more than ten feet before a memory stored in the back of his mind returned to hit him like a bolt out of the blue. *Bishop and O'Shea.* His features tightened purposefully as, instead of turning his steps toward the site of his last job, he headed back toward the hospital . . .

Dallas was certain she heard a familiar voice. She flew to the door and knelt down to peer through the keyhole once more. A lamp now burned on the table in the outer room, for darkness was closing in fast, and she could see a number of men gathered in front of the open doorway of the cabin as well as inside the room where the man who had kept guard over her all day was finally rising to his feet. She pressed closer to the hole and looked toward the opposite corner of the room, only to draw back with a sharp gasp when her gaze fell upon Justin Bishop.

Her eyes widened in horrified dismay, and she felt herself growing faint as another wave of sheer, debilitating panic washed over her. *Dear God, please help me!* she frantically beseeched. Her heart pounding in her ears, she forced herself to move back to the keyhole.

Justin and the man known only as O'Shea were alone now. She watched as O'Shea closed the cabin door and turned back to his young partner with a slow, baneful smile. The two of them began to talk, their voices drifting into the room where Dallas knelt in such fearful anticipation.

"Damn you, O'Shea, what the hell is going on?" Justin demanded angrily.

"There's been a little change in plans."

"What do you mean?"

"Just what I said. We're still heading for New Orleans, but we're taking along a 'friend' of yours." His smile deepened as Justin scowled and waited for him to elaborate. "It's a woman, actually—a very beautiful woman. You know, my boy, I always said nobody could pick them like you," he added with a soft laugh, then quickly sobered. "The only problem is, this one has a husband by the name of Ross Kincaid."

"*Dallas?*" Justin's dark eyes shot to the bolted door.

"That's right," said O'Shea, his own eyes gleaming with triumph.

"Why?" Justin demanded suspiciously. "You're the one who warned me against having anything more to do with her, so why—"

"Because I'm not going to let you ruin everything, you little bastard! You forgot the most important thing I ever taught you—you let your emotions get the better of you. You damned near blew everything to hell because of *her!*" he accused, jerking his head toward the door where Dallas still listened.

"Why do you think I arranged that setup in Fort Worth?" O'Shea went on. "I took a chance, Bishop. If that son of a bitch I hired to frame the Kincaids' foreman hadn't hightailed it out of the county in time, I might have been in one hell of a mess! And all because of you, because you couldn't keep your hands off Kincaid's wife. You're the one who made it necessary

492

for me to get them out of town for a few days. You're the one who brought Kincaid snooping around!"

"You can't pin it all on me, damn you!" Justin snarled, his gaze kindling with a feral, menacing light. "The operation was breaking apart because you wouldn't listen to me! You got too many others involved, took on too damned much. If anyone's to blame for our having to make a run for it, it's *you!*"

"No, Bishop," the older man argued with a deadly calm. "Your first mistake was having that derrick blown up. It was a stupid, careless little job, but not nearly as stupid or careless as the attack you set up. Those bastards you hired brought the law down on us by shooting that roughneck of Kincaid's. That was the beginning of the end for us."

"Neither of them talked, did they?" countered Justin.

"Not yet. But that doesn't matter anymore." O'Shea moved leisurely toward the inner door now. Dallas, her head awhirl with all she had just learned, gasped in alarm and jumped away from the keyhole.

"Why did you bring her here, O'Shea?" Justin demanded once more, stalking across the lamplit room to his partner's side.

"It's very simple, my boy," the other man replied with insolent sarcasm. "I'm hedging my bets."

"Against what?" Justin's piercing, hawkish eyes narrowed in renewed suspicion.

"Against two possibilities—the first one, that Kincaid gets wind of our plans and thinks about trying to stop us; and the second, that you think about trying to run out on me. You see, Kincaid's not likely to make any fast moves if he knows we're holding his wife. And you," he added as his mouth curved into a hard, knowing smile, "you might prove a little more agreeable if you know your 'heart's desire' will be your reward!"

"Damn you, what are you planning?"

"You owe me, Bishop. I've spent years teaching you everything I know. We had a deal, remember? And the deal was that just as soon as the two of us cleaned up here, we were to head back down to New Orleans and open up that place I've been looking to own for a long time. That's where Mrs. Kincaid comes in." He paused for a moment while Justin eyed him rancorously. When O'Shea spoke again, his voice was laced with malicious humor.

"You're going to do exactly as I say, my boy. Everything will go according to plan. Now that I've paid off the men here, you and I can leave for New Orleans—with the woman."

"Are you saying you arranged all this for me?" Justin challenged in obvious disbelief. "Because if you are, I'm not buying it!"

"It *was* for your benefit, in a way. You're lucky I didn't leave you here to get what you deserve. But I need you. With your energy and my know-how, we'll make a killing in New Orleans, the kind that'll keep us in the high stakes for the rest of our lives! As long as you do what I tell you, you'll not only get your share of the money, you'll get the woman. But if you cross me in any way, I'll see that you don't go near her. If things get bad enough, I might have to do far worse," O'Shea threatened coldly. "You know me, Bishop. You know I'll not hesitate to kill her if you force the issue. But I don't think you will."

"What makes you so damned sure I care what

happens to her one way or the other?" Justin retorted with deceptive nonchalance. *In spite of the fact that Dallas had betrayed him, he still wanted her more than he'd ever wanted anything.* "And what makes you think Kincaid won't hunt us down?"

"You never could fool me, Bishop," the older man replied with a low chuckle. "I happen to know for a fact you've been eaten up with her ever since we rolled into town. You've caused a lot of trouble because of that. As for Kincaid, once we're safely away, he's going to meet with an unfortunate little 'accident'. Right now, however," O'Shea then said as he lifted a hand to the bolt, "just to show you I'm a man of my word, I'm going to let you have a look at our prisoner. I certainly wouldn't want you to think I was trying to put anything over on you."

Dallas, her throat constricted painfully and her eyes full of horror because of what O'Shea had said about Ross, stood poised for flight when the door swung open. Her only thought was to get away so she could warn her husband, and it was this single-mindedness that provoked her to such desperate measures.

"Well, Mrs. Kincaid—" sneered O'Shea as he and Justin stepped into the darkened room.

"No!" she screamed, hurtling her body forward. Although the two men were taken completely off-guard by her action, she only managed to get through the doorway and into the outer room before Justin caught her. She cried out in helpless fury when she felt his hand closing about her arm, and she brought her fist smashing up against his face while struggling violently within his grasp. "No, damn you, no!" she screamed again.

"It appears that your vixen needs taming, my boy," Justin's partner observed caustically.

"Shut up!" growled Justin. He seized Dallas's wrist and wrenched her arm cruelly behind her back, making her sob in mingled pain and defeat. Tears streamed freely down the flushed smoothness of her cheeks as she thought of Ross. Her love for him served to renew her spirit and give her courage. She knew what she must do.

"I'll go with you, Justin," she proclaimed, turning her face up toward his with a sudden calmness. For Ross's sake, she forced herself to gaze imploringly into her tormentor's dark, menacing eyes. "I'll do whatever you want, if only you'll spare my husband's life. I . . . I can even send him word that I have gone with you willingly. He'll believe me, Justin. He knows you and I once cared for each other, and I know I can convince him that—"

"You little fool!" Justin ruthlessly cut her off. "I'm not the same naive boy you once knew! You know as well as I do that Kincaid would come after you no matter what you said. No, Dallas," he ground out, his eyes glittering with an almost maniacal light, "your husband will soon be dead and you'll be mine! And no one, *no one,* is going to take you from me this time!"

Suddenly, he pulled a gun from his vest pocket and leveled it at the other man. O'Shea took a startled, instinctive step backward while Dallas inhaled sharply.

"I'm getting out of here, O'Shea, and I'm taking her with me!" decreed Justin, his left hand tightening about Dallas's wrist while his right clenched the small silver derringer in defensive readiness. "Now get your hands up!"

O'Shea hesitated only a moment, his narrowed eyes
stened unwaveringly upon the gun, before doing as
e younger man bid. He slowly raised his arms.

"I don't owe you a damned thing, you double-
ossing son of a bitch!" Justin snarled at the man who
d been both teacher and enslaver for the past several
ars. "Whatever payment you had coming to you, you
ok long ago!"

Forcing Dallas along with him toward the door now,
instructed her to open it. Her trembling hand closed
out the knob. She turned it, then was pulled back by
stin, who used his booted foot to send the door
ashing back against the inner wall. Keeping his gun
med directly at O'Shea's heart, he commanded, "Tell
ose two curs of yours to come inside!"

"Ames! Cassidy!" the gray-haired man roared in
edience. The men who had abducted Dallas imme-
ately came stomping into the cabin. The other
embers of the gang had been paid off and were now
ding in varying directions across the countryside as
ey followed O'Shea's orders to scatter.

"Hands up and back against the wall!" growled
stin. Ames and Cassidy, looking to O'Shea for
nfirmation, lifted their arms at a curt nod from him
d moved into place beside their boss.

Dallas stifled a sharp cry of pain as her arm was
nked higher. Nearly blinded by her tears, she felt
stin pushing her through the doorway and into the
thering darkness outside. She held her breath and
gan praying once more for Ross to find her before it
as too late . . .

It was then that Justin Bishop made a fatal mistake.
arting out the door, he turned his back for a split

second in time—but that was all it took.

O'Shea's hand flew up to close upon the gun he ke[pt] hidden within the inner pocket of his coat. He whipp[ed] the derringer out and fired at his young partner.

Justin gasped and tensed, then crumpled facedow[n] upon the dusty floor, a dark crimson stain alrea[dy] spreading outward from the bullethole in his bac[k.] Dallas staggered weakly back against the wall a[nd] stood gazing down at Justin's lifeless body in stunn[ed] horror, but she was given no time to think about wh[at] had happened, for O'Shea suddenly moved forward [to] take her captive once more.

"Let's get the hell out of here!" he told the other me[n.]

Ross pulled up short as the sound of a gunsh[ot] echoed across the gently rolling countryside. Eri[k,] Sam, and Billy Joe drew rein just behind him in t[he] next instant.

"Damn, but that sounded close!" pronounced Sa[m,] trying to control the impatient pawing and swinging [of] his mount.

"God in heaven, I hope we ain't too—" Billy J[oe] started to express a very real fear, only to break off [as] Ross suddenly went riding hell-bent for leather in t[he] direction of the shot. Erik and Sam took off as we[ll.] Billy Joe, cursing the fact that his shoulder still pain[ed] him, brought the reins slapping urgently down up[on] his horse's neck and galloped after them.

Moments later, Ross topped a tree-covered rise [in] the land and pulled the chestnut stallion to a halt on[ce] more. There, a short distance away down the grass[y] knoll, lay the cabin he sought.

His smoldering gaze narrowed as it traveled about in swift reconnaissance of the cabin and its surroundings. Then, every muscle in his body tensed, and the expression on his handsome face grew savage. *Dallas!* He watched as she was dragged from the lamplit cabin by O'Shea.

"Dear God, Tex, we have found her!" Erik whispered as he drew up beside his friend and caught sight of Dallas. Sam and Billy Joe arrived soon thereafter.

Ross wasted no time now. Swinging down, he drew the shotgun from its scabbard just below his saddle and commanded the others in a terse undertone, "Stall them. I'll circle around and come up from behind. If you find it necessary to do any shooting," he added by way of caution, his voice tinged with a dire resonance, "choose your targets carefully." With that, he was gone, crouching low as he set off beneath the cover of darkness.

Dallas, meanwhile, was adamantly resisting O'Shea's efforts to pull her across to where the horses were tied up. She knew her struggles were futile, and yet she refused to surrender without a fight. There was little doubt in her mind that, with Justin dead, O'Shea was planning to dispose of her once they reached New Orleans. Her fears, however, were not focused on herself—*she had to get free so she could save Ross!*

"No!" she cried in furious defiance, holding back and twisting violently within O'Shea's brutal grasp. Ames and Cassidy merely chuckled and turned away to mount up.

"Damn you, you little—" O'Shea ground out.

"Hold it right there!" a man's voice suddenly rang out.

Dallas's heart leapt wildly, for she recognized t
voice as Erik Larsen's. If Erik was there, she to
herself, then Ross must be with him! She ceased h
struggles at once and gazed joyfully up the hill to t
grove of trees where Erik called out again.

"We've got the place surrounded, O'Shea, so y
and your men drop your guns!"

All hell broke loose after that.

A loud gasp broke from Dallas's lips as O'She
yanked her in front of him and jabbed the derring
against her left side. Ames foolishly whirled, his gu
blazing into the darkness, only to take a bullet in t
chest as Sam returned his fire. Cassidy swung up in
the saddle and tried to make a run for it, but Billy J
took aim and sent the man toppling from his horse

That left only O'Shea. Using Dallas as a shie
against the type of retribution Ames and Cassidy h
just suffered, he hauled her back toward the cab
doorway with him.

"Let her go, O'Shea!" shouted Erik, still conceal
within the cover of trees a short distance away. "It's
use now! You can't get away, so let her go!"

Ross! Dallas's mind cried frantically as hot tea
stung against her eyelids. *Dear God, where is Ross*

"I'm riding out of here!" O'Shea roared back. "Y
make one move to stop me, and the woman dies
Dallas stifled a cry as he rammed the barrel of the g
even tighter against the soft flesh below her ribs. "N
put down your guns and show yourselves! I'm warni
you—I'll kill her!" he reiterated fiercely.

There was nothing but silence for several lo
moments. Then, Erik, Sam, and Billy Joe came out
the trees with their hands up.

"All right, O'Shea. Now let her go!" Erik called out again. The man who held Dallas gave a derisive snort of laughter.

"What kind of a fool do you take me for? I'm well aware of the fact that there's nothing to keep you or Kincaid from coming after me if I let her go!" As soon as Ross's name passed his lips, it suddenly dawned on O'Shea that the driller was conspicious by his absence. "Where is Kincaid?" he demanded, his eyes shifting nervously about now.

"I'm right here, you bastard." Ross stood near the corner of the cabin, his gun leveled directly at O'Shea.

"*Ross!*" breathed Dallas, her initial relief giving way to renewed alarm as O'Shea tensed and jerked his head toward him. The beefy, gray-haired man laughed in malevolent satisfaction once more as his gaze flickered meaningfully downward to the shotgun in Ross's hands.

"Go ahead and shoot, Kincaid! You don't stand a chance of missing either me *or* your wife!"

"Maybe not," drawled Ross, only the savage gleam in his eyes betraying his inner turmoil. His eyes met Dallas's, and his rugged features tightened when he glimpsed the anguish within their luminous sapphire depths. He looked back to O'Shea. "But we both know she doesn't stand a chance of staying alive if you ride out of here with her. I propose an even exchange—her freedom for your life." It was a bluff and he knew it, but it was their only hope.

"You're not in a position to bargain!" snarled O'Shea. "We both know you'll kill me as soon as I turn her loose!"

"Not if I give you my word."

501

"Your word?" the other man echoed scornful
"Your word is worth about as much as—"

The loud, startling report of yet another gunsh
suddenly rent the warm night air.

Dallas gave a breathless cry and stumbled forward
she was abruptly released. O'Shea fell heavily to t
ground, dead, a bullet lodged in the back of his sku

"Dallas—" Justin Bishop gasped out, the gun in
hand still smoking. The life force slipped from
body at last. Collapsing in the doorway of the cabin,
joined his partner in death.

Ross sped to Dallas's side and caught her up agai
him, his strong arms enveloping her with their ha
warmth.

XX

The door swung open, and the four occupants of the room—all of them female—stopped talking to gaze expectantly upon the man who sauntered inside. Ross's mouth curved into a faint, roguish smile as he tossed his hat atop the chest of drawers.

"Ladies," he said with a slight nod. His fathomless green gaze traveled past three of the women to the one who was lying tucked securely between the covers of the bed. A soft blush rose to Dallas's cheeks as her eyes met his.

"Good night, honey," Ruby Mae suddenly proclaimed, bending down to press a kiss upon her friend's silken brow.

"Good night, Ruby Mae," replied Dallas. She caught the older woman's hand for a moment and added with heartfelt sincerity, "Thank you for all your help." Ruby Mae smiled warmly back at her, then looked to the two young women perched on the side of the bed.

"Cordi, Etta, it's time we was gettin' ourselves back

503

downstairs." Neither of them chose to argue, for t
simple reason that they had not failed to notice t
special glow that came over their older sister when I
husband entered the room. True to their oft-repeat
claims, they had indeed grown up.

"Good night, Dallas. I . . . I'm so very glad you
safe!" Cordi murmured tearfully, turning to give I
one last hug before rising from the bed. Even Ett
smile was somewhat watery as she, too, embrac
Dallas and declared impishly, "I don't care what Sa
thinks, I've simply *got* to kiss Billy Joe for finding c
where you were!"

The three visitors hastened from the room, leavi
Dallas alone with Ross for the first time since he h
brought her home earlier that same night. Her e
followed his every movement as he closed the door a
walked around the foot of the bed to stand gazi
intently down at her.

"The sheriff just left. It seems he shares my opini
that things ought to settle down now that O'Shea
dead." He turned and pulled up the chair Ruby M
had just vacated. Bending his tall frame down into it,
released a strangely ragged sigh and confessed, "I kn
the son of a bitch was shrewd, but I never thought h
go this far. If Billy Joe hadn't overheard tl
conversation down at the hospital, we never wo
have found you in time."

The merest ghost of a smile played about his l
now. Leaning forward a bit, he rested his forear
upon his knees and remarked quietly, "I'll have
remember to thank the doctor for placing that or
armed bastard's bed within earshot of Billy Joe's.

and his 'visitor' got careless. Thank God Billy Joe put two and two together when he recalled what they'd said about a big payoff. Because of that, we were finally able to make the other man talk."

Dallas, not trusting herself to speak, merely nodded. *Why is he keeping his distance?* she agonized in silence. More than anything in the world, she wanted him to hold her just as he had done all the way home. Her eyes glistening with a fresh rush of tears, she watched as his handsome visage suddenly tightened with renewed savagery.

"Damn, but I was a fool to underestimate Bishop and his partner!" he ground out. He met her wide, luminous gaze, and she was startled to glimpse the pain in his eyes. Releasing a strangely ragged sigh, he added in a low voice edged with raw emotion, "If anything had happened to you, I'd have torn them apart with my bare hands!"

"Oh, Ross," murmured Dallas, choking back a sob. "I was so frightened! O'Shea said that he . . . he had arranged for you to be killed, and I was afraid I wouldn't be able to escape in time to warn you!"

"Why?" he unexpectedly demanded.

"Wha—what?" she faltered in bewilderment.

"Why were you so concerned about warning me?" *The time for the truth has come.* He drew himself slowly upright to stand towering above his wife. His magnificent green gaze fastened upon her with such firm yet loving insistence that she felt her pulses start to race. "Tell me why, Dallas," he commanded, the deep-timbred resonance of his voice sending a shiver down her spine.

505

Staring dazedly up at him, she eased herself higher against the pillow. Her beautiful face was becomingly flushed above the high collar of her white lawn nightgown, while her lustrous auburn hair cascaded unrestrainedly down about her shoulders. She took a deep, steadying breath before answering, "Because I . . . I love you," she finally admitted. Her eyes flew back up to his face. She told herself it didn't matter whether he cared for her as much as she cared for him—she could no longer keep her true feelings concealed within her heart. "I love you, Rossiter Maverick Kincaid!"

"And I love you," he told her softly, his own heart swelling with triumphant joy at the sound of those long-awaited words on her lips.

"You *do?*" Her eyes grew enormous within the delicate oval of her face, and every fiber of her being came vibrantly alive with the dawning realization of his love. "But when . . . why didn't you—" she tried to question, only to break off as Ross took a seat on the edge of the bed and drew her gently onto his lap. His powerful arms cradled her possessively against his lean-muscled hardness, while his eyes, gazing down into the radiant sapphire depths of hers, seemed to bore into her very soul.

"I never had a chance," he said, his mouth turning up into a tenderly crooked smile. "I was lost from the first moment we met, though I didn't admit it to myself until the night Bishop's men attacked us."

"You mean you . . . you knew you loved me *before* we got married?" At his wordless nod, she demanded in a rush, "Then why didn't you tell me? Why did you le me think you only wanted a marriage in name only? And why in heaven's name haven't you said anything before *now?*"

"I wanted to give you time, my love. I didn't think you were ready to hear the truth, just as I didn't believe you were ready to admit your love for me. But damn it, you were mine, and I had to do something! Willoughby's visit presented me with the perfect solution. I had planned to be patient, to woo you slowly—but not *too* slowly," he added with another devastating smile.

"Oh, Ross!" she sighed, her whole body trembling as she buried her face against his chest. "I thought I would have to make you fall in love with me! I was thoroughly convinced that you had only married me because of the trusteeship! Then, afterward, when we were at the ranch and you told me there would be no divorce, I thought you had changed your mind because you felt a certain obligation, or perhaps because you . . . you suspected I might be carrying your child. It was then that I finally realized how much I love you." Her arms tightened about his neck, and she sighed again before wondering aloud, "Why did we have to put ourselves through so much misery?"

"Because we're two proud, independent, damnably bullheaded people, Mrs. Kincaid, and I doubt that we'll ever change," he replied with a soft, mellow chuckle. His arms swept her even closer, and he held her as though he would never let her go.

Dallas tilted her head back to gaze up into the rugged perfection of his features. Her deep blue eyes sparkled as he smiled tenderly down at her.

"Proud, independent, and damnably bullheaded you

may be, Mr. Kincaid," she told him with an answering smile of pure enchantment, "but I love you with all my heart."

"And I you, wildcat," he whispered hoarsely. His lips claimed hers at last, and heaven met earth once more . . .

Epilogue

Three years later

On January 10, 1901, near Beaumont, Texas, a roaring gusher atop a small hill called Spindletop electrified the whole nation and opened the gates to the oil age.

Ross and Erik were active participants in the wildest rush since the discovery of gold in California. Dallas and Cordi, refusing to be left behind in Corsicana, shared in the excitement with their husbands.

Much of the feverish activity was captured on film, and Dallas was able to make good use of the skills she had learned from Jacob Kauffman. Little did she know that her photographs would someday be recognized as among the most historically significant of the era.

For Ross, Spindletop signaled both an end and a beginning. A few months after the initial discovery, he and Dallas moved to Fort Worth and started building the ranch he had long dreamt of owning. Dallas gave

birth to their first child, a boy, shortly after they lef
Beaumont.

Erik and Cordi decided to stay with the boom i
Beaumont. They had married six months to the da
after meeting—Erik had finally been persuaded to pu
aside his requirement of a house—and Cordi wa
expecting *their* first child in the summer.

Sam and Etta, married less than a year, lived alone i
the big old house in Corsicana. Ruby Mae was
frequent visitor. Much to everyone's surprise, Sam ha
settled into domestic life with relative ease. He held
good, steady job at the refinery, where he wa
advancing rapidly. Etta made no secret of her desire t
start a family soon.

Dallas, meanwhile, remained convinced that he
father and George Proctor were enjoying themselve
immensely over the way things had turned out. Indeed
she could have sworn the stars shone brighter abov
her new home than anywhere else. And with Ross a
her side, she knew they always would.

BESTSELLING HISTORICAL ROMANCES
From Zebra Books and Sylvie F. Sommerfield

MOONLIT MAGIC   (1941, $3.9█
How dare that slick railroad negotiator, Trace Cord, bat█
in innocent Jenny Graham's river and sneak around h█
property? Jenny could barely contain her rage . . . th█
her gaze swept over Trace's magnificent physique, and t█
beauty's seething fury became burning desire. And once █
carried her into the refreshing cascade and stroked her s█
iny skin, all she wanted was to be spellbound by ecstasy
forever captured by MOONLIT MAGIC.

ELUSIVE SWAN   (2061, $3.9█
Amethyst-eyed Arianne had fled the shackles of an a█
ranged marriage for the freedom of boisterous St. Augu█
tine — only to be trapped by her own traitorous desires. Ju█
a glance from the handsome stranger she had met in █
dockside tavern made her tremble with excitement. But t█
young woman was running from one man . . . she dar█
not submit to another. Her only choice was to once aga█
take flight, as far and as fleet as an ELUSIVE SWAN.

CATALINA'S CARESS   (2202, $3.9█
Catalina Carrington was determined to buy her riverbo█
back from the handsome gambler who had beaten h█
brother at cards. But when dashing Marc Copeland nam█
his price — three days as his mistress — she swore she'd nev█
meet his terms, even as she imagined the rapture just o█
night in his arms would bring! Marc had vengeance in h█
mind when he planned Catalina's seduction, but soon h█
desire for the golden-eyed witch made him forget his lu█
for revenge against her family . . . tonight he would re█
the rewards at hand and glory in the passionate delights █
CATALINA'S CARESS.